CONFESSIONS: A SECRET DIARY

AMBER STEPHENS

Confessions: A Secret Diary

AVON

This novel is entirely a work of fiction.
The names, characters and incidents portrayed in it are
the work of the author's imagination. Any resemblance to
actual persons, living or dead, events or localities is
entirely coincidental.

AVON
A division of HarperCollins*Publishers*
77–85 Fulham Palace Road,
London W6 8JB

www.harpercollins.co.uk

This paperback edition 2012

4

First published as *The Secret Diary of a Sex Addict*
in Great Britain by
HarperCollins *Publishers* 2008

A catalogue record for this book is
available from the British Library

ISBN-13: 978 0 00 750192 2

Set in Minion by Palimpsest Book Production Limited, Falkirk, Stirlingshire

Printed and bound in Great Britain by
Clays Ltd, St Ives plc

MIX
Paper from
responsible sources
FSC™ C007454

FSC™ is a non-profit international organisation established to promote
the responsible management of the world's forests. Products carrying the
FSC label are independently certified to assure consumers that they come
from forests that are managed to meet the social, economic and
ecological needs of present and future generations,
and other controlled sources.

Find out more about HarperCollins and the environment at
www.harpercollins.co.uk/green

With special thanks to Tom Easton.

Chapter One

'Every now and then you should sleep with someone considerably less attractive than you.'

Shelley looked up at Briony across their cluttered, back-to-back desks. 'Er . . . what?' She hadn't really been properly listening to her friend twittering on, but sometimes Briony said stuff you just couldn't let by. 'Why?'

'You've got to give a little bit back,' Briony said, flicking over the pages of a magazine. 'Haven't you heard about that Random Acts of Kindness movement?'

'Yes, but that means buying someone a cup of coffee, or helping an old lady across the road,' Shelley pointed out. 'Not yanking your pants down at a Star Trek Convention and shouting "Get it here, Scotty!"'

Briony was about to say something else but Shelley held up a hand.

'What's up with you?'

'I'm totally bricking it.'

'About the announcement?'

'Of course. How come you're so chilled?'

Briony shrugged. 'Que sera, sera.'

Shelley bit her lip. The office was wired tighter than

Joan Rivers' face. A general e-mail had been waiting for all the staff that morning from the Chief Operating Officer of West End Magazines, their parent company, requesting their punctual presence at eleven o'clock for an important announcement about the future of *Female Intuition*, the magazine Shelley had been working on for nearly four years.

Shelley tucked her unruly brown hair behind her ears and picked up a Styrofoam coffee cup, clutching it in two hands as though she feared it might escape. 'Do you think Kate's sick or something? She's been so quiet lately,' she said.

'Don't be a div, Shell,' Briony said, rolling her eyes. 'She ain't coming back.'

'*Isn't* coming back,' Shelley corrected. She could never let a grammatical slip go by. She knew it was sad, and was convinced she'd end up alone, with a dozen cats, writing letters to the *Guardian* admonishing them for typos and punctuation clangers.

'She's been given her P45,' Briony said.

'You don't know that,' Shelley replied.

'So why is there a padlock on her office door?'

Shelley looked over at the glass office Kate had been in for two and a half decades. The office must have had cutting-edge décor back then, glass and steel everywhere, midnight-blue carpets, pastel vertical blinds, open-brick walls. *Female Intuition* had been the first London magazine to give computers to all the editors.

Now the décor looked shabby, many of the vertical blinds were lying horizontally amongst the mouse droppings on the faded carpet, and Shelley sometimes wondered if her computer were one of the original ones handed out – it was practically steam-driven.

Shelley sort of knew it must be over, but didn't want it to be true. Kate Hurley had given Shelley her first job in journalism, straight out of university, or at least her first job writing for magazines, which is not necessarily the same thing. She'd been editor here at *Female Intuition* for as long as anyone could remember and was legendary in the business.

'I need a drink, fancy anything from the kitchen?' Shelley asked.

'I have a splitting headache,' Briony replied. 'Get me a strong coffee would you?'

'Coffee's not good for headaches,' Shelley replied.

'Who says?'

'Everyone says. It's a diuretic, isn't it?'

'Don't give me any of that Scientology crap; get me a double-strength aspirin and a triple espresso.'

Shelley wandered off to the manky little kitchen to get the drinks. She passed Freya Wormwood's desk on the way back and the Fashion and Lifestyle Editor looked up, catching her eye. Though pretty, and with a figure to die for, Freya made the mistake of going with whatever hairstyle was currently in vogue, regardless of its suitability for her. Freya currently sported an enormous fringe that made her look a little like the Dulux dog.

'Not nervous are you, Shelley?' Freya asked in that sly, sardonic voice she used with people she felt threatened by. Other women, to be specific. Shelley glanced at the myriad photos of her perfect boyfriend, Harry, on her desk, so many it looked like a shrine.

'No,' she replied, trying not to sound defensive and failing. 'What would I have to be nervous about?'

Freya looked away, but not before Shelley caught the beginnings of a smirk on her face. Freya was one of those women who claim moral superiority simply because they have a boyfriend when you don't. Not that anyone in the office had ever been allowed to meet the saintly Harry. Briony suspected he didn't exist and the photos in the frames had already been there when she bought them. *Harry bought me a divine new coat the other day – far too good for work, though. Harry's whipping me off to Bruges on the weekend, first class on the Eurostar. Harry's such a sensitive lover, unless I ask him to treat me roughly, that is!*

'Have you heard something?' Shelley asked, immediately regretting it. If there was something Freya loved even more than Harry, it was knowing something that other people didn't.

'I've heard a few things, Shelley,' she said. 'But I've been asked not to share them with anyone else for now.'

Shelley didn't believe a word of it, and slumped down back at her desk. Briony arched an eyebrow.

'I wonder who's going to take over?' Shelley said. 'They might close us down altogether.'

'Oh don't worry about that,' Briony said, putting down her magazine, which Shelley couldn't help but notice was a rival publication with considerably higher circulation. 'They'll just get a new editor in who'll make a big fuss about New Beginnings and a Radical New Focus before changing the logo slightly, adjusting the font size and putting the handbags section on page 240 instead of page 170.'

'Really?' Shelley asked hopefully. 'No redundancies?'

'Nooooo,' Briony said, shaking her head vigorously. 'Apart from firing a couple of columnists, maybe.'

'Briony!'

'What?'

'I'm a columnist!'

Briony paused. 'Oh, yes. So you are. Oh don't worry; I think there's at least two columnists more likely to go than you.'

'Who?' Shelley asked, coolly.

'Oh erm, Robin and, um . . . um . . .' Briony cast her eyes around the open plan office desperately. 'Erm, and Toni.'

'Toni left three months ago.'

'Really? Oh . . .'

'Never mind,' Shelley said, saving her from further embarrassment. 'Maybe redundancy is exactly what I need. Sometimes one needs a kick up the bum to make one sort one's life out.'

'Oh does one?' Briony asked. 'What needs to change in your life then?'

Shelley thought it over. She was twenty-five and had only ever had one job. She wasn't at all sure she was particularly good at being a columnist. How could she have anything important to say to women when she'd never done anything with her life? She'd postponed her gap year until she had some money, and had never got around to going now that she had. She'd never really had a proper long-term boyfriend, unless you counted Rob at university who she went out with for six months before sleeping with him, only to discover the next day that he'd been having a string of affairs, including a quick shag with her best friend in the toilet while Shelley was in the kitchen studying for her Eng Lit exam.

She rarely went out and had no romantic interests, apart from a crush on the fit South African behind the bar at The Crown where they drank after work. In two years she'd ordered fifty-seven bottles of Pinot Grigio from him but never plucked up the courage to ask his name. She was sure she wouldn't be his type anyway. Antipodeans were used to wildcat lovers with bodies supple as springboks, according to Briony's magazine. Shelley was as timid as a springbok and the only thing wild about her was her tousled, shoulder-length hair.

'You just need a good shag,' Briony said, interrupting the reverie. 'You need to be fucked till you fart.'

Shelley went bright red. 'Briony!' she hissed.

'You're hung up on sex. You need to face your fears.'

'I don't have a hang-up about sex,' Shelley said, primly.

'Sure,' Briony said. 'Have you ever thought about therapy?'

Shelley looked up at her friend sharply. 'Read my lips, Briony. I. Do. Not. Need. Therapy! We've had this before.'

'Mmm, touched a raw nerve I think,' Briony said, tight-lipped.

She would have gone on but was interrupted by the arrival of Sonia Bailey. The Chief Operating Officer came bustling in, exuding a no-nonsense, bottom-line kind of attitude.

Bailey was the sort of person, and Shelley suspected there was one in every large organisation, who was never happier than when delivering really bad news, and her heart sank as she saw a glint of joy in the COO's eye. Cutting out 'dead wood' and hiving off unsuccessful parts of the business were what she excelled in, having little knowledge of the actual business of publishing magazines. Briony claimed she got off on it and could only gain sexual satisfaction when she was firing people.

Bailey cleared her throat to get the room's attention, which was unnecessary as everyone was waiting, hearts in mouths, wondering if they'd have time to gather the photos off their desks before being shown to the lifts. Shelley had looked up the employment terms last week when the latest circulation figures had come through. 'One week's pay for every year I've worked here, plus one month's notice period, plus unused holiday . . .'

'Now people,' Bailey began, 'I have some bad news. Kate Hurley has taken early retirement with immediate effect. The Board of West End Magazines were saddened to hear of this . . .'

Briony snorted, then fought to disguise it as a cough.

'. . . but we have accepted her decision. Kate's contribution to this magazine and to West End has been immense over the last 25 years and she will be sorely missed, but . . .' and at this Bailey's eyes narrowed '. . . it has been evident for some time that *Female Intuition* has been haemorrhaging readers and making a net loss for the Group which is deepening month on month, year on year.'

As she spoke, Shelley noticed Bailey's breath getting heavier. She was almost panting now.

'From a height of nearly one million in 1986, the circulation has dropped to less than seventy thousand,

and many of those are giveaways. People just don't know what the magazine is trying to do anymore. It has lost focus and the numbers don't add up.'

She took a deep breath, taking her time, cheeks slightly flushed.

'This magazine has become no longer sustainable and the Group can no longer support it.' Her eyes were nearly closed as she reached the climax of her speech. 'And so it has been decided that . . .' but at this point she paused and came back from the brink. When she opened her eyes, Shelley saw with interest that the glint was suddenly gone. Bailey looked disappointed. Deflated. This is the part of the speech she hadn't wanted to make.

'. . . the magazine will be re-branded, with a radical new focus.' Briony gave a flourish and a bow in Shelley's direction. '*Female Intuition* will be given one last chance to re-invent itself.'

Bailey picked up a phone on the desk next to her, dialled and spoke. 'Could you come down now please?' she asked and returned the receiver. 'We're going to discuss the new direction of the magazine. I wish you all the best and know you can make this work.'

Bailey made a gesture with her hand.

'Was that a *fist pump*?' hissed Briony.

There followed a couple of minutes of awkward silence, then the door opened and in walked Aidan Carter. Shelley frowned. Aidan was the Marketing Director for the Group.

Only fair to consult on the new direction, I suppose.

Not that she was disappointed. Aidan was easy on the eye and so, well . . . big. The way he carried himself made him seem even taller then he was, and he must have been 6′ 3″. Carter was notorious for his brash management style and forceful opinions and had apparently had several stand-up rows with other board members, at the actual conference table. He was the sort of man who, when he came storming into a room, eyes flashing, you both feared and at the same time secretly hoped he was coming for you.

Shelley watched as he walked over to Sonia, confident and long-limbed. Freya just *happened* to be in his way and simpered sweetly at him as she moved aside. Carter took the COO's proffered hand and clasped it in both of his.

Briony kicked Shelley under the desk, trying to get her eye but Shelley ignored her. Briony had been convinced Aidan fancied Shelley ever since the Group Christmas party last year. She had tried to explain that just because someone dances with you didn't mean he fancied you. 'He's just about the only decent prospect in a company made up of eighty per cent women and could have his pick of the ladies. He was only being polite in trying to dance with as many women as he could. He did the "Macarena" with Sonia Bailey for God's sake,' Shelley had pointed out.

'So why did he come back later to dance with you again?' Briony asked, knowingly. 'When "Careless Whisper" was on?'

Shelley had just blushed and got on with her work, not wanting to think about it.

Now Aidan stood tall, next to the tiny Bailey who, Shelley couldn't help noticing, sneaked a look at his crotch, to her at eye-level. She spoke again.

'Ladies . . . and err gentlemen,' peering over at the

post-room boys, the only other males on the floor. 'You probably all know Aidan Carter, Group Marketing Director. Aidan has taken a keen interest in the fortunes of *Female Intuition* over the past few months, and has personally determined to turn this magazine around. I give you your new Editor-in-Chief, Aidan Carter.'

A set of gasps escaped around the room like timed pistons. Aidan had no experience as an editor, he was abrasive and demanding, he already had another job and worst of all . . .

He was a man.

'Thank you, Sonia,' Aidan began, putting a hand on one hip, which had the effect of brushing his suit jacket open and offering a glimpse of his chest muscles through an ever-so-slightly too tight shirt. Another chorus of appreciative breaths.

'Firstly a couple of words about Kate Hurley,' Aidan began. 'A hero of mine. One of this country's finest journalists, and a pioneering feminist. She had a mind like a razor, a heart like a lion, and balls of steel. She will be missed.'

Though unsure about the third simile, Shelley found herself muttering 'hear, hear' along with everyone else.

'Do you know? My mother used to read this magazine,' Aidan continued, lifting the latest issue and waving it at the team aggressively. 'She loved it. This magazine helped her through some difficult times.' Freya nodded sympathetically and put her head to one side, blinking those doe eyes. Bailey nodded sagely.

Aidan walked over to the windows and everyone swivelled to follow. 'She read this magazine in hospital when she had breast cancer,' he continued, gazing meditatively out over North London. 'She read this magazine at home after my father left her. She read this magazine in the nursing home as she watched over her own mother dying.'

He turned back to face the group, hands at his sides, his face simultaneously full of loss and warmth. Shelley felt a little funny, and squeezed her legs together and glanced around the room. Even Briony was staring at Carter, mouth open. Freya looked like she was about to have an orgasm.

'Unfortunately my mother doesn't read this magazine anymore,' he said. 'Do you want to know why?'

Briony hissed and mouthed 'Dead?'. Shelley frowned back in distaste.

'She thinks it's too boring,' Aidan said.

Grumbling and shaking of heads.

'Things have changed. My mother has changed. The world has changed. She wants more from her magazines these days. More stories about having fun and not so many about illness, more stories about love and not so many about heartbreak, more stories about life and less about death.'

'Fewer,' Shelley said automatically.

'What's that?' he said.

'*F-fewer* stories about death,' Shelley stammered. 'Not *less* stories about death.' Why had she said that? Was she to get herself fired just as the magazine was being saved?

He stared at her hard, a strange look on his face, then he snapped out of his trance and walked off towards the window again. His square-jawed, brooding face shadowed before the May sunlight pouring in.

'My mother is tired of sickness, sadness and saying goodbye,' he continued. 'That was the past. People choose life these days. People choose . . . happiness . . . and people choose *sex*.'

He spun for the finale.

'Ladies and gentlemen, let me introduce you to your new magazine.' And with that he stepped over to an old ad board lying against the wall and flipped it to reveal a blown-up magazine cover.

Briony had been wrong. The new editor wasn't just going to faff about with fonts and page orders. He'd changed everything, including the name.

The cover was an almost naked Mimi Corvair, the model recently dropped by most of her sponsors when she was filmed having a coke-snorting threesome with the boyfriends of two other models. Her days as a cover-girl had been declared well and truly over, and now she was relegated to the name-and-shame pages only. The lads' mags still wanted her, but for what her agent considered the wrong reasons.

If Aidan wanted her on the cover it meant he was trying to make a mark. He was trying to kill *Female Intuition* and get the revamped mag back in the press. That was shocking enough.

But it was the new title that hit Shelley hardest.

In hot pink, and crowding the raunchy image beneath with huge letters was the new, bold title.

VIXEN.

Aidan paused for a moment, and then continued: 'I can't let this magazine die, I owe it to West End, I owe it to you and I owe it to my mother.'

A solitary clapping from Bailey was taken up by the rest of the room, and soon even the post boys were joining in.

But Shelley reckoned she wasn't the only one who was totally terrified. If sex was the new direction this magazine was taking, then she wasn't at all sure it was the right place for her. Sex wasn't really her thing. She'd only done it a few times, and if we were talking, y'know, proper sex, she'd only done it with two different men.

As they stood and applauded, she wasn't thinking about the future of the magazine, or the fresh opportunities she was being presented with.

She was trying to remember if she'd even had any actual sex at all in the last year.

Chapter Two

Briony and Shelley went to Dino's for lunch, like they always did. Shelley toyed with a salad while they talked about the events of the morning. Aidan had told them that after lunch he was going to speak to each of them individually and define their new roles. Dishy as he was, Aidan was still management, and he used lots of phrases like 'going forward' as in, 'We'll roll out these new synergies, going forward,' or, 'We'll revise our budgets quarterly, going forward'. The editor in Shelley wanted to point out that you could hardly do these things going backward.

'Do you fancy him?' Briony asked.

'Do you?' Shelley replied.

'Yes, of course. The question is, do you?'

'Why is that the question?'

'Because Aidan's obviously not interested in me, he's interested in you.'

'Don't be ridiculous,' Shelley said. 'If he looked at anyone today, it was Freya.'

Briony snorted, 'Only because she hung off him and kept getting in his way. Aidan Carter wouldn't go for a girl like her anyway.'

She chased a troublesome cherry tomato around her plate with a fork as she spoke.

'Why not?' Shelley asked, intrigued.

Briony speared the tomato savagely, splattering juice over the plate. Then she looked up and eyed Shelley mischievously.

'Because he's the kind of man who likes a challenge.'

Shelley shivered.

'So I suppose that's why he wouldn't be interested in you,' was the best comeback she could manage.

Briony laughed. 'Yes, I suppose so. So what are you going to do about it?'

'Nothing,' Shelley replied, pouring herself more Diet Coke to avoid having to look at Briony's smirk. 'Anyway, how do you know so much about Aidan?'

'I've been looking at his CV.'

'What?'

'Don't play the innocent, I know you googled him after the Christmas party.'

'Don't be disgusting!' Shelley snapped. 'I did not!'

Briony sighed and rolled her eyes. 'I mean you looked him up on Google.'

'Oh . . . yes. Yes, I did,' Shelley agreed. 'I thought googling meant something else in that context.'

Briony looked puzzled for a moment.

'People these days like to write about themselves on social networking sites, you know, like Facebook or MySpace. If you want to know about someone, you just look them up. Aidan Carter's MySpace page is very revealing.'

'Really? What does it say?'

'It says he's single and looking for love. His ideal woman is his intellectual equal, someone who gives as good as she gets, in the office and the bedroom.'

Shelley wilted.

'Well that's me out then,' she said.

'You're not his equal in the office?' Briony asked, smirking.

'I meant the bedroom,' Shelley replied.

'Nonsense,' Briony said. 'You're just out of practice.'

'Fat chance of getting any of that in the near future, the hours I'm working,' Shelley said.

'You're making excuses. Your problem is that you don't put yourself out there enough, you never go out these days, you've had three dates in the last two years . . . how many times have you had sex in the last year?'

'I had sex at my birthday party,' Shelley retorted a bit loudly, drawing interested looks from the neighbouring tables. 'With that accountant,' she went on, in a hushed tone.

Briony went back to smiling. 'So that was a fumble in the cloakroom at Jerusalem, with a spod, two days after your 25th birthday, and when was the time before that?'

Shelley had to think hard. Then it hit her. 'It was at my 24th birthday party. With the guy from the video store.'

'Which was a week before your actual birthday,' Briony said. 'So that means . . .'

'I didn't have sex once during my entire 25th year,' Shelley completed, now thoroughly miserable.

As a coup-de-grace, Briony whipped out her magazine,

already open at an article titled 'Women's sexual peak now at 25'.

'That's not true!' Shelley cried. 'Everyone knows it's 40 for women. I was looking forward to it.'

Briony shrugged. 'Sorry, Bird. Scientists are never wrong about these things.'

Shelley took a mouthful of lettuce and munched thoughtfully. It wasn't that she didn't like the idea of sex, it was just that . . . well, just she had never been any good at it. As soon as she got naked with someone, she just froze up. She'd read all the magazines. She had a collection of steamy novels and she even had some videos. She knew the theory, but that almost made it worse, she knew the things she was *supposed* to be doing, and the fact she wasn't doing them preyed on her mind and caused her to seize up even more. All she could think about was how awful the man must be finding it. There had even been times back at university where men had made excuses and left without finishing. Even back then Shelley had known that for a man not to finish was a pretty big deal.

Briony interrupted her thoughts. 'So what about Gavin?'

Shelley stared at her, outraged. Realisation crept in.

'So that's what this is all about? You still want me to go out with Gavin?'

'Actually, Shelley, I want you to stay in with Gavin and fuck him till his cock breaks off.'

Gavin was Briony's ex-boyfriend's best mate. Shelley had been introduced to him at a party. She suspected that, being slightly geeky herself, she was paired off with him in the way that one might pair off the only two estate agents at a magazine launch. *They'd better fancy each other cos there's no-one else.* Shelley had fumed. Didn't they appreciate there is a geek hierarchy? Shelley was slightly geeky, Gavin on the other hand was an uber-geek. He looked the sort of person who'd designed and built a robot to cut his hair. And he was positively chubby; not that looks were everything. Gavin spent the evening following her about talking about Manga, which, as far as Shelley was concerned, were misogynistic Japanese comic books with terrible punctuation.

Briony had apparently told him that Shelley was single and a real Manga fan.

'Why did you tell him that?' Shelley hissed at her while Gavin was off on one of his regular toilet breaks.

'I didn't know Manga was comics,' Briony had said in self-defence.

'What did you think it was?'

'I thought Manga was a Spanish film director,' Briony replied sheepishly. 'You're into that kind of thing, aren't you?'

To make matters worse, Briony had given Gavin Shelley's phone number and told him to call her to arrange a date. Shelley and Briony had had a falling out over this that involved ashtrays being thrown and the subject was still raw.

Briony went on. 'I sort of told him you might like to see him tonight.'

'You did what?!'

'Well you told me you weren't busy. He said he had tickets to the Abba thing, you like musicals . . .'

'I don't like musicals.'

'Course you do, you're always off down to Theatre Land.'

'Yes, to the theatre, I like going to the theatre. Do you ever actually listen to what I say?'

'Theatre, musicals, same thing. Anyway, I thought that since you can't seem to get your act into gear then I'd have to do it for you. I'm going to make sure you get some sex soon, and I'm not fussy about who you do it with.'

The man at the next table was definitely interested now. He kept trying to catch Shelley's eye. She shook her head in disbelief. 'Honestly Briony, you're a good mate and you've always stood by me, and I know you're trying to help, but not Gavin. There's just no way. Sorry.'

'Look, he fancies you. What more do you want? How many other men have asked you out lately?'

'Oh God,' Shelley groaned, head in hands. 'You know you're a minger when only other mingers ask you out.'

'You're not a minger, Shell,' Briony said. 'You're actually very pretty and you know it, but you need to start off on mingers until you get your groove back, then you can play with the big boys again. You know, work your way up through the grades.'

'You sound like a boxing coach.'

'That's how you should think of me. I'm your coach, I know what's good for you and I'm going to make sure Gavin gets into your ring.'

'Oh you're vile, Briony. Stop it.'

'It's not as if he's an axe-murderer,' Briony pleaded. 'We *know* him.'

'Yes we know him,' Shelley hissed, 'and may I just

remind you that it was only a couple of weeks ago that you yourself referred to Gavin as a "cartoon-reading salad-dodger". Now let's drop it.'

'Okay,' Briony said grabbing her bag. 'Let's pop to the pub after work, you can see if you feel the same way after a couple of bottles.'

'I'd feel the same way after emptying Oliver Reed's drinks cabinet,' Shelley said as she marched past Briony and out the door.

After lunch, they were too nervous to do any work. Shelley didn't see much point in continuing with her column – 'Noughties Loving' – if everything was going to be changed around. And as far as she knew, she might end up getting the sack after all, especially after correcting Aidan's grammar during his grand speech.

Aidan had posted up a schedule on the notice board giving everyone a 15-minute slot for an individual meeting in his office. Shelley was about half-way down, just after Freya who in turn was straight after Briony. She and Briony sat and watched as people filed in nervously and came again a quarter-hour later, some looking happy, some looking glum but most just looking gob-smacked. Stella Stargazer, who did the horoscopes (real name Moira something), stormed back out to her desk, packed up her things in a cardboard box and stomped straight out muttering 'disgusting' under her breath every few seconds.

Shelley looked on wide-eyed.

'She didn't predict that,' Freya reflected as she passed, then giggled at her own joke. Shelley watched her go.

'What a cow!' she muttered. 'And why is she so confident?'

Maybe Freya *did* know something.

'You know what else I read about him on MySpace?' Briony said, out of the blue.

'What's that?'

'He has a back, sack and crack done every three months.'

'What!' Shelley spat. 'He wrote that on MySpace?'

'Well, as good as. His blog said he visited Jen's Unisex Hair removal salon last week for his quarterly treatment.'

'That's not necessarily to have his . . . ball-hair torn out,' Shelley protested.

'What else would he go for? His nostril hair?'

'Why would someone write that on a blog? Is there no personal space anymore?'

'Not everyone is as prudish as you, Shell, Aidan has over two hundred friends on his space, he can't possibly keep up with all of them all of the time, so he writes a blog letting everyone know what he's up to. Anyway, the reason he mentioned the trip to the salon was to recount an amusing anecdote about what happened while he was there. I don't think he's one of those losers who keep a meticulous log of his every waking move.'

Shelley wasn't really listening though, she was thinking about Aidan's sleek, well-muscled back, his rock-hard, hairless buttocks, and two shiny-smooth . . .

'Bollocks!' someone shouted from Aidan's office, which happened to be situated right behind Shelley. Then the door was flung open and Maya, one of the sub-editors, marched out. Then she turned around and shouted back through the open door. 'It's all bollocks, Aidan Carter, and I'm not having it!'

She followed Stella Stargazer down the stairs.

The other subs went back to checking copy. It was Briony's turn next; Aidan popped out before she went in and said:

'I'd love a coffee, anyone else want one?'

The room went as quiet as a library. No editor had ever made even their own coffee, let alone made one for someone else. No one replied except Briony.

'Yes. I would, thanks. White with three,' she said.

'Righto,' Aidan said cheerfully and disappeared into the kitchen.

Shelley looked at her quizzically. 'You already have a coffee,' she pointed out.

'I know. I want to see how well made *his* coffee is. Is he just trying to create a good impression by offering to make a cup? Is this the first cup he's ever made? Or does he make a habit of it? If it's shit, we'll know he's a fraud. If it's good, we know we can trust him.'

Almost without thinking Shelley answered. 'I trust him.'

Shelley surfed the net absently while she waited for Freya's interview to be finished. Briony had come out of Aidan's office looking thoughtful, but told Shelley she wanted to think things over before talking much about it. All she'd say was that Aidan had presented her with a challenge, an assignment tougher than anything she'd done before.

'We'll talk about it tonight, yeah?' Briony said absently, checking her phone for messages. This of course made Shelley even more nervous and she tried to do some work to take her mind off it.

She was half-heartedly researching an idea she'd had for her column, which she was sure would never see the light of day again, at least not in its current form, but she needed to do something. Her column was supposedly about twenty-something singletons looking for love in the big city, but she was no Carrie Bradshaw and sometimes wondered if she should rename the column 'Sad in the City'. For the past three issues she'd written pretty much the same column, how difficult it was to meet a man who wasn't gay, hygienically-challenged, socially inept or carrying more baggage than a kleptomaniac Sherpa. She needed something new.

She had an idea to write about the new craze supposedly sweeping the singles bars – Nude Speed Dating. The reasoning was this: why go through all the trouble of spending five minutes finding the right life partner, only to find when you got them into bed that they had an unpleasant mole somewhere intimate? Or that the blonde hair came out of a bottle? It's the future after all, who has that kind of time?

Shelley clicked on the site of one of the companies that organised the evenings and waited for the page to load up on the crappy old Mac, only to be greeted by a full-screen, hi-res image of the naked torsos of a man and a woman, each holding a drink. Shelley stared in horror at the well-toned bodies, the woman's perky breasts and the man's only partially flaccid penis. She stabbed with the cursor to close the image, but the computer was old, and had to think a while before attempting to perform the simplest tasks.

The door to Aidan's office opened behind her and

Shelley turned, feeling her face turn crimson. Aidan stepped out first and turned to wait for Freya to emerge, glancing curiously at Shelley's monitor as he did so. Freya came out afterwards, beaming and shook Aidan's hand warmly.

'Thanks so much, Aidan,' she said ingratiatingly, 'I really appreciate this opportunity.' She walked back to her desk, swinging her hips and looking very much like the cat that'd got the cream.

'I hate her,' Briony whispered. Shelley nodded.

'Come on then Shelley, let's be having you,' Aidan said. Briony snorted as she walked into Aidan's new office and the door closed behind her.

'Now we have met before, haven't we?' Aidan said as he ushered Shelley into a comfy chair.

'You held the lift for me yesterday,' she replied. 'Such a gentleman.'

Oh God, she thought, *who do I think I am, Elizabeth Bennett?*

Aidan smiled, then immediately frowned, 'Yes, but I'm sure we met before that, properly . . . ?'

'Yes,' Shelley confirmed, 'at the . . .' and she blushed again. What was wrong with her? '. . . at the Christmas party last year.'

'Yes of course,' Aidan said beaming, '"Macarena", wasn't it?'

'I . . . no. That was . . .' she said.

'Good,' he said, looking down at the sheaf of papers in front of him. 'Now, I'm going to cut to the chase here, we don't have much time. Your column, though well-written and very funny, is not going to be suitable for the new look of the magazine.'

Shelley was disappointed, even though she'd been expecting this. She'd half-hoped Aidan would say something like 'Yours is the only bit I'm not going to change – it's brilliant!'

'Instead,' Aidan went on. 'I'd like you to do more investigative work. There's no point having you stuck in the office writing . . . well, what you have been writing. I want you out there on the streets, undercover, getting me some grade-A hot stories.'

Could it be true? Could Aidan really want her to do hard-hitting investigative reporting? This is what she became a journalist for. This is what she'd dreamed of as a girl, and throughout university. She imagined herself hanging around the bars in Westminster looking for ministers willing to speak off the record, or blagging her way into the retinue of a gangsta rapper crime lord in South London.

'I've already arranged your first undercover role,' said Aidan.

Shelley sat forward in her chair.

'It's a lot of work. I'll want a few thousand words a day.'

Shelley raised her eyebrows, but nodded. She could do that, she could do anything.

'There'd be a bonus in it if you deliver,' Aidan went on.

Shelley tried not to think in terms of bottles of The Crown's finest dry white. 'A few thousand words on what?' she asked.

He sat back in his chair, grinned broadly.

'The Secret Diary of a Sex Addict!'

A lengthy pause followed. The tick-tock of Kate Hurley's ancient clock counted the treacherous seconds away as Shelley stared at her boss.

This couldn't be right. 'I'm sorry, I think I misheard you,' she said. 'You said Secret Diary of a . . . *What* Addict?'

'Sex Addict,' Aidan repeated, gazing back at her steadily.

Shelley was floored. She'd been hoping to move away from love-soaked frippery and gossip; she desperately wanted to do hard-nosed, real journalism. Instead Aidan seemed determined to take her backwards. How could she, of all people, write a column from the point of view of a sex addict?

'I need you to pretend to be addicted to sex.' Aidan said, leafing through some pages on his desk. 'We'll come up with some convincing story for you. You can join a group, I already have most of this arranged, by the way. You'll take a week to put together some stories. Feed them through and I'll put them up on the blog site, when the next issue comes out we'll run the best. We want them sexy, you understand? We want details.'

Shelley's head spun. Was Aidan testing her? Or was he hoping to get rid of her? Did he want another walk of shame? Should she follow Stargazer and Maya the Sub down to Benny's wine bar to drown her sorrows and draft her resignation?

Aidan didn't speak.

No, she couldn't bear the thought of walking out now. She wouldn't let smug Freya have the satisfaction, for a start. They'd given her a challenge they thought she'd fail, because they thought she was weak. But she wasn't weak. She was a tough journalist, she could handle any assignment.

Even sex?

'I'll do it,' she said, firmly.

'Great,' he said looking down at his papers again. 'The course starts on Monday but you have to be at the centre on Sunday for orientation. Take a BlackBerry, you'll need to smuggle it in. You're to use the BlackBerry to e-mail your copy in and to communicate with us if necessary, but only by e-mail please. The IT department tell me they're bound to notice if someone starts using a phone, but they're unlikely to monitor wireless e-mail communications.'

'You make it sound like I'm infiltrating the Kremlin,' Shelley protested.

'The centre's clients are strictly forbidden to contact the outside world, Shelley,' Aidan said, earnestly. 'They're very clear about that. They will be watching you closely and if they catch you they'll throw you off the course, we'll lose the story and a lot of money.'

What Aidan left unspoken was what exactly might happen to Shelley's job if this happened.

'Thanks for your time, Shelley,' Aidan said, signalling the end of the interview.

She left the office feeling about as confused as she'd ever been in 25 extremely confusing years.

Chapter Three

'I don't see what the problem is with landfill sites,' Freya was saying to Briony in her squeaky, we're-all-matey-in-the-pub voice. 'If they don't fill the land we'll just have big holes everywhere.' Briony and Shelley stared back at her, trying to work out if she was serious.

Freya was almost never invited to the pub after work. She was intensely irritating at the best of times and if you went around inviting her to things, she'd just take it as endorsement of her obnoxiousness.

Shelley and Briony would normally be baiting her and trying to get her onto the subject of immigration, where she leaned slightly to the right of Hitler, and if she'd include the Polish girl who cleaned the loos, but tonight Shelley's heart wasn't in it. The buzz at the table was of the changes Aidan had wrought at the magazine. Everyone's job had changed. Even the post-room boys, who had been asked to start a blog about being the only men in an organisation stuffed with desperate young women, with a particular focus on all those 'special deliveries' they made to the girls in marketing.

The common theme of course was sex. The fashion

shoots were going to feature more scantily-clad models, sliding over buff-torsoed men. There were to be more features on sex tips, marital aids and true-life experiences. Jen DuCroix, Features Editor, was excited about the prospect of road-testing the new vibrator on the block, the Berserk Bunny. Poor old Monica Bellamy, ad-sales executive and within spitting distance of retirement, had been asked to up the tit-count in the classifieds. *Vixen* was going to allow, and indeed encourage, phone-sex ads, albeit targeted at the female market. This meant ads for lingerie, dildos and even male escorts.

'But it's just pornography,' Shelley protested, as Karen told them about her new feature, 'How to Make Him Think You're a Virgin'.

Freya snorted. 'Don't be such a prude, Shelley. All the women's magazines these days have a bit of slap and tickle about them. It doesn't have to be crude. What's wrong with a bit of tasteful erotica?'

'She's right,' Briony said. 'As much as I hate to admit it. It's not as if the mag's going to be wall-to-wall cock.'

'Yes,' Freya continued. 'Look at my new role for example.' None of them had asked her about her job, not wanting to give her the satisfaction. 'Aidan knows I have a psych degree as well as my Masters in Journalism. Well, he's asked me to write a series of feature articles on the psychology of relationships. Each is practically guaranteed to be a cover story.'

'The psychology of relationships?' Shelley butted in. 'Sounds a bit vague. Any particular aspect of relationships?'

Freya appeared momentarily shaken but quickly rallied. 'The physical side, mostly.'

'Aha!' Briony cried triumphantly. 'You're writing about sex like the rest of us. Let me guess, "What He's Secretly Fantasising About", or "10 Psychology Tips to get him Interested". That sort of thing?'

Freya scowled. 'Well, sex is important in a relationship, it's certainly one of the main things that keep the spark alive between Harry and me.' This last was delivered while she stared coldly at Shelley. 'A satisfactory love life is essential in being fulfilled as a woman.'

'So what's your new assignment?' Shelley asked, pointedly turning away from Freya. 'You still haven't told us.'

Briony smiled and very nearly looked embarrassed. 'Aidan wants me to write a monthly column in which I describe a sexual experience. A new one every time.'

'What, one of *your* experiences?' Freya asked.

'Yes, I basically find a willing partner, or partners, once a month, shag them and write about it.'

Shelley couldn't believe what she was hearing. 'He's asking you to prostitute yourself.'

Briony rolled her eyes. 'No he's not; he's just asking me to write about my life. I'm a shagaholic already.'

Shelley had to admit this was true. Despite having a sort-of boyfriend, who didn't seem to care what she got up to, Briony had slept with an enormous number of people, including the occasional woman, during the two years they'd shared the dishevelled flat near the tube station. Sometimes Shelley was woken in the night by vibrations and was never quite sure if they were caused by Central line trains pulling into the station, or her energetic friend.

Why hadn't Aidan asked Briony to go to the clinic?

She was a real-life sex addict. Maybe he had asked her and she'd refused? Or maybe he didn't want her cured? Aidan wasn't stupid, and it was obvious he'd done some background checking on his new staff to find out how they might be useful to him.

Shelley was sitting with her back to the bar. The pub was nothing special, just one of those interchangeable inner London pubs. But it sold a decent house white and there were generally big tables available if you got in early enough, which Briony and Shelley normally did. Freya was looking over Shelley's shoulder and smirking. Shelley groaned inwardly, she knew what was coming.

'Your boyfriend's here,' Freya said. Shelley didn't have to look. It was her favourite barman, the South African.

'Oh drop it,' Shelley said, shaking her head.

'Yes,' Briony added, coming to her rescue. 'Shelley already has a date tonight.'

One of Freya's eyebrows raised itself just enough to make Shelley want to kill her.

'Really?' The fashion editor asked in the same disbelieving tone she might have used had Briony just told her Shelley had invented salt.

'Yes, she's going to a party with Gavin,' Briony said. Shelley's mouth dropped open as she stared at her former friend. 'What on God's blue-green Earth made you tell her that?'

Freya's smirk had reached warp factor nine by now. 'I don't think I know Gavin.' she said.

'He likes Manga,' Briony explained.

'I see,' Freya said in a tone that suggested it all made perfect sense now.

'I do not have a date with Gavin,' Shelley ground out through gritted teeth. 'I find him hugely repulsive on both physical and intellectual levels.'

Freya nodded, after a slight pause.

'I did think Shelley would have been a little out of his league,' she said to Briony.

Shelley swallowed slowly. She wasn't used to support from Freya, albeit lukewarm.

Briony was on her third super-sized glass by now though and apparently oblivious to how close she was to having the ice bucket rammed down her throat.

'Remember our discussion though, Shell, start a few rungs down the ladder, until you get your confidence back.'

Freya nodded in appreciation of this soundly-made point.

'Just out of interest, Briony,' Shelley said in as reasonable tone as she could muster. 'To what sort of level would you say I should aspire?'

'On the Hollywood celebrity gauge?'

'Naturally.'

'What about Jim Carrey?' said Karen.

'You can do better than that,' Ash from Accounts called from further up the table. 'What about James Woods?'

'How about we leave the Jims behind?' said Shelley. 'Let's start thinking in terms of Brads and Georges.'

'George Lucas?' Freya suggested.

Shelley shook her head.

'George Bush?' Briony said.

Shelley kicked her. 'He's not Hollywood.'

'Ouch!'

'Oh we're getting nowhere,' said Shelley. 'What about you then, what's your celeb level?'

Briony considered for a moment. 'Matt Damon,' she said confidently.

Shelley laughed out loud, but then realised everyone was nodding along in agreement.

'What? You think you could get Matt Damon?'

Briony shook her head. 'You've missed the point Shell, the idea of the game is to find your level, not to speculate on who you might be able to get into bed. I'm a Matt Damon, Freya here is a Bill Pullman, physically that is, personality-wise she's a Steve Buscemi, Ashley is a Gene Hackman – no offence Ash – and you are an Elliott Gould, or possibly one of the Baldwins.'

Shelley stared back icily.

'But if you go up to that barman and get his number, then maybe I can bump you up to a David Schwimmer.' Briony snatched the bottle from the ice bucket sitting in the middle of the table and poured the last of it into her enormous glass. 'Your round I think.'

All conversation had stopped and everyone watched smiling as Shelley got to her feet and walked to the bar. As she went, a path opened up magically before her in the busy pub, a path which led straight to a gap at the bar itself. Beyond the bar stood the South African, who, along with one of the other young bartenders, was dancing to a track pumping from the stereo. She watched his hips move and wondered briefly what it might be like to have those hips gyrating between her thighs, before crushing the thought like a grape. He saw her coming, stopped dancing and smiled broadly as she approached.

Another punter waved a twenty at him from stage right but he kept his eyes fixed on Shelley.

She reached the bar and smiled back. This was it. She didn't need sex therapy; she didn't need Briony to fix her up with comic-reading nerds. She was quite capable of forming romantic liaisons with attractive young men.

She could feel the eyes of her colleagues burning into the small of her back. They were expecting her to fall to pieces again. But she knew exactly what she was going to say and do. She was going to ask him his name then she was going to ask him what time he finished. Two simple questions. She'd show them she wasn't to be trifled with. She was a David Schwimmer, no, better than that, she was a David Duchovny.

The barman leaned towards her. Too close.

'What can I do for you, beautiful?' he said and looked directly into her eyes, smiling at her as if she were a childhood sweetheart.

She froze.

His smile dropped a millimetre. 'Do you want something to drink?'

'Ub . . . ub . . . ub.'

She could smell his aftershave. She wanted to cradle his rough-looking head against her flat, naked stomach and at the same time she wanted to run screaming into the night.

He peered quizzically at her. 'Sorry?' he said. 'What was that?'

'P-Pinot Grigio?' Shelley squeaked.

He looked disappointed and gave her a bemused stare

before nodding and turning away. 'Coming right up,' he said.

'I don't want to talk about it,' Shelley said, slamming the new bottle back in the ice bucket. She felt like crawling inside the bucket herself, freezing herself solid. There had been a girl at university with Shelley whom everyone called the Ice Queen. She hardly spoke to boys and rumours flew that she was a lesbian, or a man-hater, then a vampire. Shelley sat next to her sometimes, discovered her name was Jane and they became casual friends. Jane was neither lesbian nor vampire, nor did she hate men. She was simply the most focused person Shelley had ever met. She didn't care what people said about her, or what they thought. She was there to excel in her chosen field and she did so.

Shelley admired her immensely and wished she had even half her self-possession. The problem was that Shelley *did* care what people thought. She *did* care what people said. She was terrified of rejection, desperate for approval and, not to put too fine a point on it, horny as hell a lot of the time. She didn't freeze at the first sign of male attention because she was an ice queen, too cool for school. She froze because she was screwed up.

And she hated herself for it.

Shelley slumped in her seat, trying to avoid Freya's simpering look of faux-sympathy, and Briony's told-you-so eyes. She felt the welcome buzz of her phone in the purse she had on a lanyard round her neck. She checked the text.

'Oh hell', she muttered under her breath. *Bloody Gavin.*

She popped off to the loo, not wanting Briony peering over her shoulder while she tried to rid herself of the pest. She locked herself in a cubicle and read the text.

Hi Shel, U gong 2 Alex prty then? CU there?

She rapidly texted back

Sorry am busy tonight.

She sat and closed her eyes for a while trying to clear her head of racing thoughts. Then she pulled herself together and made to put the phone away. It buzzed in her hand. Gavin again.

U at pub near ur work? We could meet there?

She groaned and flexed her thumb, trying to figure out the best way of getting rid of him, she didn't want to be rude, but . . .

Am on way home with tummy ache.

That should do it, she thought. She snapped the phone shut and made to open the door, but stopped when she heard someone enter. She wasn't in the mood to have a loo chat just now so decided to wait. Someone barged into the cubicle next to hers and sat down heavily.

Then she heard Freya's voice.

'I really can't see Shelley staying, you know?'

'Why do you say that?' Karen said from the next cubicle.

'Well, the new focus of the magazine, it's not really her thing, is it? What does she know about sex? She doesn't even have a boyfriend.'

'She's a good writer,' Karen said. Shelley smiled at this surprise bit of support. 'Excellent grammar.'

There was a pause as Karen flushed and moved to the sink. 'You're right about her being sex-starved though, according to Briony, she gets as much action as a comatose nun.'

Freya giggled while Shelley fumed. She took a deep breath and prepared to fling open the door when her phone buzzed. Gavin again.

Oh sorry to hear that – RU going to the Manga convention on Sun?

She heard the toilet door slam, her opportunity to confront Freya and Karen now gone.

No.

As she pressed send, she felt a brief pang of regret. She wasn't sure though whether that was because she was being unnecessarily mean to Gavin, or because she was wondering whether she shouldn't just do exactly what Briony was suggesting and sleep with him. No, she wasn't that desperate.

Not yet anyway.

She finally left the cubicle and re-joined the table.

'So go on then, Shell,' Briony said, apparently having realised belatedly it was time to change the subject. 'Tell us about your new assignment. You can't keep it secret for ever, you know.'

'Yes, Shelley, what's it all about? We've all told you what we're up to,' Freya pouted.

The others, further up the table leaned in, anxious to hear this. Shelley shrunk in on herself. She hadn't even decided if she was doing it yet. How could she pretend to be a sex addict when she wasn't even a David Schwimmer?

'Erm, it involves being away for a few weeks, going undercover . . .' Shelley began, hoping to keep it vague.

'Undercover as what?' Karen asked.

Shelley's phone buzzed again, offering an escape route.

I h8 prties, wanna cum to mine instead and shag till dawn?

Shelley flipped the phone shut and turned to Briony. '*What* have you been telling him?'

Briony blinked innocently. 'Who?'

'Right, that's it,' Shelley said finally, pouring herself a large drink. 'I'll tell you what I'm doing. I'm getting the hell away from London, away from Gavin the pervert, Aidan the sex fiend and you bunch of unsympathetic, unamusing nymphomaniacs. God alone knows what I'll find at the sex addiction clinic Aidan's booked me into, but I doubt they can be any more obsessed with knobbing than you lot.'

And with that, she drained the wine, grabbed her bag and walked out, but not before she heard Freya screeching behind her.

'Sex addiction clinic! Old maid's clinic, more like. What a joke!'

'Sorry about last night, Shell,' Briony said the next morning. 'We took it a bit too far. We were only teasing.'

'It's fine,' Shelley replied, smiling at her across the debris covering the sitting-room floor. It looked like rooms in films when the hero returns to find mysterious agents have turned the place upside down looking for a secret diary. Something had happened here last night involving at least two men and an electrical device. Shelley had woken to hear crashing, giggling and the occasional screech. Well used to this, she'd stuffed her ears with two sets of earplugs and turned on Classic FM. Even so, after the wall behind her head started wobbling in synchronism with someone getting a firm rogering she began to wonder if she shouldn't have gone to Gavin's after all.

'Are you going to be writing about this, er, encounter?' Shelley asked as Briony buttered some toast for her.

Briony snorted. 'God no. Neither of them was very inventive. I had to finish myself off in the end. Literally.'

Over coffee, and trying to ignoring the gentle snoring from one of the men behind the sofa. Shelley fired up her BlackBerry and checked her mail. As she'd hoped there was a message from Aidan.

'He's sent me my cover story,' she told Briony who'd come to join her. Briony eagerly peered over Shelley's shoulder at the tiny screen. The girls read for a while, Shelley scrolling. Aidan hadn't gone into too much depth but nonetheless had included a small amount of quite raunchy background information.

'Hmmm, interesting that Aidan would think this sort of thing when he thinks of you.'

Shelley was to tell the psychologists at the clinic that she was a nurse with a tendency to hop into bed with her patients. That she had some kind of deep-seated urge not only to nurse sick men back to health, but to nurse them to orgasm too. Not just patients either, doctors, other nurses, anyone vaguely connected with the medical profession. Aidan was acting as her concerned brother trying to save her sanity as well as her career after a complaint had been received from her previous hospital.

Aidan promised more details later. In the meantime,

she was to make her way to the clinic, start getting some sizzling real-life stories and e-mailing them back to the office via her BlackBerry.

'Shell,' Briony said softly, from behind her left shoulder.

'Yes?' Shelley replied, waiting for the snide remark.

'I think you're going to be brilliant at this.'

Shelley turned around to look at her friend, expecting to find her suppressing a sarcastic cackle. But Briony returned her gaze levelly. 'I mean it, Shell. You're a great writer, a great journalist.'

'Thanks Brie,' Shelley replied filling up a bit. 'That means a lot. I'd made up my mind to do it anyway, but it helps to know I have some support. I'm leaving today in fact. I won't be back for a couple of weeks.'

Briony smiled. 'That's probably just as well, really. You don't want to hang around here too long.'

'Why's that?'

'I may have texted Gavin last night and told him you liked it . . . er, you know, in the backdoor. I was drunk!' she added, by way of explanation.

Shelley paused for a moment, and then leapt at Briony over the back of the sofa, knocking her over. The man behind the sofa was woken by two women crashing on top of him, but not in a good way.

Chapter Four

Shelley took a train out to Northampton, then jumped in a taxi to the gates of the centre, which was somewhere near the border with Warwickshire. She stared thoughtfully at the discreet plaque on the right fence post as the driver turned in the road and drove off.

'Fresh Paths' was all the plaque said. This was the place. An Edwardian manor house set in two-hundred acres of sprawling countryside. It was a grey spring day and the daffodils were well past their best, standing slightly flaccid, petals turning brown.

Shelley shrugged, hefted her case and crunched her way along the gravel path towards her new beginning.

Shelley's first sexual experience of any account had happened at school. Her friend Rhianna had told her Tom Broachfield fancied her and would she be at all interested in meeting him at lunchtime behind the toilet block. Rhianna was to come too, with her boyfriend, Rod. Though perhaps not the place you might first consider as a love den, the toilets had the advantage of being underused, due to the smell, as well as being out of sight of the school buildings. The bike shed was otherwise engaged, being the place to go for illicit smoking.

Shelley had gone along out of a mixture of boredom and curiosity, as well as loyalty to her friend. The boys were duly waiting for them behind the shed, looking nervous.

'All right?' they said.

Rhianna and Rod got right down to business, having dispensed with the formalities on a previous occasion. Shelley sat next to Tom and tried not to listen to the thick glooping sounds coming from the snogging couple. She wasn't sure what was supposed to happen next, and neither, as it turned out, did Tom. Eventually he hissed in a sort of 'Oh-sod-it-I'm-going-in' kind of way and made a lunge at Shelley. As she was facing forwards, and made no effort to turn to meet the kiss, he ended up planting a smacker half on her cheek and half on her lip. She sat, stunned. Then he sort of grabbed her face, twisted it in a way supposed to be sensual, but more clammy in effect, and managed to plant one on her lips, which she kept firmly closed.

This went on for some time, and then the bell went. Shelley left, feeling a bit underwhelmed.

'You'll be fine next time,' Rhianna assured her as they walked back to double maths. 'So do you fancy him then?'

Shelley hadn't even considered this. Was she supposed to? She liked boys, at least, boys in magazines, and on the telly. The thought of wanting to kiss one of the ones in her class seemed a bit different though. These boys were real, not fantasies. It was as though someone had just told you had to marry your brother.

'S'pose,' she replied.

Shelley walked in to the grand, Regency-style reception area and was greeted by one of the most attractive men she'd ever seen, standing behind a counter. He had madly stylish hair, loose sculpted curls, and wore a blue Paul Smith shirt with the top button undone, revealing a tuft of chest hair. He also looked vaguely familiar. Had she seen him on the centre's website?

'Hello,' he said, smiling broadly at her. 'I'm Cian.'

'Hello, Cian,' Shelley replied. 'I'm Shelley and I'm here for the Sex Addiction programme.'

And then, extraordinarily, the man winked at her. 'I bet you are, my darling,' he said, rather suggestively, and then looked at her breasts. 'Ready for your examination?'

This didn't seem right. Surely the last person you need on the counter at a sex clinic is Casanova's less-reserved brother.

'Mr O'Connor!' A voice shouted from the other side of the entrance hall. 'I've told you not to talk to the other patients yet, and get out from behind there. That's for staff only.'

'Sorry!' Cian giggled and winked at Shelley again.

The owner of the voice arrived, a short, blonde lady of indeterminate age carrying a clipboard and with her hair in a tight bun. The dowdy suit wasn't just snug on her, it was tight in all the wrong places, making her torso look like a collection of over-filled water-balloons held together by a woollen sack and secured with tightened belts.

'Verity Parrish,' the lady said, proffering a hand.

Shelley shook it and smiled. 'Shelley Carter,' she said.

'Of course, you're the last to arrive,' Verity said, ticking something off on her clipboard.

'Of course? Am I late?' Shelley asked in alarm.

'Not at all, everyone else was early, that's all, must be doubly keen to get on with it, I suppose.' She frowned at Shelley, eyes seeming to ask a question.

'Me too!' Shelley said, as enthusiastically as she could. 'Let's beat this damn addiction.'

'Leave your bag here. The porter will take it up to your room. You need to just pop along to see Dr Jones, who will chat with you and ask you to sign a couple of forms, and then we'll see you in the Mounting Room for an introductory session at three sharp.'

'I'm sorry,' Shelley said. 'Did you say the Mounting Room?'

Verity gave her a stern look. 'Oh dear. I can see we'll have our work cut out with you. First floor, room 103,' she said and walked off.

Shelley trudged up the sweeping staircase. Behind her a tubby woman in a tabard stomped out of a side door, saw Shelley's bag and sighed. 'Oh fan-fucking-tastic, another pervert's arrived.'

Shelley inspected the fire-escape plan on the wall, trying to memorise the layout of the centre. The building was composed of three floors, the conference, dining and treatment rooms were on the ground floor along with the kitchens. The first floor held offices and staff quarters. The second floor was mostly patient accommodation.

Shelley counted twenty of these en-suite rooms in the building's two wings.

In addition to the main building, there were outbuildings including the drug and alcohol rehabilitation centre, a pool and gym complex and some sheds and what-not. She had already noted the entire complex was enclosed by a twelve-foot wall, useful for keeping people in as well as out. Shelley started to wonder whether Aidan's plan wasn't just to stick her here out of the way while he got on with re-organising the magazine. Why hadn't he just fired her? Did he want to force her to resign, giving up any redundancy she might be entitled to?

She stumped down the neutrally-decorated corridor, feet silent on the plush carpet and reached room 103. She knocked.

'Come in!' a voice called from inside.

Shelley found the director of the centre, Dr Janet Jones, sitting behind an enormous desk almost empty apart from a tiny laptop and a single sheet of paper. Shelley judged she might be in her late fifties, though perhaps younger as the menopause might explain her florid complexion. She had light brown hair, probably dyed.

'Shelley Carter?' Dr Jones asked. 'Sit down,' she said slowly, without waiting for a response.

Shelley did as she was told.

'So,' Dr Jones said, pulling a manila folder out of a drawer. She peered into it.

'You're a nurse?'

'Yes,' Shelley replied. She had been worrying she might get found out, but if this was the level of the questioning, she had no concerns.

'You have a penchant for sleeping with patients.' Dr Jones said matter-of-factly.

'And doctors, and other nurses,' Shelley replied.

'You are bisexual?' Dr Jones inquired. 'The file doesn't make it clear.'

'Err yeah, sure. ' Shelley said, realising she was making it all up anyway. 'In for a penny.'

'Who's Penny? A lover?' Dr Jones inquired, an eyebrow raised.

'No, just an expression,' Shelley replied.

Dr Jones pressed a button on the intercom. 'Nurse Smith, could you come to Dr Jones' office for an examination please?'

Shelley froze. Examination? Was this to be a physical examination? Worse yet, was she to be searched? Suddenly the BlackBerry in her inside jacket pocket felt enormous, she was sure Dr Jones must be able to see the bulge.

'It's a little stuffy in here,' Shelley said. 'Do you mind if I remove my jacket?'

'Not at all,' Dr Jones said absently, still reading through Shelley's file.

Shelley stood, took off her jacket and walked over to the hat stand in the corner, she popped the jacket on a hook and sat back down just as the door opened. The plump nurse came in, saw Shelley and rolled her eyes.

Dr Jones looked up. 'Thank you Sandra, please could you . . .' and she waved airily at Shelley.

'Behind that screen please,' Sandra said. Shelley did as she asked, terrified she'd notice the jacket and want to check that too.

Behind the screen, Sandra looked her in the eye and whispered, 'You'd better not look like you're enjoying this.'

Shelley blinked by way of response.

'Cos most of your lot do, you know. I'm not here to give you cheap thrills. Now turn around and spread your legs.'

Shelley was too shocked to do anything but obey. Sandra had one of those authoritative voices possessed only by senior nurses and royalty. Shelley heard Sandra's knees crack and then felt rough hands running up her leg. She found herself wishing she'd shaved. As Sandra's hand slid between her legs, Shelley tensed and was sure the nurse must realise what she was feeling was the exact opposite of someone enjoying the experience. Surely she'd be found out.

Sandra ran her hands up Shelley's sides, cupped her breasts and patted down her back.

'She's clear,' the nurse said and stumped off. Shelley straightened herself and went back to Dr Jones's desk.

Dr Jones suddenly sighed, as if tired of the whole affair. Shelley noticed her eyes flicker to the desk drawer. She pushed a couple of forms over to Shelley. 'Would you mind signing these?'

'What are they?' Shelley asked. Not that she really cared. Aidan would sort out any legal difficulties she got herself into. He'd promised her and though she wasn't at all happy with her assignment she trusted him to not let her get into any serious difficulties.

'One's a Section Four voluntary admission form, the other is for insurance,' Dr Jones replied, speaking slowly, now openly staring at the desk drawer. Shelley felt as if she were intruding.

She signed the forms and pushed them back.

'Right, good luck and all that,' Dr Jones said vaguely. Shelley realised she was expected to leave now.

'Right. Am I supposed to go to the Mounting Room now?'

Dr Jones peered at her intently, nodding slightly. 'The Mount*ain* Room, I think.'

'Ah. That makes more sense,' Shelley replied, relieved.

'Downstairs towards the back of the building, follow the signs,' Dr Jones said as Shelley grabbed her jacket and left.

'My name is Shelley . . .' Shelley was saying. Seven expectant faces looked at her interestedly, urging her on. She paused and looked around at the room. It said 'Sales Conference' to her. Bland décor, boring furniture, tedious pictures on the wall. And the inevitable brainstorming pad on an easel.

Verity Parrish coughed beside her.

'. . . and I'm a sex addict,' Shelley finished.

She shrugged and looked around at the group. Everyone wore a name tag. To Shelley's right sat an attractive if slightly used-looking lady, probably in her forties, called Rose. Shelley vaguely recognised her, she thought, from some long-forgotten tabloid story.

To Shelley's left was a smooth forty-plus man; his name was Will. Facing her, from left to right, were Abigail, Cliff, Cheryl, Cian, and Larry. Verity hadn't done formal introductions yet. The idea was that they were all supposed to give a little bit of a self-introduction before the main session got underway. During the course of the next week, each would have to give a full and frank account of why they were here. This would be a no-holds barred descent into the excesses that had led to them deciding they needed help. The magazine wasn't really interested in how these people might be helped, or what happened to them later. *Vixen* was after the salacious 'before' details, not the more worthy but duller 'after' picture.

Shelley tried to inspect her fellow inmates without making it obvious she was doing so. The others all seemed to be doing the same, apart from Larry, who was staring out the window. Shelley reckoned he was the only one younger than her.

Shelley was first to speak that day – she'd agreed to that on condition she'd be last to give her full story, for which she was grateful. She figured she'd have till Friday before she'd have to make her 'confessional'. The thought of it was already making her nervous. She was rubbish at lying and it wasn't as if she had any appropriate life experiences to draw on. She was supposed to be a sex-obsessed nurse who'd spent the last eighteen months in Australia. Instead she was a sex-starved journalist who'd spent the last eighteen years in Clapham.

'Just a little about yourself for now, please Shelley, you don't need to go into detail just yet,' Verity said in an encouraging, and slightly patronising, tone.

Shelley took a deep breath and tried to remember the cover story Aidan had put together for her. 'Er,' she began. 'I'm a nurse, and I got in trouble because I slept with a patient.' She saw Cian nodding at her, grinning; he gave her the thumbs up. 'Actually, I slept with more than one,' she said, causing Cliff and Cheryl to prick up their ears. '. . . and also some doctors . . .' Will stroked his chin and looked at her legs, '. . . and some nurses . . .' Rose raised an eyebrow, '. . . and once a video of me ended up on the internet,' Larry sat bolt upright, '. . . and then I was found tied to a hospital gurney with some straps, stark naked.' This last brought interest from Abigail. '. . . and I had to leave the hospital in disgrace.' She went on. 'My brother paid for me to come here: he's trying to stop me dragging the family name through the mud.'

By the time Shelley had finished, all seven of her fellow addicts were gazing at her in various states of interest, from the openly lecherous (Larry) to the disbelieving (Abigail).

'That's it,' Shelley said weakly, and sat down.

'Thanks Shelley,' Verity said. 'Who'd like to go next?'

'I will,' said Rose, She had long blonde ponytail, and she had a strong cockney accent, like someone hamming it up on *EastEnders*. She wore a pair of tight jeans and a top that showed off her considerable cleavage. She didn't stand, but leaned forward and placed her hands on her knees, as if she'd been preparing this for sometime and wanted to get it just right.

'I was a porn star,' Rose said. 'Some of you might know me – I went by the name Rose Saintly.'

'Oh yes,' Cian said. Larry, sitting next to him, nodded as well.

Rose winked at them and continued. 'All that's behind me now, at least the film work. I'm too old. Problem is,

I developed certain . . . habits, or shall we say tastes, while I was in the business. And I've been indulging them a bit too much in the last few years. I need to break out and have a proper relationship, while there's still time.'

She sat, and Shelley wondered if she was talking about wanting to have children. She wasn't sure if the new magazine would be interested in that side of the story, or whether they just wanted the sex stuff. She determined to try and find out anyway.

Next was Abigail. Tall, raven-haired and exquisitely beautiful in a cold way, she'd been watching Shelley with an appraising eye since she'd entered the room. Abigail wore a miniscule skirt and thigh-high boots. She'd stood and announced clearly and confidently, 'My name is Abigail, I'm a sex addict. I'm thirty-four and have been a dominatrix for the past four years, full-time; before that I just dabbled. I love inflicting pain, and have got to the point where I can't enjoy a normal sex life. I need help.'

She sat, and resumed staring at Shelley.

Next to speak was Will. He wasn't bad-looking though wore an expression that said he knew it. He introduced himself in a Northern accent as Will Trewin, a merchant banker. This caused giggles between Cian and Larry, who seemed to have become firm friends already. Shelley wished she were sitting next to them. Will glared at them and went on. 'I'm ashamed to say I'm a serial adulterer. I love my wife, Mand, and our little lad. But I just can't help myself. I've sworn off the affairs so many times, and Mand's forgiven me nearly as many. But she's finally put her foot down. If I can't mend me ways, she's off. So here I am.'

After Will, Cliff and Cheryl stood together. Verity explained:

'Cliff and Cheryl are here together, as a couple. This is not unusual. We often have couples here at the clinic hoping to improve their sex lives. But it *is* unusual to have a couple in an addiction programme, please make them feel welcome.' She waved at them to begin.

'We are most definitely sex addicts,' Cliff laughed. 'We're swingers and like to take part in threesomes, foursomes and more-somes regularly. Now that would be okay, as we both feel the same way about it . . .'

Cheryl nodded. They were a good-looking couple, Shelley couldn't help but notice. Cheryl was slim, with boyish hips and short, sandy hair. Cliff was average height, with wide-set eyes and the sort of familiar, even face that made him look an actor you spend the whole movie trying to remember what you've seen them in before. Most of the swingers Shelley had read about looked like they'd fallen out of the ugly tree, hit every branch on the way down, been stung by bees and landed on their faces.

Cliff went on. 'But the problem is we want our own sex life to be just as good, like it used to be. And we're increasingly finding we're just not interested unless there are other people involved.'

'We want our own sex life back,' Cheryl finished. They smiled at each other and sat down.

Next was Cian. 'Wotcher,' he said rising to his feet. 'Right, I'm Cian O'Connor, lead singer of The Cossacks.'

That's where I've seen him before, Shelley thought to herself.

'I'm here because I can't stop knobbing endless lines of women. It's not that I don't like it, but I think I've had enough really and need to settle down. My career's suffering and me old man's not too happy with the direction my life's taking. Tada!' he finished with a flourish and sat down. God, he was good looking. Briony would say he was the sort of man you wanted to bite bits off of.

Last to speak was the Larry, the young Asian man sitting to Cian's right, and Verity's left. He introduced himself as Larry Bala. 'I'm a Singaporean sex addict,' he proclaimed, with a shy grin. He had lovely jet-black hair and perfect skin. 'Or at least I'm a wank addict cos I just can't stop masturbating. I spend up to twelve hours a day on the internet, looking at porn and quite frankly, ladies and gentlemen, the stuff I'm looking at is just getting weirder and weirder. Plus there have been some, er, incidents in public. I need to turn my hand to something else, my father said. So here I am.'

Now Shelley realised why everyone had taken an interest in her story. There was apparently something there for everyone. Well that was okay, she could use that to her advantage, get them to open up more outside the formal sessions.

'Thank you everyone,' Verity said, shuffling her papers. 'Now, if you'd all like to help yourselves to a cup of tea or coffee, and use the facilities. Then we need to press on with the full confessionals. Shelley has already said she wants to go last. But would anyone like to volunteer to go first?'

'Yes,' said Rose without hesitation. Shelley turned to look at her. 'I've been thinking about how to tell this story for ages now, and it's all ready to fall out my head if I wait any longer.'

'Fine, let's reconvene in fifteen minutes, and we'll hear what Rose has to say. I know you've all been fully briefed on the content of the course, but let me just reiterate that you are all expected to give a warts-and-all account, what we call a 'confessional' of the events that led to you coming here. If you can't open up to us and tell us the truth, then you can't open up to what you are for yourself.'

Shelley winced at the appalling sentence structure. It sounded like so much cod psychology to her. But she nodded along with the rest, her mind wandering and thinking of the BlackBerry in her jacket. She wanted to hide it in her bag, but was worried Sandra would search it, looking for pornography or sex toys. Any kind of recording device or means of communication with the outside world was forbidden.

Rewriting the story later would be long-winded on the BlackBerry's tiny keyboard, but unless Rose turned out to be the Catherine Cookson of the porn industry, her story would need editing anyway. Aidan had asked Shelley to do her best to relate each story in the style and vernacular of the person telling it. In the old days reporters used to phone their copy through to sub-editors back in the office.

Shelley was actually quite glad she didn't have her own mobile, and not just because she didn't have to read any more embarrassing texts from Gavin. Briony had a tendency to download intensely irritating ring tones and set them up to go off at top volume on Shelley's phone, which she'd then hide at the bottom of Shelley's bag. Last week she'd had to endure a mortifying forty-five seconds on the tube rummaging through her bag, flipping tampons everywhere while looking for the damn thing as it played 'Too Drunk to Fuck', by the Dead Kennedys.

'So Rose, we want *everything*!' Verity was saying to the voluptuous blonde.

'Don't worry,' Rose replied, smiling. 'You're gonna get it.'

Chapter Five

'God I love Hobnobs,' Cian said, 'Hey Verity, are we allowed to fuck biscuits?'

She stared back at him in astonishment. 'What?' she said.

'Well I know we're not allowed to shag each other,' and he waved a hand at Cheryl, who giggled. 'So maybe we could transfer our passions onto non-threatening, inanimate objects like biscuits. I quite fancy knobbing my way through a packet of Jaffa Cakes.'

Will shook his head and snorted. Abigail looked a bit green and put her biscuit back on the plate, from where Larry snatched it up.

'And the best thing is you can eat them afterwards, saves the cost of putting 'em in a cab and sending them back to Mummy.'

'I don't think that kind of talk is really appropriate,' Verity said as they took their seats again. 'Now everyone quiet down please. Show Rose some courtesy. Rose?'

Rose stood, and Shelley smiled at her as their eyes met briefly. Rose cleared her throat and began to speak.

* * *

Home was Whitechapel and I left it when my mum told me I couldn't be a model. She was right, though it took me a long time to admit it. My tits and arse were too big to fit into those tiny frocks, but I was sixteen and knew nothing. I'd met this bloke you see, a photographer who told me my cheekbones were just right for that season, and that he wanted me to sign up with him. He asked for £150 for photos and I emptied my savings account. He gave me a place to stay too, with some other girls, mostly from Eastern Europe. I thought I had it made right then, but someone took those rose-tinted glasses off me after a few days and chucked 'em in the canal. First of all nothing happened. I just stayed in the flat with the other girls. Horrible dingy place it was. Out near Ilford and you can't hear the Bow Bells from there.

I had next to no money, and survived on nothing much more than brown rice and water. That was all the other girls ate as well. It was okay with me, I knew I needed to lose a bit of weight. The flat was owned by an agency the photographer was connected with. It didn't cost anything till you started earning, then they took it all back.

The photographer brought this clothing designer around one day after a few weeks, said he was looking for new faces for a show. Me and a few other girls were herded into a van and taken to a freezing cold warehouse somewhere near Canning Town in the East End and we were asked to strip down to our knickers. I wasn't so keen but the other girls did it straight away like they were used to it. I took off my bra and it hit me then that I didn't fit in. The other girls hardly had a tit between them; I saw a row of tiny nipples poking out in the cold air, and then looked down at my melons. Pretty fine they were, no implants then but firm enough to fool a blind greengrocer. The designer was staring at them and said something to the photographer who looked over me, said something back and they both laughed. I felt pretty cheap.

But later, the designer called me into another room and asked me to try on some clothes. He came up behind me as I was getting myself into this tiny little frock. Horrible thing it was, all colours of the rainbow, like something Joseph's slutty sister might have worn. God knows what he was thinking when he came up with that idea. Anyway, he 'helped' me into it, acting all business-like of course, but his hands went everywhere. I didn't know what was normal, so accepted it. But then I found his hand up my skirt.

'Oy!' I said, 'No pot of gold up there, mate.'

'Don't be silly,' he said in this toff voice. 'I need to see what it looks like without the panty line,' and then he whipped me keks off! I was too surprised to say anything.

He stood behind me again and felt my tits, making out that he was just positioning them for best effect. I figured something was wrong, but I still had this stupid idea I'd be a top model. Now let me say right now that he wasn't bad looking. I don't want to pretend he was some big, fat creep with a face like a bulldog. And if he'd just asked, then I might just have said yes. I'd been stuck in a grotty flat with a bunch of Polish tarts for three weeks at that point, and would have appreciated some attention from someone who spoke English. What I didn't like was the liberties he thought he could take. Still that's the business isn't it? Models are just tarts without the cream at the end of the day.

'You're very beautiful,' he said. Finally someone being nice to me. I felt a bit better after him about that, especially when he told me he'd probably have some work for me. He poured me a glass of wine and asked me to sit down.

'Now you're young,' he said, 'and you may not know how things work in this industry, but there are certain perks of the job for designers like me.'

I looked at him, standing in front of me. I was starting to guess what he was talking about, but I wasn't going to serve it up on a plate, was I?

'I mean for designers who are hetero. You know, straight?' He sipped his wine and winked at me. 'There aren't many of us, and we get to choose from a large pool of pretty young girls.' He reached out and stroked my chin. 'You see, I could choose anyone for this job I have in mind, someone with a less feminine figure, for example, it would make things easier for the dressmakers.' He shrugged, like he didn't care, but I knew he was acting. 'But on the other hand, maybe someone with your more, er, ample charms is what the fashion world is looking for. Do I take the risk? And get my reward? Or do I play it safe?'

I'd got it by then.

'You'll be expecting this reward from me, then?' I said.

'That's right,' he said, stroking my hair. He moved closer to me, took my hand and moved it to his fly. He wanted me to do the deed, to put the responsibility on me.

I made a decision then. That I'd do what I needed to do to make it. I didn't want to piss about with the scrawny Poles for the next year. I took hold of his fly and pulled it down. His cock was already trying to burst out. He wasn't wearing pants, he'd planned it all. I'd seen penises before of course, round my way the lads aren't shy about whopping it out in the hope you'll grab hold of it. But I was still a virgin. I'd never even had one of them in my mouth. It sort of made its own way out of his fly, rising up and pointing straight towards me, like it was saying hello. He moved even closer and I could smell him, a musky scent.

As I watched, a tiny drop of fluid appeared at the tip.

'You look like you've been starving yourself,' he said. 'How about a bit of sausage?'

I rolled my eyes, opened my mouth and gingerly moved my head forward. He sighed as my lips made contact with his cock. I had no idea how you were supposed to do this sort of thing, but how hard could it be, I thought. You just take as much in as you can and try to chew without using your teeth. He seemed to like it anyway. He wasn't really that big, but it felt enormous in my mouth. I remember thinking it tasted a bit salty, or not salty, but . . . well, most of you know what it tastes like. Thing was, I didn't mind the taste. And I liked being able to make him react, you know? It was like I had some power in this exchange too. Though he was trying to dominate me, I wasn't completely under his control. I pulled my head back, letting the slippery head come out and he tried to stick it back in, but I held him back, then slowly licked the end. Little feathery dabs with my tongue. This drove him wild and I liked that even more.

Eventually he couldn't stand it any more. He stood back, took off his trousers and grabbed a condom from the nearby table. I watched him, nervous, but also ready for what was going to come.

Now I reckon I was quite lucky to get the guy I did. Plenty of girls have it much worse on their first time. Sure he was pushing me into something I hadn't asked for, but he had given me a choice; it wasn't like he was raping me or anything. I could have walked out anytime I liked. Also, I was lucky he used a condom, and lube. God alone knows the places his old feller had been. Further afield than Canning Town anyway.

He came back, knelt down before me and kissed me. He pushed me back a little and I had to lift my leg so as not to overbalance, then I felt his hand slip between my thighs. He was good this guy. I only hope he'd dry-cleaned the couch recently because I reckon it got a lot of use.

I remember the feeling as his hand touched my pussy lips. It felt wrong, sort of invasive, but at the same time it felt so good, it was what I wanted. I opened my legs a little more as he bore down on top of me and I gave up the fight and lay flat on the couch. I felt his lubed-up fingers sliding across my labia and then one of them popped briefly inside me. I would have squealed but his tongue was down my throat. His breath smelt fresh and I felt my body relaxing as his mouth moved against mine and his fingers explored inside my vagina.

Then, almost before I knew it, he was on top of me

sliding my tight skirt up my thighs and exposing my bare arse to the elements. He lifted my legs up and over, so my ankles were around my ears and he positioned himself over me, I could feel his big purple head throbbing and tickling my open fanny lips.

'How old did you say you were?' he asked softly, gazing into my eyes.

'Sixteen,' I replied quietly. He smiled and nodded. Then he thrust himself inside me. We both closed our eyes and groaned. He with pleasure, I with pain.

Jesus, it hurt. I've had some huge things jammed in there since which hurt more, but I was ready for those, I knew what I was getting. This took me completely by surprise and knocked the wind out of my sails for a bit.

I wish I could say it stopped hurting after a while, but it didn't. He took some time to finish off and each thrust hurt, despite the lube. Could have been worse, I suppose, but could have been a hell of a lot better too.

Afterwards he gave me the details of the job. It was a shoot for a no-name lingerie catalogue. Not quite what I was expecting, but I was hopeful it would lead to better things, and better sex.

I got quite a bit of work from that designer, and he put me in touch with a different, more up-market agency he used who put me on their books. They also fixed me up with a better place to stay. It was a big house with half a dozen models in it, a couple of 'em were top shelf or second shelf at least. They were snooty bitches and didn't talk to the likes of me. I got loads of lingerie work, they like big tits you see. Also some magazine work for fuller-figured girls and a few ads including one on the telly. So all in all I think I got the better end of the deal with that designer. Problem was he'd turn up from time to time expecting sex. We weren't supposed to have men at the house, but he wouldn't take no for an answer. Eventually one of the other girls blabbed about it and I got thrown out.

I wasn't sure what to do, I didn't have much savings and without the agency the work was drying up. But then Bob came along and saved me. I'd met him before; he was a photographer on one of the lingerie catalogues. I told him about my misfortune.

'Don't worry,' he said. 'I'll get you some jobs. Lovely girl like you should never be out of work.' I liked Bob. He took me for a drink and was a perfect gent. Nice-looking too, which helped, though he had a bit of a beer gut.

He told me to meet him at a place in North London. When I got there I realised at once this was a different sort of modelling. In the studio was a king-size bed, and next to it was a clothes rail stuffed with a bewildering variety of lingerie. Crotchless panties, see-through negligees and what-not.

'You're shooting porn?' I asked him, more surprised than shocked.

'It's glamour modelling,' he insisted. 'I'm not asking you to fuck anyone. Not yet anyway.'

So apparently that's the line of distinction, ladies and gents. If you just take your knickers off, then you're a glamour model. Stick something up you and you're a porn star. Anyway. I'd already made my decision, weeks before in the studio with the designer. I modelled the crotchless panties, a leather bra that chafed something wicked, the see-through camisole, the frilly knickers, everything. Then we did some shots with me starkers.

'How do you feel about touching yourself?' he asked.

'How do you feel about doubling the money?' I replied.

We negotiated a bit, but it soon became apparent that the more I did, the higher the price went. It was all the same to me. I'd stepped over the line and was determined to make sure I got my money.

So there I was. Lying on a bed at some anonymous address in North London. Legs spread wide while I rubbed my clit and tried to look sultry for the camera. Fact is I was getting worked up, and Bob could see this. He took a couple more snaps, and then he put the camera down and just stared at me for a while as I continued to work my clit. I could see the bulge in his trousers and wondered what he might be like naked.

I stared back for a good thirty seconds, thinking it over, then said, 'Come on then.'

He didn't need to be asked twice, and had his trousers and pants off before he hit the bed. He kissed me and I rolled him over until I was on top of him. I was determined this time to do it my way. I wanted to be in control, you see.

I reached down between my thighs as I kissed him and took hold of his cock. He was a bit bigger than the designer, but as I was wet and ready, I figured he'd go in easy enough, and I was right. As I slid down over his pole I moaned without meaning to. He seemed to like it too and thrust his hips up at me. But I told him to lie still while I did the work. The designer hadn't just got me my start in fashion; he'd shown me a few other things too. I got me arms around his back and lifted him up, leaning back at the same time so we were both half sitting, with my legs crooked over his thighs. In that position we rocked back and forth, slowly, while I kissed him, the four or so inches at the end of his cock sliding gently in and out of me. He seemed to like that and I could feel him getting even bigger. Then he held me close to him, sat stock still and shuddered as he came. His orgasm lasted a long time and I don't think he'd had anything quite like that before. The look I saw on his face after was gratitude, not satisfaction. I think from that moment on he'd decided he'd do anything for me.

I'm sure Bob did well out of that little photo session, I saw those pictures floating around for years afterwards, and they weren't bad. I moved in with him that night. I had nowhere else to go and he seemed nice enough.

Truth is, he wasn't a bad bloke. He was just in a bad business. A couple of days after he moved in, he told me he had some more work for me, if I was interested. This time though we were talking films rather than pictures. Was I interested? I shrugged, what difference did it make to me?

He took me to another warehouse, this time in West London. Inside there was a film studio. I didn't think much of the set, just a few shabby old sofas in a fake living room. The lights were too bright and there were too many people about. I started to have second thoughts, especially when Bob introduced me to the bloke I was supposed to be in the scene with. He was dodgy-looking. He wore a manky old dressing gown and he hardly acknowledged me.

'This is Trevor "The Truncheon" Collins,' Bob said. 'He's been in this business a long time and he's a total professional.'

I must have looked nervous, because Bob said, 'Hey, don't worry love; I'll make sure you're okay. And think of the money. Look, have some of this if you like.'

He offered me some pills. 'They're happy pills,' he said. 'It'll get you in the mood.'

This is in the days before ecstasy, or even Viagra. God knows what he was giving me.

I thought about it for a second, and then decided no. I needed to be in control. If I was going to do this, I wanted to do it knowing exactly where I was, who I was and why I was doing it. I shook my head.

'Look,' he said. 'I've got to be honest with you; you only got this job because another girl pulled out. She had an overdose so won't be back anytime soon. The money's bloody good. These sorts of jobs don't come up too often. You turn this down and it's back to the crappy lingerie stuff.'

I knew he was right, back in those days there was no internet. It was all about VHS and there was good money to be made in the right niche, but there were a lot of hungry girls out there ready to do pretty much anything. I couldn't afford to be squeamish.

I stripped off and got into the skimpy dress they wanted me to wear. It didn't fit at all well, but that was okay I suppose, my boobs were so far out my top it looked like I had two bald men in there head-butting each other, which I suppose is about right for this kind of film.

Anyway, there wasn't much of a script. I was supposed to be this horny housewife playing with herself when suddenly, by massive coincidence, the doorbell rings and there's a bloke to fix the washing machine, or tune the piano or something, I don't remember exactly.

In fact, the only thing I do remember about that film was the size of Trevor's truncheon. It was more like an axe handle really, in length and shape. I was a bit scared when I first saw it, and the director loved the look on my face. I wished I'd had the pills then. The Truncheon had certainly had his. I'd been well lubed though and he was pretty good with it. When they say size doesn't matter, it's what you do with it, that's true only to a certain extent. Size helps a lot, and if you've got a big dick *and* you know what to do with it, well, most girls wouldn't say no to that.

He was a professional, and he certainly tuned my piano, I can tell you. I didn't have to act. I forgot about the lights, I forgot about the crew, I forgot about Bob. I just closed my eyes and felt that huge cock pounding into me from behind and I knew I'd found what I wanted to do. That was the first orgasm I'd had from a bloke. On screen. There were to be many more over the years.

It wasn't that I hadn't enjoyed the sex I'd had with Bob, or even the designer for that matter. It was mostly okay. But it wasn't until that day on that mouldy old sofa in an echoing warehouse in Acton that I understood how good sex could be.

And how much I wanted more.

Chapter Six

After the day's shoot, the director invited everyone back to his pad for a party. The film was finished apparently, and the entire cast came along, there were a dozen or so girls and three guys, but the numbers were evened up by the crew, who were mostly men apart from the make-up girl, who didn't seem entirely happy with the whole situation, but she came along anyway. I liked the look of her; she seemed down-to-earth and not far off my age.

The director's pad was huge. A giant loft-style apartment in Shadwell, it was, overlooking the river. There were drinks, and cocaine for those that wanted it, but I stayed away. Bob got stuck in to the Charlie though, as did most of the girls and the crew. It was just me and the make-up girl who stayed straight. I'd done my own for my scene, so we hadn't properly met. I smiled at her and she came over to chat, introducing herself as Maya. She was attractive, petite and olive-skinned.

'How'd you get mixed up in this?' I asked.

'He's my brother,' she said, indicating the director. 'I got into a little trouble and needed a straight job, or at least, as straight as you can get in this business. He helped me out. I don't know much about anything but I do know how to put on make-up.'

I saw her eyeing the cocaine being hoovered up by a gaggle of actors off the glass coffee table. She had a wistful look in her eye. I didn't need to ask what sort of trouble she'd been in.

It was pretty rowdy by that point, and the heat was stifling. 'Shall we get some fresh air?' she suggested. I agreed and we went out on to the balcony. I sipped my wine and gazed out over the twinkling lights of south London, ended beneath by a sweep of the inky Thames.

'You seem different to the others,' Maya said. 'A bit more . . . straight?'

'Really?' I laughed, looking at her in surprise. 'I'm anything but straight.'

'Good,' she said, and then she leaned forward and kissed me on the mouth.

I was too surprised to push her away, but I didn't kiss her back. She pulled away, a questioning look in her eyes.

'I'm sorry,' I said, 'I think I must have given you the wrong idea. When I said I wasn't straight . . .'

'But you're a porn actor,' she said, 'You've done girls haven't you?'

I hesitated for just a second, and then nodded my head. 'Sure,' I lied, 'Sure I have.' Then she kissed me again, and this time I kissed back.

What I started off thinking, as the kiss began, was that keeping the director's sister happy was a good move for my career. What I ended up thinking, as she slid her slippery little tongue into my mouth and licked my teeth, was that I wanted to fuck this girl. I had a rough idea what you did with other women, but absolutely no experience. Luckily she took control. She turned me around so I was standing at the rail. She dropped to her knees behind me and I felt her delicate hands slide up my thighs, under my skirt and take firm hold of my panties, I parted my legs slightly and she slid them down in one smooth movement.

Then she hefted my skirt up so my backside was exposed to the cool September air and after a pause, during which she ran her hands gently over the smooth globes of my behind, I felt her lips kiss me at the spot where my spine slips down between my cheeks. She was so gentle, and her face so soft against my skin.

She worked her way down, licking each cheek in turn, and then forced my legs still wider. She paused again for a moment. I stood there, arching my back, and gazing out over London.

Then it happened. I felt her mouth against my pussy and my knees buckled with the sweet ecstasy of the sensation. I felt her jaw moving against my mound and her tongue slipping out and flicking against my clit. She knew exactly what she was doing.

Suddenly a flash of light over the rail distracted me: it was reflected London light off the wine glass I'd been holding. I'd lost control of the muscles in my hand and let it slip. I watched it tumble down away from me, in slow motion, as I was tongued from behind. I came when it hit the ground, both the glass and I shattering into a million pieces simultaneously.

Then we heard cheers from inside and we turned to

see the others had drawn the blinds before the glass doors to the balcony and were standing there watching us, whooping and hollering. I smiled despite my embarrassment – I didn't mind being watched – but Maya hissed in disappointment.

After that we went in and the party really started. It just seemed that all of a sudden everyone was naked, or next to, and getting it on with everyone else. Looking around I could see Bob and another guy roasting a bird like it was Christmas come early. The director was being worked on by three girls, hands, mouths, pussies, everything they could think of to get into his next film. I found myself on a couch between Maya and the lighting guy, who wasn't much to look at, tell you the truth, but what the hell? He certainly knew how to handle a boom.

He slid me on top of him, so I was facing away and he slipped his cock inside me. I was still horny as hell and, while I'd enjoyed the girl action I'd had from Maya, a good, firm cock helped a bit too. Maya rubbed my clit as I rode him. Never did learn his name. I remember his big, strong hands reaching around and holding my tits as he grunted and thrust himself into me. I liked that. I guess he'd had a bit of Charlie cos he kept it up a long time. I came again. Then hopped off while Maya had a go. She was watching me the whole time. I dropped to my knees in front of them and leant forward to get closer to the action. I watched him pump that cock into her tight little fanny for a bit while I got myself worked up again, then I lowered my face and started lapping at her clit as she rode. She pushed herself forward into my face, groaning, still grinding his slippery cock.

Then I felt someone behind me getting into position and before I knew it I had another cock inside me. I didn't bother turning around. Maya and the lighting guy came at the same time and I settled back onto the mystery man's pole behind me. I came for a third time as he fucked me from behind. When I turned around I saw it was the director, he'd been doing me doggy style while I licked his sister's pussy. Now that's a bit weird. But whatever floats your boat. I'd already stopped being surprised by this point. It was anything goes as far as I was concerned.

Anyway it did the trick, because I got plenty of work out of him over the next couple of years. He went to jail eventually, after they found some of the girls he'd been using were underage.

In hindsight, I suppose my success in porn wasn't that surprising, when I look back at pictures of myself from that time. I looked pretty good, slim, but not too thin, big tits, nice and firm even before the boob job in '92. I was willing to do anything. My first anal scene opened my eyes and more besides that, but it wasn't long before I was doing double penetration. Remember I was still a teenager and everyone wants a good-looking blonde eighteen-year-old willing to do DP and girl-on-girl on the same day.

The thing was I loved it. I was enjoying the sex. Most of the other girls said they liked it, but when they got drunk they'd tell you what they really thought. Some of them hated it, some were in it for the drugs, some for the money, some cos they'd got mixed up with the wrong man. They mostly hated the actual sex, especially the rough stuff. Some preferred doing other girls, but a lot of them were squeamish about that.

So I was kind of the exception. I loved what I did and I wanted more of it. I soon lost interest in Bob; the only time we'd have sex was when he brought other people back to the flat. Once I had enough money I moved out and got myself my own pad. I didn't bother giving Bob the address. I didn't feel bad about it. He'd used me, after all, and ultimately I'd used him to get where I needed to be. I had a fantastic big flat in Chelsea, a burgeoning career and sex with beautiful people whenever I wanted it. I'd stayed off the drugs and didn't smoke and apart from the odd glass of wine didn't drink either. I was self-contained and in control.

I got myself an agent and started to make some real money. I was in demand. The reason I was able to ask for such big money was that I never bothered with a cunt double like some girls did. Everyone gets sore after a while, sometimes the big names would ask for another girl to do some of the close-up work, particularly when the guy was big, or there were massive dildos involved. I did it all myself, which gave the director the freedom to pan up and show my face as I was pounded from behind.

Also, I think it was always clear that I was genuinely into it on screen. I rarely had to fake an orgasm.

I started to accept more hard-core stuff, including an S&M flick. They dressed me up in leather and I had to whip some bloke, and then walk all over him. They made me stand on his balls which seemed a bit odd, but the guy seemed to like it. That was a rough set. In one scene two girls held me down while some guy pretended to anally rape me. I was lubed up so it wasn't too bad. For once I had to act, but in this case like I didn't enjoy it. The handcuff stuff was great. But it was always better when I was the one calling the shots. I guess it's this control thing again.

Around this time I started to get a little voice in my head telling me something was wrong. Quiet at first, and I couldn't make out what it was saying to me. Just that my life wasn't as perfect as I was telling myself.

I was offered a lead role in *Tiberius*. You might remember it, it was the biggest-budget porn film ever made, still is, I think. This was the time when internet porn was just starting to damage the movie business, and this was the industry's response. I was Marissa the Slave Girl, cruelly abused by her master, then rescued by a courtier and taken to live in Tiberius' palace in Rome.

The orgy scenes were incredible. One of them took three days to film. We stayed on set pretty much the whole time, the food they brought in was real and we were drunk most of the time. Most of the sex was undirected. My character is brought into the ballroom as the orgy is underway. I was inspected by the Emperor and his wife Vipsania, who decide to break me in on a low dais in the centre of the room as everyone watches. Tiberius was played by Johnny Brooks, possibly the best-looking male porn actor there has ever been, with a massive 10-inch sword spoiling the line of his toga, so I was happy about that. Vipsania was played by Jessie Pink, legendary in the business. She was nearly forty by then but still had a fantastic body and a wrinkle-free, beautiful face.

I was wearing a short tunic, with no knickers underneath. Firstly I lay down on the dais and a male slave came over with a bowl of hot water, soap and a razor. He was actually one of the make-up guys and he was totally uninterested in my snatch other than in a professional way, if you get my meaning. Most of the make-up guys travelled the wrong way up the Bakerloo line. I was glad about that because it meant his hand was steady. He gently rubbed foamy soap between my legs and shaved me quickly and expertly. I'm glad he knew what he was doing because that razor was damn sharp. As I lay there I was kicking myself for not getting my clit insured for a million pounds. It was a weird feeling, and I was surprised to find the heat from that sharp blade got me wet. Maybe it was the danger of it, or the novelty. I'd never been shaved before.

Then they told me to sit up on my knees. Jessie lay naked on the dais and I shuffled forward till I was knelt over her face. I lowered my head until we were in a 69 position. I dove in and started eating her out while she jabbed her hot little tongue into my pussy. I could feel my juices dribbling out over her face as she slid her mouth across my smooth, shaven mound.

Then Johnny got into the action. He came around and presented his cock to my face. I left off licking Jessie's snatch and took him into my mouth. I could only fit half of it in and his girth was such that it was all I could do to avoid choking as he slid himself in and out of my mouth. I focused on his bronzed six-pack twitching before my eyes. Jessie was all the while working on my pussy, but I wasn't ready to come.

Johnny pulled out and went around to the other end. I returned my attentions to Jessie's dripping snatch as I felt her fingers opening me gently so that Johnny could slide in between my wet pussy lips. I felt myself being stretched as he thrust himself deep inside. Ten inches is a lot to take, even for a girl like me. As he fucked me, Johnny held my hips better to force my haunches back against his pelvis. Jessie reached around and fingered my ass. I was dimly aware of the other actors watching intently, and beyond them the cameras and lights, but mostly I was thinking about the massive penis pumping slowly into me, the nimble, mischievous finger in my anus and the hot, wet mouth working against my labia.

I exploded in an orgasm as bright as a supernova. I honestly felt I was going to die, it was so good. I swear my life flashed before my eyes. Johnny never stopped his rhythmic, steady fucking and Jessie never let up with her finger and tongue. Eventually I had to pull away and I collapsed on the dais, sobbing with relief and emotional release. The director loved it; it seemed the little slave girl was finally satisfied.

But when the shooting stopped for the day and the cameras were shut off, most of us stayed on; enough eating, drinking and fucking to make the Romans themselves blush pinker than a tart's fanny.

I had sex with dozens of people that night, working my way through the cast, then the crew. Everyone else was on coke, or ecstasy, or something. I got through on coffee and naked lust. I woke the next morning, stark naked, sleeping on top of two enormous spear carriers.

Later that day one of the producers approached me and asked me if I was interested in something a bit different. I was out of my mind with exhaustion and I felt like someone had stuck a broom up inside me, brush end first. I shrugged, and told him to contact my agent.

'It's a farmyard scene,' he said, when I called him the next week.

'What, you mean I'm shagging some farmhand on a horse?' I asked.

'No, I mean you'd be shagging the horse.'

I burst out laughing. I'd thought I couldn't be shocked by anything but I was wrong.

'Actually I'm all right, thanks. I'm not that fussy about who I have sex with, but at this stage in my career, I think I'd prefer to stick with the human race.'

It was an eye opener though. What I was hearing was that people saw me as a girl who'd do anything. I decided that I was going to go for the high-class stuff from then on. My agent got me some auditions for some softer stuff, arty films, you know. Still real sex, but not so hard core. I was comfortably off by then and I could afford to do fewer and better films, just two or three a year. I wrote a couple of books, or at least I had a couple of books ghost-written for me. They made a joke about me on the News Quiz, they said I was the only woman ever to have written more books than I'd read. I had a guest appearance on a soap opera, I even got on a couple of late-night talk shows and nearly made it into the mainstream, but then the tabloids started printing double page spreads of my early pictures and stills from some of the hard-core stuff I'd done. They'd known about my background all along of course, but they obviously decided to wait until I'd become reasonably well known before they splashed on the story.

That was it for going mainstream. I ran away to LA for a while. The industry over there is much more professional, and if you've got your shit together, you can earn a lot. I quite liked it there, but everything just seemed fake, the tits, the tans, the teeth, even the sex. You could never be sure whether the director really thought you were hot in a scene, or whether he said the same thing to all the girls. You could never be sure if the guys were that into you, now Viagra was commonplace. 'Oh yeah, that's so good,' they'd say in a monotone. 'Yeah suck it, bitch,' in a voice like they'd rather I did anything but.

Some of the stuff was good. I did one film which was a take on David Cronenburg's *Crash*, and the cast and I drove around in flash cars giving each other oral sex and shagging against the steering wheel. We didn't actually get to do any crashing though; the budget didn't stretch that far. We had to give the cars back at the end – just as well the seats were leather or else the dry-cleaning bill alone would have bust the budget.

Mostly though, the films were uninspiring and mediocre. No proper story, just a series of gratuitous excuses for shagging. Not turning my nose up, you understand, a cheque's a cheque and a cock's a cock, whichever side of the Pond you're on, but, y'know, I guess I'd known for a while I was missing something in my life. I didn't understand what, but I figured I wasn't going to find it in California.

So a couple of years ago, once I'd earned a decent pension, I came back. I'd intended to retire, maybe meet a nice guy who didn't watch porn and who didn't know who I was, if there were any. Maybe even have a kid? I didn't know. I dropped right out of the business, or at least I dropped out of the sex part. I needed to keep myself busy somehow, so my agent hired me as his assistant, it helped him to have someone who knew the business from the inside, so to speak.

Problem was, I missed the sex too much. I'd never stopped enjoying that. The money wasn't so important. I had control of my life, I had my comfortable house, I even had some friends. I'd always stayed in contact with Maya, and there was my agent and some others from the early days. But it wasn't enough. I found it easy enough to find men at clubs, or on the net, but they were either dull as shit, or crap in bed, or both. I had a string of one-night stands and to be fair I never gave 'em a chance I suppose. I was like an alcoholic trying out different sorts of fruit juice. I missed Johnny Brooks, and Trevor the Truncheon. I'd send these young, hopeful girls out to shoots around the country, and all the while I'd be wishing it was me going off, not knowing quite who I was going to be working with, or what I'd be asked to do. It was that slight sense of wrongness that I missed. The sense of danger I loved. Like the feel of that hot razor against my pussy lips.

So I talked to my agent and he shrugged and said I should go for it. I made a comeback. This time on the internet. I'd never done this kind of thing before but there's good money in it. There's this company that does interactive stuff. Where you and some bloke, or some girl, sit on a bed and wait for the punters to e-mail you what they want you to do. I found it pretty dull. Most of 'em didn't have any imagination.

'Do it to her doggy style', or 'suck her tits'. And there'd

be long periods where nothing would happen so you'd just sit and look at each other trying not to laugh.

I tried to get back into films but I wasn't eighteen any more, and of course I'd lost my reputation as the girl who'd do anything. There were plenty of girls who would. I stumped up some money to produce the sort of things I wanted to do. Films with a story. We did a hospital thing, *Erection Room*, and a lawyer one called *Banging the Gavel*, but they never came to much. We lost money in the end. I kept it going longer than I should have, I didn't have my mind on the numbers, just on the opportunities to have sex. My after-shoot parties were legendary, there's footage of me on the internet at one of my own parties being penetrated by three men at once while drinking a glass of champagne. Think about it.

Eventually it was Maya who brought me down to earth. No one else had the balls to tell me the truth. 'You need to stop now,' she said. 'It's time to leave the set.'

I'd always thought I wanted control, that I just needed to be in charge of myself. But that wasn't totally true. Or at least it was true in my head, but down between my legs it was different. Down there I've always needed a bit of risk. I've needed to be coerced, or pushed, or surprised, or . . . or something, I don't know. I'm not explaining it well. It was all sorted in my head before I started talking, but I can't get the words right. I need help. I need to understand why I can't be happy with what I've got. Or why I can't learn to just love one man, or one woman for that matter.

And so I came here.

Chapter Seven

Eight pairs of eyes stared back at Rose in utter silence. Shelley was gobsmacked. She hadn't expected anything like this. She'd thought it'd be all 'His hand caressed my knee and we went back to his for a nightcap'; not 'He fucked me with his pick-axe handle of a dong until I was red-raw and mewing like a kitten.'

Nor had she expected such intimacy and openness. Rose had really given it everything and Shelley was filled with admiration for her bravery. Confident, articulate and fiercely intelligent. Totally unfazed by the random people sitting staring at her, open-mouthed.

Maybe it was easier that way. Maybe talking to strangers is less terrifying than talking to people you know? People you have to work with, or live with.

Shelley almost wished she'd been the one to go first. Almost.

Cian broke the silence by initiating a round of applause. Everyone joined in, muttering of appreciation. Larry whistled loudly, and Rose finally looked embarrassed, though she smiled sweetly through the blush. They'd walked into the room strangers, but already it seemed they'd formed a bond. Verity walked over and touched Rose lightly on the shoulder, whispering something to her Shelley couldn't hear. Rose looked up and nodded.

When things had calmed down a little, Verity spoke up. 'Now, we've overrun a little. We were to have some rec time, but as dinner will be served in half an hour, I suggest you get yourselves comfortable in your rooms first. Here are the keys. I should point out at this time that you will be sharing rooms.

There were intakes of breath and a bit of grumbling from Will.

'I expect you to help each other out here, during this course,' Verity went on. 'You have to keep a close eye on one another. If someone starts to waver, then I expect the others to step in. Your roommate has been selected carefully, as the person you are most likely to find more of a help than a hindrance in this regard.'

Shelley shrugged, it made sense. Having someone else in the room not only made it less likely you'd sneak out to molest a poor unsuspecting cleaner, it also meant you were less likely to give yourself a little treat. Putting Cian in with one of the girls might have backfired of course, so he was in with Larry. Will was sharing with Cliff, Cheryl with Abigail and Shelley was sharing a room with Rose.

Shelley smiled shyly at her new roommate as she held the door open for her. She was terrified Rose might start asking her about her own experiences.

'Sorry I went on for so long,' Rose said as they went up the stairs. 'I've been wanting to tell that story for years. The books they wrote for me were just wall-to-wall sex.'

'No, I loved it,' Shelley said, thinking to herself that Rose's version of the story was hardly *The Princess and the Pea*. 'I mean, I feel for you, but you seem like such a strong person, so . . . together. I wish I had your confidence, I don't know how I'm going to manage when it's my turn.'

As they reached the door of their shared room, Rose paused and looked back at Shelley, smiling. 'Well, if you want, you and I can work on it together, if you'd like to share?'

'That's very kind,' Shelley replied, 'I may well take you up on that.'

The room was basic. Just two beds, two cupboards and a tiny en-suite. Nothing sexy about it – the beds were so narrow as to make it inconceivable two people might be able to share, unless they were size-zero models but then they wouldn't have got much sleep, what with all the sharp elbows.

'Do you mind if I hit the shower first?' Rose asked.

'Not at all,' Shelley replied, eyeing her bag, apparently untouched, on the bed. 'I'll have one after dinner.'

'Great,' said Rose and lifted her top off in one smooth motion. Shelley couldn't help but stare. Half the porn stars on the planet had had their lips wrapped around those babies, she thought.

Rose winked and walked off into the bathroom. Shelley noticed she left the door slightly ajar.

As the shower started up Shelley snapped out of her trance and took the BlackBerry out of her jacket pocket. She wouldn't have time to write Rose's story out now, not with two thumbs, certainly, but she needed to check it worked.

Hey Binster, here I am at Shag General. Hot stuff already. How are things?

Briony's must have been at her desk: the reply came straight away.

Hi Shel, nice to hear you're getting some action. Any idea where my pink vibrator is? Need it for my article.

Shelley decided not to go into details about whatever column her friend was cooking up.

How would I know where your pink vibrator is? Not getting hot action! Getting hot story! Have to go. Roommate getting out of shower.

Shelley snapped the lid shut. That should keep Briony intrigued, and no doubt the *Vixen* office as well, knowing Briony's less than strict approach to discretion. She found herself hoping Aidan too would want more details. Opening the gadget again, she fired off a quick text to Aidan.

Help, need more details of my past sexploits.

Shelley turned the BlackBerry off, hid it carefully in a tampon box and shoved it deep into her bag, just as Rose emerged from the bathroom. She was wearing a towel, but then immediately took it off and began burrowing into her own bag. Shelley was left staring at the porn star's rounded, peach-like backside. She closed her eyes and tried to stop thinking about arses, Aidan and axe-handles.

On the way down to the dining room, they passed Nurse Sandra. She was muttering as she stomped along. 'Could have been a psych nurse, but no, here I am waiting hand and foot on a bunch of deviants who can't keep their hands to themselves . . .'

Shelley and Rose glanced at each other and burst into giggles.

Shelley sat and stared at the enormous banana split in the dish before her, by now certain this was some kind of test. Two ice-cream scoops were positioned at one end of the seductively curved fruit. And a splodge of cream decorated the opposite tip. Someone in the kitchen had an odd sense of humour. The first course had been asparagus spears, which Shelley was sure were supposed to be an aphrodisiac. Second had been fat sausages, and now this. She looked over to the kitchens and thought she spotted Sandra through the serving-hatch.

Shelley had wanted to sit with Larry and Cian, or failing that, Rose. But instead she'd been button-holed by Verity as she came in and found herself sitting with the prim counsellor on one side while Will had plonked himself down on the other. She glanced down the table to see Larry and Rose falling about over something Cian had just said. Meanwhile Will chattered on beside her.

'. . . I'm a romantic at heart. You know what my favourite film is?'

'*Brief Encounter*?' Shelley said, taking a wild stab.

Will blinked. 'Er, yes. Isn't it fantastic?'

'It's okay,' Shelley said, guardedly. 'A little unrealistic maybe.'

'What, that Trevor and Celia would have risked everything because of a chance encounter on a station platform?'

'No, that British Rail would have managed to get them both to the station in the first place.'

Will smiled faintly. 'I love it though. Such a beautiful love, and they never even kiss. Do you know, Trevor Johnson only touches her once in that film. Right at the end he lays a hand on her shoulder as he leaves for the last time.'

Shelley frowned. 'That's not true, he kisses her in the tunnel.'

'He kisses her in the what?'

'In the underpass. At Woking. Hardly the most romantic of places, I grant you, but they definitely snog.'

Will was about to say something else, but Verity cut him off, perhaps wondering, like Shelley, whether Will was edging toward flirtation.

'So Shelley. I hope your reluctance to speak will not cause a problem. You should let Rose's performance today be an example and an inspiration. It really is important for us to get a full picture of the awful excesses . . . Ooh, Dr Galloway!' Shelley looked up to see a rather dishy-looking man had just entered the dining room. He wore a pristine white coat over a black shirt that looked as though it might have cost more than Shelley's car. Galloway had sweeping black hair, tanned skin and an air of gravitas. Seeing Verity, he waved and came over.

'This is Dr Mick Galloway,' she told the group, a little

breathlessly. 'He works mostly with the drug addiction group but has *extensive* experience in sexual matters.'

'You flatter me, Dr Parrish,' Dr Galloway said, in a smooth Western Irish accent. Shelley could see why Verity was a-flutter and began to warm to the counsellor. Going to pieces in front of attractive men was something Shelley and she had in common.

'Pay attention to this fine lady,' the dishy medic continued. 'There's nothing you can teach her regarding sexual excess.'

'Sounds like a challenge,' Cliff said, grinning at Shelley.

After dinner was coffee in the lounge. Alcohol was forbidden of course. Though none of the patients had many inhibitions left, it was better to err on the side of caution. Shelley was gagging for a glass of wine – one of those enormous glasses the Government says you shouldn't have. She couldn't understand that one, and had written an article about it. What difference did it make how big the glass was? A smaller glass just meant you'd fill it up more often.

Shelley waited until everyone else had sat before she positioned herself next to Rose. Cian looked a little disappointed. About her, or Rose, she couldn't tell.

Everyone was tired, and conversation ran mostly to discussions about the programme over the next few days. Each day varied. There were gym sessions, more confessionals, lectures and seminars on various subjects, with the occasional bit of free time. In addition, there were to be one-on-ones with Dr Galloway. *Great*, Shelley thought, *another thing to be nervous about.*

She tried to put it out of her mind and sank back into the luxurious sofa, letting the hubbub of the conversations wash over her. Again she found her first romantic attachment swimming back into focus.

It was a month after Shelley's first kiss, and she was at a party with Rhianna, Rod and Tom, who now seemed to think he was Shelley's boyfriend though she wasn't entirely sure how he'd got that idea. Still she was curious about what would happen next, and she didn't hate him, per se.

Having a boyfriend helped get you invited to parties, especially someone like Tom who was popular in the school on account of how his parents owned a record shop to which he owned a key, and which was curiously prone to stock control problems.

They were in someone's bedroom sitting in a circle on the carpet, a bottle in the middle. Someone spun it and it pointed at Tom. Someone spun it again and it pointed at the wall between Shelley and Rhianna.

'Shelley!' everyone cried out. Shelley squinted doubtfully. It was really pointing more to Rhianna than to her, but she guessed that wasn't the way the game was played. She shrugged inwardly and stood up. Tom looked like he was about to faint, he was so pale. God alone knew what he was expecting, but Shelley was pretty sure her intentions weren't a mirror image of his. Nonetheless, she stepped into the wardrobe and helped Tom into the narrow space after her. Rod closed the door behind them, leering. 'Sixty seconds,' he said, almost drooling over the implausible fantasy running in his head.

Then he shut the door. It was pitch black.

Shelley sat stock still. Tom didn't move either. He just said, 'Er.'

'Ten seconds!' Rod called out.

Shelley realised she was going to have to kick this off and leaned forward. Unfortunately, Tom did the same. Crack! She sat back, rubbing her head and giggling. Tom grunted in annoyance. Then she felt him lunge towards her, his slobbery lips colliding with her cheek. He shifted until his lips were on hers and began trying to eat her.

'Twenty seconds!' Rod called out gleefully.

Is that all? Shelley thought.

Then she felt one of Tom's hands on her right boob. She stiffened in surprise. She'd never been touched intimately before. Before she could decide whether she liked it or not, he suddenly squeezed it, hard, and she yelped in pain.

'Sorry!' he said.

'What the hell are you doing?' Shelley asked. *It's not a fucking avocado!*

'Sorry,' he repeated desperately.

'Thirty seconds!'

Shelley was beginning to realise Tom was no more experienced than she was. She fumbled about until she had his hand, and then took hold of it.

'It's okay,' she whispered, warming to the boy. 'I'm nervous too.'

She held his hand until Rod opened the door again. They emerged, blinking into the light, transformed from innocent wannabes to tentative allies, together against the world. A world of confusing, contradictory messages of sex and relationships.

Shelley was snapped out of her memories by Rose.

'You look like you're dropping off,' the ex-porn star said with a smile. 'It's making me tired just watching you. Think I might head up.'

'I'll come too,' Shelley said, yawning, though she was wondering if it was a good idea. She was trying not to think about the fact that Rose had earlier that day admitted to being unable to stop fucking even after a three-day orgy that nearly made her bleed. They were now to share a cramped bedroom.

They said their good nights and left the room, nearly bumping into Sandra as she headed for the door, coat on.

'Goodnight, ladies,' Sandra said, smirking. 'Keep your hands to yourselves tonight, eh?'

'As attractive as my friend Shelley is,' Rose said coolly, 'Some of us are capable of professional restraint.'

Sandra glowered, and then turned to Shelley. 'Dr Parrish told me you were a nurse,' she said, looking Shelley up and down with a dubious look that suggested she'd sooner have believed she was an astronaut.

'That's right,' Shelley said, feeling herself flush slightly. 'In Australia,' she added to forestall the inevitable follow-up questions.

'Oh yeah?' Sandra said. 'Whereabouts in Australia?'

'Oh it was a pretty small place,' Shelley said, floundering a little.

'I lived there for a couple of years and worked in a few small hospitals,' Sandra pressed. 'What was the place called?'

'Erm, Warrumbungle . . . burra Hospital, Infirmary,' Shelley offered.

'Warrumbungleburra?' Sandra repeated. 'Never heard of it.'

'There you are,' Shelley said in triumph. 'Told you it was small.'

'Leaving so soon, Sandra?' a voice said from behind them. It was Cian, come to save the day. 'I'd hoped you and I could share a quiet moment in one of the consultation rooms.'

Sandra glared at him. 'I don't care who you are outside, Lover Boy,' she snapped. 'In here I'm in charge and I'll thank you to keep your perverted ideas to yourself. You're supposed to be in a sex addiction group and you're coming on to the nurse?'

'I haven't started the course properly yet,' Cian protested. 'Until I've done my story I'm still a sex pest and I'm determined to make the most of it.' With that he stepped towards Sandra, who squealed and rushed off through the front doors, slamming them behind her.

The girls laughed, and Cian winked at them. 'The charms are fading. Goodnight, ladies.'

Up in the room, Rose yawned and announced she was exhausted, to Shelley's relief.

'I'll pop in the shower,' Shelley said, 'and get changed in there, so as not to disturb you.'

She took her bag into the bathroom and closed the door firmly behind her. She planned to take her time in the shower, have a good scrub and then, hopefully, Rose would be asleep and Shelley could write out her confessional and e-mail it to Aidan.

She slipped off her clothes and leant into the shower to turn the knob. As she waited for the water to warm, she inspected herself in the mirror. As ever she was neither particularly pleased nor dreadfully disappointed. She was happy being a brunette, and she could see she had a pretty, if unexceptional, face. Shivering slightly in the cool room, she ran her hands down over her waist, with just a trace of a tummy. Her boobs were small but firm; she cupped her hands under them and massaged them gently, wondering what it would be like to have sex with a camera lens shoved into your nether regions.

Shelley looked down there. Her lady-garden needed a bit of pruning, she decided. Months of neglect were making themselves known through excess growth. Imagine a hot razor scraping at your most tender spots, she thought. The idea made her shiver, though with disgust or excitement she didn't want to think about.

She slipped a hand down between her legs and felt wetness. Rose's story had turned her on more than she'd admitted to herself. Shaking her head to clear it, she stepped under the powerful shower..

Shelley soaped herself up. She was trying to get sexy thoughts out of her head, but it was difficult while lathered and while thinking about the best way to write the cock-filled narrative she'd listened to earlier in the day.

She found herself rubbing herself between her legs a little longer than was strictly necessary and she stopped suddenly. Shelley grabbed the shower head and directed it down there to remove the soap. She opened herself up with a couple of fingers. 'I'm just washing,' she told herself and continued rubbing.

Just then the door swung open with a bang and Rose marched in. Shelley, who had been crouching a little, stood straight up and dropped the shower head with a clang.

'Don't mind me,' said Rose through the steam. 'Just needed to brush my teeth.'

Shelley felt the blood rush to her cheeks. She wasn't sure how much Rose could have seen though the foggy glass but dropping the shower head in surprise probably gave the game away. She also couldn't help but notice that Rose was wearing a see-through negligee. Not the sort of thing first on the list of things to pack when attending a sex-addiction class, but maybe it was all she had. For her part, Shelley had brought a pair of track-suit bottoms and a selection of baggy old t-shirts.

She turned her back on the other woman and began washing her face instead.

'Night, night,' Rose said eventually and closed the door behind her.

Shelley decided that not only had she better keep her hands *to* herself, as Sandra had suggested, she'd better keep them away *from* herself too, especially when there were others about.

The thing was that she was horny as hell. She tried to think of something else as she dried herself. After taking her time getting dressed and brushing her teeth, she peeked out through the door and saw Rose curled up in bed, sleeping soundly. Shelley took out her BlackBerry. Noticing a power point, she went back into her bag for her charger. She rummaged for a good five minutes before she finally admitted to herself she hadn't brought the damn thing. The battery on the device would give her a good few hours, but there was a lot of copy to write, she would probably need to charge it up at least once.

She rolled her eyes, sat on the loo and turned it on. There were e-mails from Aidan and Briony.

Shelley, still working on your cover story, apologies for the delay. We've had the auditors in looking through last year's accounts. But if pressed, say you were at the Queen Adelaide Hospital in Cairns. If they ask who your supervisor was, tell them Jane Masson, she's an old friend who'll confirm your story if anyone calls.

More soon, currently working on your character's early sexual exploits. Good luck.
Aidan Carter

Well, that didn't help, she thought. The idea of Aidan sitting in his flat writing about Shelley having sex with ambulance crews on deserted Australian beaches wasn't doing anything to dampen her flames.

She read the e-mail from Briony

Hey girlie, still haven't found that dildo, seem to remember inserting it into someone on that Friday night before you left. Maybe it's still where I put it. Oh well, must pop down to Ann Summers for a replacement, I've heard good things about the Berserk Bunny; apparently it has three extra prongs. Can't think what the third is for but looking forward to finding out.
Miss you,
Brie

Shelley smiled. 'I miss you too,' she whispered. Rose would know what to do with the third prong, she thought.

Then Shelley opened a new e-mail and started to write Rose's story.

Two hours later, thumbs sore, Shelley crawled into bed. Her mind still racing, she glanced over at the sleeping form in the bed next to her. Rose's shoulder raised and lowered gently as she breathed. Shelley slipped into a doze.

When she awoke, she was lying on a hospital gurney. Through a window to her left she saw a glorious blue sky and heard the haunting sound of didgeridoos. A boomerang whistled past the window, only to return a few seconds later pursued by a bouncing kangaroo.

How did I get to Australia? Shelley thought, and made to sit up. But she couldn't. She was strapped to the gurney. As she looked down at herself she realised in horror that she was totally naked. Then, to make matters worse, the door swung open and in walked Aidan Carter and the staff of *Vixen* magazine. Shelley desperately tried to close her legs but found these strapped to the side of the gurney.

'Good morning, Ms Matthews,' Aidan said cheerfully in a dreadful Australian accent. 'I hope you don't mind, but I've brought some students in to have a look at you today.'

Freya leaned forward and had a good old stare. The post-room boys were taking pictures on their mobiles. Briony gave her the thumbs up.

'Actually,' Shelley said, 'I bloody well do mind! And can I have a gown?'

But Dr Carter, as he was, ignored her and reached over to a tray, picking up a sleek black truncheon that was over a foot long.

'What the hell is that?' Shelley asked. Despite her position, or maybe because of it, she felt a tingling in her loins.

Aidan looked at her in surprise. 'This is for your treatment, Ms Matthews. Don't you remember? This is what you need. To get better.' And with that he strode forward and stroked the tip of the truncheon across Shelley's naked belly. She shivered involuntarily.

Aidan leaned over and kissed her on the lips as she felt the truncheon slide down towards her open legs. She closed her eyes and imagined she was Rose, being penetrated by three men and drinking a glass of champagne. Think about it, Rose had said.

When it happened she came quickly and hard, thrusting up against the pressure of the rigid, black instrument.

The orgasm woke Shelley up and she lay there for a few moments wondering how that had happened before she realised she had a hand down in her trackie bums. Her dream self had decided she needed a little treat after all.

Chapter Eight

Next morning after breakfast, Shelley felt surprisingly good.

They'd been woken by Sandra, which had been a bit of an unpleasant surprise.

'There you are,' she said, setting down to steaming mugs. 'Two cups of *medicine.*' Then guffawed at her own 'joke' before leaving them to it.

Rose glanced over at Shelley, puzzled. 'Is she serious? Is there something in the tea?'

Shelley sniffed it. 'What was it they used to put in schoolboys' tea to stop them playing the wrong sort of games with each other? Bromide?'

'I think so, does it smell funny?'

They decided not to drink the tea. Shelley poured it down the sink and they went down to breakfast in the canteen. Abigail, Cliff and Cheryl were already there. The swingers smiled and gave her a cheery welcome. Abigail just nodded. Shelley realised she'd barely spoken a word beyond her introduction since the course started.

Sandra wasn't around so the breakfast was mercifully free of phallic objects, not even sausages. Shelley was ravenous and chose bacon and scrambled eggs with toast after she'd failed to satisfy her hunger with a bowl of muesli. In fact, she thought, looking around, the centre was almost entirely free of anything even remotely sexual. There were no red-tops available, only the *Guardian* and *Independent* were allowed, and even they had the arts sections removed so no errant tits could sneak through. *Cure by broadsheet*, Shelley thought. The magazines were all *Horse and Hounds*, or *Provincial Kitchens*.

Shelley's admittedly hurried research on the centre had informed her it didn't just cater for sex addicts; there were other addictions catered to as well, drugs and alcohol being the most extensive programme. Also the sexual health clinic dealt with a huge variety of other sex-related psychological problems. All in all, it was clear the interior designers had been given a brief to keep everything as neutral and flat as possible. The most erotic thing in the room was an uncovered, though admittedly rather shapely, table leg.

Will popped up behind her as she reached the end of the queue for the hot food. 'Carry your tray, Shelley?' he said, but he was interrupted by Dr Parrish who wanted to ensure he wasn't pestering Shelley.

'Save your strength for your confessional today, Mr Trewin,' she said primly, and led him away by an elbow. *Hmph*, thought Shelley. *Carry your tray indeed. Did he think this was the 1950s?*

'I'll take that for you, Madam,' Cian said, grabbing Shelley's tray and motioning for her to lead the way. Shelley tittered like a schoolgirl, instantly charmed by the offer. The difference between a gallant offer and a sexist one has a great deal to do with how much you fancy the bloke making it.

Shelley couldn't help but notice that Cian looked a little rough, like he hadn't had much sleep. Then Larry entered and Shelley realised he too looked awful, unshaven, with bags under his eyes and a pale, puffy look. Were the boys ill? Had they smuggled a girl into the room, or some magazines?

'Great,' Verity said, once they were all there, munching away, 'We didn't lose anyone in the night, then? Don't laugh, it's happened before. One course we lost three in the first week.'

After breakfast, Shelley spent a couple of hours in the gym and pool trying not to think about anything in particular. Then there was a brief session in the River Room, at the front of the building, where there was a projector. Verity closed the blinds and Cian clapped at the back. 'A film,' he squeaked happily, 'starring Rose Saintly, perhaps?'

Verity ignored him. 'The film we're about to watch is called *It's Okay to be Alone*.' She pressed play and went to her seat.

'Being alone isn't my problem,' Larry muttered from his seat behind Shelley.

The film began; it had the feel of one of those dreadful corporate videos you have to watch at company training days. The acting was terrible and the plot involved a woman meeting a moustachioed man at a bar, then agreeing to go home with him before waking up the next day feeling used and guilty.

Then the narrator popped out and suggested they go back in time and try it again, only this time the woman was to refuse to go with him. All ends happily. Shelley found herself yawning, looking at her watch and cursing Aidan's name. Verity turned the lights back on. 'I hope you all enjoyed that, just a bit of fun.'

'It *was* fun, Verity,' Cian said. 'But educative as well.'

Verity smiled back at him uncertainly, not entirely convinced of his sincerity.

Immediately after lunch, they re-assembled in the Mounting Room, as everyone now insisted on calling it after Shelley had told them of her mistake over dinner the night before. Verity waited until they were all seated, then began.

'We've all had a chance to think and reflect on Rose's confessional. Let's hear from another member of the group. Will? Would you like to share the reasons you're here?'

Will stood up, thought better of it and sat down again. Then changed his mind again and stood up. He ran his hands through his hair nervously.

He hasn't put as much thought into this as Rose, Shelley thought. Out of all of them in the group, Will was the one who seemed most uncomfortable here, herself included.

'Where should I start?' Will said absently.

'Ahem,' Verity coughed, meaningfully and gave him a pained look that reminded Shelley of the look her mother had given her once when she'd painted go-faster stripes on the dog.

'Please why don't you tell us why you cheated on your wife,' she suggested calmly.

'God,' said Will. 'That's not an easy question to answer.'

'It's why you're here,' Verity said gently.

Will nodded. His eyes met Shelley's briefly and she gave him a quick smile and a nod. He clenched his fists and began.

Chapter Nine

Okay, so I'm not proud of what I've done, but I'm here to tell the whole truth, so I'm going to tell you exactly what I did, who I did it with and how I felt about it at the time. I've told my wife a lot of this, but not with the details, you know what I mean? And there are some parts I haven't told her at all.

Now the way I see it, men are hunters, right? It's biological; you can't do anything about it. It's not natural for a man to sleep with just one woman. I know that having a bloke about the place is good for a kid when they're little, but it doesn't really matter if it's your real dad. My real dad was never around and it didn't do me any harm.

I've always liked to get my end away. One girl was never enough. Everyone does it at school, don't they? It's just lads, trying to sow their oats, get a bit of a reputation, shag as many as you can and keep score with your mates. You blokes know how it is.

Where I grew up, in Bradford, everyone lived in terraces, we all knew each other. Fridays and Saturdays you'd go out with your mates and try to score, Wednesday was ladies' night, when you'd go out with your lass. We all had steady girlfriends, me and my mates, it didn't mean you couldn't snog other girls, or shag 'em if they'd let you. The girls were all doing the same on the weekends, they'd go to different pubs in different parts of the city, everyone knew the score.

I've always been confident, so I always got the girls. I never had any problems and my mates used to get me to go over to a group of ladies and get talking to them, then they'd come over once I'd got in there. I got to choose whichever one I wanted as payment.

My dad left when I was little and Mum worked all hours, so I could usually bring a girl back home with no one bothering us. I lost my virginity on my Captain Caveman duvet cover when I was fifteen. She was a lovely lass, big boned, but still young and firm back then. She's probably pushed out fifteen kids by now and slack as a wizard's sleeve, but she felt pretty good to me. She knew what she was doing, older than me you see. She took off her clothes and lay down on the bed, pulling me down on top of her. She kissed me for a bit. My head was full of questions. What do I do next? Can she tell I'm a virgin? What time did Mum say she'd be home? Can you get a girl pregnant by kissing her?

Then she shoved my head down between her legs. I was so shocked I froze, until she said: 'Go on then, lick it.'

I was such an idiot: I licked the hairs at the side.

'Not there you div! Between the lips!'

Lips? What lips, I thought. But I had a good look and a bit of a feel and saw what she meant. I prised apart her sticky labia and gingerly stuck my tongue in. I expected it to taste disgusting, but it wasn't at all. Like something alive, do you know what I mean? She wriggled a bit and I stuck my tongue in further; she really liked that so I started licking harder.

'Are you a dog?' she asked, and showed me where the clitoris was. Once I'd got my head around the idea and my tongue around her clit I sorted her out quite quickly. She spasmed silently, her mouth half open and her eyes fully closed. I remember looking up at her as I lapped away thinking this was pretty cool. She felt her tits as she came, fingering the nipples and pinching a little. I thought that was really sexy, like Kim Basinger in *9½ Weeks*.

Then it was my turn. She laid me back on the bed and got on all fours to one side of me. I stroked between her legs as she wrapped her lips around my cock-shaft. I could hardly believe it was happening as she started sucking me off. I'd never imagined it was going to be this good. I'd heard older boys talking about this at school, using that old chestnut 'Did she spit or swallow?', and it had taken me a while even to believe girls were willing to do this at all. Her mouth was hot, not just warm but hot. She gagged a bit as the tip of my penis stroked the back of her throat, but she kept going. She didn't swallow or spit as it happens, but I hardly noticed. She stroked me off as I shot my load and ended up with a milk glove for her troubles.

I lay there in a daze while she got her clothes back on. 'Gotta get back,' she said. Then she was gone. I cleaned myself up and went back down the pub for last orders. And to tell my mates of course.

Anyway, there were plenty more like that over the next few years. I had a few 'proper' girlfriends, some of whom I slept with, some I didn't. On the weekends we went out in a pack, hunting. Everyone did it.

By the time I met Amanda at college, I'd calmed down a bit. Still liked the ladies, but I was tending to stick with one at a time mostly. They never lasted long; I was always on the look out for the next one. I'd done well in maths and had this idea I'd be an accountant. The mills had all pretty much closed by then, so I was keen to move away once I'd qualified. Not to London, full of poofs, I thought. I wanted to go to Leeds, or Manchester. Home was getting a bit crowded with three sisters and Mum's new boyfriend, so I moved out of Mum's and into student digs in Wakefield. Well, I didn't want go too far; I still needed to go home on the weekends to get my laundry done. Amanda was there doing bookkeeping. She was the most beautiful girl in the college. Hell, she was the most beautiful girl I'd ever met. Still is.

I asked her out as soon as I'd met her. 'How you doing?' I said.

'Sorry, what?' she said. She had a southern accent, not real posh, but posher than anyone I knew. 'Bollocks,' I thought. I didn't know any southern girls but I knew the rules were different. Rumours were they all had sticks up their arses to start off, but if you got one in the sack, she'd suddenly transform into the most perverted hell-slut you'd ever imagined. Well, I've never backed away from a challenge and I wanted to find out if the rumours were true.

'Do you fancy a drink?' I said. 'Would you like to go for a drink with me?'

She stared at me. 'What, on a date?' she said, as though I'd suggested we swap heads.

'Er, yeah.' Feeling unsure of myself wasn't something I'd had much experience with before.

'Are you the chap with the souped-up Ford Capri?' she asked.

'That's me,' I replied proudly. Girls loved that car.

'No thanks,' she said.

'Why, because of the car?' I asked, stupidly.

'No, because of the driver.' She replied. 'Sorry, but I don't think we're compatible.'

Stuck-up cow, I thought. I was furious. So you know what I did? I asked her best friend out. Now this was a northern gal. Jules her name was. Big arse and no tits but she banged like a mental carpenter. When I stayed over at their flat, I made sure Jules squealed nice and loud to show Mand what she was missing. I was an arse. I told you I'm not proud of myself. Mand probably didn't care, but I did. I hated to see her with other blokes, especially when she brought them back to the flat.

I tried to become friends with Mand, wheedle my way in, you know? But she was always polite without ever seeming to warm to me. Sometimes I'd just be sitting on the couch with her, watching telly, and I'd say something, then she'd just walk off into her room and slam the door.

She used to mock me, too. She'd mimic my accent, singing 'Ilkley Moor' and calling me Geoffrey Boycott. Worse yet, she'd make jokes about my car. 'What holds a Ford Capri together? All the screws in the back.'

So I realised after a while that I was wasting my time. There were plenty of other girls out there and that I had to get used to the fact that I couldn't have just anyone I wanted. Some girls would always say no. I decided to dump Jules and give up on the project.

But then Jules got hit by a car and ended up in hospital. It looked like she was going to die. Mand and I would sit there by her bed, waiting for her to open her eyes, and just chatting. I felt awful, I'd lied to Jules, I'd lied to Mand and now here I was, sitting, pretending I felt something more than I did for a dying girl. I made up my mind that, whatever happened, once I'd got out of it all, I'd stop lying, stop shagging and just find one nice girl and stick with her.

But as the days went on, and Jules didn't look like waking up, Mand and I would spend more time together. Now I didn't have an agenda, now I felt some shame. I was more like my real self, I think. That's what she said to me later. We just talked about normal stuff. We'd go for coffees together, then for meals. We'd walk by the river to get the stuffy hospital air out of our lungs, and one day we found ourselves stood in the park and hugging each other, she had tears running down her face and I was blubbing like Gazza when he got that second yellow card in the '90 World Cup.

Then she was kissing me and I still don't remember how that happened but everything was mad just then and my head was screwed. Jules died the next day. Amanda and I slept together for the first time when we got back to the flat after the funeral. The rumours about posh southern girls were true, she was like a demon. I put it down to the fact she was out of her head with grief, but I woke up with scratches down my back and she was walking funny when she got up to go to the loo.

She cried for most of that day.

'Are you crying because she's gone, or because of what we did?' I asked her quietly.

She shrugged, hiding her puffy little face from me behind that soft black hair of hers.

I didn't feel too good about what we'd done, at least in terms of guilt. I hadn't loved Jules but it did feel a bit like being unfaithful; especially with her only a few days cold.

But we needed the physical contact. We both did. I bet that sort of thing happens a lot. And remember, I genuinely had feelings for Amanda. I didn't think she felt the same way but that was her problem.

'I'd better go,' I said. 'I'm sorry.'

She sat up and looked at me like I'd stabbed her.

'That's it? You're just going to wipe your cock on the curtain, jump in the Capri and ride off to find some other poor cow?'

I stared back. What was she on about? 'I thought you hated me?' I said. 'All those jokes about my accent and my car?'

'Did it seem like I hated you when I had your dick in my mouth last night?' she snapped.

'I thought . . . I thought you just hopped into bed with me because you were upset about Jules,' I said, totally floored by now.

'Is that what you think of me?' she said. 'That I'm so

shallow I'll just fuck whoever's nearby when I'm feeling a little sad?'

'Then why?'

'Because I love you, you . . . moron!' she spat, in a voice that didn't sound like she loved me, but then again maybe it did.

I didn't get it, and told her.

'When I told you I didn't want to go out with you that time, of course I wanted to go out with you.'

'Eh?'

'I didn't expect you to give up just like that. You were supposed to pursue me.'

'Oh.'

'You had a reputation back then. You seemed to be trying to get as many notches on your bedpost as you could. I didn't know you like I do now: I believed what people said about you.'

I sat down and waited for her to go on, amazed at what I was hearing.

'How do you think it made me feel when I was the only girl in the college you didn't seem interested in?' she said.

'I was interested. I *did* ask you out!' I protested. 'The moment I first saw you, but you said no.'

'You only asked once,' she replied. 'Then you gave up and went out with my best mate instead. How do you think it was for me lying in bed listening to you two together? I hated you, and I hated her.'

'Jesus,' I said. 'Why didn't you move out?'

'I don't know. Because I hoped that one day, if I stayed around you and Jules, one day something would happen.

And of course I didn't hate you all the time. I didn't hate Jules. I just . . . hated how things were. You used to try to be so nice to me, to be my friend, and I knew I was being cold with you, but I couldn't get closer because of how I felt about you. I'm sorry.'

Then she started crying again, so I took hold of her, stroked her hair and waited for her to look up at me. Then I kissed her. It had been a bit of a roundabout journey, but I'd got what I wanted.

She was wearing a baggy t-shirt, full of holes. I tore it off and threw it on the ground, then I lifted her and carried her back to her bed. She lay beneath me, my prize for all the time and effort I'd put in. My cock was pushing hard, trying to find its way out of my boxers to see what was going on. I slipped them off and climbed on to the bed, shuffling towards her on my knees. I lifted her legs and swung them over so she was lying on her side, jack-knifed across the bed. I leaned over her and kissed her hard, pulling her head back by the hair and working my lips over her chin and down her soft white neck. As I leaned across the tip of my cock tickled her backside and she reached down to take firm hold. Her breasts were firm but busty and they hung heavily to the side. I took hold of her left breast and took the nipple in my mouth, massaging it with my tongue. I caressed the other breast gently as I worked the dark brown nub with my teeth and lips. Then I lifted myself up and looked at her. She tried to sit up but I pushed her back down in the same position.

She looked up at me, her nostrils flaring as she wondered what I had in mind. I rubbed a thumb against her labia to check she was wet enough, and then positioned myself. By stretching one leg out behind me and hooking the other over her bent upper thigh, I had just enough access to her vagina, once I'd lifted her leg up a little. I worked my cock in gradually. In that position, with the weight of her right leg bearing down on my cock as it forced entry, she felt very tight. She moaned in appreciation.

It was a slightly awkward position for me, but I knew she'd like it. It was comfortable for her and I could reach around and play with her nipples or clitoris as I pumped into her. We could also kiss and I wanted to make sure we did a lot of that. I knew she was still vulnerable and I would have done anything to make her feel happier.

Soon though we both wanted to shift position and she turned face down on the bed. She spread her legs, giving me better access and I lay on her back, holding her shoulders tight as I thrust myself into her, eyes closed in effort and lust.

'I want to look at your face as you finish,' she whispered. So I got up and let her turn around before re-entering her. I finished off quickly, supporting myself with my elbows as I gazed into her eyes. She smiled and thrust back with passion as I climaxed, flooding her with my come.

That's when I started to think I was in love.

It wasn't the only time I came that night. I generally don't manage more than one, but that night I had three. The third time, I was sure I couldn't manage it, and my old feller was complaining a bit, so she flipped me over and snuck a couple of fingers up my arse. I was too surprised to resist. 'Wait,' she said as she felt around inside me. It felt weird, but I liked it. I liked the fact she was doing it more than anything. These posh girls knew a thing or two.

'What am I waiting for?' I said. I was breathing heavily.

'This!' she said and jabbed at a spot inside me somewhere.

Something flipped inside my head and I found myself coming again. It was extraordinary. The feeling was so good, I just couldn't bear it. I wanted it to be over but it just kept going on and on. I was thrashing my legs on the bed and clutching the pillow so tight. It went on for what seemed like a ridiculous amount of time, totally different to a normal orgasm. If that's what gay blokes are feeling then maybe I should think about biting the pillow.

'What was that?' I panted, when it was finally all over.

'That was your Chakra,' Mand said. 'Learnt about it in India.'

'Did you now?' I asked, 'what else did you . . .' but she cut me off.

'Let's not talk about what we've done before. We're starting from scratch, yeah?'

I nodded. 'Yeah.'

Anyway, that's when I knew I was definitely in love.

Chapter Ten

When college finished, Amanda and I moved to Manchester together. This was in the boom during the late 80s and we both got jobs straightaway, good money too. I worked for financial services, Mand was in white goods. We rented a small terrace east of the city centre and before I knew it we'd been together a year. The longest relationship I'd had before that was about three weeks. You can see why I thought this was different. I'd been such an idiot thinking all that stuff about men being hunters, of course that was what little boys think. When you grow up you realise that you're supposed to pick one woman and stay with her forever, don't you?

My mates were discovering the same thing, seemed like there were weddings every weekend and after Mand caught her third bouquet I figured I'd better get on with it. We were married in a little church in Bournemouth, where Mand comes from. We honeymooned in Barbados – told you the money was good – and when we got back we bought a huge modern apartment in the centre of Manchester. Mand was doing well for herself and I made a move into sales where there was more money. I did a brokering course in the evenings to get my qualifications.

Anyway, everything was fine for a couple of years. I sometimes watched girls go by, with short skirts and low-cut tops, and I'd think about the old times, but then I'd think about Amanda, and what she could do to me and I'd think, why go out for hamburger when you can have steak at home?

Then Amanda announced she was pregnant. I was over the moon. 'Can we still have sex?' I asked

'Of course,' she said. 'It's recommended during pregnancy, as long as you're not too rough. In fact, my libido will probably be increased, plus no periods.'

So we had to cut out swinging from the chandeliers, but we did everything else. When she got big, she liked to rest her bump on a pillow while she lay on her side. I'd enter her from behind and reach around so I could rub her clit. I found I could make her come over and over again by doing that.

If she took it easy, she could go on top as well, if she went reverse cowboy she could support herself with her arms while I thrust up into her and stuck a couple of fingers up her arse, looking for that damn Chakra.

'I love you, Will,' she'd say, as she came.

'I love you Mand,' I reply. And I did. I loved her more than anything in this world.

But when Jamie came along, things changed a bit. Now I love my son. I'll do anything for him. It's for him as much as for Mand that I'm here today. But by God that kid could scream. Hours and hours every day. Always something wrong with him. First colic, then teeth, then ear infections, then chickenpox. I spent half my life in the waiting room at the clinic, listening to the little bugger scream at some poor doctor who hadn't warmed her stethoscope enough. Mand was exhausted. And of course that was the end of the sex for a long, long time. Even when things calmed down a bit, she didn't seem interested.

Home wasn't fun and now Mand wasn't working we needed extra money so I started working longer hours, trying to get my commissions up. It was around then that we got this new junior dealer. Young girl by the name of Jenny. She was tiny, blonde with perky boobs she didn't mind showing off. Confident and smart too. I liked her straight away. She made me laugh, whereas Mand just moaned at me as soon as I walked through the door. I went for a drink with Jen and told her how bad things were at home. I'd had a bit too much to drink and as we said goodbye I leaned in and kissed her on the lips. She seemed surprised but she didn't scream, just smiled in a thoughtful way and walked off.

Well, to cut a long story short, the next day Jen came into my room and closed the door.

'I'm sorry,' I said. 'About last night. I didn't mean to kiss you, I was just emotional.'

'Don't worry about it,' she said. 'I didn't mind.' She kept looking at me.

'What?' I said.

Then she shut the door, closed the Venetian blinds and walked around to my side of the desk. She stood over me, with a faint smile on her face, and then leant over to whisper in my ear.

'I think you and I are the same,' she said.

'How's that?' I asked. I could smell her perfume. It was something I'd smelt before, on some girl's pillow years ago. I couldn't remember the girl, but I remembered what I did with her. My cock shifted in my trousers at the memory.

'I think we're both hunters,' she said. 'We both see what we want, and then we go and get it.'

I shrugged, 'All good brokers have that quality,' I replied. 'Anyone who wants to be successful in business needs to be able to focus on their goal.'

'I'm not talking about business,' she said. 'As you know full well.' Then she slipped a soft hand inside my shirt and kissed my ear. I tried not to turn my head.

She nibbled my earlobe and stroked my chest. I wanted her so much. I hadn't had sex in weeks, longer than I'd ever gone since I first lost my cherry. She was beautiful. Smooth, pale skin, dead-straight blonde hair pulled back in a cute little ponytail. Icy-blue eyes. Amanda on her best day was betterlooking. But Amanda's best days were behind her. Steak she might have been, but sometimes what you really feel like is a nice, juicy hamburger.

I turned my head and she kissed me, biting my bottom lip. She took her hand out of my shirt and wrapped her arms behind my head, pulling me towards her as our kiss became more urgent. She had a wicked little tongue, fencing with mine and trying to get itself down my throat. Then, without breaking the kiss, she swung a leg across me and sat astride me, her skirt riding up, showing her little panties. She never stopped kissing me but managed somehow to unbutton my shirt and take it off.

Then finally she stopped kissing my mouth and moved to my nipples. I lay back in the chair, trying not to think of my little family at home. There was no going back though. If she'd stopped and tried to walk out at that point I think I would have forced myself on her, I was that worked up.

I placed my hand on her narrow waist and ran it up to her right breast. I, along with all the other men in the office, had been dreaming about these breasts since they'd arrived in the office, and I felt a brief pang of regret that I wouldn't be able to tell anyone I'd been first to touch them. Or maybe I wasn't the first. It didn't matter.

Her shirt felt too tight so I started fumbling with the buttons. I made a mess of it though and she just leant back and ripped the front open, firing buttons across my office and exposing her white cotton bra. She reached behind and unclipped it, exposing her small, perfect tits, nipples pink and erect. I leaned forward and took one in my mouth, sweet as a peach. She held my head against her and rocked as I suckled, stroking her back.

Then she stood up and took her skirt off.

'Those, off!' she said, pointing to my trousers. I obliged, and then removed my boxers, releasing my cock, by now stiff as a statue.

She stuck a hand down her knickers and felt herself to see how wet she was. Then she smiled, turned around and leant over the table, turning her head back to watch me approach. 'Leave the panties on,' she said.

I came up behind her and stroked my hands across her narrow hips. She had almost a boy's body, apart from the tits of course, and her pert, round little arse. I hooked a thumb inside the elastic and pulled the crotch aside, exposing her peach-fuzzed pussy lips. She sighed as I used my fingers to part her lips gently and I rubbed my cock head up and down between them. She was certainly moist enough. I positioned myself carefully, then grabbed hold of one of her shoulders and yanked her back onto me. She let out a low, guttural moan, like she'd been waiting for this as long as I had. Maybe she had. I felt like I was so big I was going to split her in half, though I'm not bragging ladies. I'm average size, nothing more, but I felt enormous that day, like I was expanding in her, like every last drop of blood in my veins was thrusting into that cock shaft just as I was thrusting into her.

I took hold of her ponytail and pulled her head back. She loved that. With my other hand I reached around and could just get my fingertips to her clit. I tickled it as I fucked her hard from behind and she came just a little before me. I fired my load into her, out of my mind with the intense pleasure as I kept pounding away into her slippery pussy.

Afterwards she slipped her skirt back on but finally took the panties off and left them in my top drawer.

I showered in the office gym and went home to my wife and child. I dealt with the guilt by ignoring it, putting it out of my head. I told myself that what happened at work, stayed at work. It was part of my male life, the hunting part. I didn't need to bore Amanda with the details of what I got up to at work. I just needed to bring the bread home.

At first Jenny and I just saw each other at work. I'd work late two or three nights a week, and if she was around she'd pop into my office and we'd fuck. Sometimes on the desk, sometimes under the desk, sometimes both. But soon enough we got bored with this: what's the point of having an affair if you're just going to get into a rut like at home?

We arranged to go off on trips together and we'd have marathon sex sessions in the hotel in between meetings. Conferences I liked the best. Mand was invited to come sometimes but I never told her that. Why take sand to the beach? We had to hide the affair from everyone else of course, so we'd be sneaking around the conference centres late at night trying not to be seen by a senior manager. It was part of the fun.

Mand never suspected anything. Jamie had settled down and things were starting to improve at home. Speaking for myself I reckoned I was happier and more relaxed at home on account of getting a regular shag at work. I didn't pester Mand for sex so much, so things were easier between us. Mand started to come across once or twice a week, so I was getting some most nights in the week and was pretty happy.

Then one night it all went tits up. Funny thing really. We'd just landed a big deal, and we went out to celebrate. Loads of us had been working on it, including Jenny, so we all went to a local bar and got wasted on champagne. Someone suggested we hit a strip joint. Jen was the only woman, but she seemed up for it, so we went along.

Problem started when one of the dancers came over

to me and asked if I wanted a lap-dance. Of course I said yes and gave her a twenty. She was a lovely bit of crumpet, I tell you. Her name was Jackie. Beautiful tits. Anyway, as soon as she started I could tell Jen didn't like it. The boys loved it of course, whooping and cheering. They didn't notice Jen sitting in the corner, giving me evils.

Jackie knew her stuff. She ground down on me with her pelvis and stroked her nipples across my lips. She leant back to give me a view and every time she shifted position, her hand seemed, just accidentally, to brush against the swelling in my trousers.

To be honest, I was a bit annoyed at Jen's attitude. I was drunk, we were having fun. Why couldn't I have a bit of a laugh with a stripper? It wasn't as if Jenny had the moral high ground, shagging a married man, and I'd never assumed the two of us were supposed to be faithful to one another. I had a wife, for God's sake.

Anyway, when Jackie invited me into the back room, I said yes, when normally I wouldn't have. I wanted to teach Jenny a lesson, but also, I wanted to milk the jealousy a little. I liked it. What man wouldn't want a cute little blonde like her to be jealous of another woman?

So I went in the back room with this girl, while the boys chanted 'Trewin! Trewin!' behind me. Now I thought I was pretty experienced with women, but that Jackie taught me a thing or two. Girls in strip joints make most of their money by bringing blokes back to private rooms and doing private dances for them. Sometimes they'll agree to do other things too, depending on the club and the girl. The key is for them to keep you there as long as possible. If a quarter-hour costs £50, then if they keep you there for longer you'll have to pay for the full half an hour.

Well, Jackie certainly kept me there for the full half hour. It didn't bother me; I was putting it all on my company credit card. I'd claim on expenses and Mand would never see the bill. Jackie danced slowly, and languidly. She moved so gracefully, like a properly trained dancer. And her body was incredible, well-muscled and toned, almost feline. She stalked around the room, coming back from time to time to sit astride me, or to make out like she was going to blow me before moving off again.

Eventually she got on top and bore down on the ridge in my trousers. She was wearing just a tiny little G-string. She grabbed my hands and put them on her breasts. I was incredibly turned on. She stared into my eyes, her nostrils flaring as she reached down and undid my trousers with one hand. She raised an eyebrow and I nodded. Then I felt her hand on my cock.

I thought that I'd go off in her hand straight away, but she was an expert, she kept me going without quite letting me finish.

'What's your name?' she asked.

'Will.'

'Do you like me, Will?' she asked.

I nodded.

'Do you like what I'm doing to you?'

'Yes,' I said, my voice cracking.

'Do you like it when I dance for you?'

'Yes.'

'Do you like the sensation of my fingers dancing on your cock?'

'I do,' I groaned.

'Would you like to come now?'

I nodded 'Yes, yes!'

I thrust my hips upwards to meet her hand and gripped the chair arms as I exploded. It seemed to last for ever. She had a tissue handy to collect the fluid.

She continued stroking me off, gently, looking me straight in the eye as I juddered and shook. Eventually I had to grab hold of her wrist to stop her.

'That was amazing,' I said.

'See you next time,' Jackie replied and disappeared through a side door. I went back to join my mates, accompanied by a round of applause. Jenny was gone.

And that was that between Jen and me. The next day she sent me an e-mail, saying 'It's been fun but I'm seeing someone else now and think we should end it.' I don't think she was seeing anyone else but she could see I wasn't someone she should get too close to.

I missed her, but in a way I didn't mind so much. If I was going to have affairs I wanted them to be casual, meaningless things, not substitute marriages. I was just glad I'd got out of it without any tearful scenes and revenge attacks. I only had one wife. I decided to take Mand away on a weekend to Paris; probably I felt guilty deep down and wanted to make amends.

But when I got home that night, the house was silent. On the kitchen table were two pieces of paper. A note from Mand telling me she'd gone to her mother's. The second was a printout of a picture that looked like it had been taken by a mobile phone. The picture was of me naked and asleep, with Jen lying next to me holding my cock in one hand. The devious little bitch had taken this picture at one of the conferences, maybe to use as blackmail, maybe just to screw me over when I ended it. No warning, no screaming matches, no begging. Just a *Fuck You, Will.* A spiteful gesture of hate.

Jen was wrong about one thing; she and I were not the same. She was too emotional to be a hunter. Women get too involved. Only men can separate home and work properly. She'd told me she didn't expect me to leave Mand for her and didn't want me to. Her words were, 'A man who marries his mistress is creating a job vacancy.' So why she felt she had to ruin my life I don't know. But that's women for you, who knows why they do the things they do?

Amanda was gutted. She'd never suspected a thing. I don't think I'd realised before then how much she loved me. How much she *had* loved me. Maybe I'd never really believed she felt that way about me, even after what happened the day Jules died. I never forgot how I felt that day when I first saw her, and asked her out. I felt low, rejected. I didn't like that. Maybe a shrink would tell me I was angry at Mand for what she did to me, that the affair was a way of punishing her. But I don't think so; I understand that my cheating is about something in me, not what anyone else has done.

Anyway, Mand did forgive me eventually, Lord knows why. I'd like to think not just because she wanted Jamie to be with both of us, but because she still loved me. I don't know for sure. We slowly rebuilt our life together, went to counselling and things seemed to be getting back to normal. Problem was, she wasn't coming over in bed. I was frustrated. I couldn't think of anything but sex. I didn't want to push it with her, but I was desperate.

Then I ran into Debbie one day just outside my office building. Debs was a girl I used to see at college, before I met Mand. Thing about Debs was that she was a friend, rather than a girlfriend, or a one-night stand. We had a right laugh me and her, and we did used to sleep together sometimes. Bed-pals, we used to call ourselves, though I guess the other term is fuck-buddies.

I didn't have time to talk right then, so we arranged to meet for lunch. As soon as we sat down and ordered I realised I was in trouble. She looked fantastic, had filled out a little bit maybe, but she looked good with it. She was looking back at me, eyes twinkling a bit mischievously like they'd used to before she suggested we pop back to hers. I didn't want to hurt Mand again, but I was so horny, and I knew I could count on Debs not to say anything. It was a safe bet. If you ask a hundred men whether they'd have an affair, maybe ten of them would say yes. If you asked a hundred men whether they'd have an affair if it was cast-iron they'd never get caught. Ninety of them would say yes.

So I called the office and told them I'd got an important sales lead and wouldn't be back in. Debs and I checked into the Hilton. I remember lying in the bath with a glass, both full of bubbles, when Debs walked in, naked and stepped in to join me. I felt her feet slide up inside my legs and her toes tickled my cock. Then she slipped one foot under and gently worked the toes between my arse cheeks. I smiled at her, she was always a wicked one and it looked like she'd learned a few things since I saw her last. She wriggled and shifted her big toe and eventually got it into my hole. It felt weird, different and exciting cos it was a bit wrong. It was the sort of thing Mand never did these days. Something I didn't expect her to do, anymore.

Debs sat on my lap and pulled my dick up between her legs and squeezed it between her soapy thighs. Then she began shifting up and down a little and I could feel her slick pussy lips rubbing against the shaft of my cock. She stroked the tip, which just about poked out of the water. My hands went around her and massaged her slippery globes. Her tits were sagging a little more than the last time I'd seen them, but I didn't care. There was something nostalgic about the experience.

She stayed in that position for a long time, clearly enjoying the sensation. She craned her neck around so we could kiss over her shoulder and one of my hands slid down the gentle roll of her tummy and found its way down into her dark thatch. I rubbed gently and she grunted in appreciation. Then she lifted herself up, leaned forward and stuck her backside into my face. It took me a bit by surprise, but I got into it after a while. I nuzzled against her cheeks at first, and then slipped my tongue into her soapy crack. She was clean and it didn't taste of anything, and she loved it, pressing her arse back onto my face. She had one hand on my cock all the time. She reached one hand back around and I felt something wet pour down her back and between her cheeks, it was champagne. The bubbles tickled my nose and I dived in, lapping up the sweet nectar.

Once she was well and truly wet and ready, she sat back down, more slowly this time, guiding me with one hand. She moaned as my cock pressed into her tight anus. She seemed to want more and she forced herself down onto me. I was a bit taken aback, I didn't expected this, but I wasn't complaining, it felt tight in there and it hurt a bit, but I expect it hurt her more – she was wet back there but she'd not used any lube.

She worked herself up and down, clenching her muscles in a way that suggested she'd done this before. I found it hard to gain any purchase though, so when she asked me to go a bit harder, I grabbed her round the belly and flipped her over, staying inside her all the time. Then I was on my knees, behind her as the bath water sloshed over the side, and I had more control. I began pounding into her. I could see her heavy breasts swaying as I fucked her in the arse. Just yesterday I'd been counting my lucky stars that Mand had forgiven me and I'd been sure I'd never so much as look at another woman, and here I was twenty-four hours later in a hotel bathroom, fucking an old flame up the jacksy.

What's most strange though was that I didn't really feel guilt about it. I didn't feel anything except animal lust.

I didn't see Debs again. She didn't live near; she'd just been in Manchester on business. We kept in touch by e-mail, but neither of us made any attempt to arrange another meeting, she was married too and we both knew the score, always had.

I'd like to tell you Debs was the last affair I had, but I'd be lying if I did. She wasn't even close to the last. There was my secretary for example, a few months later. I'd employed her specifically because she was the only one of the three I interviewed who I didn't fancy. So why was it I was caught shagging her in the plane toilet on the way to a meeting in Frankfurt? It was only the flight attendant who caught me, so that didn't matter. In fact, I'd left the toilet unlocked because I wanted to be caught. It got me horny, the thought we might get seen by someone. Felt sorry for poor old Fiona, the secretary, though. She had her skirt up and her knickers down. I was standing on the toilet with my cock in her mouth when the door opened. I had to jam a fist in my mouth to stop myself laughing at the sight of her face.

And after her there was the hotel receptionist at a conference in London. I hardly said anything to her, just winked and asked her if she was going to turn my sheets down personally. She was waiting for me when I came back into the room that night. What was I to do? A hunter takes every opportunity. You never know when there's going to be another.

Anyway I won't list them all. I'll just mention the last one, because it was her that Amanda found me in bed with. It'll make you cringe when I tell you; it's a bit of a cliché. I only went and shagged the au pair, didn't I? Mand was visiting her mum with Jamie, and I couldn't go for some reason, can't remember why now. The au pair came back late, a bit drunk and sat up with me watching telly. Something saucy was on and we had a couple of drinks and, well, I don't need to spell it out, one thing led to another and Mand found us asleep on the couch together, naked and with two used condoms on her nice new carpet. Luckily Jamie was behind her and didn't see. She shoved him back outside, closed the door and told us to get cleaned up.

Two days later the au pair was on a flight back to Russia and I was filling out the application for this place.

I know I'm supposed to tell you everything, but please don't make me describe the look on Mand's face when we sat down to discuss what had happened. Don't make me tell you what she said to me, or the snot-nosed begging I did in return. All you need to know is that I love Mand and I desperately want to change. I need to change. I need to find this bit of me that makes me behave like a hunter. I see that other men don't have it so much as me. I need to find it and cut it out so I can be more like them. I need to stop hunting, because I've found the woman I want.

And that's it. That's all I'm saying. Sorry.

'Well done, Will,' Verity said, breaking the silence. Will sat back down and put his head in his hands. Shelley could understand why he'd been nervous. No one likes a cheat. The rest of them were betraying no one but themselves, but Will's addiction was tearing a family apart.

'Good for you, Will,' Cheryl said.

'That was very brave,' Cliff added.

Then Will stood and left the room, head down. Shelley thought she detected a tear running down his cheek. No one said anything. They were lost in their own reflections.

Shelley could hear the April wind rushing through the copse of laurel trees out on the lawn.

'There's a time and a place for jokes and fun,' Verity said, eventually. 'But we must remember why we're here. Sex addiction isn't some tabloid fantasy. It is real, and it destroys lives. Now we must support Will, and not judge him. I'll see you all back here in half an hour for our next session.'

Chapter Eleven

Shelley wasn't sure how to feel about Will after his confessional. On one hand she was appalled by his misogyny and his arrogance. He evidently believed that biological processes were to blame for his behaviour, that he was genetically predisposed to be unfaithful, and the implication was that men who didn't behave in this manner were emasculated. It wasn't just in the bedroom that Will felt he had Alpha male status, but in the boardroom too. The obvious relish and attention to steamy detail in his account suggested he felt proud of his conquests. He wasn't just being honest, he was boasting.

On the other hand, Will was a more complex character than Shelley had originally given him credit for. Everyone had their good points, but Shelley was surprised to find them in such abundance in Will: it was like popping into an Aldi, hoping to pick up some cheap kitchen towels, only to find they also had an excellent selection of goats' cheese.

He was unreconstructed, sure, but he obviously loved his wife and child deeply, and genuinely wanted to change in order to keep his family together. The story of how

Will and Amanda had come to be together in the first place was tragic, yet beautiful. There was tenderness and compassion in the man.

Will was asking for help and had taken a brave step coming here in the first place. As they left the room and headed towards the canteen for lunch, Shelley reflected on the fact that however awful someone's actions seem to the casual observer, there's always a back story, always some reason why they do the things they do. Will justified his actions to himself, but at the same time recognised they were unacceptable not just to his wife, but to society at large, hence the efforts to hide his affairs even from his colleagues.

Most people left the room and wandered out to use the loos or grab a coffee, Shelley went off by herself to the dining room. She wanted to sit by herself to get her head around what she'd just heard. She wanted to be true and fair to Will when she wrote it out later that night, but as she sat down with her muffin and tea, someone came up to her. She looked up to see it was Will.

'Hi,' he said. He looked different. Nervous and a little worried.

Shelley smiled, guessing he was concerned about how he had come across, and whether they'd all laughed at his tears. A man with an ego the size of Will's cared very much how he appeared to others. 'You were fine, Will,' she said. 'You were honest and very . . . graphic.'

He smiled. 'Great!' he said and sat down. Shelley frowned, it hadn't been an invitation. She wasn't quite sure she was ready to be friends with the serial adulterer yet. He was about to speak when Verity appeared from nowhere and plonked herself down next to him. Verity frowned on people sitting in pairs and usually managed to insinuate herself into such situations before they descended into rampant sex.

Will's attempts at small talk suggested to Shelley he was anxious to speak with her, but not with Verity there. As it happened, she began to wish Verity wasn't there as well. There were a few details of Will's story she wanted clarification on for her article, particularly the parts involving Debs and the bathtub, but she couldn't very well ask him about that with the stern-faced counsellor present.

Shelley sipped her tea, let her mind drift and found herself wondering what Aidan would do if she tried to jam a toe up his hairless bum. Maybe she'd get her P45. Maybe he'd shoot his load over her ankle.

The thought took her back to her first proper date with Tom. He'd taken her in to Bristol to see a 'thinking film' as he put it. It turned out to be *Casino*, with Robert de Niro and Joe Pesci. Shelley enjoyed the film, but wasn't sure it struck quite the right note for a romantic evening with a new person in your life. Still, it kept Tom transfixed, and apart from the awkward moment when he put his arm round her just as Joe Pesci's character forces Sharon Stone to give him a blow job, it felt okay. In fact, it felt comfortable and easy, with just that little hint of 'what-will-happen-after-the-film' anticipation to liven things up.

Tom rode with her on the bus back home, even though he lived in a different direction, and when they got to her house he got off even though he would have done better to stay on and change at Redland Station. They stood out on the footpath, the night warm and heavy with expectation.

'I really liked it tonight,' Shelley said.

'Yeah, me too,' Tom replied, looking at his feet.

Shelley felt odd. There was a warm, tingly feeling in her lower abdomen. She wasn't due a period. Maybe this was the feeling her parents had told her about when they'd given her the birds and the bees lesson. They'd left it far too late of course, she knew the salient points already and she'd been old enough to want to run screaming out of the room in embarrassment. But they'd told her, and she remembered. You were supposed to feel something like this when you liked a special person.

'Don't suppose I can come in?' he mumbled. So that was why he was looking so nervous.

'No,' she said shaking her head sadly. He looked up, a flash of annoyance in his eyes, and she grew scared, was he going to turn out like all the others? But he nodded, 'No, of course, I understand. Anyway, see you.'

He turned and walked off.

'Hey,' Shelley called. He stopped and spun around.

'Where's my goodnight kiss?'

He grinned and jogged back. They kissed properly, as if they were both ready and could see each other, for the first time. It was nice, Shelley thought afterwards, but at the time she was just thinking about whether she was doing it right. She broke off first and hugged him.

'Thanks for being lovely,' she said. He shrugged. She kind of guessed he wouldn't be so lovely given half the chance, but boys are pragmatic. Keep plugging away and eventually you might get there, they think.

Then she did something impulsive. She whispered into his ear. 'My parents are going shopping with my sister on Saturday, they'll be out of the house all day, wanna come over?'

He nodded like a toy dog on a parcel shelf.

'See you then,' Shelley said and walked off, swinging her hips, realisation suddenly dawning that she was a woman now. She could do things like this.

The afternoon session was called 'Sex? No Thanks. What Else Have You Got?'

Shelley had to fight the urge to walk to the whiteboard and change the last part to 'What Else do You Have?', but that would be taking the grammatical guerrilla war to an entirely new level.

On the way to the room, Verity had fallen into step beside Shelley. 'You seem to have attracted an admirer in Mr Trewin.'

Shelley blushed a little. She wasn't sure she entirely agreed with Verity but kept her own counsel. Will obviously felt some kind of connection with her, but Shelley wasn't accustomed to getting much male attention, and she wondered if maybe Will just wanted to talk to her, as a friend. Surely part of the recovery process was learning to have friends of the opposite sex without trying to sleep with them? She had to button her lip. Too many questions and Verity might get suspicious. The counsellor turned around to make sure they weren't being overheard.

'Please try and stay away from him, let's keep temptation as far away as we can.'

Shelley nodded, feeling a little uncomfortable. What was all the talk about helping each other out? She didn't think it right two members of the group should be told not to talk to each other.

In the Mountain Room, Verity began taking them through a list of distraction techniques to avoid temptation. 'Why not try riding a bike?' she suggested, 'or heading down to the gym?'

Shelley doubted these activities would help much. Her gym was always filled with attractive, well-toned young men fighting over the weights. If she were a genuine sex addict, the gym would be the last place she'd want to be. She'd be better off staying at home and watching the Shopping Channel. Riding a bike though? Cyclists were very clubby; Shelley felt a little intimidated by them, but maybe once you were in there would be plenty of opportunities to meet new friends, male friends specifically. She found herself thinking about cyclists' bodies, those powerful piston legs pumping tirelessly . . .

'Shelley?' Verity was saying. She snapped out of her fantasy. 'What other methods could you think of for avoiding sex?'

Manga conventions, Shelley nearly said. But instead she offered, 'Er . . . gardening?'

'Yes,' Verity replied, beaming. 'Do you have a garden, Shelley?'

'I certainly do,' Shelley replied, thinking of the tangled shrubbery in her pants. 'And there's nothing I like more than to get the old hedge trimmers out of an evening and hack away at the undergrowth.'

'Excellent!' Verity said, and moved on the next person.

Shelley smiled to herself. Well, you had to make your own fun around here.

During the session, the group members were popping off, one by one, to see Dr Galloway. Rose arrived back, a little pink-cheeked, and plumped down next to Shelley. Verity had cornered poor old Larry and was trying to get him to name five pursuits he could do to spend a Friday night other than surfing the internet for hard-core bondage porn. He wriggled uncomfortably.

'Amputee porn?' he suggested, after some consideration.

'You'll like the sesh with the Doc,' Rose whispered to Shelley, winking. 'He asked me to send you in next.'

Shelley excused herself and walked down to Dr Galloway's office wondering what Rose meant.

She knocked and Dr Galloway's rich Irish baritone called her in. She stopped short after entering though. Dr Galloway was perched on the edge of his desk, obviously having chosen the pose as more welcoming and informal. What it did though was expose a large bulge in his tight trousers. Shelley felt like she had to say hello twice.

Galloway motioned her into a seat immediately in front of him and she sat down, now eye-level with the lump in the doctor's chinos. How on earth were you supposed to distract yourself from sexual thoughts when dishy doctors were shoving their over-stuffed tackle boxes into your face?

'Thanks for popping in, Ms Carter,' Galloway began.

'Call me Shelley,' she said immediately. She always said this in formal situations as she'd been trained to do at university. The idea was that by making the situation more chummy the other person would open up more readily. Shelley hoped to get something usable for her piece out of the doctor today.

'Okay, and please call me Mick,' he said, twinkling a little and shifting position slightly. Shelley tried to keep her eyes up and away from his crotch.

'Now, I need to ask you a few questions about your medical history,' Mick went on. 'Just to make sure there are no physical causes for your addiction, you understand?' Shelley nodded, a little nervous. As a nurse, she was going to be expected to know terms and names for things that the other group members wouldn't.

'Now, you've recently returned from Australia,' Dr Galloway said, peering at a sheet of paper in his hand.

'Yes, that's right,' Shelley replied. 'I worked for a number of small, community hospitals. Paediatrics mostly, that's my area of specialisation. I did work for a large hospital in Cairns, the Royal Adelaide.'

'That's great, that's terrific,' Dr Galloway said without looking up from his paper, in that infuriating way doctors have that makes you suspect they haven't listened to you at all and are therefore just about to give you the wrong medicine.

'Any bites from animals out there? Spiders, or cats?' he asked.

Cats? 'No,' she said. 'No bites from animals, only from humans, ha ha.'

He ignored the joke.

'Any history of insanity in your family?' he asked, somewhat out of the blue. Shelley sniffed at the insinuation.

'No!' she replied coldly, wondering if she should tell him about her mother's tendency to go mental at Christmas and attack her father with the electric carving knife. Surely everyone's mother did that?

'Any STDs?' he asked.

Shelley paused for a moment while she struggled to remember what STD stood for. Then it came to her and she stiffened.

'How dare you?' she asked, before she remembered who she was supposed to be. Galloway looked up at her in surprise. 'I mean no,' she said. She covered up her error with bluster. 'Should you not have got all this information from my GP?' she asked. 'Why are we taxpayers spending all this money on new IT systems for the NHS when you can't even get your computers to talk to each other?'

'This is a private centre,' Galloway protested, reasonably.

'But you do plenty of lucrative NHS contract work, don't you?' she followed up, her journalistic instincts taking over.

'Well . . . yes, but the NHS doesn't allow us to use its computers.'

'You do have phones though, don't you?'

'I'm not really sure what all these questions are about,' Dr Galloway said.

'I'm just making sure you know what you're talking about,' Shelley said, enjoying the row. Attack is the best form of defence after all. 'My brother is paying a lot of money for me to be here and if I think he's wasting that money then I shall simply walk through that door and expect full reimbursement.'

'Ms Carter,' Dr Galloway said firmly, 'I can assure you your brother will get his money's worth. Now please calm down. I think it best if we continue this session at a later time, when we've both had time to reflect.'

Shelley took a deep breath and stood. As she reached the door Galloway spoke again. 'And might I just remind you, Ms Carter, that when you entered the centre, you signed a Section Four voluntary admission form?'

Shelley turned around and looked at him quizzically. 'So?'

'So that means you specifically *cannot* walk out that door whenever you feel like it. You have been sectioned under the Mental Health Act and will leave this centre when a qualified doctor says so and not before. Is that clear?'

Shelley was stunned. Of course, that's what Section Four was! The bit that said they could hold you against your will. And she'd signed it like a muppet. Oh God, what had she done? Deciding that defence was now the best form of defence, she nodded dumbly and left.

She was happy to have escaped without having had to answer too many difficult questions, but she felt she might have gone a bit overboard with the whole lunatic act. Considering she was basically a prisoner here now, she'd better be careful or she'd find something worse than bromide in her tea. She didn't want to end up like Jack Nicholson in *One Flew Over the Cuckoo's Nest*. In fact she didn't want to end up like Jack Nicholson in anything.

That night in bed, Shelley dreamed about Aidan again, he was still carrying the truncheon, but this time, as she called out to him, she saw Dr Galloway was standing there at the foot of her bed, carrying an enormous syringe with no needle, just a blunt, rounded end. He came around the side of the bed and approached her as she struggled to break free. Mick Galloway smiled as he looked into Shelley's eyes and squeezed the plunger. A thick jet of fluid shot out the end.

'Are you going to inject me with that?' she asked breathlessly.

He nodded. 'It's a truth semen,' he replied.

'Truth *serum*, you mean?' Shelley said, nervously.

'That's what I said,' Galloway replied and slid the end down between her naked breasts, over her flat belly, which was beaded with sweat, and down towards . . .

Shelley awoke in a sweat just before Galloway could plunge the syringe anywhere. She breathed heavily and tried to put the image out of her mind.

'Are you okay?' Rose said from the other bed.

'I'm fine, just a bad dream,' Shelley said.

'I can't sleep either,' Rose said. 'I can't stop thinking about Galloway's bulge.'

There was then a long pause as they listened to each other breathe. Eventually Rose broke it. 'Maybe we should . . .' she said, before tailing off.

For an instant, Shelley considered it. What might it be like to feel another woman's hand sliding across your tummy? What might it be like to kiss her soft lips?

But no, she put it out of her mind. 'I'm really flattered, Rose, but I don't think it's a good idea for us to hop into bed together.'

There was another long pause. Again Rose broke it.

'Um,' she said. 'I was only going to say maybe we should . . . drink the tea tomorrow.'

Shelley giggled. Then Rose said, 'I do fancy you though, if you were wondering. And if we weren't in the middle of a sex addiction course I'd definitely seduce you.'

Shelley had to remind herself Rose was under the impression that she, Shelley, was bisexual fuck-addict. Having said that, even as a straight sex castaway, Shelley thought Rose wouldn't have to work too hard to get her into bed.

As she drifted off, the images of the truncheon-wielding Aidan and the syringe-plunging Galloway were joined by a bare-breasted Rose falling out of a nurse's uniform. The course was having the opposite effect to the one intended. It'd be just her luck, thought Shelley, to end up with her hang-ups cured just as all the shaggable people here swore off sex forever.

At breakfast the next morning Verity stopped by to tell them the next confessional, from Abigail, would begin at eleven sharp.

'I'd like you all to pop into the gym after breakfast, so don't eat anything too heavy.'

Shelley stopped mid-chew and looked down at the full English she was halfway through. Rose smiled at her across the table.

'I'm hungry,' Shelley said defensively.

'A tired body is a satisfied body,' Verity went on. 'Replacing a bedroom workout with one in the gymnasium is an excellent way of distracting both the mind and body.'

'Surely we're allowed to have sex sometimes though, Verity?' Will asked. 'I mean, I can have sex with my wife, can't I? I don't have to pop down to the gym every time I feel a little frisky?'

'Of course not, Will,' Verity said rather frostily. 'A moderate love life in the matrimonial bed is a very healthy thing.'

'Moderate? What's moderate?' Cian asked. 'How often do you do it with Mr Verity?'

Verity flushed. 'There is no Mr Verity, Cian. I have been celibate for three years now.' And with that she turned on her heel and departed.

They sat in reflective silence for a while before Cian broke it.

'Three fucking years! I thought three days was bad enough.'

Shelley changed in her room and wandered down to the gym. It was well-appointed, with long rows of cross-trainers, running machines and bikes. The gym and pool complex was in an outbuilding, attached to the rest of the mansion by a corridor. They had a lovely big bank of windows that let the light in.

Shelley watched low white clouds dancing across the motorway-grey background as she pedalled her bike madly, trying to burn off the black pudding she'd eaten.

After twenty minutes she switched to a cross-trainer and fiddled about with the needlessly complicated settings for a couple of minutes. What on earth did the machine need to know how old you were? Did it vend cigarettes if you reached your target? She was getting hot and bothered. She didn't need this. Bloody Aidan.

Someone came into her field of vision and she was mildly concerned to see it was Cian, who'd stepped up onto a cross-trainer right in front of her. He turned back and grinned, then wiggled his bottom. Usually Shelley found nothing remotely sexual about sweaty men in tight shorts down the gym, but Cian wasn't sweating as he wasn't actually working out. He stopped stepping and bent over, scratching his knee. He looked back at her again. 'Itchy cock,' he said, causing her to snort with laughter.

'I can't concentrate with you there,' Shelley said, smiling. It was impossible to get angry at Cian. It was also impossible not to find him attractive, but whether there could ever be anything else, Shelley wasn't at all sure: she imagined his cheeky-chappie routine could get really old, really quick. 'I'm going to the rowers.'

As she wandered down to the other end of the room, she was distracted by the sound of Abigail shouting at someone. She stopped to watch. It turned out Will had finished his weights then gone off to do something else, leaving a pile of dumbbells scattered about the floor.

'Why can't men ever tidy up after themselves?' she barked at him. 'I wish I had my whip.'

'Calm down,' Will replied soothingly. 'They have people who do that for you.'

Abigail closed her eyes. 'Onetwothreefourfivesix . . .'

'I have to agree, Will,' Cheryl said. 'It is kind of annoying to have to move someone else's weights out of the way, especially if they're really heavy.'

Will rolled his eyes. 'I need to use heavy weights. I'm a man, and anyway . . .'

Shelley, who didn't like the gym at the best of times, decided to leave. Rather than walk back to her room, dripping sweat all over the shag pile, Shelley decided to shower in the communal facilities. She peeled herself out of her Lycra and stepped into the shower, flinching at the wonderful heat. She lathered up, but dropped the soap when she heard someone else come into the ladies' changing rooms.

'Bastard!' spat Abigail, stepping into the shower. She frowned at Shelley, making her feel as welcome as a giant verucca. Thank God she *didn't* have her whip, was all Shelley could think. What she did have, though, was a spectacular body. It was almost too perfect to be sexy. She was tall, with high, shapely breasts, which, if they were false, had been made by a plastic surgeon whose phone number alone would be worth the price of a Lamborghini. Her straight hair flooded down her back, coal black on porcelain. She was neatly shaved between her legs and her steel eyes burned back into Shelley's.

Shelley was too transfixed to realise she was staring until Abigail coughed.

'Sorry!' Shelley cried. 'It's just . . . you have a lovely body.' Shelley winced at her own comment.

'Maybe you should look the other way,' Abigail replied. Shelley did so, embarrassed.

As she finished up hurriedly and got dressed, she reflected that maybe it wasn't such a bad thing that Abigail had caught her looking. It would help to convince the cold fish that Shelley was who she claimed to be.

* * *

Later that morning the group assembled in the Mountain Room, the routine starting to help them feel comfortable. They chatted amicably, though Will seemed a little distant and pouted when Shelley pointedly sat well away from him. She sat next to Larry, in fact, who rubbed his crotch involuntarily as he stared at her breasts. Poor old Will, Shelley thought, it can't do a mature businessman's confidence any good to be rejected by a sex addict in favour of a teenage toss-pot. She wondered if she should ignore Verity's advice and get closer to the banker, but if he did fancy her, that might give him the wrong impression. It sure was complicated being a frigid journalist pretending to be a sex addict.

'I'm looking forward to this,' Larry whispered to Shelley.

She eyed him narrowly. 'I'm not sure you're supposed to be enjoying this so much, as learning from it.'

'Yes, I suppose so,' Larry said, looking thoughtful. 'She's a hell of a woman though.'

'She is,' Shelley returned. 'And I'm looking forward to finding out more about the real Abigail. Maybe she'll be less intimidating once we've heard her story.'

'Not sure about that,' Larry said. 'God knows what she does to her clients, but she scares the be-jesus out of me.'

'Now, hush everyone,' Verity said. 'Abigail would like to tell us her story.'

Abigail stood and gave a little bow to Verity. Shelley tried to think of her as a real person rather than a terrifying ice queen standing naked in the shower. The dark-haired dominatrix smiled stiffly and went straight into the story without betraying a hint of nerves.

Chapter Twelve

When I was a little girl I liked to play school with my dolls and stuffed toys. But this was no ordinary school; it was a school for wayward toys, an Academy for Bad Bunnies and Troubled Teddies. I was a strict teacher. You had to be with these toys, turn your back for a second and they'd be fighting, or running away, or chewing gum. I made them pay attention to me. Every week they'd get a report card and the naughtiest would be punished, by a few slaps with a ruler, or the really bad ones would have some stuffing removed.

When I got a bit older, I moved on to my cat. I'd try to make her roll over, or miaow at me. If she didn't do as I asked, I'd throw water over her. She ran away soon enough, and we got a dog instead. He was much easier to dominate, and I trained him to obey my every whim using a choke lead and an old slipper.

Now let me make this clear. There was nothing sexual in this. I don't have a kink for stuffed animals, or household pets. That's sick. But I do like to control. It was only later on that I realised sex could be a tool. A tool for punishment and a tool for reward.

I went to a rotten inner-city school in Bermondsey. Horrible place, the sort of town where anyone with any talent or work ethic moves away from as quickly as they can, then they spend the rest of their lives saying things like, 'I wasn't always successful you know, I grew up in Bermondsey; we had nothing.'

Anyway the kids there were a rough crowd. I was a bit of an oddball, I suppose, and I got bullied for most of my time there. When we all got a bit bigger and started being interested in sex, that's when I realised I had some power, and used it to get my own back. I was pretty busty even as a sixteen year old and the boys stopped bullying me when they noticed. I'd lead them on, I knew what they wanted and I had no intention of giving it to them. I enjoyed making them beg. There were three boys who'd bullied me mercilessly in fifth form and I chose these three to make an example of. I led them into a deserted classroom during break and took my top off. They just sat there, leering, waiting to see what I'd do next.

I made each of them sit on a straight-backed school chair and I unzipped their flies, each in turn. These were sixteen or seventeen year old boys, you understand, they were gagging for it. I had them totally under my control and I loved it. Remember, these were boys who'd been bullying me. I hated them, and I wanted my revenge. Having power over them, having something they wanted, felt good to me. I felt strong.

'I'll give each of you what you want if you let me do what I want,' I said. They all nodded furiously. So I walked behind the chairs and, using plastic zip-ties, strapped their arms to the chair legs. Then I came back around to the front and knelt down in front of the first boy. He was a rotten so-and-so. Craig, I think his name was. Used to throw twisted staples into my hair, which took forever to get out.

I slowly reached into his trousers as he twisted in his chair nervously. Craig was the sort who'd talk a good game when it came to sex, but it was well known in the school he'd never had a girlfriend. I took hold of his virgin cock and brought it out; he shut his eyes and groaned in pleasure. The other two boys stared at what was happening, unable to believe what they were seeing.

I looked into Craig's face, his eyes still shut and features contorted. Then I began stroking him off. It doesn't take much to make a sixteen-year-old male virgin come, and soon enough great wads of white fluid were spasming out of his engorged cock. He looked down at me as he came, naked lust filling his eyes.

I wiped my hand on his shirt and moved to the next one. His eyes followed me, wide as saucepan lids. I reached into his trousers, about to pull his tool out, only to find he'd fired his wad into his underpants the second I touched him. I laughed in his face.

The third boy didn't take much longer; he nearly cried as he orgasmed. He was a spurter, this one, and I had to duck to avoid getting a load in my eye. Giving these boys what they wanted had been easy. I put my blouse back on and walked for the door.

'Hey!' Craig said. 'Aren't you going to untie us?'

'Oh, I'm sure one of the teachers can do that for you.

I think Ms Pearson has a Geography class in here in a few minutes.'

And with that I walked out, and down the hall, listening to them shouting my name. The power felt so good. Debasing those three boys got me wet. Though I didn't realise it at the time I think I may even have had a mini-orgasm as I walked away, leaving them to their fate.

The story of how those three were found in that situation became legendary in our school. You can look up the story on the internet, they reckon it's an urban myth.

Anyway, from then on I continued to explore my interest in domination. The orgasm I'd had proved to be an aberration. Dominating people didn't at first help me to achieve sexual satisfaction. That's not why I did it. It's hard to explain why; maybe Dr Parrish can help us all to understand. I started off visiting sex shops, where I'd pick up magazines and books called *Bound Maiden*, or *Curl of the Lash*. When other girls my age were reading *Heat*, or *Cosmo*, I'd be flicking through rubber-suit catalogues, or dungeon design pamphlets. The sex shops in Soho stock contact magazines as well. It was through a cheaply-produced, black and white brochure that I got involved with my first BDSM club. For the uninitiated, that stands for Bondage, Domination and Sado-Masochism.

They met once a week at someone's house, and everyone would dress up and have a few drinks and a chat to loosen up. Then the negotiations would start. I was amazed and excited to find how different everyone was. It seemed everyone had a totally different fantasy and a different set of instructions. We first decided who wanted to dominate and who wanted to be dominated:

there weren't many who wanted to try both. There were far more there wanting to be dominated. I began to understand that for some people, being bound, and maybe hurt, was the only way they could achieve satisfaction. I filed the information away for later. I was there because I wanted to dominate and just then I wasn't really interested in anything else.

There were more men than women and I ended up with two guys, Michael and Jonathan. Neither of them was attractive but that was irrelevant. They gave me loose instructions about what they wanted me to do, and where I was to draw the line. They each had a code word. We drove back to Jonathan's house. He was something in the City and had a big flash pad not far away.

In the house, we split up to get ready, and then reassembled in the living room. My submissives looked at me expectantly and, I'd like to think, appreciatively. I was wearing a leather basque, fishnet stockings and thigh-high boots. I also wore a rather fetching black leather cap and carried a whip. The men had taken off their shoes and ties, but otherwise were dressed normally, in their trousers and shirts. I swallowed nervously. This was it. I was confident though, I knew what I was doing and I craved it.

'In the bedroom,' I snapped at Jonathan. He scuttled off. 'You, on the floor,' I snarled at Michael, who dropped to the carpet, a worried look on his face.

'Crawl towards me, worm,' I said. He did so. 'Head down!'

'Do you like my boots?' I asked, resting the whip on the nape of his neck.

'Yes,' he said.

'Yes, Mistress!' I screamed, slapping his backside with the whip. He squealed. 'Yes, Mistress,' he said hurriedly.

'Now, back to my boots. I would like you to lick them . . .'

Michael took hold of my left boot and thrust his tongue out eagerly.

'Wait until I say!' I cried, kicking him hard in his shoulder. He cried out and went down on to the floor, clutching his shoulder. I waited a second to see if he would use the safety word but he just moaned. 'Sorry, Mistress!'

'Take off your trousers, and get back on the floor,' I spat. 'I'll be back later.'

I stalked off to the bedroom, to find Jonathan.

He flinched as I came in, obviously having already worked himself up into a state anticipating my arrival.

'Hands behind your back,' I said calmly, not looking at him. I walked around him and deftly snapped a pair of handcuffs tightly around his wrists.

'On your knees, you piece of shit.' He dropped, and I wrapped a scarlet scarf around his eyes and secured it at the back of his head.

Then I took out a large pair of heavy, steel dressmakers' scissors and snipped them menacingly in front of his face. He groaned and began to quiver. 'Please no,' he said.

'Shut up, Slave!' I said. 'I didn't give you permission to speak. You shall have to be punished.'

'Sorry, Mistress, please don't punish me,' he cried. He was a good actor, Jonathan, no doubt a fine upstanding member of the local amateur dramatics society when he wasn't being dominated with a bunch of other freaks.

As he opened his mouth to continue, I popped a red rubber ball in, shutting him up. The ball was attached to a set of straps that went around his head. I tightened them with a hard yank, making him wince and grunt in pain.

Then I took the scissors again and cut his clothes off bit by bit until he was totally naked. I snipped the scissors in front of his stiff penis and he swayed his hips back to get away from the cold steel.

I left him there and walked back to see how Michael was getting on.

He was in exactly the same position I'd left him in, except with his trousers off.

'You moved!' I said.

'No!' he replied. 'Mistress, no. I didn't.'

'Shut up,' I replied and kicked him between the legs. He collapsed, groaning, and I thought I'd really hurt him for a moment. But this kind of thing is tame compared to what some of them want. Michael was an amateur, as was I back then. Soon he was back on his hands and knees, licking my boots as I flicked the end of the whip against his exposed backside.

And so the evening went on, I divided my time between the men, the periods where they'd wait for me nervously being an important part of the punishment. Eventually Michael used the code word that meant I was to bring him off. I was a little disappointed; I could have done this all night.

I lifted a booted foot and shoved him so he toppled

over onto his back. Then I stepped over him so I was straddling his now naked torso. I lifted a foot and positioned my stiletto over his groin; he stared up at me, desperate, nodding.

Then I brought my foot down and twisted the heel into his fleshy scrotum. He screamed in agony and I nearly backed off, but he never once said anything, just lay there climaxing, his face a twisted mixture of pain and pleasure. I was fascinated. I had to wipe the fluid off the sole of my boot onto his backside.

Jonathan had heard Michael's orgasm and wanted to be finished as well. I forced him to bend over face down on the bed and began whipping him hard. It wasn't a full-on, proper whip like a cowboy would use, much shorter and less painful, but the one I was using produces a nasty sting and marks that last for a week if you whack it hard enough. I thrashed him until he was red-raw before he finally came. I never laid a finger on him.

Over the next few months I worked my way steadily through that group, learning the techniques, finding out what made men tick. Not that it was just men of course, some women liked to be dominated too. It made no difference to me. I learned how to use chains, how to use various whips and straps, and how to put on a rubber cat suit without hurting myself. Suffice to say I got through a lot of talc. Some people liked more conventional sex aids, like dildos, vibrators and love beads. I had to learn how to use them safely too. I wasn't interested in these things for myself, just in how to use them to get what I wanted out of my submissives. I did quite enjoy wearing a giant strap-on dildo, mostly to put the fear of God into my slaves rather than to actually use it on them.

While all this was going on. I must stress that I had a normal job, a normal life and a normal boyfriend. He didn't know about the BDSM club. I didn't want to weird him out and he wouldn't have understood. The two parts of my life were totally separate.

I loved it. I wanted more. And when one of the women in the group asked me if I wanted to come and check out her dungeon, I jumped at the chance.

The dungeon was a whole new ball game. It was in the city and catered for paying customers who wanted things done properly, and who were willing to pay considerably for what they wanted. The clients were generally public-school educated businessmen, doing well for themselves and looking for a bit of kinky relief before going home to the wife in Woking.

The woman's name was Vanessa; she was part-owner of the place. She showed me around first. There were rooms full of chains, for hanging clients up. There were tables that looked like something from the Spanish Inquisition; there were orgy rooms and private cells. We stood in the props room, looking at rack after rack of bondage gear and rubber wear.

'I hear you're pretty good,' Vanessa said to me.

'I'm only just starting,' I replied.

'You're a natural, is what I hear. There aren't too many beautiful, intelligent women ready to do this kind of thing.'

Was she after something, I wondered. 'Do you want me to dominate you?' I asked, eyebrow cocked.

She laughed. 'Maybe sometime, but actually I'm asking you if you want a job. The money's good,' she added.

I was surprised. I'd honestly never considered I could make a living at this. But instantly I knew that this was what I wanted – no, what I needed – to do.

'Yes,' I said. 'The answer's yes.'

Quitting my job was a breeze, less easy was telling the boyfriend. I was pretty sure he wouldn't understand, so I decided to end it. I didn't want any complications; all I could think about was getting into that dungeon and making some scumbag of a City trader crawl on the floor like a dog.

A week later that's exactly where I was, though the trader was a minor politician and the guy hanging by his arms from the chains above me was a well-known film director.

I made the politician get up on the table and strapped him down. He was wearing leather underpants and I jammed the handle of my riding crop inside them and left it there while I turned the wheel that tightened the straps. He grunted against the gag and I heard his joints pop sharply. Tight enough.

I consulted the mental checklist of instructions he'd given me. Ah, that was it. I unbuckled the leather pants and whipped them off, exposing his swollen cock. I patted it with my crop, eliciting another groan.

'Ha!' I said. 'That wouldn't satisfy a gerbil.'

Then I began thrashing his genitals with the crop. He stiffened first, then began thrusting himself upwards, he was about to come. I stopped, leaving him suspended, yearning desperately for the release.

I turned to the film director; he was watching me, fear in his eyes. His cock and balls were imprisoned in a zippered rubber thong, far too small for a man of his size.

I stared up at him contemptuously. 'Look at you,' I sneered. 'Look at you. If only your mummy could see you now.' He closed his eyes in shame, but I wasn't finished. 'Here he is, the great movie maker, hanging from the ceiling with his cock in a squash ball.'

I took out the special prop we'd had to prepare earlier that week. A super-size Oscar award.

'Open your eyes,' I snapped. He did so. They widened in alarm as he saw the size of the Oscar. I snapped my fingers and two burly dungeon guards came over and grabbed a leg each. They flipped him around and spread his legs; one of them unclipped the thong and took it off, leaving the man exposed and vulnerable to attack from the rear.

'Now this is going to hurt,' I said softly as I approached and positioned the Oscar's head against his puckered hole. He mewled in fear.

Vanessa told me later that the scream, as I'd inserted the luckless statue into the director's backside, could be heard three levels up, outside on the street.

I stayed working at the dungeon for three years. Vanessa had been right, the money was good, and I soon gathered a collection of regulars who tipped me well. I got a bit of a reputation. One man liked me to call him Dorothy and hurl rotten fruit at him. He paid me extra if I'd smear him in putrid banana flesh while he jerked himself off.

Some men wanted to make love to me, and offered crazy amounts, but I never allowed that. I didn't need their money, and a dominatrix who acts like a prostitute loses her reputation pretty sharp. The guys who begged me to fuck them always came back even when I'd refused them.

It was around this time that I started to find myself enjoying my job in a different way. I started to become aroused by the beatings I was dealing out. It started out gradually, but as time went on I began to find myself growing wet and turned on when I inflicted pain. One time, after a particularly brutal beating of some pathetic wretch, I found myself so worked up I retreated into a private room and tried to collect myself. I sat on the cot in there and felt something under me. It was a large dildo. I shrugged, well, why not? I slid down my tights and lay back on the bed. I felt between my legs and my fingers came back soaked with juices. I ran the dildo down between my breasts, across my exposed stomach and down to my pussy lips. It was a fat toy but it slipped in without too much pressure. I began pumping it into myself, rhythmically, gradually increasing the pace. All the while I was thinking of the pain I had inflicted on my client, the red welts on his back, and the pleading look in his eye.

I was about to come when the door opened and Vanessa walked in. She didn't look surprised. She walked over to the bed, grabbed hold of the end of the dildo and pulled it out smoothly.

'James, Ryan,' she called over her shoulder, never taking her eyes from mine.

'You've been working too hard,' she said as the muscle-bound, well oiled men came into the room, faces deadpan. 'You need a treat. I'll take care of your client.' And she stepped out. The two guards dropped their trousers and moved into position. Ryan adjusted the bed so my head was raised at around a forty-five-degree angle.

James grabbed hold of my hips and lifted my haunches up. Then he pulled me back and impaled me on his rigid, ribbed shaft. I groaned with appreciation as the muscular blond began thrusting himself deep inside of me. Ryan, at the other end, presented his long, thin cock to me. I opened my mouth but he shook his head and handed me something.

It was my riding crop. I gripped it tightly, enjoying the feel of the rough leather against my palm.

Vanessa knew exactly what I wanted. As James pumped into me, I lashed Ryan's cock, matching him stroke for stroke. Ryan winced with pain, so I lashed him harder. His cock shrivelled and retreated, so I lashed him harder.

I came so hard I nearly gave myself a hernia. As my body convulsed, James never stopped thrusting into me and I never stopped whipping poor Ryan's shrunken penis. James shot his load into me as my fire began to die. I sank back against the cot and closed my eyes, enjoying the afterglow.

I gave Ryan half my tips that night. I reckoned James had got the better end of the deal, so I didn't give him anything else, he'd seemed happy enough.

* * *

I hadn't thought things could get any better but, after that first time, the floodgates had opened and I enjoyed the job even more. Now that I was gaining sexual, as well as professional, satisfaction from kicking people in the genitals, I was over the moon.

Then things went wrong. Not seriously wrong, but . . . well, I'll tell you the whole story. I had a couple come in, Guy and Natalie. Nice people they were, good looking, successful, and well spoken. They liked to try out stuff in the bedroom, and they'd read in this magazine that BDSM was the new thing everyone was trying.

They asked me to dominate the two of them together, and to force them to do things to each other they might feel funny about asking each other in real life. This isn't that unusual a request as it happens. So that's fine, I'm wearing my strap-on, thinking Natalie might worry I'm going to use it on her and the guy might worry I'm *not* going to use it on Natalie.

First I tied them both back to back and hit them with the pretend whip; they didn't want any marks you see. Then I forced Natalie to lick my boots. She was wearing nothing but a G-string and Guy had a little leather hold-all.

'Come over here,' I said to Guy, who was on his knees, watching us with a hungry look. He stood up.

'I didn't tell you to stand up!' I hissed. I shoved Natalie over with my boot and stalked over to Guy. 'On your knees!' He dropped to his knees.

'Now you, bitch, get over here and show him your arse.' Natalie shuffled into position. I dropped a spot of lube into Natalie's cleft and said, 'Fuck her like a dog.'

Well, Guy jabbed his dick in his girlfriend's pussy and

started sliding it in and out. She groaned. Then I started thrashing the two of them with my crop. I tried to get a few good blows in on his cock as it showed itself from time to time. I built up the speed and felt the familiar warmth in my crotch as I lashed out more and more violently.

Then I don't really remember perfectly what happened. The red mist came down and the next thing I knew was that I had eight inches of my fat strap-on jammed in Natalie's virgin backside and was beating the screaming girl over the shoulders with a cane while Guy was pulling at my arm, shouting out the safety word over and over again.

Chapter Thirteen

Vanessa would have fired me if I hadn't left of my own accord. She promised to give me a good reference if I promised to get some help. I saw a shrink for a few weeks while I sorted my head out. She told me I needed to separate my work life from my home life, and that included sex. Easier said than done. But one of the things she pointed out to me was the fact that while I'd had a 'normal' boyfriend, I didn't find myself frustrated in the dungeon. Maybe, as I was finding satisfaction at home, I could keep a clear, professional head at work.

I didn't think too much of that at the time, but a few weeks later, I met Rob. I'd taken a temp job as a secretary in some dull office in Docklands and he was an American stockbroker on my floor. And not long after we met he was quite literally on my floor, my kitchen floor, as I sat on his thick cock and pinched his nipples. I know you're not supposed to, but we slept together on the first night. Or at least we fucked each other all night, and then slept together as the sun came up.

Rob was amazing. Attractive, rich, funny and with a bit of a kinky side that made me feel I could open up early on and tell him about my past. He was a little surprised, but appeared to accept it. I was quite pleased to see he didn't appear to be massively turned on by the stories I told. He wasn't freaked out, but neither was he extremely curious.

A few months after we started seeing each other, Rob said he had been called back to New York and would I like to go with him? I didn't have anything to stay in London for so I agreed, after a few days' consideration. Rob's bank had fixed him up with an apartment in Lower Manhattan with spectacular views out over the Hudson. He asked me if I wanted him to get me a job at his office, but I declined, saying I wanted to find my own way. The money wasn't important, I had plenty in savings and Rob was loaded of course. Rob brought me to work functions and I grew friendly with some of the other wives and girlfriends, these were stick-thin *Sex and the City* types, quick-witted and funny. I liked them but wasn't sure I really fitted in. Rob's boss' wife, Cara, took me under her wing. She was attractive and bright, and just getting to that age when she was starting to worry that her husband might be looking for a younger model. She spent a fortune on creams and, as far as I could tell, never ate anything at all.

She took me to her favourite restaurants where she drank water and the occasional vodka and she invited me to girls' nights out where we'd get tipsy and tell each other what our men liked to do in the bedroom. It was on one of these that I had a little too much to drink and let slip the fact I'd been a dominatrix.

Cara raised her eyebrows but took it calmly. 'I knew there was something about you,' she said. A few days later she picked me up for a night out and said as we left the building, 'I want to show you something.'

We hopped in a cab and went uptown, to somewhere in the mid-fifties, on the East Side. Cara paid the driver and took me down a narrow flight of stairs to a tiny door at the bottom. My stomach clenched in nervous excitement as we approached. I knew what was on the other side.

A little plate slid across after we'd knocked and we were inspected. Evidently Cara was recognised because we were let in and found ourselves in a waiting area, lined with red velvet and silver chains.

Cara and I looked at each other; she had a strange smile on her face. I was keenly aware of the fact that this was the boss' wife. I felt uncomfortable there, but I could hardly run off and risk offending her.

After a time a woman came out to see us. She was wearing a cat suit and carried a vicious-looking whip.

'Hello, Mistress Venetia,' Cara said. 'This is Abigail.'

'I know why you're here,' Venetia said sternly. 'But why is she here?'

'She's from England,' Cara said. 'She used to be into the S&M scene over there and wants to see how New York dungeons compare.'

I had wanted no such thing, but I held my tongue. Rob would hardly thank me if his boss' wife came home complaining about how I'd embarrassed her. Anyway, it wasn't as if I was going to be shocked by anything tonight. I decided to just go along with it; I might even end up enjoying myself.

Venetia smiled. 'Come this way, ladies,' she said staring

at me. 'You can get changed in there. Cara led me into a changing room, with a variety of outfits. I'd never been a submissive before and I wasn't sure what I wanted, but Cara went straight for a rubber maid's outfit. It didn't surprise me. It's generally those who hold power over others in real life who most love to be dominated, and someone used to shouting at the home help in her two-storey apartment overlooking Central Park, was naturally drawn to dressing as such a maid when play time came around. She stripped off, glancing at me shyly as she took off her knickers. She had a great body, though a little stringy from too much gym time.

Eventually I chose a harem-girl's skirt and jewelled bra, as it was the easiest to put on. I was finding myself a little turned on, to be honest, and as I slipped off my panties, I could feel that the crotch was moist. I turned around and saw Cara staring at me as I fastened the top. I wondered if she was going to try and seduce me. I didn't hate the idea, but I would have preferred she got her kicks from the dominatrix, to avoid the awkwardness next time we went out for drinks as much as anything. Plus I liked Rob and I didn't want to cheat on him, even if it would help his career.

Ten minutes later we found ourselves in what looked like a torture room. Nothing too dissimilar to the dungeon back in London, though they seemed to really like dog collars here.

Cara wore one, and one of the guards clipped a leash to a ring at the back. Venetia reappeared and immediately forced Cara to her knees. Venetia slipped a stockinged foot out of her stiletto and offered it to the rubber-clad society lady. Cara began licking Venetia's feet, running her tongue up and down the arch and taking the big toe into her mouth, sucking frantically. Venetia watched me as she held Cara's leash taut against the older woman's throat.

'Get on the rack,' she said. I turned around, looking for what she meant. Too slow – she snapped her fingers and two guards rushed up, grabbed me by the arms and frog marched me to what looked like some kind of gym equipment in the corner. They quickly strapped my arms and legs to the contraption, which consisted of a series of interlocking steel struts all resting on gimbals which allowed it to swivel, spin and tilt. The guards left me there.

Venetia dropped the leash and kicked Cara in the stomach, doubling her over. Then she stalked over to me.

'The safety word is Geronimo,' she whispered. 'Now open your mouth.'

I did as she asked and she jammed a plug in; the end tickled my throat and I had to fight not to gag. How was I to say the safety word with this in my mouth? Maybe she'd intended that, to heighten my fear. She strapped the plug in tight around my head. She inspected me, using the end of the whip to lift the skirt and have a good look at my pussy. 'Very nice, I bet you cost a good few shekels at the slave markets.'

The cool air of the dungeon tickled my lips and I yearned for some more physical attention. But she wasn't ready yet. She left me there, my shoulders aching and my pussy dripping as she slowly walked back over to inspect Cara, still lying on the floor.

'What sort of shitty maid are you?' Venetia shouted. 'Asleep on the job again? Get up, bitch, on your hands and knees.' Cara obliged. 'Now clean this floor, using your tongue!'

Cara began lapping at the floor, which was covered in thick matting. Venetia walked behind her and slid the whip down between the blonde woman's thighs, tapping against her rubber crotch. Then she snapped her fingers and one of the guards rushed over to hand her a small, black object. I couldn't quite see what it was, but as Venetia reached down and yanked Cara's knickers down, exposing her bony backside, I realised it was a butt plug. Venetia didn't bother with lube; she just worked the end of the plug into her submissive's anus and forced it in to the hilt. Cara moaned.

'Keep licking!' Venetia snapped. She then pulled Cara's rubber knickers back up and turned to look at me. She cracked the whip over the slobbering Cara. I moaned softly and lifted my hips in a desperate attempt to find some kind of relief for my intense arousal.

'You like that, little concubine, don't you?' I nodded. 'You like it when I hurt her?' I nodded again.

Venetia began whipping Cara frantically. I wanted to stop looking, the desire was unbearable. Then Venetia came over to me and, without a moment's hesitation, she slipped a hand under my skirt and stuck three fingers inside me. I was side-swiped by this, I generally didn't touch my clients in such a straightforwardly sexual manner, but I was grateful for the attention. I would have preferred one of the guards to use his cock on me, but concubines have to take what they can get. I pumped my hips, trying to get purchase on her questing fingers, wishing she'd use her whole hand. I tried to recall the image of her thrashing Cara. I wanted more pain to be inflicted.

However, Venetia soon realised some spark had gone from my eyes. And she nodded. 'I see,' she said. 'I know what you need.'

She moved away and spoke to the guards briefly, who dragged the unresisting Cara over and strapped her to some bars on the wall in front of me. Then she handed a crop to one of the guards. He began slapping the crop against Cara's rubber-bound breasts. I breathed heavily through my nose, the ball restricting my air flow. I wasn't getting quite enough oxygen, which is the whole point of course. To induce low-level panic and to heighten the eventual orgasm by restricting oxygen to the brain. My eyes must have told the story as Venetia stepped up to the rack and unzipped the front of Cara's outfit. Her small and perfectly round tits sprang out. They looked fake to me, but a damn good job. The guard resumed his strokes, this time against Cara's bare breasts. She groaned in arousal. I was as hot as a deep-fried chilli.

Venetia decided to put me out of my state of delirium. She called the other guard over. He had a fantastic body and I wished I could see his face. He flipped the rack over until I was face down. He swivelled it so I could see the violation of Cara across the room, and stepped into it and in between my spread legs. I felt his cock spear me from behind as Venetia joined in the lashing of Cara. It took just a few strokes for him to bring me off and I hope he wasn't disappointed. He certainly satisfied me.

I thrashed and groaned, trying to scream against the ball jammed into my mouth. He clutched my hips tight as if I were a beast trying to escape his death grip. Afterwards I collapsed against the harness and closed my eyes in exhaustion.

Cara paid.

Cara was well known in the BDSM community, and it was through her that I set up my own little cottage industry. There were plenty of people interested in being dominated but who didn't want to go to a dungeon. Over the next few months I developed an extensive client list. Rob knew all about it. Once I'd explained I had no intention of actually sleeping with any of my clients, he accepted it. Have I said before what a great guy he was? I think my openness helped. From day one I'd told him what I was. I think he was just happy I had something to keep me busy.

I rented another apartment, uptown, where people could go without bumping into their neighbours or friends. I fitted it out with a few tables, wall-racks and chains, but most rooms were just tastefully furnished, with nice comfortable carpets. My clients on the whole weren't looking for the full dungeon experience, which is why they came to me. I had one guy who liked me to bathe him, then suddenly grab his head and hold it under the water for what seemed a scarily long time. I had to be very careful with my stopwatch.

A female client I had, some big-name Wall Street financier, liked to dress as a schoolgirl and lay herself face down over my knees while I spanked her with a hairbrush. I had to install cable so she could keep her eye on the stock-market channel as I whacked her wobbly backside.

The sessions would get me hot, but I was always careful to leave myself an hour or so between appointments so I could masturbate to release the tension. I set up a CCTV system so I could watch re-runs of myself hurting people while I lay on the floor fingering myself to climax. Then I'd be ready for the next client.

Even with regular self-relief, Rob would usually be met with a wet and horny girlfriend when he got home. He was young and fit and I don't think he minded. I was like Cato in the *Pink Panther* films, he'd come in to a dark apartment, not knowing where I was, then I'd leap out at him screaming like a banshee. Though unlike Cato I'd be naked and would fuck my man where he lay.

Please understand, sex with Rob was entirely straight, we didn't even use blindfolds and silk scarves. It was important to me to keep the two parts of my life separate, and Rob just didn't want to go down that road. But it's not quite that simple either. I'd be horny because of what happened at work, and though I could certainly become aroused and achieve orgasm without even thinking about leather straps, I'd be lying if I said I never fantasised about bondage or domination while I was having sex with Rob. So it wasn't entirely absent from our bedroom. But for all intents and purposes, my relationship with Rob was entirely normal. He was good in bed. Perhaps not very inventive, or experimental, but I quite liked that about him, he had no real kinks; he grounded me, I guess. And what he lacked in adventure, he made up for in enthusiasm. He could go for hours when he wasn't too tired from work. Some weekends we hardly left the flat and never bothered to put clothes on. I used to love it when he fucked me from behind as I stood at the floor-to-ceiling windows, hands pressed against the glass, looking out over the New York skyline, twinkling with a million lights.

I loved New York, I loved Rob, I loved my job and I loved my life.

So of course I had to go and screw it up again, didn't I? One day Rob came home to find me even more horny than usual. Two of my sessions had overrun, leaving me sopping wet and dazed with lust. I'd beaten one man until he'd had to use the safety word and my final appointment had asked me to kick him repeatedly in the balls with my sharp-toed boots. He'd left a bit mangled and my pussy was throbbing with desire. I rushed home and waited for Rob.

As luck would have it, he was late that day so I tried to put sex out of my mind by doing some housework. Our maid was dreadful and I often thought she could have done with some lessons from Mistress Venetia. I was vacuuming like a maniac when I heard the door slam. He took one look at me and raised his eyebrows.

'I think I might get lucky tonight,' he said.

I said nothing, my chest heaving and my nostrils flaring. I needed his cock inside me immediately and told him so. He shrugged and dropped his trousers and pants showing me his beautiful, silky smooth cock, stiffening before my eyes.

I didn't realise I was still holding the vacuum cleaner pole as I stumbled towards him.

'Er,' he said, half nervously. 'What are you going to do with that?'

I had no intention of doing what I did do, which was to detach the pole from the machine, raise it over my head, and bring it down on his stiff penis. He screamed in agony and fell to his knees. I didn't stop and began raining blows down on his head and shoulders, out of my mind with lust and . . . well, maybe just out of my mind.

And that's it basically. He didn't press charges but told me I had to get out of his flat. I had no stomach to stay in New York alone and I knew I needed help. Proper help this time, not just weekly sessions with a shrink.

And so here I am. I hope I haven't shocked you, or scared you. I'm not usually violent. But I know I'm not totally in control. And that is something I can't bear the thought of. A dominatrix who loses control is fit for nothing.

Abigail sat down and appraised the other group members coolly. She caught Shelley's eye and, caught out, Shelley gave her the thumbs up, immediately feeling like an idiot. Abigail had this weird power over her, over everyone probably. She just had to look at you and you'd collapse in a wobbly mess, ready to do whatever she wanted.

They filed out, Larry patting Abigail on the shoulder gingerly. Shelley couldn't help but notice him walking a little awkwardly. This must be even more difficult for him than the others, she thought as she followed Rose and Cheryl to the dining room, listening to them chattering about the new Madonna album, as though they heard tales of violent domination before lunch every day.

Chapter Fourteen

After Abigail had finished, Shelley snuck up to her room and locked herself in the little bathroom. She was keen to get down in writing some of the technical terms and scenarios Abigail had mentioned. She was an odd one, Shelley thought. Of all of the group, she was the one Shelley felt least close to, even after the intimate confessional they'd just been through.

When she turned on the BlackBerry she noticed two things, one was that the battery was running low, and the other was that Aidan had sent her an e-mail.

Dear Shelley,

Just a quick thanks for the excellent copy you've been sending through. Everyone here is most impressed with your endeavour. The edited extracts on the blog are going down a storm and we've had a lot of interest from the media wanting to know who you are and whether the story is genuine.

Already a number of new advertisers on the strength of the extracts and publicity.

Keep up the good work.
Aidan

Shelley flipped the gadget shut and sat on the bed. She was flattered by the professional kudos but, as usual, she couldn't just enjoy her triumph; she had to ruin it by panicking about her own confessional again. The reason the stories she'd written so far were good was because they were true. How could she compete with that? She knew she was going to disappoint everyone.

Not only that though, but if her story was patent rubbish, she'd be torn limb from limb by the rest of the group. She didn't care about Fresh Paths, but she was beginning to think of the others in the group as her friends. How would they feel if they found out she was lying to them all? Shelley tried to put the thought out of her mind and sent a quick e-mail to Briony.

Hi Brie. Hope you found your vibrator. Need info on BDSM dungeons in London and New York. Re latter, please try to locate underground clubs in mid-town East. Need for story urgently. Thanks

Shelley decided not to attend the rest of the morning's session but to try and find a quiet spot to type up the story, which she suspected would take her longer than the others. She decided to send a message to Verity saying she had a stomach upset and needed some fresh air. She phoned reception and Sandra answered. Predictably, she was entirely unsympathetic.

'You need to be a bit more careful what you put down your throat.'

Shelley rolled her eyes thinking of nurse's physique.

'I think that's a piece of advice we both could do to heed. Now please pass my message on.'

Shelley smiled. She liked being the new Spicy-Shell. Maybe she'd keep up the hard-nosed bitch act when she got back to the office. Who was she kidding? It was easy to be tough down a telephone line.

Shelley wandered around the grounds. It was a bright, breezy day and it was good to get outdoors and clear the stuffy institutional air from her lungs.

She made her way around the back of the stately home, past the glass-house where the pool and gym were located and headed towards some outbuildings. As she arrived she was surprised by Dr Galloway, who popped out of a side door. This must be the drug rehab centre.

'Ah, Ms Carter,' he said, smiling broadly.

'Shelley, please,' Shelley replied. 'Dr Galloway, I do think I owe you an apology.'

'Whatever for?'

'I was dreadfully rude to you yesterday, in your office. You asked me a perfectly reasonable question, under the circumstances, and I reacted most outrageously. Please accept my apologies, sir.'

'Not at all,' Dr Galloway replied, bowing a little. 'I won't hear of you apologising for such a thing. Whatever the circumstances, it is an uncomfortable conversation for any lady, and I apologise to you for my insensitivity.'

Shelley wasn't sure how long she could keep up the Austen shtick.

'The answer's no, by the way.'

Dr Galloway gave her a sideways smile, 'Well, that is good news,' he said.

Is he coming on to me? Shelley thought. Surely not. Dr Galloway obviously realised he might have gone too far because he changed the subject.

'I've just been seeing a patient, a young lad, most unfortunately mixed up in the wrong crowds. His case may interest you, with your experience in paediatrics?'

'Oh?' Shelley replied, suddenly panicked. 'Perhaps we could chat about it another time, I am due for . . . a swim.'

Dr Galloway looked disappointed, and perhaps slightly suspicious? But he nodded politely and Shelley scuttled away.

Waking briskly round the corner of the building she bumped into Cian.

'Hello, my darling,' he said. Cian's face had a charming tendency to light up like a pinball machine when he was pleased to see someone. 'In a rush?'

'Hello, Cian,' she said, turning around to make sure Galloway wasn't right behind her. 'Got button-holed by the Doc back there, thought for a sec he was coming on to me.'

'Ah, now that's interesting,' Cian said. 'If it was anyone else but you telling me that, I'd remind them of what Verity told us the other day in the "Establishing Boundaries" workshop.'

'What was that?' Shelley asked.

'That those of us inflicted with this terrible curse tend to have difficulty differentiating ordinary friendly banter from sexually-charged negotiation. We see everything as a flirtation and an invitation to move towards the physical.'

'Oh,' Shelley said. 'I see.'

'But as it's you, I don't think that is necessarily the case,' Cian added. 'Because you are so damn sexy that I have no doubt the doctor wanted to bend you over then and there and give you a thorough internal examination.'

Shelley blushed and hit him on the shoulder, immediately feeling like a love-sick schoolgirl.

'I say, by the way, Carter,' Cian said suddenly, with his best RAF-Brigadier accent, looking about to see if they could be overheard. 'Did you find the tunnel yet?'

'What tunnel?' she asked.

'One of those damn orderly Johnnies told Larry there's a tunnel under the wall. The entrance is in the woods behind the pond. You can sneak out without the CCTV spotting you and walk down to the town; it's only half a mile. Private Larry and I went out on the first night and got hammered down the Fox and Goose.'

Aha! Shelley thought. *That's why they'd looked so shattered the following day.*

Cian leaned forwards so that his face was close to Shelley's ear. She felt his warm breath on her earlobe and a little thrill went down her spine. Cian continued, still in the *Great Escape* voice:

'We were thinking about popping out again tonight, but not making it such a late one. Maybe you and Rose could come out with us? Larry's taken a bit of a shine to her if you get my meaning. Think he wants to act as her tail-end Charlie, what, what?'

He was wearing one of Shelley's favourite scents and it was all she could do to stop herself burying her face into his exposed neck. She was flattered by the invitation, and was just about to agree when she remembered her assignment. There was no way she would be able to go out, have a drink or two, then get back in time to type out Abigail's story.

'I'd love to, but I think I'd better not,' she replied, regretfully.

Cian shrugged. 'Oh well, can't blame a guy for trying. See you later.'

Shelley watched him go wistfully. The job came first; she didn't want to disappoint Aidan.

As she walked back to her room, hoping to write a few hundred words before lunch, the BlackBerry in her pocket suddenly vibrated, making her jump. She nipped behind a bush and looked at the display.

It was Briony.

How the hell am I supposed to find out about sex clubs in New York?

Shelley rolled her eyes and thumbed a response.

I guess that's a real stumper. If only there were some kind of giant global computer database you could access to look this kind of thing up. Maybe some kind of . . . I don't know web, or net or something. But I guess it's just impossible. Thanks anyway!'
Shel

Thirty seconds later the device buzzed again.

U sure are sarcastic now ur a sex fiend. Will get onto it.
B

Shelley walked back to the path and popped the BlackBerry back into her pocket. As she looked up, she saw Sandra approaching.

Oh bugger! she thought. *Did she see me with the BlackBerry?*

She waited for the standard unpleasantness from the nurse as she passed, but Sandra just smiled knowingly at her and carried on walking.

Uh-oh, Shelley thought. *She* must *have seen me.*

She determined not to carry the thing around with her anymore, and also to find a better hiding place in case they searched her room. Whether it was Cian with his silly accents, or Galloway with his talk of the Mental Health Act, she didn't know, but she was starting to feel a bit like a prisoner.

She got back to the room, planning to check her messages again, but as she turned the BlackBerry on, it bleeped at her. The battery was nearly flat. She sat on the bed and considered what to do. She needed to get out of the centre to find a recharger. That was easier said than done though; the nearest town was hardly more than a village.

There was nothing else for it – she'd have to escape through the tunnel. She decided she would find Cian and take him up on his offer after all. With the last of the juice in the machine she sent a message to Aidan telling him about the missing charger and warning him he might not get his bed-time story tonight. Then she spent the next half an hour wondering if that last comment had crossed the line from harmless joke to unwanted flirtation.

'I knew you'd come around,' Cian said. She'd tracked him down in the dining room, where he was trying to score some biscuits before the next session started in a few minutes.

'But we need to go now,' she said. In a rural town, the shops would close early and she wasn't even sure she'd be able to get the right charger.

'Now?' said Cian in mock alarm. 'But that means missing "Saying No to Sex Doesn't Mean Saying No to Fun" this afternoon with special guest, Dr Verity Parrish.'

'Oh okay,' Shelley said, turning away, 'I can always ask Will.'

'Now, hold on just a minute there, m'lady,' Cian said quickly. 'No need to go do something drastic. I don't mind going now, but what about Larry? He wants to come too.'

Shelley thought for a minute. 'Leave him a note?' she suggested. 'I can leave one for Rose too.'

'Great idea,' Cian said. 'Meet you behind the potting shed in fifteen.'

'The potting shed?' Shelley asked, puzzled. 'I thought you said the tunnel ran from the woods behind the pond.'

'Yeah it does,' he replied. 'But I thought we could have a quick fumble behind the potting shed first, you know; make sure we're sexually compatible before we do something serious like go on a date.'

'Hmm,' Shelley said, hand on chin. 'I've thought it over and I think I'll give it a swerve, thanks. Meet you in fifteen in the woods.'

He shrugged, and turned to go.

'You see, I prefer to do things the other way around,' Shelley couldn't help calling out as she sashayed off in the other direction.

Maybe this course was doing her some good after all. She was flirting with rock stars now.

Shelley nipped back up to her room and scribbled a note for Rose, which she left on her friend's bed. She then dabbed a bit of perfume behind her ears, straightened her hair and tried not to look too hard at her eyebrows, which had needed doing since before Christmas. She felt nervous, though whether this was because she was sort of going on a date for the first time in months, or because she was frightened of getting caught, chucked off the course and possibly fired once Aidan found out, she wasn't sure. She slipped out of the room and crept down the stairs, watchful for staff, particularly Sandra. She stopped at the bottom, considering her options.

She couldn't go out the front doors because that would lead her past the Mountain Room's open door. If she went out the back, she'd be likely to be seen by someone in the canteen. Checking the fire-escape map, she saw there were doors out to the putting green. She'd have to go through the River Room. Slinking down the hall, she peered through the door. The room was empty.

Suddenly she started as she heard footsteps behind her. And without thinking she darted into the River

Room, rushed across and hid herself behind the heavy red drapes. Just in time, because the footsteps followed her into the room and she heard Dr Galloway's voice.

'Now, Mr Draper, this is the River Room, this is where the sexual dysfunction group meets. It's a more secluded and intimate room than the Mountain Room.'

'It's very nice,' Mr Draper responded. 'Er, will the group be very large? It's just that my problem is rather . . . delicate. I'd prefer to not have to share it with too many people.'

'I quite understand, Mr Draper, but please be assured that difficulties of this type are extremely common, you won't be sharing anything the other members of your group haven't also experienced, some of them far worse.'

Shelley was desperately curious to have a peek but couldn't risk showing herself. She waited until the poor Mr Draper was led off by Dr Galloway.

'Your course begins Monday week, Mr Draper . . .' she heard the doctor saying.

Shelley turned and tried the doors, they opened easily and she popped her head out, checked the coast was clear before emerging into the weak afternoon sunshine. She skirted the building and made her way to the meeting point in the woods over the road without further incident.

But as she waited for Cian to arrive, she saw Dr Galloway and Mr Draper exit from the front doors and walk to the car park, just a dozen feet from where Shelley was hiding behind a rhododendron. They shook hands and Draper turned towards Shelley to open his car door.

For the first time she saw his face and when she did she stiffened in amazement.

It was Harry. Freya's Harry. Perfect Boyfriend Harry.

The tunnel turned out to be less mysterious than she'd thought. It was simply an electrical substation sunk into the ground by the wall. There was a door and steps on each side. Shelley was quiet on the walk down. She was busy looking about, nervously expecting to see Fresh Paths staff leap out of the bushes. She was also torn between smirking at Harry's – and by extension Freya's – little problem and sympathising with them. She settled for feeling sorry for Harry, and smirking at Freya. Apparently not everything about Harry was perfect.

The Fox and Goose turned out to be a charming little pub, all low beams and smoke stains on the plaster. Shelley gazed in rapture at the glass of Chablis Cian had just plonked in front of her.

'So,' he said sitting down opposite her with a pint of best. 'You like to keep a man guessing, don't you?'

Shelley wasn't quite sure how to respond. Firstly, she needed to keep up the pretence of being a sex addict and so flirting with Cian fitted with that; on the other hand she genuinely liked him and didn't enjoy lying.

On the *other* other hand she *genuinely* genuinely liked him and enjoyed the attention he was giving her. She was left in the unfamiliar position of being the one who called the shots. She could do whatever she wanted and she knew Cian would accept it. She glanced at the clock over the bar. 4.39pm. Hmm, she'd better run now if she was going to find a shop that sold power adaptors. She took a gulp of wine.

'Oh,' she said, standing up suddenly. 'Would you excuse me? I've just remembered I need to pop to a shop for something.'

'I can come with you if you like,' he said, rising to his feet gallantly.

'No, I'd rather go alone.'

He looked a little hurt, so she added in a whisper, 'Ladies' things.' He nodded quickly and sat back down.

As she left the pub, Shelley smiled at her unintentional brilliance. She now had two excuses in one. Apart from the privacy she'd bought, Cian thought she was having her period, which could be useful if he started to get too fresh later on. Now the problem was in finding an electronics retailer in this sleepy town. Shelley thought she must be blessed when she saw a cab turn into the street. She flagged it and hopped in. The driver told her that the place to get such a thing was on the commercial estate just out of town and twenty minutes later she was back at the pub, finishing her wine.

Cian watched her, grinning.

'What?' she asked.

'This is great,' he said. 'I never get to do this.'

'You never get to drink in a pub with a girl?'

'No,' he replied earnestly. 'Not like this. Not just two people, having a quiet drink, just chatting.'

'We're not chatting, you're staring at me and grinning like the village idiot.'

He pretended to look hurt.

'But seriously,' he continued. 'This is what I want. I

want to be normal, to not be wondering where I can take whatever girl I'm with, and what she might let me do to her. I just want to sit in an old pub, where no one knows me, and chat.'

Shelley wasn't sure how to react to this. Was Cian suggesting he had no interest in her at all? He must have realised how his words might be taken and quickly followed up.

'I'm not saying I don't . . . I mean, I'm not suggesting . . .'

'Okay, maybe we need to change the subject?' Shelley said.

'Yes, great idea. What shall we talk about?'

'The weather's always safe,' Shelley suggested.

'Look, don't get me started on the weather,' he said, rolling his eyes. 'Every morning I watch the telly or listen to the radio trying to follow the reports but they just ramble on for ages about showers in Aberdeen or hail in the Orkneys and I find my attention wandering. I start thinking about all the people in those charming-sounding places going about their lives, gutting fish or fighting off massive seabirds or whatever it is they do and then all of a sudden I realise the weather-person is talking about London and I try to concentrate but then they've moved onto Belfast and I've missed it again.'

Shelley looked at her watch, trying to figure out how long they'd been away.

'Oh God, I'm sorry,' Cian said.

'What?' she asked.

'I'm boring you, aren't I?'

'Boring? No, why would you say that?'

'Because you're looking at your watch.'

She shook her head. 'I'm just wondering if they'll be missing us back at the centre. You're not boring me at all.'

'You sure?'

'Yes. Now go and buy me a drink.'

He stood, looked sheepish and headed off to the bar.

He was a nice guy, Shelley realised, when you cut through the bluster and the cheekiness. He was simply a nice young man, well spoken, intelligent and desperately insecure. She wanted to take him home and make him a decent supper, then tuck him into bed with a glass of hot milk. She suspected though that this little boy wasn't one to stay in his own bed for long. Maybe she wouldn't mind so much if he found his way into hers.

After a couple of hours, there was no sign of Larry or Rose and they decided they must not be coming. Shelley suggested they get back. She needed to write up Abigail's story. Cian agreed reluctantly and they made their way out on to the street. The sun was going down.

'Hang on,' Cian said. 'Is that Sandra?'

Shelley spun in panic and turned to look. 'I'd know those saddle-bags anywhere,' she said. Sandra was facing away from them, scanning the street. As they watched, she turned to look in their direction and Shelley felt Cian drag her back into the pub. He peered around the doorway. 'She's coming!' he hissed.

'She's looking for us,' Shelley said. 'How did she know we were here?'

'The notes we left,' Cian said.

'The note I left, I think,' Shelley replied. So Sandra had been searching in her room, going through her things and looking for the BlackBerry. She sucked in her breath as she contemplated the invasion of her privacy. But Cian was pulling her back into the pub.

'Come on,' he said, 'there's a back door.'

They crashed out into the beer garden, stumbling against each other and giggling. Shelley felt Cian's strong arm tuck itself around her waist and help to keep her steady as they ran over the unsteady paving stones in the gloom.

They finally made it back to the centre well after dark. They stopped just outside a side door and turned to face one another.

'Wait here for a couple of minutes before following,' Cian said. 'If I get busted, I'll make a lot of noise and you can try a different door.'

'My hero,' Shelley said, giving him a hug. 'Thanks, I enjoyed myself.'

'That . . .' Cian said, grinning, '. . . was the best date I've had since . . . well, since I can remember.'

'Yeah right,' Shelley said, rolling her eyes.

His face hardened. 'No, I mean it. Wait till you hear my confessional tomorrow. You'll see what I mean. I don't have . . . well, I don't do this sort of thing usually.'

Shelley stared back at him, unsure of what to say. Cian kissed her, quickly, on the cheek and turned to go. But then he stopped, turned and said, 'Oh, by the way. This came out of your bag in the pub, thought I'd better bring it along for you.' And he tossed a little package to Shelley.

It was the power adaptor. She looked back up at him.

He moon-walked backwards, waving as he disappeared into the building.

Cian came into Shelley's room later that night. He was wearing a black rubber mask. She tried to sit up but found she couldn't move.

This happens to me a lot, she thought to herself. *Why am I always stuck to the damn bed every time some sexy beast walks through the door?*

Cian was wearing a pirate hat, for some reason, and carried her power adaptor.

'Didn't you already give that to me?' she asked, puzzled.

'I'm going to give it to you now,' he replied and climbed up on to the bed.

He reached over and plugged the power adaptor into a wall socket. Then she realised it was plugged into something. A long black something that looked a little like her BlackBerry, but also a lot like a vibrator. Cian turned a switch and the machine buzzed. Shelley tried to close her legs but found she couldn't.

'Hey look, Cian,' she said. 'I like you a lot, but I'm not sure I'm ready for this.'

'Oh you're ready,' he said moving the thrumming device down between her legs. 'You're so ready I can smell it a mile off. We all can.'

She lay back and waited for the vibrator to enter her. But nothing happened.

She looked up, she was alone, apart from the gently snoring Rose in the next bed. Shelley curled up into a foetal position. A dream analyst wouldn't have too much trouble with me, she thought.

Chapter Fifteen

Shelley was grumpy the next day, and worked her aggression out by running around the grounds just inside the perimeter wall. She staggered back and showered as the others were assembling for breakfast, and when she finally walked into the dining room only Will was still there. She had no choice but to go and sit next to him. He was eating a plate full of fruit and looked like he'd rather swap with Shelley, who was having two rounds of toast and a blueberry muffin.

'Watching the weight,' he said, patting his stomach. Shelley smiled and took a bite of moist muffin.

'You wanted to talk to me the other day?' she said, munching.

Will frowned. 'Yes, I . . . I'm not happy here, Shelley. I miss my wife.'

Shelley nodded in sympathy, wishing she had a wife to miss. Or a husband, preferably.

'I don't get on with the others so well. I'm not sure this sort of thing is for me.'

'I know what you mean,' Shelley said absently, thinking about sitting on the sun-trap terrace of her sweet little flat in London and wishing she could be back in The Crown, sharing a bottle of Pinot Grigio with Briony. Hell, she even missed Freya a bit.

'Do you?' Will said. Shelley looked up and was surprised to find him staring intently back at her.

'Of course,' she said. Will looked to be about to say something else when Shelley noticed the clock on the wall. 'Shit, we're supposed to be in the Mountain Room.'

They gulped down their tea and rushed off. Verity frowned at them as they came in and they apologised profusely for being late. Cian didn't seem bothered. He was playing a painful-looking hand-slapping game with Larry. If he was nervous about having to give his confessional, there was no sign of it.

'Cian? Cian?' Verity said.

'Eh? Oh right yeah, miles away. Okay, here we go then.' He stood and stepped into the centre of the circle, turning to look at each member of his rapt audience as he began to speak.

So, a lot of what I'm going to tell you might sound like bragging and this is part of my problem. Every time I try to talk to someone about my . . . issues with sex, it seems like I'm just showing off. My mates look at me in disbelief when I tell them I want to stop with the endless knobbing. 'I wish I had your problems, mate,' they say. 'You play to packed houses night after night only to go home afterwards to your flash pad in Primrose Hill with an endless parade of short-skirted teenagers!' It seems . . . what's the word, churlish? It seems churlish to complain when most men would sell their first-born for what I've got.

And I haven't got any female friends I can talk to, either. I've shagged them all and they either won't talk to me afterwards or else they stalk me and I have to get security on to them. The sort of girls I pick up after my gigs aren't the talking type if you know what I mean. I tried talking to some of them, you know, afterwards, about wanting to stop shagging so much, but no girl likes to think she's put you off sex.

I guess that's it. I don't want to disappoint anyone. People expect me to want to fuck them, so I do. I'm no different to anyone else really, I want to be loved, and needed. And sex is what people love me for; it's what they need me for. Oh, and the music as well, I suppose, but it doesn't seem to me that that's what I'm really good at. Just the sex. I know I can give good sex.

Sorry for this rambling, I'd better go back to the beginning.

I guess it started with the au pair. Lena. She was from Slovenia, or Hungary, or some other place in Eastern Europe where the girls have fantastic tits. My father was, is, rich and we lived in a massive house in Hampstead. Lena had her own loft conversion, with great views out over London, but I didn't bother looking out the window too much when I was up there.

I didn't have too many friends and certainly no girlfriends, my spare time was spent either in the gym in the basement, or rehearsing with the band I was in then – Adverse Camber – Goth sort of thing to start with, but we got over that after a while. My father was the usual. Hardly ever around, never paying much attention to me, except to give me a disapproving look when I told him how the music was coming along. He wanted me to be a doctor I think, or something in the City. His second wife and I never got on too well, though I don't want to pretend she was some archetypal evil stepmother. She was better than my real mother, who's an alcoholic and lives in Brighton.

I'd noticed before how stunning Lena was of course, I was a teenager and sex was pretty much all I thought about, just like now really. One day I came into the kitchen where she was scrubbing the floor, facing away from me. She was wearing a tiny skirt and I could see the little white triangle of her panties, tight against her mound. She swayed back and forth as she scrubbed and I stood and watched for ages, my cock rock-hard in my pants.

Then suddenly she turned and winked at me. She'd known I'd been standing there watching. She'd been giving me a show. I stammered an excuse and ran up to my room where I masturbated furiously for an hour or so. The image of her swaying arse and panties went straight to number one in the wank bank.

On my sixteenth birthday she told me at breakfast she had a present for me and she wanted me to come up to her loft after school. I didn't think anything of it, like I said, we were rich and there didn't seem much chance she was going to give me something I didn't already have. How wrong I was.

My stepmother used to get home around four, and I tended to get in a half-hour earlier than her; for that half hour Lena and I would be the only people in the house. When I got home from school, I wandered up to her room and knocked.

'Come in,' she said, softly. I walked in and stopped dead. She was standing before the windows, wearing a thin dress. I could see just about everything, certainly enough to know she wasn't wearing underwear.

She didn't mess about. 'Your uniform is dirty; I will need to clean it tonight.'

I looked down, it didn't look too bad, and anyway, I had spares. What was she on about?

'Take it off,' she whispered.

I knew what was happening, but it was like looking down from above, like I was hypnotised. I did what she asked.

'And the pants,' she said, staring at my crotch. Now, again it'll seem like bragging, but when I took my pants down, her eyes widened. I'm not lacking down there, as any number of ladies have been happy to tell the gossip mags for a few quid. I had a good body even back then; me and the mates were always down the gym.

She walked over to me and dropped to her knees, still staring at my cock, standing proud and hard as a ship's cannon and just as likely to go off in her face if she so much as touched it.

She looked up at me and I stared lustfully at those perfect pale globes down the top of her dress. She had the smoothest skin I've ever known and perfect tits with little rose-bud nipples.

'Happy birthday, my big boy,' she said.

I nearly fainted as she took my cock in her soft, warm mouth, or as much of it as she could manage, anyway. I think the shock of realisation delayed my coming for a little while but even so it was just a few seconds before I shot my load against the back of her throat. She gagged slightly but swallowed the lot and kept on mouthing me gently until the spasms had died away.

Then she stood up, turned me around, slapped me on the arse and told me to go back to my room and get dressed.

'See you tomorrow,' she said as I left, stark-bollock naked. A few minutes later, still in shock, smile as wide as a cut throat, I heard the door slam downstairs as my stepmother arrived home. Lena even cleaned the uniform.

I made up my mind to walk a bit faster on my way home from school the next day. She was ready for me again. This time she was wearing a little red outfit, with a short skirt. And she was on the floor, scrubbing.

'You remembered,' I said.

'Do what you like with me,' she said.

I was nervous, and at first I just watched while I shoved my hand down my pants and rubbed my stiffening cock. Then I got a bit closer and reached out a trembling hand toward her rear end. I brushed against the red fabric of the skirt then slowly slid my hand down. With one finger I pressed against the mound hidden by the white panties. She sighed as I fingered the moist cotton. I didn't understand this and wondered if she'd peed herself. It didn't stop me though and I began rubbing her pussy through the material. She stiffened, then moaned gently. I cupped her mound with my hand and explored the soft contours of her crotch.

I was determined to last longer than before, and I wanted her to have an orgasm if possible. But of course

I didn't really know what I was doing, so I just did what I'd done in my fantasies about her; after all, she'd said I could do what I liked with her.

I lifted her skirt. She had a nice big bum with rounded, smooth white cheeks exposed by the G-string. I pulled the G-string aside and felt my first pussy. The lips were soft and sticky-wet. I was fascinated and inserted an exploratory finger, she gasped and shifted back slightly so as to get more of it inside her.

I remember that scene so vividly, you know? The afternoon light was pouring in through the windows; I could hear kids playing in the park across the road, the sound of traffic. And there I was with three fingers jammed up the au pair's sopping wet vagina, my cock like a tent-pole straining in my pants.

I couldn't bear it any more. I took off my trousers and pants and told her to take off her panties; I remember my voice cracking a little as I said it. She giggled and wriggled out of her G-string and got back into position. As I knelt down behind her again, she lifted her arse up and spread her legs, exposing herself to me. Then it got a bit awkward as she had to help guide me inside her. You don't just slap in a cock as big as mine. But it felt amazing. She was so hot inside and groaned as I filled her up. I watched in delirious fascination as my shaft pumped in and out of her wet pussy. She was breathing more and more heavily as I thrust it in deeper and deeper. Faster and faster.

I didn't last too much longer than the first time, small atom bombs went off in my head as I climaxed. Exquisitely sensitive, I could feel my pulsing cock stretch her labia and she grunted as I shot my load inside her. She hadn't orgasmed, so afterwards she turned over, pulled me down on top of her and kissed me roughly as she took my hand and showed me how to bring her off. I'd heard of a clitoris before, but I had no idea where it was, or what you did with it. I was too rough at first so she showed me how to use a gentle circular motion. Her clit felt soft, slick and vulnerable under my fingers and as she came she wrapped her thighs around my hand and thrust herself upwards. I watched her beautiful face, eyes closed in ecstasy.

Then it was time to go, and again I got back into my room and into the shower just as my stepmother arrived downstairs.

From then on it was a different lesson every day. I tell you one thing about these Eastern Europeans; they sure have a hell of a work ethic. I couldn't wait to get home, couldn't concentrate on my lessons. All I could think about was her body, her lips. Sliding my cock hard into her as we kissed roughly. She taught me so much. God knows where she'd learnt it.

My schoolwork suffered and I stopped going out with girls from my school. They all thought I was weird. The only social contact I got was through the band, I think the confidence and the self-regard I gained from Lena helped me on stage. I turned from a shy teenager into a swaggering young adult and I guess it was that, plus the fact that we weren't half bad, that meant we ended up with hundreds of groupies. These weren't just girls from school either, these were university babes, Camden chicks, even Sloane Rangers, slumming it in the seedy pubs of

North London and private parties we played in Hoxton. They'd throw themselves at us after the gigs, and I hated to say no but I had Lena waiting for me at home.

Again, it sounds like boasting, but the fact that I wouldn't take any of these girls home made me into even more of a sex object. There were rumours I was gay, and for a while I played up to being celibate like some latter-day Morrissey, but the other guys in the band knew the truth, and the record label would send on fanmail from girls who wanted to fuck me. I was flattered, and intrigued, especially when I read all the things they wanted to do to me, but I stayed loyal to Lena. I didn't love her; we hardly ever spoke except to tell each other to turn over, or to do something harder, or faster. But I was grateful to her and, most importantly, I didn't want to disappoint her. She was the first person who ever really showed me love, of a sort, and I didn't want to let her down.

One day I came home and she was completely naked, blindfolded and lying on the bed. Wrapped around each wrist was a silk scarf. I knew what she wanted. I tied her arms to the bedposts, and began kissing her. I moved from place to place, surprising her, teasing her, never letting her know where I was going to tongue her next. She parted her thighs, begging me to kiss her there but first I lifted her shapely legs and pushed them back until her ankles touched her ears. Then I lowered my head and tickled her wet outer lips with my clean-shaven chin waited until she could bear it no longer, then rammed my tongue into her wetness.

It was just then that I heard the door open and a shriek filled the room.

'Cian! What the hell are you doing?'

It was my stepmother. I looked up, Lena's juices dripping from my chin, then turned back to the bound au pair, anguish on her face. She knew it was over.

And that was the end of my first affair. Lena was sent packing back to Rumania or whatever, where I've heard the men make less sensitive lovers. I actually cried periodically for a few days, and then one night I flicked open the fanmail, made a list of phone numbers and sent a few texts.

We had a gig soon after. And most of the girls I'd selected showed up. Afterwards they came crowding up to the stage. I had a few beers with the boys first, then when I came out the back door there was a mob. Girls were fighting. Over me! I picked two pretty much at random, and we escaped in a cab.

I took them to a hotel, my stepmother kept a pretty tight rein on me at home. I tapped out some coke and we got a few bottles of fizz from room service. At first we just whooped and cheered and rushed around the room; MTV on full blast through the room's entertainment system. Eventually though we found ourselves lying entangled on the bed and I kissed each of them in turn.

You read stories in the tabloids about three-in-a-bed romps, but I wasn't totally sure how to do this. The girls were keen but young; they were looking to me to lead the show. As usual I didn't want to disappoint. I told one of them, Kayleigh her name was, to sit on the armchair and watch while I did her friend Bianca. Kayleigh was thin, with a hungry look in her eye. I remember she had the tiniest skirt, hardly thicker than a belt, but was expert at crossing her legs just so to stop you getting an eyeful. It drove me crazy.

Bianca was beautiful, slim waist but curvy everywhere else. I massaged her soft breasts through the thin material of her top and kissed her gently at first, then rougher. I was desperate to get inside her, but I needed to go slowly, I had determined to give each of them an orgasm before I came. Girls like a bit of the rough stuff now and again, but they also like to be warmed up first, especially the young ones.

Gradually the clothes came off. Both girls sighed when they saw my cock for the first time. Bianca reached out slowly and took hold of the throbbing monster. She looked a little nervous. I had lube with me though and reached over to my bag to get it. Bianca lubed up my cock slowly. I looked over at Kayleigh; she was touching herself, watching us.

Then Bianca lay back and spread her legs, I knelt down and kissed her inner thighs, she quivered under my moist tongue. I began kissing closer to her pussy. She had a Brazilian, leaving just the thinnest patch of wispy blonde hair running down the lips. I used my fingers to open her up slightly and kissed her clitoris. She gasped and wriggled. Then I began lapping at her pussy. She started breathing more and more heavily.

At this point I felt a hand push between my thighs and grab hold of my engorged cock. The naked Kayleigh had decided she couldn't wait. Soon enough her hand was replaced by her mouth. The sensation was fantastic. I'd had a few drinks, so was able to control myself, and tried to concentrate on tonguing Bianca's clitoris.

'Fuck me,' Bianca moaned. Always ready to please, I shifted position, kissed her on the mouth, so she could taste herself and flipped over so she could ride me. Kayleigh helped direct my slick cock into her friend's wet pussy as Bianca lowered herself onto me. Even with the lube it was a tight fit. She began fucking me, slowly at first but gradually building speed as her pussy stretched to accommodate my girth.

Kayleigh moved around and without waiting to be asked, lifted a leg over my head and positioned her pussy over my mouth. She was facing Bianca so she could watch me fuck her friend as I licked her.

Kayleigh came first, as it happened, she was a real sex kitten that one, as I discovered later in the night. It was the time when I first discovered rubbing a bit of coke into the end of your penis keeps it hard for hours. I wouldn't recommend it though. I stayed semi-hard for days and was red-raw for a week after that. But that night my old friend served me well. I finally came after each of the girls had had a couple of orgasms. I stood up on the bed as the girls knelt before me, wet mouths working on my shaft, fighting over it. Kayleigh slipped a finger up my arse and Bianca stroked my balls as I fired what seemed like gallons of come over their faces.

I woke the next morning with an aching head, a still hard and hugely painful penis, a whopping hotel bill and a beautiful young woman on either side of me.

If this was sex, I was hooked.

Chapter Sixteen

Kayleigh's and Bianca's smiles as they left the hotel room were much more important to me than the good review the band got for that gig. From then on I went home with a different girl, or more, after every gig we played, and sometimes in between. It wasn't long after that that we switched to Sony and released *Crumpin'*, which you may remember went Gold. I moved out of the house in Hampstead, of course, and got a shag pad in Chelsea. At first I let the girls stay overnight, or even for the weekend, but as we became more successful, they seemed to get more clingy and eventually I got a security guy and he'd get rid of them afterwards.

I couldn't stand to do it myself. I couldn't deal with the look of disappointment I'd get. What were they thinking? Why would they imagine I'd fall in love with them? They knew I shagged a different girl every night. I hated to disappoint, but I was definite about not wanting anything long term. It was just the sex I needed, and not even that, just the feeling of wanting to be loved. I wanted to know everyone felt it, not just one or two girls with tiny skirts and smaller IQs.

I got better at it too. I read what they wrote about me in the kiss'n'tells, about my performance. Though I never responded to journos myself, if I detected any hint of dissatisfaction, I'd work on it the next time. One girl said she felt I was less keen to go down on her than to make her suck me off, so the next night I tongued a girl for so long she came three times then begged me to stop. Another time I read I'd been a bit too gentle so the next girl found herself strapped to the bed as I rammed my dick into her harder and harder until the bed collapsed. In hindsight maybe there was a hint of overcompensation there.

That year is pretty much a blur though. I must have slept with more than a hundred girls. Maybe two hundred. Two gigs a week on average and one or two girls after almost every one. The only times I didn't score were the times I suffered from nervous exhaustion, and a period of a couple of months when I was getting over a mild STD. That's right, I was sometimes so out of it that I didn't use a condom. Still, sitting with the nurse in a cold exam room was enough to change my habits in that regard. Now I toggle up every time without fail. Sometimes I even keep one in my underwear if I know it'll be a big night.

Coke, music and sex were the only things I was interested in. And the music came a distinct third, as any of you who listened to our second album would probably agree. I ended up in rehab eventually. And though that helped my drug addiction, it did nothing for the lust for sex.

On the third or fourth night I was in the clinic, I'd

just got to bed when the door opened and a nurse walked in. Now this was my fourth night of cold turkey, so for once I wasn't thinking about sex so much as the drugs, so I didn't immediately pay much attention to the fact she was hot. It was only once she pulled open her uniform blouse and revealed two magnificent tits that I stopped thinking about shoving something up my nose and instead started thinking about shoving something else.

'I'm here to take your mind off your problems,' she whispered, before shrugging off her uniform and sliding up onto the bed. Coming off drugs does funny things to your body. I hadn't had a hard-on for days, and it took her a while to get me up, but she managed it. Back before they had Viagra, they used to have these girls in the porn industry whose job it was to get the men hard before their sex scenes. They called them fluffers, and they knew all the tricks. Well, I reckon this girl must have been an ex-fluffer. I wish I could remember all the things she did; I'd try and teach them to every girl I met. The only thing I do remember for sure is that I thought she'd swallowed my entire tackle at one point. I was seriously worried I'd never get it back out of there.

Anyway, she sorted me out and got herself into the reverse cowboy position. Girls usually like it that way cos the guy can reach around and stroke her clit while she controls the pace and length of the strokes. It's generally harder for the guy to come, and I think she probably knew that. I went for ages, she came twice in the meantime and just as I thought I was about to come she hopped off me and started getting dressed.

'Wha . . . wha . . .?' I sputtered.

'All part of the treatment, Mr O'Connor,' she replied primly and walked out.

Well, in a sense it really did work, because I'd stopped thinking about the drugs, and started thinking about the sex again. But she didn't know about the sex addiction, or at least I think she didn't.

Her name was Gloria, I found out, and over the next few weeks she continued the 'treatment', the hot little piece of ass. She'd pop in when I was asleep sometimes, and wake me up with a hand job. Or when she was on day shift she'd ambush me in the corridor, pull me into a supply cupboard and bend over a stool for me. She finished me off from time to time, but always left me wanting more. She was the first woman since Lena I wanted to keep seeing. And gradually it seemed to be that she wanted something more as well. I'd thought she was just another slapper at first, wanting to get her kudos and go running to blab to her mates about how she shagged a rock star. But she wasn't like that. She hardly knew who I was, for a start. She had awful taste in music, all eighties stuff like Madonna and George Michael. We went for walks through the grounds together and got to know each other, in between quickies in the bushes.

She made me understand, or perhaps made me remember, that two people in a relationship together, however unusual it might be, can explore each other, can learn from each other and work together to improve the sex. Do you know what I mean? I mean that it's better when you know the person. When you know what she likes and she knows what you want. She reminded me of Lena in that way.

One night I received a message to go to a treatment room. When I arrived I knocked and was told to enter. Gloria lay on the gurney, totally naked. On another gurney lay a little mirror with white powder and a rolled-up fifty. I looked back and forth, like a spectator at a tennis match.

'Choose,' Gloria said.

There was no contest. I shrugged off my clothes and hopped up onto the gurney with her. We just kissed at first, while she caressed my cock gently. 'I want to try something different today,' she said. She handed me a tube of lube and rolled over on to her front, lifting her haunches and displaying her peachy arse. I didn't need to be asked twice and squeezed a generous helping of lube into her cleft. I rubbed it in gently, and then slipped an exploratory finger into her anus. She pursed her lips and moaned.

'Can I go on?' I asked. She nodded. I'd never done this either. To be honest I'd never really thought about it much. I was thinking about it now, worried that I might hurt her but fascinated to know what it would feel like.

I pulled my finger out and rubbed the excess lube onto my cock. Then I positioned the tip at her puckered hole. She rocked back slightly on her knees, invited me in. I pushed forward firmly and felt the end of my cock pressuring her resistant arsehole. Then I felt something give and I was in, the tip at least. It felt damn tight. She groaned a little, with pain or pleasure I couldn't tell. Probably both. I waited a while as she got used to it, then began gently sliding the first couple of inches inside and out again, careful not to let the tip slip out.

Gradually I worked more and more into her, I could hear her grind her teeth, and her knuckles gripped the edge of the gurney like she was afraid to let go. But she began thrusting back. It was almost painful for me as well, her sphincter muscle clenched tight around my cock head and I had to shove hard to force my way in.

It was different, and interesting, but neither of us came. Not that first time anyway. I pulled out after a time, cleaned off and we finished in more conventional style. As I lay in her arms afterwards, both of us a little sore, but happy, I wondered if I'd found The One.

Once I got out of the clinic, my rehab a resounding success thanks to Gloria, I kept seeing her. I was still obsessed with sex, but so was she. She moved in with me and it was bliss. I spent the days practising and the nights gigging, she spent the days sleeping and the night working. We spent the mornings fucking each other's brains out.

She was experimental, though not kinky. She liked to surprise me. She cooked me a dinner once, making me wait until I was starving, then she swept my plate onto the floor just as I was about to tuck in. Then she hopped up onto the table and spread her legs, inviting me to feast on an entirely different meal. I was angry, as she'd expected and I fucked her senseless, our passion filling my empty belly and eight pints of blood flooding into my engorged cock rather than my stomach.

My musical career started to improve as well. We brought out the *Original Victim* album and went on tour. Gloria came and joined me for part of the tour. That was wild. Sleeping and shagging in the back of the bus as we travelled from town to town across the US. She had to get back to work after a while and we went on to Japan. Tokyo was mad. I stayed faithful to Gloria, truth was there wasn't time to screw around, we were that busy. But about a week in, we were in Kyoto and there was some problem with the venue so it was cancelled and we had a free night. We went to a karaoke bar of course, got bladdered and somehow ended up in a strip club. Well, to cut a long story short it wasn't long before I had half a dozen dancers hanging off me, and what's a guy to do? I went in the back room for a private dance with two of the girls, not planning on asking for anything more, but the girls had other ideas.

They were beautiful, and could have been sisters. Each had the clearest, smoothest skin and shimmering straight black hair. Shortly they were naked and came over to my chair. One of them sat astride me, rubbing her bare pussy against the swell in my trousers. I'd like to say I was thinking of Gloria and fighting against my conscience, but I wasn't. All I could think about was how I was going to make them squeal.

The second girl was behind me, she adjusted the chair so that it leaned back, and I found myself looking into her smiling, upside-down face. She kissed me, tickling my lips with her darting tongue as her friend continued grinding her pelvis across the ridge in my jeans.

Then suddenly my flies were open and the one on top had swivelled herself around so her pussy was over my face. She hefted my cock out of my pants, and uttered an astonished cry. Her friend said something in Japanese and they laughed a little nervously. A pair of lips attached themselves to my member and I shuddered. The one on top lowered herself onto my face and I nuzzled her. She smelt sweet and her fuzz was soft and silky, I slipped a tongue inside her and she squeaked.

The other lifted my haunches up and began tonguing my balls gently. I felt them tighten as an orgasm built, but the girls weren't ready for me to come just yet. They stood off me, and giggled with each other. The longer they held me there, on the edge but unsated, the more money they would earn.

'You heartless bitches,' I said.

And so it carried on. They'd wait for my hard-on to subside slightly, then start working on me all over again. It was torture, but sweet torture. I'm not sure I would want to repeat the experience now, but I'm glad I went through it. Those girls knew exactly what made men tick. Well, it's an art I suppose. They say that oriental girls have all this mystical knowledge; well, they used it all that night.

I was in there for three hours. Eventually I told them I'd pay an extra £500 if they'd finish me off. They agreed and set to work. One took hold of my cock again, but further down. She still had control, but less so. The other one took as much of it into her mouth as she could and used her tongue to good effect. She stared right into my eyes, watching for the signal. As I tensed up ready for the final act, she sucked hard while her friend squeezed my shaft and stroked my balls.

I'd been worried she might choke on the gallons of fluid I thought I must have produced by now, but her friend regulated the speed of the release with her grip and it came out slowly over a good thirty seconds. I released a long, guttural groan as I came, writhing in helpless ecstasy as the Asian beauty sucked me dry.

They left me drained of money, energy and semen, but it was the most incredible experience I've ever had. I slept like a baby once I finally got back to the hotel, and I can't say I felt guilty.

Problem was that experience seemed to reawaken something in me. I'd thought I was happy with Gloria, that I didn't need anyone else, but once the floodgates had been opened, as it were, I couldn't help myself. I kept telling myself that it was just while were on tour, that once I got back to London I'd be a one-woman man again. The other guys in the band just laughed. Someone decided, I can't remember who now, maybe it was me, that we should spend the rest of the tour trying to plumb the depths of East Asian depravity before we cleaned up and went back to London.

We made a thorough job of exploring the fleshpots of south Asia over the next couple of weeks. We did three nights in Manila where we visited a dwarf brothel. That was pretty weird. Then in Shanghai we went to this place where hollow-eyed opium addicts had sex on stage with animals. I wasn't so keen on that. In Phnom Pen we were presented with a couple of girls with red marks all over their arms. I didn't realise what was going on until one of them took a burning cigarette and stubbed it out on her wrist.

I ran. Why I wanted to see all this stuff I don't know, I guess I wanted to see how sick other people were, so as to make me feel better myself. I wasn't into all this sick shit, I just wanted sex. Straight sex, normal sex. That's okay isn't it? That's healthy, isn't it?

When I got back Gloria wasn't there. I wasn't too surprised. I'd hardly called her in the last few weeks. Chances were she'd figured out what was going on.

I was a little hurt, but more than anything I was angry. I'd been unfaithful, but only with prostitutes; that didn't count as far as I was concerned. I'd passed up the chance to have sex with dozens of normal girls for her. And she couldn't even be bothered to tell me to my face when it was all over. After the gig the next night, I went out the stage door, pointed to half a dozen girls and took them all back to mine with a bottle of Viagra.

As it happens, six girls turned out to be too many even for me so I sent a cab to pick up the guitarist to come over and help me out. We had ourselves quite a little party that night. The guitarist and I had this little bet to see if we could bring three girls off all at the same time. I got the first one, a little brunette with a tight arse, to sit on my cock. Then I asked a tall African girl to sit on my face and I buried my head between her legs, lapping at her pussy hoping to lose myself in there, hoping that when I woke up I'd be back in Kyoto. She kept squirming and lifting up, so I took hold of one of her thighs and held her against my working jaw. That left one hand free, which I used to stroke the third girl's mound as she knelt, facing away from me. I realised after a while that she was kissing the brunette. The third girl, a plump blonde, grabbed hold of my hand and began grinding herself against my wrist bone.

They didn't all come at the same time, but I didn't really mind losing that bet. The blonde came first, and she helped the brunette to finish off by flicking her tongue against her perky little nipples and stroking her clit as she rode me. The African girl took longest. We finished up lying on our sides, with me behind and her with one leg raised slightly, offering me access. I rubbed her clit as I slid in and out gently and she moaned softly as she came. The two other girls were working on giving each other a second orgasm by the time I'd finished.

Gloria was standing in the doorway, watching the proceedings. That shrunk me quickly than an ice-bath. Even from my position ten feet away I could see the tears in her eyes. Then she turned and left and I never saw her again.

I never did find out what had happened. Why she hadn't been there when I got back and why she turned up that night unannounced. She never contacted me again and the hospital she worked at told me I wasn't to visit.

I fell into depression after that. I managed to stay off the drugs, apart from Viagra obviously, but the sex just got more and more out of control. I became less discerning about who I invited back and then, one crazy night, I gave my address out on a girl's MySpace page and was swamped by hundreds of them, and even a few guys. It was fun at first, but there was a three-day orgy and half my stuff had been nicked. The rest had food, booze and other unidentified stains all over it.

I swore off casual sex again after that, and determined to find myself a nice, normal girl. But within a week I caved in and found myself deflowering a seventeen-year-old virgin on her parents' kitchen table.

Something snapped at that point and I went home afterwards, cried for three hours, then phoned my dad. He came around straight away. I hadn't seen him for over a year, but he never mentioned that. I expected him to give me a lecture, but he just gave me a hug. A stiff hug, but a hug nonetheless. Then he told me not to worry, that he'd phoned a doctor friend of his who was sorting me out with some help, if I wanted it. I told him I did and, well, here I am.

I know I'm capable of having a normal relationship. I had a sort of normal relationship with Lena, then another one with Gloria. I was happy at both those times. And I was never properly happy when I was single and shagging endless lines of women. I just don't know . . . I don't know how I should be. How I should act? How I can stop myself being . . . who I've been. Do you know what I mean?

Chapter Seventeen

Cian's words were greeted with sympathetic murmurs and a big hug from Cheryl. Shelley felt stunned. Part of her wanted to be that au pair, getting a good rogering from behind, another part was listening to the alarm bells his tale had set ringing in her head. Cian was a troubled soul. While he obviously wanted to get help, and get his life organised, the fact that he was still a world-famous rock star living the life suggested this would be no easy road. This was the second time he'd been institutionalised and probably wouldn't be the last if you listened to the statistics.

The man himself, after a few moments of uncertain silence, pointed with a thumb towards the door.

'I'm starving! Lunch?'

He and Larry raced for the door, trying to trip each other up. The others followed behind. Shelley was last to leave. She was already composing the story in her mind, writing it mentally before transferring it to the BlackBerry's electronic brain via her thumbs later that night.

Outside the door, she came across Verity and Will

standing just outside the door, Will was angry, jabbing his finger at the counsellor.

'I'm telling you I've had enough,' he said. 'I don't see the point in sitting here listening to this filth day after day, then doing these idiotic exercises when half the group doesn't bother to attend.' He caught Shelley's eye. 'Shelley, you're a smart girl. I see you sitting there trying not to laugh during the lectures, it's a joke, isn't it?'

'Will, please calm down,' Verity said. 'I am here to listen to your concerns about the course, but there is an appropriate time and place for such a discussion. Why not take a break, then come and see me in my office? We can talk this through.'

Will opened his palm towards Shelley, as if to say, 'Why don't you back me up?'

'Look Will,' she said. 'I think you should listen to Verity on this one. Take a walk and get some fresh air. You need to clear your head before you make a decision like this.'

Will's brought his hands against his sides in frustration, and his eyes widened, giving him the look of a puppy she'd just kicked. Shelley knew Will saw her as an ally in all this, and now a turncoat one. He stalked off.

'Thank you, Shelley,' said Verity. 'You handled that maturely.' She too walked away. Shelley frowned, she wasn't sure she wanted Verity's approval on this, having some sympathies for Will's point of view. Plus Verity had said it in a tone that suggested Shelley was normally as mature as a Beaujolais nouveau. Had she been talking to Galloway about Shelley's temper tantrum?

She walked towards the dining room, rounded a corner

and bumped into someone very tall and hard. She bounced off and fell to the carpet. 'For the love of buggery, why can't you look where you're going?' she shouted as the clumsy oaf helped her to her feet. She looked up at him.

'Aidan!'

'Sorry to surprise you like this, Shelley. I didn't know I was coming either until this morning. I had to drive up to Wolverhampton for an urgent meeting and I had time to spare so I figured I'd pop in and see how you're getting on.'

'Fine,' Shelley said shortly. She knew she was pouting a bit but she couldn't stop. It was all very well for Aidan, swanning about, dropping in on people at a whim. She was the one trapped here with people shouting at her and attractive men with complicated love lives throwing themselves at her. She wasn't at all sure she had forgiven him for dropping her in it like this.

'How did you get in?' she asked, looking around. 'We're not allowed visitors.'

'I told them it was a family emergency. The girl on the desk wasn't sure at first but I talked my way in.'

Charmed your way in, more like, Shelley thought.

'The column's going down a storm on the website,' Aidan said in a low voice. 'I'm posting extracts and people are voting for the story they like the best then we're going to print the full text of it in the first magazine.'

'Great,' sniffed Shelley. 'So these people's personal lives and private tragedies are now the subject of some vapid popularity contest.'

Aidan frowned and stood back a little. 'You seem to

have forgotten you're a journalist, Shelley. You're here, at the expense of the company, to do a job for us. You're not here to make friends.'

Shelley, slightly stung, sat back in her chair. Then she pulled herself together. She nodded. 'I know, I'm sorry, I guess I've just become . . . institutionalised.'

Aidan leaned forward again. 'Go on,' he said, softly, looking into her eyes and nodding in a reassuring manner. Shelley melted a little.

'I feel different, Aidan. I feel this place is changing me. Not quite sure what into yet,' she said with a smile. 'I keep losing my temper,' she said. 'I'm more emotional, more . . . passionate, I suppose.'

He smiled, his face lighting up.

'A bit of passion's no bad thing,' he said. 'And I don't think you wanted for passion before.'

'Really?'

'On the dance floor at that party last year. I liked what I saw that night.' Aidan stopped and looked uncertain for an instant. His face was a closed book again, his tone brash. 'I realised you had balls, Shelley, and I knew you were the person for this job.'

Shelley nodded, her head a whirl. What had just happened there? Had she just seen a chink in his armour?

'Anyway, there are plenty of other things happening in the office. Briony's column is perfect. The sort of things she claims to get up to . . . you live with her, don't you? Is she really like that?'

Shelley nodded. 'Whatever she writes, I dare say it's all entirely true. She probably cuts out the raunchiest bits in case her PC sets on fire.'

Aidan laughed. 'The post-room boys are blogging like demons down there between deliveries. They certainly have some . . . er, interesting and strongly-worded views, particularly on some of the younger ladies in the office.'

'What about Freya?' Shelley asked as casually as she could.

'Some good stuff,' Aidan said, looking at his feet quickly. *Hmm*, Shelley thought, *why so coy?* 'She's giving me some really deep, some really long . . .'

'Yes?' Shelley said encouragingly.

'. . . pieces on the psychology of love. I may give her the cover story . . .'

'May?' Shelley asked.

'May . . . unless I decide to put another story on the front.' And with that he looked Shelley in the eye. A tiny current of something passed between them. She was sure of it.

'Oh, by the way,' Aidan said. 'Have you encountered a Dr Galloway yet?'

'Yes, he heads the alcohol and drug rehab centre, but also does one-on-one sessions with the sex addicts.'

'Great. I want you to get close to him. See if you can get anything useful on celebrities who may have had need of his expertise.'

'Anyone specific?'

'I heard a rumour they may be a rather well-known actress who comes here from time to time, as well as an aging rocker, but I'm not fussy. Get me some dirt on anyone C-List and up.' Aidan looked at his watch. 'Must run, good to see you, Shelley.'

They stood, their eyes locked. Aidan leaned in slowly towards her.

Oh my fucking God. He's going to kiss me!

Shelley felt her lips part and she craned her neck.

'I am enjoying your stories, Shelley,' said Aidan in her ear. 'You have a real gift for writing . . . erm, action sequences.' He broke away. 'Keep up the good work.'

Then he turned and strode off down the hall to the front door. Shelley followed him for a couple of steps, then watched him go, her head a battlefield of emotions.

It was strictly professional. Aidan did not see her like that. *Damn you, Matthews. Think of the cats.*

'Now food,' Shelley said out loud, heading for the dining room along the winding corridors. As she rounded the corner she found Abigail, holding Sandra in a head lock and bashing her skull against the doorjamb.

'Stop!' Verity called, running up and flapping like a drunken ostrich. Cian and Cliff were there too, grinning madly and egging the girls on.

'Fight, fight, fight!' Larry called from inside the room.

Abigail let Sandra go and eyed her menacingly, fists raised. *One of her rages?* Shelley wondered.

'She started it,' Sandra spat. 'She's always bossing me about. Put the tea there, Sandra, bring me a glass of water, Sandra, carry my bag, Sandra. She treats me like I'm a fucking slave!'

'You're supposed to be a nurse!' Abigail snarled back at her. 'You're supposed to be sensitive to our problems and speak to us appropriately. But you're as sensitive as an iron clitoris and your language about as appropriate as a chocolate tampon.'

The red-faced Sandra glared back at her then suddenly made another lunge at Abigail. In a flash Galloway was there and pulled the dominatrix out of the way. At the same time Dr Jones arrived and tried to grab the flailing nurse, missed altogether and fell to the floor with a crash. She lay there, moaning weakly. Eventually an orderly turned up and wrapped his burly arms around Sandra. 'Calm down, love,' he said, gently.

Dr Jones was led away, for a cup of tea, or probably something stronger if Shelley was any judge of character.

Shelley slipped past the mêlée into the dining room, hoping they hadn't stopped serving. She managed to scrape together a few bits and pieces Larry and Cian had left and sat down for a well-earned meal. Sandra came in holding an ice pack against the side of her head and plonked herself down opposite. Shelley peered at her, a forkful of cold quiche half-way to her mouth.

'Someone was here for you,' the nurse said slyly.

'Yes, he found me, it was my brother, Aidan.'

'Not him, someone else. Strange-looking bloke. Told him you were in a meeting.'

'Well, come on, don't be so mysterious, who was it?'

Sandra paused for a while, savouring the moment.

'Funny hair. Said his name was Gavin.'

After lunch they were given some free time to settle down and most of the group headed for the pool. Everyone except Abigail and Will were already there by the time Shelley had changed and made her way down. She'd sat in her room for a while, trying to work out who could have told Gavin she was here. She took out the BlackBerry, and typed an email.

Briony Binns, did you tell Gavin I was here?

A knock on the door made Shelley plunge the device under her pillow. The handle turned, and Verity entered without waiting for permission.

'Hope the little fracas didn't upset you today, Shelley.'

'Not at all,' she replied. 'I appreciate that sometimes tensions run high in these groups, particularly after a few days when people are starting to miss their . . . well, whatever they were addicted to.'

Verity nodded. 'And that man you were chatting with in the Mountain Room?'

'My brother,' Shelley said, levelly. Verity seemed to accept this.

'Good. Good,' said Verity. She looked around the room as though it was the first time she's seen it. 'The others are at the pool. You should join them.'

As she left, the BlackBerry beeped. Shelley looked in panic at the door, expecting Verity to reappear with a triumphant gleam in her eye. Thankfully, she didn't. Shelley let her heartbeat slow, then pulled out the BlackBerry.

No, of course not, what do you take me for? Gavin did come into the office looking for you though. I saw him talking to Freya. Miss you.

'No running, Larry!' Shelley heard Verity shout. 'And put some trunks on!'

Given the lengths the centre had gone to remove any form of sexual temptation, allowing a bunch of sex addicts to wander around wearing skimpy bathing suits seemed to Shelley a little foolish. It was like laboriously going through a dieter's cupboard, throwing away all the bad stuff only to leave them a pizza menu and a credit card. They evidently thought that the wholesome qualities of good, old-fashioned exercise outweighed the potential for underwater fumbling.

Shelley tried not to look at Cian's taut belly. She looked the other way only to see a muscular Cliff lifting the lithe Cheryl out of the water. She briefly wondered what it would be like to run her fingernails down those firm back muscles.

She dived straight in at the deep end and made good speed up the pool. She tumble-turned and pushed off again at the far end, head down, arms stretched out in front, then she powered down to the deep end again. Half-way, she collided with someone, or more specifically two someones. She pulled back, suddenly swamped, and found herself taking hold of Cliff's shoulder. Cheryl had accidentally on purpose got herself entangled in Shelley's legs and snaked an arm round her waist to stop from dipping under. 'Can't swim,' she gasped, grabbing hold of Shelley's left breast.

'Hey, what's going on?' Verity called. 'Come away from one another.'

Shelley frowned, then smiled in spite of herself as Cliff slipped an arm under each woman and lifted them up out of the water so their upper bodies were exposed. Turning to Verity he called out 'Just rescuing these maidens, Verity. Nothing sexual going on.'

As Shelley was resting at the deep end, supporting herself on her crossed arms, Will walked in with Mick Galloway. Both were fully dressed.

'Will has something he'd like to say,' the doctor called out, and the hubbub died down.

Will cleared his throat. 'Look, everyone, I'd just like to apologise for my attitude and my threat to leave. I see now that we're a team, and that I need to support you all if I'm to receive support in return. That's it, really.' He smiled sheepishly.

'Good for you, mate,' Cian called.

'Hear, hear,' Shelley added. 'Welcome back, Will.' He grinned at her gratefully and went off to sit on a lounger. As Shelley turned around, she couldn't help but notice that Cliff, for one, didn't look overjoyed to hear Will had decided to stay. Presumably he'd been looking forward to having the room to himself.

Abigail came in a little later too. She shrugged at Shelley's inquisitive look. 'We kissed and made up. She's still a cow though.'

It was nice to have them all back together, Shelley thought as she climbed out of the pool and headed for the changing rooms, Larry watching her as she went.

While showering, Shelley felt as if she were being watched. She looked around the communal showers, wondering if there might be gaps or holes through which an enthusiastic voyeur might be able to peer. She couldn't see anything but had given herself the creeps. She wrapped a towel around herself, grabbed her gym bag and decided to look for a private cubicle to change in. She tried a couple of doors that were locked but the third opened and she peered in. It was a boiler room. It looked rarely used and she popped inside and closed the door behind her. It was warm and felt safe. She got changed and found herself a comfortable spot to sit on some old foam mats in the corner. Then she pulled the BlackBerry out of her bag. After Sandra's little visit while she'd been at the pub, Shelley made sure she took the device, and the charger, everywhere with her.

She settled down and began composing her next text to Aidan.

If my mum could see me now, she thought. *Sitting in a boiler room at a sex addiction clinic writing a saucy account of the exploits of a rock star and e-mailing it to a boss I fancy a bit. Or a lot, if I'm honest.*

She chuckled to herself as she wrote, but then her smile disappeared as she remembered it would be her turn to make her confessional in just two days' time.

She didn't want to lie to her friends. But what else could she do?

Chapter Eighteen

Sunlight poured in through the windows of the Mountain Room. Shelley gazed out over the fields, watching a bird of prey hovering, waiting for some unsuspecting mouse or rabbit to come out from its hiding place. Shelley felt like the mouse.

'We're running late,' Verity called out through the door as the stragglers dawdled. Cliff and Cheryl were whispering to each other, discussing their confessional. Will and Abigail were already seated. Shelley made her way to her seat as the boys and Rose hurried in smiling sheepishly at the mumsy counsellor.

'Right-o then,' Verity said, smiling at the couple. 'No time to waste. Please begin when you're ready.'

The couple glanced at each other nervously and stood together, holding hands. Cliff said:

'I hope you don't mind, but we're going to tell the story together. And we made some brief notes, just to keep us on the right track.'

'That's fine,' Verity said, 'Please begin.'

Cheryl: We were childhood sweethearts, I suppose. We lived in the same street in Portishead, a suburb of Bristol.

Our parents were friends and we played together in the park. We played the usual games, and explored each other's bodies. We went to the same school, Cliff is a year older than me but we saw each other in the playground, he was like an older brother and looked after me. We first kissed outside the McDonalds in Bristol. Later, at secondary school we each went out with different people but we always stayed firm friends. We got together properly in sixth form and lost our virginity to one another under a blanket at an end-of-school party. Then we went off to different universities.

Cliff: We drifted apart then, naturally, I had quite a serious girlfriend, by which I mean we were serious about each other, not that she never smiled. Though she was a bit of a punk I suppose. Anyway, I have to admit I didn't think too much about Cheryl. We met up from time to time when we came home to visit our respective parents, so we kept in touch. I suppose I figured she'd always be there, do you know? Cheryl was part of home. Part of my life and part of me.

Cheryl: After university I went on a gap year and Cliff moved to London as he'd been offered a graduate trainee position for an insurance company. When I got back from Asia I decided to move to London myself. Cliff's mum gave me his address and I just turned up one day, to surprise him. He opened the door and gave me the loveliest smile, like he'd never been happier to see anyone in his life. He looked great, fit, his hair shorter than the last time I'd seen him when he was in his hippy phase. He invited me in and we sat, ate chocolate Hobnobs and drank gallons of tea while we caught up.

Cliff: Cheryl looked amazing when I opened the door. Tanned, slim and just so pleased to see me. It lifted my spirits, which had been a little deflated I have to say. The job was tough and London can be a bleak place when you don't have much money and no friends. It was like I was suddenly home again, but I also felt very attracted to Cheryl. I don't want you to think I just saw her as a familiar old face. She looked different, exciting. We'd both grown up and changed a lot since that night under the blanket at Sharon Jones' party. I suggested we sit on the sofa and Cheryl plumped herself down virtually on top of me. Before long we were kissing and she lifted a long, bare leg and curled it around my waist. She wore a short denim skirt, this was July, and I slid my hand up her smooth thigh until my fingertips were tickling her back-side. Her mouth was hard on mine, urgent and hungry. I shifted my hand to her breasts and she loved it. It was like old times. So easy. I laid her back on the sofa and unbuckled my jeans.

Cheryl: I couldn't wait to feel him inside me. I hadn't planned to sleep with him when I'd come over, though the thought had crossed my mind. I lifted my hips and hooked my thumbs into the waistband of my G-string. I slid it off and threw it across the room. He looked down lustfully at the tuft of hair peeping out from where my tiny skirt had ridden up and he yanked his jeans down in a hurry, falling and knocking a lamp over. I burst into giggles and he looked a little embarrassed, he was so sweet. I got up and helped to get him undressed. He took off my top, exposing my breasts, but he left the skirt on. We knelt on the Persian rug, kissing, just holding each other for a while.

Cliff: I grabbed hold of her sweet little backside and lifted her up onto my lap as I knelt back on my haunches. She used her hand to position my cock and she slipped down onto it quickly, wet as an English summer. In that position we could continue kissing and looking at each other as we gradually built to orgasm. We rocked back and forth gently and eventually came at the same time.

Cheryl: He felt so hard inside me, so big. It hadn't been like this before. Neither of us had known what we were doing back then, we'd each gained experience since then and the sex was so much better. I'm glad I lost my virginity to Cliff, but I'm even more glad he slept with a lot of other girls before we did it again.

He invited me to move in with him soon after that, and we've together ever since. I got a job as an assistant editor with a publisher and Cliff finished his trainee programme and got a well-paid position as an underwriter for one of the country's biggest firms. We bought a flat together and married a year or so later. Everything was perfect, particularly the sex.

Cliff: We both have healthy libidos. We had sex almost every day, sometimes twice in a day. I know it's normal for the sex to tail off a little in frequency as the relationship goes on, but that didn't seem to happen with us. It was always just assumed that we would have sex before sleeping, or on a Saturday morning, or whenever we found ourselves in the same room together with a few minutes to spare, we didn't think anything of it. Very gradually, we began to introduce more and more variety into our sex. Not that we were getting bored with each other, but you know, it's fun to explore.

We tried anal sex, which I liked but Cheryl wasn't so keen on. Then I bought a vibrator and Cheryl loved that, but it wasn't so much fun for me. Handcuffs were great for a while, but we got bored with that. We tried tantric sex, sensual massage, butt plugs and cock rings. Everything really. Then I started buying porn, which we'd watch together.

Cheryl: I was a little unsure about that at first. It felt like bringing other people into our perfect little world. But Cliff chose some classy stuff, including a film with Rose, and we discovered watching it really added to our sex life. I'd get so wet watching those beautiful girls and those muscular young men. I had this picture in my head like *Boogie Nights* with moustachioed men with hairy chests and seventies clothes, but these men were good-looking, even if they weren't going to win any Oscars.

As we watched, Cliff would slowly undress me, then stroke my clitoris and finger me. He'd wait until I was panting hot and the film had got to a good bit, then he'd dive between my legs and using long, hard strokes, lick me from bottom to top. I'd come quickly, pumping my crotch up against his hot tongue, never tearing my eyes away from the girl getting a pounding from the man hung like a police horse on the screen.

Cliff: It became obvious after a while that we both particularly liked watching the same sort of movies – group sex, threesomes, orgies, that sort of thing. I'd notice Cheryl would always get so worked up whenever there were more than two in a scene. One day I straight out asked her if she'd like to try it for real.

Cheryl: I was shocked at first and asked myself whether this meant Cliff wasn't finding me attractive anymore, whether this was just his way of having his cake and eating it too. But I didn't dismiss it out of hand, I thought it over. I tried to imagine what it would be like to watch my boyfriend's head between another woman's thighs, or another man with his hard cock thrusting into me, while Cliff looked on. I had to admit to myself that the thought was exciting. Once I'd started thinking about it I soon couldn't think of anything else. I asked Cliff to describe, in detail, what he'd like to do.

Cliff: I wanted to get another woman to join us, at least to begin. I thought that would be easier. I knew Cheryl was curious and had had some same-sex experiences at college. Lord knows I'd asked her to describe them to me often enough as we made love. I wasn't exactly grossed-out by the idea of sharing a bed with another man, but I'd have liked him to be bringing a lady friend if you know what I mean. We didn't know anyone we felt comfortable asking, so we advertised on the internet. Not to sound boastful but we attracted quite a few offers, because Cheryl is so stunning . . .

Cheryl: . . .because of your great body, more likely.

Cliff: Anyway, we had a few offers and we chose a younger woman, Fiona, and asked her out on a date, just so we could meet in a neutral environment. Well, she was lovely. Pretty, funny and super-sexy. We met in a wine bar in the city, somewhere we were unlikely to be recognised, though I remember hoping that someone I knew would come in and see us altogether. I wanted the other customers to notice us and to wonder about us, whether we were friends, or colleagues. I was excited by the thought that no one would suspect what we were really doing there, a married couple meeting a young girl for the first time, hoping to have sex with her.

Cheryl: She had these deep, brown eyes. I just looked at her, getting wetter and wetter while Cliff did the talking. She seemed to like us too because we all ended up back at our flat later that night. We were a bit nervous, but she seemed to know what she was doing. She took off her jeans, revealing red, lacy knickers and climbed onto our bed, resting on her hands and knees and looking back at us playfully. I grabbed Cliff and kissed him. 'Whatever happens,' I said quietly. 'I love you.' 'I love you, too' he replied. Then we stripped and hopped up on the bed with the patient Fi.

I sidled up alongside her and we kissed and rubbed

our bodies against one another. Cliff came up behind us and I watched him over my shoulder as he ran his fingers down Fi's back, over her buttocks and down between her slightly parted thighs.

Cliff: I rubbed her soft pussy through the knickers. The sight of her kissing my wife was an incredible turn-on. I'm sure all men like it when their wife or girlfriend walks into a room and all the men stop talking to look. Well, it was like that feeling but more. It wasn't just that this beautiful girl was in my bed, offering herself to me, she was offering herself to my wife as well. I slowly eased the panties down over her backside and she shifted her knees so I could work them all the way off. Then I sat back and inspected the beautiful rear view of two naked girls side-to-side. I couldn't bear it any longer, my cock was as hard as it had ever been, even harder than that time Melanie Foster let me stick two fingers in her pants outside the Portishead Rollerblade centre when I was fifteen. I shuffled forward into position. Cheryl turned around and placed her hands on Fi's bottom, prising her folds apart. I pressed forward and my cock slid comfortably into Fi's pussy. The girl gasped and put her head down, and I took up a rhythmic thrusting, my belly slapping against her backside.

Cheryl: I slipped underneath Fi and began sucking her tits. She leaned down a little to make it easier for me, and she stroked my hair as I flicked my tongue over her hard, claret-coloured nipples. Then I felt one of her hands slide down my body and a couple of her fingers stole into my moist vagina. I felt my muscles contract hard around them. I could feel Cliff's thrusts going through her body and making her breasts swing across my face. As her hand manipulated me firmly, it wasn't long before I could feel an orgasm building.

Cliff: Suddenly Fi spoke to me. 'Fuck your wife,' she said, and those words alone almost made me come. I pulled out and transferred my attentions to Cheryl, who was panting hard, with Fi's slender fingers buried in her mound. I entered Cheryl and, with Fi's help, the two of us rolled over until the groaning Cheryl was on top of me.

Cheryl: As Cliff pumped, and just as I felt the fog of orgasm enveloping me, Fi slipped a finger into my bottom and tickled me there. It was the final straw and I shouted out 'I'm coming!'

Cliff: She didn't say that at all, she said 'Uuaarrgaaggahhhrr!'

Cheryl: Well, I was saying it in my head. All I know was that it was such a powerful release it scared me. I hadn't realised orgasm couldn't be that good, and I had been really happy up until that point. I slid off Cliff and lay down on the bed, abuzz with warmth and happiness but too tired to take part for a while. I lay there and watched the two of them fucking like wild animals.

Cliff: She attacked me, just about. She leapt on just as Cheryl hopped off and seemed to be on a mission to pump the life out of me. The girl was a demon. We switched position a few times. She swivelled into the reverse-cowgirl, then after that I flipped her on to her back, hoiked her legs up over her head and fucked her senseless for a while before turning her over to one side. I did all this without ever pulling out, which I was really chuffed about.

Cheryl: He went on about that for ages . . .

Cliff: While we were in that position, Cheryl, who'd come to her senses by now, crawled across the bed until she was sixty-nineing with Fi. I lay behind the younger girl, her legs parted to allow me to enter her from behind. I pumped the tip of my cock into her rhythmically as I watched my wife lapped at her sweet juices. She came hard, thrusting back onto me, and Cheryl chased her clitoris as her hips bucked in ecstasy.

She stayed the night. The three of us cuddling up together. And in the morning, we started all over again.

Cheryl: Fi introduced us to a swingers' club she used to go to. We all met upstairs at a pub in Holborn. We were nervous the first time, but soon found that everyone was normal, like us. It was only couples allowed, which is why Fi didn't go anymore as she'd broken up with her boyfriend when he decided he couldn't deal with the thought of her sleeping with other men. Other women he was okay with apparently, especially if he was allowed to watch.

It wasn't that the club was being discriminatory, just

that they catered to couples; there were other clubs for singletons and groups as we discovered later. Anyway, at this club, everyone was very nice, but . . . well, I don't like to be judgemental, but there were a lot of couples who had rather let themselves go.

Cliff: You suspected they turned up more in hope than expectation.

Cheryl: But we did meet a lovely couple. They were older than us, and had been around the block a few times. Their eyes lit up when they saw us come in, a bit of fresh, lean meat, I suppose. Anyway we got on famously with Jenny and Mark and they invited us back to their place.

Cliff: It was strange, being in someone else's house, with a couple, and knowing what you were all just about to do. As Jenny fixed drinks for us, Mark chatted to Cheryl on the sofa . . .

Cheryl: . . . we talked about loft conversions, Mark put us on to a wonderful company who ended up doing a lovely job on our dormer . . .

Cliff: I wandered about the living room looking at pictures of their kids. These weren't weirdos or perverts, these were ordinary, middle-class people who liked to mix it up a little in the bedroom. Just like us. But still, seeing all this normality, all this happy-families business. It was just strange, that's all.

There was a slight misunderstanding, they thought it was just going to be a straight wife swap, but when we explained we were looking for something that required a king-size bed, it didn't faze them. As I told you, they'd been around the block. I was particularly nervous, I didn't know how to mention the fact to Mark that I wasn't keen on blokes, but he fixed that by looking at me and saying 'Don't worry, I'm straight as a die, me.' I breathed a sigh of relief and we took our drinks through to the bedroom.

Luckily they had a massive bed. Jenny put some Leonard Cohen on the stereo, which makes surprisingly good music to make love to, as long as you don't listen to the lyrics. Mark stepped up to Cheryl and said, 'May I?' She nodded and he began unbuttoning her top. He slipped in his hands inside the material and cupped her breasts. Then he kissed her.

Cheryl: I was thinking about Cliff when Mark kissed me, how he was feeling. But almost immediately my thoughts changed to how hot this kiss was making me. It wasn't just that Mark was a good-looking older man, but it was that and the fact that I knew Cliff was watching. Another man was kissing me passionately and feeling my breasts while my husband stood and watched. It made me feel dirty and cheap, but it also got me incredibly wet.

Cliff: For me, I felt a mixture of jealousy, anger and extreme arousal. I wasn't used to taking such a passive role, and it felt like Cheryl and I were being used by this older couple. Jenny dropped to her knees in front of me and unzipped my fly. She pulled my rigid cock out of my trousers and took a mouthful of champagne before she wrapped her lips around my shaft. The bubbles tickled and her hot wet mouth felt silky sweet on me. I groaned and looked down at her as she took in the entire length and began gently bobbing her head back and forth.

Mark was now naked and had Cheryl down on the bed and had taken her trousers off. I watched as he took her foot in his hand and began licking it. She giggled, as I knew she would, and he moved his way up into less ticklish territory. Cheryl watched him approach, and then I saw her eyes flick over to me. Just for an instant I wondered if I saw a flicker of doubt, and to be honest I was a little nervous myself, but I was determined to go through with it, so I gave her a little nod, and a smile. Just to show her I was comfortable with it.

Cheryl: You certainly looked comfortable, with your cock half-way down a beautiful woman's throat. I was loving the attention I was getting from Mark, though I wanted Cliff to keep watching. Mark took his time but eventually reached my crotch and he slipped a finger into the side and pulled my panties across. I had this impression my labial lips had grown huge and swollen, I felt so sensitive. Then Mark planted a tonguing kiss between my thighs and I melted. I remember kicking my legs out in a spasm of ecstasy and he brought me to the edge very quickly. He didn't let me orgasm though, but used his thumb to keep me hanging.

Cliff: Jenny didn't finish me off with her mouth, either. There was no hurry. She stood and kissed me. Then she led me over to the bed and we joined the others. I made sure I kissed Cheryl long and hard. Jenny took Cheryl's hand and lifted her up. Mark lay down on the bed and Jenny, after removing Cheryl's bra and panties, manoeuvred my wife until she was positioned over Mark's erect penis. Cheryl slipped down easily and Jenny kissed her and began massaging her clit as she rode him. Well, I didn't want to miss out on the fun, so I moved behind Jenny and began taking off her clothes. She had a nice body for a woman in her forties and I quite liked the little roll of flesh around her belly. She knelt on the bed, still playing with Cheryl's pussy and kissing her mouth. I watched my wife slide up and down the cock of a man she'd only just met. I knelt behind Jenny, rubbing my palm against Jenny's naked pussy, and slid my cock into her.

She seemed to enjoy it quite rough so I took hold of her hair and pulled her head back while I fucked her hard from behind. She was a talker, you know, 'Yes, yes, give it to me, fuck me', and so on.

Cheryl came first. I eased up on banging Jenny so she could go back to stroking my wife's clitoris as she screwed up her eyes. After she'd finished, she slipped off and without a pause turned over and took Mark's cock into her mouth. He wasn't sure where to look, at the blonde twenty-something deep-throating him, or me pounding brutally into his wife. It didn't take him long to come. He raised his hips and stiffened as he went over the brink and shot his load into Cheryl's mouth.

Cheryl: I was dimly aware of Cliff out the corner of my eye. I wanted to give him a great show so I made sure I swallowed every last drop. I could feel great spasms of pleasure surge through Mark as he pumped his juice down my throat. I think the sight of his wife gargling some other man's come helped Cliff to finish off himself. I heard him groan and knew it as the sound of a man, my man, finding satisfaction.

Then we all worked on Jenny. The guys were both a little tired, so Jenny opened a bedside drawer and took out a substantial vibrator. She lay back on the bed and spread her legs. Mark kissed her mouth. Cliff tickled her nipples with his tongue and I inserted the vibrator slowly inside her and switched it on. The three of us brought her off in a matter of seconds, the vibrator inducing huge, sweeping waves of orgasm that made her whole body shiver and twist.

Cliff: And that was that. We had a coffee, chatted for a while and left.

Chapter Nineteen

Cheryl: We didn't talk much on the way home. I think both of us were feeling the same thing. A mixture of emotions. Firstly there was excitement and discovery. Like we'd entered a new world together and had just realised how much there was to explore.

Cliff: But at the same time I think that car journey was the first time we started worrying a little. We've talked about it since. The problem was almost that it was too good. We both wanted to do more, but felt that this spelled the beginning of the end for our regular sex life. We didn't feel like freaks but we knew our behaviour wasn't the way normal couples went about conducting their sex lives.

We saw Mark and Jenny again, they introduced us to another club they attended. It was more exclusive, and further away, near Birmingham, but it was worth it. The members were all a lot more attractive than the one Fi had introduced us to. I guess you needed to be vetted by existing members before you could join, plus it was damned expensive. But again, it was worth it.

Cheryl: We met dozens of other couples there. And not just couples either. There were threesomes there, I mean people who lived as a threesome, all sharing the same bed. There were doms and submissives, people who just liked to watch. Anything you can imagine really. We all met in a huge basement on the outskirts of the city. There was music and a bar. Even bouncers.

There were rooms you could hire for private parties and we made good use of these. We started off just meeting other couples and having our own private sessions, but one night we were invited to an orgy. I don't know how many people were involved, maybe twenty? Roughly equal between men and women. The only rules were no violence and safe sex. There were bowls of condoms everywhere. We walked in to find things were already underway and I didn't know where to start.

Cliff: I looked at Cheryl, winked and said 'Let's split up, see you later.' Then I went off and joined a couple of girls who looked like their tongues might be getting tired.

Cheryl: I was grabbed, politely, by a huge man who'd seen me come in. He looked like he spent most of his life in the gym. All he was wearing was a pair of trainers, and his massive cock jutted out in front of him. He never said a word to me, he just threw me down and pulled a condom on. Then rammed it into me. Another man slid over and presented his member to me and I sucked this stranger off while another slowly fucked me. It was an incredible night, that first orgy. But even as I was there, doing what I loved, and happy at the thought that my man was nearby, sharing in this experience, I had this sense something was wrong.

Cliff: I had the same feeling and it took us a while to work out what it was. It was that for the first time we weren't being intimate with each other. I saw Cheryl from time to time as my cock, lips and fingers worked their way through to other people in the room, but we weren't side by side as we satisfied half the swingers in the East Midlands.

Cheryl: I felt it when I took a wander through the room and finally found Cliff on a pile of cushions being blown by a young guy. I'd never seen him even touch another man before and I realised that even though we were both travelling in the same direction, we were on different tracks.

Having said that, the sight of my husband receiving head excited me at the time. I stroked the stranger's balls from behind as his head bobbed up and down on Cliff's pole.

Cliff: I hadn't even realised it was a man at first, but when I looked down and saw this young chap sucking so enthusiastically I didn't have the heart to tell him to stop. I closed my eyes and relaxed, enjoying the sensation. You see, it isn't about the person. It's about both the sensation and also the thought of doing something you're not really supposed to. Every time we explored something new, it was exciting and arousing. It seemed like breaking new ground, stepping into forbidden territory. Problem was, each time you need to take things a little further.

When I opened my eyes and saw Cheryl there with her hand between this guy's legs I was surprised and, for a second, I felt ashamed. Like I'd been caught by my mum with a jazz mag. The guilt was quick to fade though, and I was left with that deliciously dirty feeling, and I surprised myself again by coming suddenly and violently, nearly choking the poor lad who had his lips wrapped around my pole.

Cheryl: I felt a little angry at Cliff, then at myself for reacting like that. I pushed the stranger on to his back and straddled him, grabbing his cock, and rolling on a condom. I guided him into my pussy, already well-lubricated from all the firm fucking I'd had so far that night. I squeezed my muscles as I slipped down. Cliff came up to us and slipped a finger in my arse. He knows just what I like. A finger is fine, anything more I'm not so comfortable with. We stayed long enough to finish off our new friend and then, by mutual consent, we left.

Cliff: We left it a couple of days then had a chat over a bottle of wine. We both felt the same thing. That although we were both excited by new experiences, and wanted to do more exploring, with new people, that we were both worried we might end up moving away from one another. Cheryl asked me whether I was interested in sleeping with more men. I thought about it for a while but decided that I didn't want to pursue it. It did make me wonder, though. Maybe we're all a little bit bisexual.

We decided that in future we'd not go out to clubs and parties anymore. We wanted more control over things, so we decided we'd just host events in our own house.

Oh, I should say that by now we'd moved out of the inner-city flat and bought a large modern house in the suburbs. Nothing special and much nicer on the inside than the outside, loads of space inside. Comfy couches, thick rugs and heavy curtains.

Cheryl: Yes, so we were in a position where we could have house parties without the neighbours getting suspicious. We advertised in a local contacts magazine; they're much more exclusive than the internet. And we arranged a get-together one Friday night. Six couples as well as us. Everyone could stay over if they liked. We spent ages getting everything just right, but then remembered that we had my parents coming over for lunch the next day. I made sure I set two different alarm clocks: the last thing I needed was for Mum and Dad to walk in to a house full of sex-maniacs, still in a slumbering cluster-fuck. We weren't expecting anything too wild, but we were sure we'd be happy with this new arrangement. Just to make sure there was enough spice we went on a mini-break to Amsterdam and came back with a bewildering variety of toys. God knows what they were all supposed to do, one thing looked a bit like a garlic press and I was never game to try that out. We had dinner first while we all got to know each other. The men were all okay-looking, though none of them were exactly George Clooney. The girls were better and I could tell Cliff particularly liked one girl called Sam.

Anyway, to cut a long story short, we decided to all move into the lounge for coffee and Viagra and one thing led to another. We hadn't been clear about whether or how we wanted to pair off, and someone suggested we play Sixty-Second Fumble to get the ball rolling, as it were. We all wrote a sex act on a piece of paper, pink for girls, blue for boys, and popped it into a hat. Then we passed the hat around. The acts all had to be hetero as some of the party weren't as liberal as others. First, a chap called Gary picked a slip and read it out: 'give Caroline a good tongue thrashing.' Caroline giggled and spread her legs as Gary came crawling over, growling like a sex-starved lion. He lifted up her thin blue dress and gently eased her panties down.

'Your time starts now!' Cliff called and clicked a stopwatch.

Caroline smiled at this man she'd only just met and lay back on the sofa as he dived between her legs and started lapping away. She lay perfectly still, savouring the sensation as her husband looked on, almost drooling at the sight of another man licking his wife's pussy.

When Cliff called time, Caroline looked annoyed.

Cliff: After Gary, Sam had a go, and she had to give Gary a blow job. She was a good-looking girl, short, jet-black hair with high cheekbones and blue eyes. Nice tits too. Gary could hardly believe his good fortune as this young stunner took his dick in her mouth. He was gutted when the sixty seconds was up though. After Sam was Pete and he had to fuck Cheryl from behind.

Cheryl: It was good, but over so quickly, and, to be honest, by this point I was starting to wonder if this had been a good idea. Everyone was being a little tame. We needed to turn the heat up if Cliff and I were going to find the home front an acceptable alternative to the clubs. Next was my turn. I chose one of the pink slips. As I'd hoped, it was Cliff's and it was as hot as I'd suspected it would be. 'Use a sex toy of your choice on Clive,' it said. Clive was Sam's boyfriend, and the best looking of the guys. I looked in the box we'd brought back from Amsterdam . . .

Cliff: 'Anything to declare, madam?'

Cheryl: . . . and took out a string of ben-wah balls. I'd never actually used one of these before but I'd seen it on videos and had been itching to get stuck in . . .

Cliff: Literally!

Cheryl: Enough with the jokes, sweetheart. Now Clive's face suggested he wasn't so sure about this, but what could he do? Sam seemed fascinated. I stood him up, spun him around and jerked his trousers and pants down around his knees. Then I leant him over until his backside was thrusting out at us. Cliff started the stopwatch and I popped a spot of lube into his arse. He flinched, but not so much as he did when I inserted the first ball into his anus.

Cliff: If we wanted to liven things up, this was the way to do it. These couples were just local dabblers you see, not sex-mad semi-professionals like we were. Cheryl popped another ball in, then another, until she had six in there. I looked down at the stopwatch, time was up, but I let it run.

Cheryl: I reached down between Clive's legs and took hold of his rock-hard penis. He shifted a little to give me better access, clearly enjoying it. I could see the others start to shift a little closer to one another. And I saw Sam's hand slip into Cliff's lap, rubbing his bulge. I began jerking Clive off as I slowly pulled the balls out, the smooth steel stretching the tight sphincter, then popping out suddenly, one by one. Clive groaned as the last ball came free, and I spun him round and kissed him, gripping his cock. Then I sat down.

Cliff: After that the party really got started. It would take too long to describe the whole thing, the bit I remember most was having Sam riding my cock while Caroline straddled my face. The two girls French-kissed as I jammed my tongue as far as it would go into Caroline's snatch.

Cheryl: I orgasmed from anal sex that night, which is something I'd not done before. I'm not really sure why I let it happen, maybe I'd had a bit too much to drink. But Pete was doing me up the bum, he was very gentle and lubed me up very carefully. At the same time Gary was sliding an eight-inch rubber dildo deep into my pussy. I cried afterwards with the emotion of it. I felt like something had broken inside me. Maybe it was a barrier, or maybe my last reservation.

Anyway that first party was a success, and we just managed to get everyone out the next day before my parents turned up. I installed them in the hastily-tidied lounge and went into the kitchen to give my husband a hug; it was the first time we'd really had to chat since we'd woken up in a heap of naked bodies.

I asked him what he thought. 'It was good,' he said. 'Let's do it again, but next time let's get four couples, and we'll get everyone to dress up. What about bondage games?'

I nodded, but I had my reservations – were we just starting the cycle again, only this time at home? I was just about to voice my concerns when Mum walked in with the string of ben-wah beads around her neck.

'What an unusual necklace,' she said, stroking it. 'Where did you get it?'

Cliff: The incident with the beads was funny, but in hindsight, I can see it as symptomatic of our problem. The sex addiction that we now recognise we have was always there, threatening to interfere with our 'normal lives'. Most of our spare time was spent organising parties, buying toys, surfing the internet looking for experienced swingers. I wouldn't say our jobs suffered, in fact mine was VERY secure after we chanced upon my boss wearing a rubber gimp suit at a sex fair in Germany. He must have thought he was safe going over there. But despite that, neither of us seemed to be going anywhere in our careers. There were no changes of direction, no big holidays, no friends outside our swinger groups and not even the remotest thought of babies. The swinging consumed our personal lives.

Cheryl: I should point out that by this stage it had been a long time since we'd had sex, just the two of us. I can't think when. Once we tried watching some porn, but it just didn't seem real. We were hooked on the real thing. One time we did try it, without any kind of aid and . . . well . . .

Cliff: Go on, you can say it.

Cheryl: Cliff couldn't do it. For the first time ever, he couldn't get it up. Which didn't make me feel very good, even though I understood why. So we kept going with the parties, what else could we do? They were fun, and we attracted quite a little clique. We met some genuine friends and everything seemed perfect for a while. We'd sometimes get approached by new couples who we'd break in gently, like Jenny and Mark broke us in. More often though we liked to have more experienced couples, people who were into harder stuff.

Cliff: Every time we hosted a party, we'd think up new games, or new scenarios we could introduce to get people to do the things we wanted. Some people didn't like it. Once Fi came over when she was in town, but she left after Cheryl started role-playing a rape scenario.

Cheryl: Eventually it all came to a head, we had another party, there were four other couples this time. Again, we played the paper game, only this time we'd gone for broke. I made Cliff attach nipple clamps to some poor girl. She went along with it, but she didn't look happy, and neither did her husband. They left early and as they walked to the car I heard him say 'We're not coming back here again.'

Cliff: But what I wrote down was worse. I wrote a blue paper, and asked a man to fuck my wife in the arse.

Cheryl: I told you all already I didn't like anal sex, it hurts me. At the right time, and when I'm properly lubed and ready, then it's okay, and there was that time I came once . . .

Cliff: Which is why I thought it would be okay. I was transfixed by the sight of my wife, face down on a bean bag with a big bloke on top of her, pounding into her tight backside. I loved it. And the fact I knew she was unsure about it made it even more sexy for me.

Cheryl: I did hate it. I knew Cliff wanted to see, but it didn't feel right and I burst into tears. It was very embarrassing. The poor man apologised and we ended the party early.

Cliff: And it was then that I realised that I'd gone too far, and that I'd always go too far. However good the sex is, I always want to push it just that bit further. And I was willing to see my own wife used and abused to satisfy my urges.

Cheryl: It wasn't just you, Cliff, you know that. We both went too far. I was there beside you through all of this.

Cliff: So that's when we knew we needed help. We looked up sex addiction on the internet. Found this place.

Cliff and Cheryl: And here we are.

Chapter Twenty

'Thanks Cliff, thanks Cheryl,' Verity said, nodding and smiling at them encouragingly. As had now become the practice, the others gathered around and one by one patted the couple on the shoulder with a smile or a few understanding words.

Shelley had never experienced a relationship with anything like the intensity of Cliff and Cheryl's. But she'd had a few boyfriends, and she'd watched enough boys she liked go off with other women. She found it hard to understand how two people so much in love could bear to watch each other sleep with total strangers. She had thought there'd been moments during the joint confessional when each of them briefly betrayed feelings of regret or jealousy.

This was an issue for Freya and her Psychology of Sex column, Shelley thought. Maybe she'd suggest it when she got back.

Cian shook Cliff's hand, then bent down to kiss Cheryl on the cheek. Now that almost everyone had told their story, Shelley reflected, the group was tighter, more caring. She glanced over at Larry. As the only two still to confess, they were somewhat sidelined. Larry smiled back shyly. Shelley felt for him, but she was more concerned for herself. Each day brought her closer to the time when she'd have to make her own confessional, and the time she'd certainly be found out.

'Take a couple of hours,' Verity said as they filed out. 'I have a meeting straight after lunch, so we'll meet back here at 3.30pm sharp. I recommend you get down to the gym and burn off some tension. Remember what I said, "Don't Sleep About, Sweat it Out."'

Shelley was desperate for the loo and nipped in while the others headed down to the dining room. Inside, she found Sandra inspecting her bruises in the mirror.

'Hello, Sandra,' she said politely.

'I'm here tending to my injuries, just in case you thought I might be cruising for lesbian sex.'

'Thank heavens for that,' Shelley replied. She popped into a cubicle and relieved herself. Coming out, she saw Sandra was still there, dabbing foundation onto the marks.

She washed her hands, the two women eyeing each other coldly. Shelley decided to just come out with it.

'Sandra, did you search my bag?'

The nurse glared back at her. 'Yes, I did.'

'Why?'

'Security.'

'Security?'

'You can't be too careful in this post-9/11 world.'

'What, you were looking for a bomb? What sort of terrorist would bother trying to blow up a bunch of alcoholics and sex fiends? Surely Bin Laden has bigger fish to fry?'

Sandra grunted.

'Didn't find anything though, did you?' Shelley said, smiling sweetly.

'I will, Little Miss Snooty,' Sandra replied. 'I will.' And with that, she marched out.

Shelley was quiet over lunch. She listened to the cheerful chattering of the others at the table, now a solid group, all sitting together, after Will's wobble. She was still thinking about Cliff and Cheryl, and how complex a thing love could be. She tried to think of the most intense relationship she herself had had.

'Who's Tom?' Rose said.

'Hmm, what's that?' Shelley replied, startled.

Rose peered at her, intrigued. 'You just said "Tom" out loud in a sort of resigned voice.'

'Did I?' Shelley smiled. 'Sorry, just remembering an old flame.'

They sat on her parents' suede sofa, some pop show playing on the TV. They had the place to themselves all morning because her parents had taken her sister to a mall out of town.

They kissed softly. Tom was getting quite good at this, Shelley thought. Or maybe it was that she was getting used to the idea. Kissing had seemed silly at first. Why make such a fuss about a simple saliva transfer? But she was starting to get the idea. When she kissed Tom, it made her feel close to him. It almost made her feel like they were one person, just for a second or two, when the kiss got really good. Then she'd start worrying about whether she was doing it wrong and the feeling would go away.

Today the kiss was especially good. Tom pulled back after a while and smiled at her; he looked like he was going to say something soppy and embarrassing.

'Tom,' Shelley said, saving him from himself.

'Yes,' he breathed.

'You can put your hand on my breast if you like.'

His face underwent a transformation. Before he'd been a love-sick puppy with a rubber bone in his mouth. Now, all of a sudden, he was a junk-yard dog with a raw steak. Shelley worried whether she'd made a mistake, but it was too late to back down now.

Tom kissed her again and she felt a hand groping at her chest. It didn't feel remotely sexual. She sighed, shrugged inwardly and took off her top. Tom's jaw dropped and he began pawing feverishly again. Shelley began unbuttoning his shirt.

She wasn't quite sure how it happened, but a few minutes later Tom was naked and she was down to her bra and panties. Tom was working on the clasp, grunting and tutting. 'Who designed this thing?' he said, 'Rubik?'

'Here,' she said, 'let me do it.' Though she was anything but sure that this was what she wanted, she unhooked it and whipped off the bra, then lay back, holding a hand across her firm breasts. Tom's nostrils flared as he watched.

He took her hand and gently pulled it aside. Shelley felt excited and scared. She'd never shown her body to a boy before. She was terrified he'd screw up his face in disgust, but equally worried he'd lose control and ravage her. She'd been trying not to look at his penis but, sensing movement, took a quick peek. It seemed enormous, and was getting bigger. He reached out a trembling hand and stroked her right breast. She knew he wanted her to touch his penis, he was almost jabbing it into her face. But she wasn't quite ready for that. She just sat there, wondering whether she was supposed to be feeling quite this terrified. If there was a recipe book you could follow for this sort of thing she'd be okay. She'd just look at the next instructions, check the photo of what it was supposed to look like finished, then get cracking a few eggs, but she had only a vague idea what was supposed to happen next, and she was fairly sure Tom didn't know much more.

Cian's honking laughter dragged Shelley's thoughts back to the table. She looked up to see what was going on.

'. . . so I pulled my trousers back on, took off the wig, and left through the window,' Will said, ending some tale of nefarious adultery, no doubt. Cian, Cliff and Larry looked amused, Cheryl shocked and Abigail downright disgusted. It was good to see Will had found his place within the group, Shelley thought.

After lunch Shelley made her excuses, saying she needed to stretch her legs and wandered towards the exit. Rose came running after her.

'Do you want some company?' Rose asked, smiling kindly.

'Would you be offended if I said I wanted to be alone for a while?' Shelley replied.

'Not at all,' Rose said. 'Is everything okay?'

'Yeah, I'm just nervous about telling my story on

Friday. I'm not good at public speaking at the best of times. I had to make a two-minute speech at my cousin's wedding, just to thank the caterers basically, and I burst into tears half-way through and hugged the head waiter.'

Rose laughed. 'I like you, Shelley,' she said. 'You're sweet. I can see you've got hang-ups, but you're honest about them. And you're not one of those people who masks their feelings with humour.'

'Only because I'm rubbish at telling jokes,' Shelley said.

'Anyway, like I said, I'm here to help you work through your story if you like, you can try it out on me.'

'Thanks,' Shelley said. Wondering if that was really such a good idea. Two women alone in a room, so ripe they were almost starting to ferment, talking about sexual escapades.

She headed off into the gardens. The feel of spring was in the air and the tulips were just starting to open their vulva-shaped heads. The lawn looked like it might need a cut soon.

Shelley made for the pool house. There was a side door she could enter through before popping into her boiler room to write up the story she'd just heard. She settled down on the mats and fired up the BlackBerry. Before she started she collected her thoughts. She knew exactly how she was going to write this, finding it easier as she went along and starting to believe that she could keep up the column after she returned to London, even without the confessionals to prompt her. She was more comfortable with the language now. Cocks, pussies, balls, arseholes. They were just words. She could do words.

It wasn't just professionally she had loosened up. Maybe sex didn't have to be the big deal she'd made it out to be.

She e-mailed Briony.

Hey Binns. How's it going? If you see Aidan, can you prod him please and remind him he's supposed to be sending me more details of my sexy background. If only I had half of your experiences, I'd be all right. Worried-face. Everything okay with you? Got any juicy stories you're not using in your column I can pinch?

Then she began typing Cliff and Cheryl's story. A few minutes later she got a message back from her friend.

Hi Sweetie, I'm all right, though it's red wing day. Or red wing fortnight more like, I really don't like this new coil. I'm planning to talk some poor bloke into surfing the crimson tide later so I can write about it in my column. In the meantime I'm on my high-iron 'rag' diet – lunch was four bottles of Beamish and a bag of spinach. Don't know what's got into Aidan, but since he got back from his sales trip he won't stop talking about you. Shelley this, Shelley that. Hmmm, interesting.

Will certainly prod him, but I shouldn't be too surprised if he prods you at some time in the not-too-distant future.

Love Brie

PS Did you know you actually wrote the words 'worried-face' rather than use an emoticon?

Shelley knew Briony was just teasing her, and yet maybe there had been something in the way Aidan looked at her in the Mountain Room.

Hey Brie,
Aidan does NOT see me like that. He popped in here a couple of days ago to see how things were going, and it was all strictly professional. Yes I know I wrote 'worried face', I can't figure out how to do emoticons on this stupid thing. Angry face.
Sx

She shook her head and got back to typing up the story. There was no point speculating about what Aidan may or may not feel. He was her boss and nothing more. She needeÏd to look elsewhere for romance. Maybe behind the bar at The Crown? Shelley resolved to pop in for a bottle of Pinot Grigio as soon as she got back. Maybe she'd work up the courage to ask for some cheese and onion crisps this time.

After Shelley had finished typing, she closed her eyes for a moment. The boiler room was warm and felt safe, the dull throb of the filtration system soothed her as she lay back on the mats.

Shelley and Tom were both naked. They knelt facing one another, each inspecting the other's body. Shelley was surprised to find Tom, naked, was actually pretty good looking. He had a swimmer's physique, toned and slim, with broad shoulders. She tried not to look at his stiff cock. It looked too big to fit anywhere inside her. Especially the bit where she knew he wanted to put it.

But she supposed now was as good a time as any other. She had to lose the dreaded cherry sooner or later, and why not with Tom? He was nice and didn't try to force things. A girl could do worse, she decided. This was it.

So she lay back and took Tom's hand, pulling him down on her. Then she remembered.

'Do you have a condom?'

He looked panicked for a second, before nodding. 'Yes, where's my wallet?'

He got up and tiptoed across the room, as you do when you're naked in someone else's house, and dug into his jeans, slung across a chair. Shelley lay there, feeling self-conscious, as he came back, clutching the silver packet and beaming at her like a four year old who'd just found a toy in a cornflakes box.

Tom sat down beside her, put one hand awkwardly on her left breast and kissed her. These were the bits she liked, she decided. Then he broke off and unwrapped the condom. Shelley watched nervously, sure he was going to screw up and puncture the damn thing.

He took hold of his cock and popped the rolled-up condom on like a milk bottle top, then began rolling it down. Shelley had never seen it done on a real penis before, just on a banana in Sex Ed. Tom was thicker than a banana and slightly less bent. He got it on, nodded in satisfaction at his own handiwork, like her dad used to do when he managed to put up a shelf without hammering a nail through his thumb, and climbed back on top of Shelley.

'Spread your legs a little,' he whispered. She obliged, and he slid down between them, bringing the tip of his rubberised cock to her outer lips. It tickled and she felt a surge of fear.

'This might hurt a bit,' he said. She nodded, she knew. Then three things happened at once.

The first thing was Tom shoving himself deep inside her, the second was her screaming with the pain of it, and the third was that the door was flung open and her little sister Madeleine walked in and asked her what she was doing with that boy.

Tom rolled off in surprise and tumbled to the floor, his penis rapidly shrinking as Shelley's parents followed Madeleine into the room and stood there, blinking in surprise at their daughter, legs splayed and naked on the sofa they hadn't yet begun making the payments for.

She hadn't thought about that episode in years. Though sometimes, when she was with a man, the horrified faces of her parents, full of shame and disappointment, would fly unbidden to her mind's eye.

She decided she needed some fresh air and left the room, tucking her BlackBerry safely into her pocket before she did so. It was a bright day, with a nippy little wind and she breathed in the spring air.

As she approached the drug rehab building, she saw Sandra backing out of a swing door, carrying a tray of medication. Shelley couldn't face another verbal lashing, so ducked behind a bush until Sandra had passed. As she hid there, peering out from between the fronds, she heard a noise and turned around to see a small window high in the wall and mostly obscured by greenery. She could hear muffled voices coming from inside the room.

Her journalist's nose demanded she investigate. By standing on a twisted tree branch, she could gain just enough height to peer in through the dusty window. She almost fell off again.

Through the window she could see Dr Galloway's office, a desk, a chair, charts on the wall and an examination table. Perched on the edge of the table was the good doctor himself. On her knees in front of him, sideways-on to Shelley, was Verity Parrish, looking less mumsy than usual with her hair messed up and a good half-foot of Galloway's cock in her mouth. As Shelley watched, Verity demonstrated that her experience of all matters sexual wasn't just theoretical. Her wet lips slithered up and down Galloway's pulsating member, the ridges glistening with her saliva as she pulled back, before plunging forward again.

Celibate for three years, my foot!

In a world where just about everyone seemed to be having sex except for her, she'd seen Verity as a kindred spirit.

There was also something else though and it took Shelley a moment or two to identify the emotion. It was jealousy. She hadn't had any real intention of pursuing a romantic attachment with Galloway, but she'd been enjoying characterising him as the romantic lead of the novel in her head. No one wants to see Mr Darcy getting noshed off by the governess.

The doctor had his head back and his eyes closed. One of his hands rested gently on the back of Verity's head as the counsellor gobbled him. Shelley watched in mounting amazement as Galloway began to tremble and with his hand guided Verity to move faster. Shortly he came, thrusting his hips forward and plunging his cock ever deeper into Verity's accommodating throat. Verity took the come like a professional, swallowing as she sucked and never missing a beat. When Galloway opened his eyes and brought his head forward, Shelley decided it was time to beat a retreat.

She dropped down to the ground and rushed off. The image still burned on the inside of her retinas: Verity's red cheek bulging with Dr Galloway's manhood. Shelley found a bench with a view of the pond and plonked herself down, heart thumping. A pair of swans barely rippled the water as they moved silently from left to right. The breeze whipped her hair as she thought about what she should do with the information. Briony's voice popped into her head: *Include it in the report. It's a cover story. Think how pissed off Freya will be.*

On the other hand, Shelley's sense of morality told her she should go and see Dr Jones and let her know exactly what her staff were up to. It was hardly appropriate for the two professionals in the sex addiction treatment team to be performing oral sex while they were supposed to be working.

But then again, Shelley thought, what they got up to in private was their own business. If she hadn't been sneaking around she would never have known.

Eventually she decided she would go and see Dr Jones, despite feeling this was more the action of the old, prim Shelley rather than the new, thawed version she was beginning to like.

She was angry though and began justifying her decision to herself as she entered the building and stumped up the stairs. Galloway was supposed to be available for them whenever they needed him; Verity should have been preparing for that afternoon's session, Larry's confessional. Shelley didn't want to splash this story and ruin their careers, but neither was she happy with them getting away with it. As it was she felt the course was badly run and over-priced. She felt a loyalty to her fellow group members and was determined to speak up for them.

The door to Dr Jones' office was ajar and when Shelley knocked it swung open. Shelley stepped inside and stopped, staring.

Dr Jones sat slumped at her desk, head on the table, a half-empty bottle of cheap gin on the blotter before her. Her hand clutched an empty glass. Shelley stepped up to the desk and peered into the doctor's face. It was puffy, and emanated a sharp smell of spirits.

'Geez Louise,' Shelley muttered to herself. 'The staff are either at it like bunnies or sacked out under the table. Maybe I should go to the tabloids after all.'

She shook her head and left.

Thirty minutes later and they were re-assembled in the Mountain Room. Shelley inspected Verity. Her cheeks were a little flushed and the bun not as perfect as usual, but apart from that no one could ever have guessed that half an hour earlier she'd swallowed half a litre of Dr Galloway's DNA.

'Good afternoon everyone,' Verity began. 'We're here this afternoon to listen to Larry tell us about how he came to be here. You know the drill by now. Be receptive and don't interrupt. Larry, please begin when you're ready.'

They all turned to look at the him. Larry sat, legs crossed, looking very comfortable. He smiled and held his hand out, palms up, a gesture of surrender, and began speaking.

Chapter Twenty-One

I haven't got tales of illicit conquests, threesomes or rampant roger-fests. As I mentioned briefly at the start of the course, I'm a different sort of sex addict. I'm addicted to sex with myself. I like to Bash the Bishop. Choke the Chicken. Yank the Yoghurt Pot. You know. I'm sure most of the planet, if asked, would admit to knocking one off from time to time, and the rest are probably liars. I'm a little bit different. It took me a while to realise but I now understand it's not normal to jerk off two dozen times a day. It's not normal to have a spare room full of magazines and DVDs. It's not normal to spend twenty-four hours at a stretch surfing the internet for more and more freakish porn.

Sorry, I know I need to start at the beginning. My Dad's a CEO for a big multinational based in Singapore. When I was fourteen or so he sent me away to boarding school in England. I was lonely and I felt like I didn't fit in. The weather was always grey and wet and I missed my mum so much. The school was horrible and we didn't have much to look forward to. But all that changed one day when my friend Stevie smuggled in a magazine called

D-Cup Delights. We all gathered around in the dorm after lights out, with a torch and the mag and reverently turned each page. We couldn't believe what we were seeing. Remember, we were a bunch of spotty virgins walking around with hormone-filled balloon balls most of the time anyway. The only decent material I had in the jerk bank was an image from parents' day when James Morrison's mum climbed out of her car wearing a short skirt and flashed her knickers.

So bringing this magazine into the dorm was like throwing a cat into a room full of toddlers, everyone wanted a stroke.

We took turns taking the magazine into the toilets; most boys were in and out in thirty seconds, beaming and relaxed. Then they went off to do other things. I made sure I was last so I wouldn't be disturbed. The second-to-last boy handed it to me with a wink and said: 'Sorry about the mess on page 17. I cleaned it up as best I could.'

I sat on the loo trembling with excitement and opened the first page. I made sure I read every caption, inspected each girl. 'This is Samantha, 19, from Croydon. Samantha likes dancing, meeting people and says she's right behind Mr Bush and Mr Blair as our brave boys go off to war. Her guns are loaded and she's ready to fire.'

I didn't care too much about Samantha's politics but, like her, I too was ready to fire. I reached into my shorts and pulled out my dick. I knew what I was doing. I was fifteen at this point and I'd obviously done it before, but this was different. This was special. It was me and Samantha now. Guns at the ready. I began to stroke myself off. I tried to go slowly, to enjoy the sensation, but the pictures were too much and it wasn't long before I fired my jizz across the cubicle and hit the door.

But I wasn't finished. It was rugby practice that day and no one would miss a scrawny runt like me. I had all afternoon and I used it. I whacked off to every one of those huge-breasted girls that day. Towards the end it was getting more and more difficult, and I was getting sore. I began constructing elaborate fantasies about what I'd do to each of the girls to help keep me hard. I'd make this one kiss my penis. I'd lie on top of that one and do whatever it is you did to girls when you got them back to your house. I'd get that one to do to me what I was now doing to myself.

I was on the final spread and nearing orgasm, searching for it as I yanked at my poor, abused cock. Then the door opened and someone came in. I was determined to finish, I was so close, and kept it up. Then someone spoke.

'Who's in there? Is that you, Bala?'

I had no intention of answering and I kept jerking away, trying to concentrate on my fantasy, involving Bridget and her skimpy bikini.

I finished with relief, my come no longer spurting out but merely dribbling like a half-hearted drinking fountain. As I leaned back against the cistern I looked up to see the head of Mr Blake, the science teacher, peeping over the top of the door, eyes popping out of his sockets like turtle heads as he realised I was beating the meat.

Needless to say, the mag was confiscated. Stevie demanded I replace it but I'd already made up my mind to make it my business in life, or at least at this school, to acquire as many stroke mags as I could. I don't think the school told my father what had happened. This sort of thing was commonplace, and who wants to tell a potential source of income his son spends most of the time at this £12,000-a-term boarding school tossing himself off to jazz mags.

On a free day soon after, I wandered down to town and walked into the newsagent. Twenty minutes later I walked out again with a selection of top-shelf publications and an arrangement with the owner. He'd supply me with magazines, I'd sell them to the other boys at school and we'd split the profits. I've always been good with money, I suppose it's my dad's influence, and I made a fair amount of pocket money over the next couple of years. I also got to look through the magazines and make the bald man cry before I sold them. The best ones I kept for myself, in a special hiding-place where I could go and spank the monkey to my heart's content before selling the mags on. I was always careful not to make a mess of them. No one wants to pay top dollar for something only to find half the pages stuck together.

I wasn't the only one doing this of course. We used to trade everything. And sometimes other lads would bring in magazines I couldn't get hold of at the small-town newsagent.

Once a boy named Ducker brought in a magazine he'd picked up somehow when in Italy on holiday. He showed us a little. It was dynamite stuff. Much harder than anything we could get in England. The girls looked a bit rough but that wasn't surprising considering the workload they'd been asked to perform. Ducker asked for our best offers.

I had to have it. It was a tight auction but the other boys knew I was determined; I'd already got a reputation, and a nickname – the Organ Grinder. It cost me forty fags and my own treasured copy of the '96 October *Playboy* – the one with Pamela Anderson

Me and a few of the other boys formed the Palm Club, where we swapped the best literature we had and discussed technique. Sometimes we'd watch each other, which I found intriguing at first, but ultimately tedious. Some of the other boys paired off and tried helping each other out. They weren't necessarily gay, but when you're stuck in an all-male environment, then you don't care too much what sex the hand is that's jerking you off. I tried it a couple of times. I liked doing them more than I liked them doing it to me. They never got it quite right. They didn't know exactly how hard to squeeze or where to pinch. I preferred it solo. Always have. We had competitions for speed, for frequency and for distance. I won all three, hands down, nearly every time, apart from the fortnight I had meningitis; then I could only manage around half the distance.

When I left school I had no idea what to do. I'd wasted too much time stroking the sausage to have done well in the exams. I wanted freedom, freedom to explore the wide world of pornography I knew was out there. So I needed income. Dad was understandably unhappy about paying for me to sit in a flat and play with myself, and he arranged for me to go and work in the London office of his firm. The London boss wasn't too keen when he saw my results, but Dad told him I'd work hard and he gave me a probation period. That was fine with me. I'm not stupid, and I am capable of working hard when I need to. And not just one-handed working either. Problem was, they let me have internet access. It's really been porn, and people's insatiable desire for it, that has driven the development of the internet. Forget all the worthy talk about communication, and education, and democratising the planet. It's not the part-time surfers in Silicon Valley driving this, it's the one-handed surfers in a billion bedrooms around the globe. I'd discovered this treasure-trove of porn, much of it free if you know where to look, and I was in heaven.

Now this was a few years ago and I only had dial-up at home, which meant it took a long time to download a hi-res image of a girl with big tits. Often up to a minute per tit. Short clips and streaming video could take hours. God knows how many days of my life I wasted sitting, staring at a picture assembling itself line by line on my fourteen-inch screen, hoping that the girl would be as dirty as the caption had suggested. Most times I was disappointed. It was the thrill of trying to find something truly filthy that kept me going.

But at this job, they had ADSL, much faster, though not as speedy as today's broadband, still six to seven tits per minute. I couldn't resist. I started sneaking little looks on my third day, when I could stand it no longer. Just the thought of all that young, firm flesh in the big internet pot, ready for me to access with just a few clicks of the mouse. I'd wait till there was no one else in the room, then I'd open the filthiest sites I could find and gorge myself. Problem was though that I'd get myself so hard I'd have to keep popping into the loos for a five-finger disco. If they ever used one of those CSI blue-light things the police have for showing up DNA traces they'd find that little toilet cubicle lit up like Blackpool.

So I asked the boss if he'd mind me working late. He looked surprised, but agreed. Of course he did. This is brilliant, I thought to myself, I can sit here all night tugging the todger to the world's most depraved porn and keep the boss happy at the same time. I saw some great stuff. Things I'd only dreamed about, and things I'd never dreamed were possible. Have you ever seen a woman fit two fists inside her arse? Or a dwarf fuck a giantess? Have you ever wondered how really fat people have sex? Or what gay transsexuals like to do most? Well, I've seen it all. And I know you might think this is all a bit sad, and that we should feel sorry for those people and not exploit them, but at least they were there, doing it. What was I doing? Watching it all on a tiny screen. The freaks and the weirdos were getting more actual sex than I was. I didn't mind. I was just an observer, just watching others get on with their weird lives.

And jacking myself off in the process.

I kept it up, literally, for five nights before I was rumbled. My plan was slightly let down by the fact that I was hardly doing any work, and that we kept running out of bog roll. They checked the internet access records with IT and saw what I was up to.

The boss decided he wanted to catch me red-handed for some reason, probably to make it more likely I'd just walk out without a fuss. He came in later one night and cleared his throat right behind me as I was slapping the salami to an image of a woman so flexible she'd managed to stick her head between her legs, come up the other side and give herself a backdoor treat.

This time my dad did find out what I'd been up to. Though my boss agreed not to tell him the specific image I'd been looking at. Funny thing though, I didn't really feel embarrassed about it. Everyone does the five-knuckle shuffle. Everyone hides it. Okay, so no-one wants to see what other people are getting up to, no one walks into a party and says, 'Hey, guess who I was jerking off to last night?' But hey, it happens. Let's not make a big deal, alright?

Anyway, my dad didn't see it that way. He told me to get my arse back to Singapore. Well, I don't know if any of you have ever been there? Nice place but straighter than a nun's haircut. They'll flog you for spitting gum in the streets. Anyway, my Dad and I don't get on, he's a total div, and I mean no offence to the div community when I say that. Some of my best friends are divs. So I refused to come back. He cut me off and I found myself looking for a job.

What was I going to do?

I did the only thing I knew how to do. I started up my own magazine importing and distribution company. I travelled to the darkest corners of Europe finding the cheapest, vilest, most specialist publications you can imagine and set up a direct mail service. I distributed to porn shops and even some regular newsagents too, but most of my income came from catalogue and internet sales. I worked from home when I wasn't travelling, trawling the net for filth. There's plenty there if you know where to look. And, boy, did I look. Everyone wants to do something they love as their main job. Here I could pay my rent at the same time as helping to put Mr Kleenex's kids through college.

I was responsible for bringing in such lines as *Grannies on Meth*, *Girls Who Like Dogs*, *Big-Arsed Slags*, and *Fisting World*. Made pots of money, and really dredged the depths of my own perversions. I did discover that even I have a limit. I couldn't deal with proper violent stuff, no kiddy-fiddling of course. Animal stuff I was all right with, as long as it was tasteful.

Don't look at me like that. It can be.

The upshot was I had loads of time on my hands to get to know my first love – Mrs Palm and her five daughters.

Chapter Twenty-Two

It was around this time that I met Carla. My first girlfriend.

You're asking yourselves how did a dysfunctional creep like Larry get himself a girlfriend. Well, it's not so strange. I met Carla through a sex-chat website. Sometimes, when I got bored of porn, I'd log onto one of these rooms and talk to real people. Sometimes they had webcams, and I had one too. I liked the look of Carla and she seemed to like the look of me. She also liked to watch me choke Kojak. She'd type dirty suggestions to me and I'd tell her to take off her top and stuff. Then I'd whack off while she watched. She never seemed to indulge herself at the same time, she'd just watch, fascinated. I'd try to fire my load right into the camera lens for her. She loved that.

Eventually we arranged to meet up. I think she wanted to see me masturbate for her in the flesh. I was happy to oblige.

We went out for dinner first. I'm not a complete social retard. I don't have many friends, but I know how to be with people in a normal situation. She was nice, perhaps not so sexy as she seemed on the tiny webcam display.

She was pleasant looking rather than pretty. And she was taller than I'd expected and a bit triangular. But I liked her. Especially her flashing dark eyes and her gypsy hair. She seemed exotic to me. Though I suppose any woman willing to talk to a mean fiddler like me must be a bit out there.

We had a nice time but towards the end of the meal I was horny and really needed to liquidate the inventory. She seemed keen to get home and watch. I had a couple of beers so it would take longer. I took her back to mine, where I'd spent most of the day washing sheets. I poured drink for both of us and we sat on the couch looking at each other nervously. Carla put down her drink and lay me back on the couch. She unbuckled my jeans and pulled them down, then she did the same with my boxers. She inspected my stiffening cock.

'It looks much bigger in real life,' she said, which I thought was very decent of her. I wondered for a minute if she was going to open her mouth and blow me, but she just watched, her face a few inches away.

'Go on,' she said, breathlessly.

I took hold, the practised fingers slipping into what I called position two. This would take longer, but would produce a longer, lower-level orgasm, with plenty of spurt height. She sighed as I began cleaning my rifle. I watched her watching me, fascinated by her fascination.

It felt really weird basting the ham with another person watching, but it got me going. I had to take deep breaths and restrain myself to avoid blowing my load too early. I wanted our first time to be special. But eventually it proved too much. I fell into a great well of sensation,

I almost lost the ability to move my arm (and I sometimes wake up in a sweat, having had a nightmare about just that) but I managed to jerk out the *petite mort*, as the French call it. When I opened my eyes, I giggled at the sight of Carla still there, face covered in white seminal fluid.

'What about you?' I asked. 'Are you going to work yourself off? Or would you like me to?'

She shrugged and smiled nervously. 'I don't know how,' she said.

'Really?' I asked. 'How hard can it be?'

So we did it together. I helped her slip out of her trousers and panties, feeling myself grow hard again at the sight of her dark thatch. Then I laid her down on the sofa and lifted a leg up so I could get at her. Remember, this was the first time I'd been with a real woman. It didn't occur to me to kiss her. I just parted her labial lips with my fingers and dipped the tip of my pinky into her slit. She arched her back and moaned. I slipped a finger up to her clitoris and began circling. You might think it's odd, but actually I'm a good lover. Bear in mind that I have seen everything by sitting at my computer. I could list a hundred nuanced fingering techniques, one to fit every occasion. I'd go as far as to say I was a connoisseur.

I knew Carla needed me to go slowly and gently.

But for me, it wasn't exciting. It was just an interesting exercise. I was so good at playing lightsabers with Captain Solo, now I had to do it to someone else. I rubbed her a little harder as her breathing deepened. Then she reached down and took hold of my hand.

She thrust my fingers deeper into her. 'Fuck me with your hand,' she said. I squeezed my fingers together and slid them inside her. She groaned again, deep and guttural. I pumped my fingers in hard and rhythmically. I could feel the orgasm build in her broad hips and at last she was there, thrusting back hard against my hand, threatening to envelop it as her muscles relaxed. She stiffened and raised her hips off the sofa as she came.

We moved in together a few weeks later. And on the first night in our new flat, I actually used my cock for what it was designed, rather than just mangling the midget the whole time. It was a little disappointing to tell the truth, but we kept practising and I got to like it more. The problem with regular sex, is that it's kind of dependent on the other person. They never know exactly how to move, when to thrust, what to suck. On the other hand, having someone else's hand on your pecker was a revelation for me. I'd tried the old trick of lying on my hand until it went to sleep before knocking one off in the hope it would feel like someone else was doing it. But it doesn't really work. Wearing a surgical glove works better.

Anyway, the point is that we enjoyed a proper, recognisable sex life. We both still liked to watch. I'd watch a porn flick, and she'd watch me test-firing the Death Star. This is the period I like to think of as my normal period. Unfortunately it didn't last.

The sex grew a bit stale after a while, as it always does I'm led to believe. So I went back to heavy internet porn use. I didn't try to hide it from Carla, and at first she didn't seem to mind. But as time went on and I started to get into more and more sicker things, regular sex just dried up. She didn't excite me any more. And then she started to resent the amount of tissue time I spent with my square-headed girlfriend. By this time the business was doing well and I'd bought myself a flash big-screen wank machine, with a top-notch sound system for proper appreciation of that wah-wah soundtrack and the grunts and moans of the damned and depraved.

I began spending more and more time in the computer room, with a box of tissues and a tub of hand cream. I'd discovered a site where people post their own . . . well, you can imagine. They had literally thousands of clips on there, and I made it my personal mission to watch every one and give it a rating. There was a lot of rubbish on there, but some great stuff too. Some things I watched, then wished I hadn't. But I couldn't help myself. There are a lot of sick people out there. I guess I'm one of them, maybe those of us that watch are the worst. Without an audience these sites would dry up and die.

I met another girl on the sex site as well. This one liked me to watch her while I burped the baby. She'd fill herself with a succession of toys and type the most filthy things you can imagine while doing it. I kept her existence a secret from Carla. But, as it turns out, I needn't have bothered as Carla had had enough by this point. Can't think why.

I didn't notice she'd gone for three straight days. I was so grateful she wasn't pestering me to come out and eat a meal with her that I just carried on flipping the ferret until I started bleeding. I staggered out, malnourished and dehydrated, to find a note on the table. I didn't even care. I slept for twenty-four hours straight, then ordered a pizza and headed straight back to the computer, manipulating myself to German bondage, the pizza grease serving as an unexpectedly effective lubricant. The Germans are the best at porn, by the by. They just don't care what they do, the dirty buggers. The worst are the Italians. All style and no substance. Lots of hand waving and shouting, but very little cock action.

I knew I needed help. But I didn't look for it. I felt free again. Free from my dad, free from Carla, free from my boss, my teachers. I could look at whatever I wanted, whenever I wanted. And free to continue my lap-based web-browsing till my cock came away in my hand if I so chose.

So that's what I did. I hired a guy to look after the business, and simply wandered about, finding ever more inappropriate places to masturbate. I'm sure Dr Galloway could tell me in clever language exactly why my psyche told me to go out and do it in public. All I know is that I needed to get out from behind the computer and involve myself in the world, the only way I knew how, by spurting jizz all over it.

I started off in strip clubs, the ones with cubicles where you pay your money and the slot opens for a few minutes. There's always some hollow-eyed girl in there swaying about in a drug haze, starkers. They provide tissues but I never bothered. A cleaner always popped in after you'd finished anyway, sometimes you'd pass them in the hall. 'Look in the right-hand corner,' I'd say helpfully. I'd go to adult cinemas, and to strip clubs.

I got beaten up by a bouncer in Soho for rubbing one out at the bar.

I also got busted in a park, ogling the girls. I spent the night in jail, waxing the Buick. I was banned from the Natural History Museum. What? Those Neanderthal women haven't got tops on. They look like they'd be pretty wild in the sack too.

After I was arrested a second time, for masturbating in a restaurant, I tried to pull myself together. I tried going cold turkey for a while, and gave my computer away to charity. I hope I remembered to wipe the hard disk. I lasted a couple of days, lying in a cold sweat, trying not to think about how much I wanted to butter the corn. I went to the library to take my mind off porn and to try and find something a bit more cerebral. I ended up in the indexing room pounding the flounder to a Jilly-bloody-Cooper bonkbuster.

I bought a new computer that afternoon and had another three-day wank-a-thon. My health was suffering. I couldn't sleep, just dozing, waking, milking the moose then dozing off again. I was lethargic and irritable. I had no friends left, even the guy at the local adult shop wouldn't talk to me. His best customer!

I talked to my doctor about it, and he suggested that exercise was a good way to relieve the tensions and tire me out so I could sleep properly. I took up swimming. That worked for a while. I just ploughed up and down the pool, looking down, trying to think of nothing. I swam for hours every day, exhausting myself and going straight home to sleep. But in the summer the problems started again. The place was suddenly filled with young women preening and sunning themselves by the pool as I swam up and down. The sight of all those girls in skimpy swimming costumes was just too much. One day something snapped. I snuck behind the changing block and stood on an old wheelie bin to have a peek through the old grimy louvres, straight into the showers. This was better than porn, this was real. There's something just so erotic about foamy skin and I stood there for hours, spanking the pony as a succession of teenage girls came in, stripped off and soaped their hot little bodies.

Now let me make clear that these weren't underage girls, I'm not into that kind of thing. But unfortunately I had a hard time convincing the police of that, when they caught me, which of course they did soon enough. I was arrested for a third time. The coppers came around the corner, saw me giving it the old one-gun salute and just shook their heads in disgust.

My parents flew in from Singapore, my mother crying non-stop and my dad wringing his hands, trying to stop himself wringing my neck. They knew I was a serial self-abuser of course, they weren't dumb, but they'd never expected me to turn out to be a Peeping Tom, and quite frankly neither had I. I'd shocked even myself and was chastened. I pleaded guilty of course. I've never tried to hide what I am.

The judge gave me a conditional sentence and put me on the Sex Offenders Register. I have to attend this course as part of a court order. If I screw up, I go to jail. And I don't want to go jail. I've been here five days and haven't so much as touched my winky. I've even been sitting down to pee. I have had some pills to reduce my libido, but even so, I'm really proud of what I've done so far. It hasn't been easy sitting here and listening to all your sexy stories. But it's been important for me. I need to learn how to stop treating every sexual account I see or hear as fodder for my wank-bank.

I'm here not just because the judge told me to come. I want to be here. I want to get better and lead a normal life. I know I can do it.

Chapter Twenty-Three

After Larry had finished, Verity told them they'd have recreation before dinner.

'I suggest you do something as a group. I can see you're all bonding well, but I want to keep that going throughout the confessionals, and beyond. I need you to look after each other. It's a lovely afternoon, why not pop out onto the croquet lawn?'

'Croquet!' Cian shouted enthusiastically. 'Whacking my opponent's balls with a bloody big hammer? Count me in.' The others agreed and they made their way down the hall to the double doors out onto the croquet lawn. Shelley tapped Rose on the shoulder. 'Just got to pop to the loo, I'll catch up with you.'

In the toilets she locked the cubicle and sat down, her head in her hands. *Poor Larry*, she thought. What an awful story. She felt terrible, and not just through sympathy. She felt guilty at her deception, and a crippling, stomach-wrenching fear about her own confessional the next day. She knew now that she couldn't do it. She'd have to leave the group, tonight. She'd have to let her new friends down.

She decided she was going to march up to Dr Jones'

office, and use her telephone. It seemed unlikely she would have woken up considering the amount she'd drunk. And if she did, so what? Shelley was leaving, come hell or high water, and bugger the Mental Health Act. As she stood to leave though, she felt her BlackBerry buzz. She wavered for a second, then sat down and flipped it open. A message. From Aidan.

> *Hi Shelley,*
> *Sorry about the delay on this. I've been thinking it through carefully, trying to get it just right. Thinking about what sort of things you might get up to and trying to write them in your brilliant style. I've aimed to strike the same kind of level as the confessionals you've been sending back, so some of it is pretty raunchy. I'm no writer, but I hope what I've been able to do will give you enough material to make a good fist of it. I know you won't let me down. I'm confident your story will be the best of the lot and will round off the series well and merit the cover. You deserve it for the work you've put in. Just one more push.*

And after that Aidan had provided a detailed, involved and explicitly-written story for Shelley. As she read it through, she felt herself flushing. It wasn't just the jaw-dropping sex he'd described, but the fact that he was thinking of her when he'd wrote it. She imagined him late at night, in a flash pad somewhere in Chelsea, sitting in boxers and a tight vest tapping away with his strong fingers. All the while thinking of her naked, with another man's hand between her legs, or another man's cock in her mouth.

She read it through twice, and as she finished the second time, she realised she had her hand hard against her crotch. She let her middle finger trace over her swollen clitoris, then pulled it away hurriedly.

'Well, I guess I could stay for one more day,' she told herself. Then she checked her make-up, washed her hands and went off to join the others.

'That's what I'm *talking* about!' Cian yelled as Shelley stepped out of the doors and walked over to the croquet lawn.

'You plonker!' Will shouted at him.

'I'm allowed to do it!' Cian shouted back, grinning madly. 'If your ball ends up touching mine I can whack it as hard as I like.'

'Not with a fucking cricket bat!'

'Sussex rules,' Cian said, shrugging.

'Where did you get that bat anyway?' Abigail called over. She'd apparently taken charge as soon as they'd reached the green and was busy ordering everyone about.

'I found it with the other gear in the games room,' Cian said, hefting and spinning it, forcing Will to duck.

Shelley joined Rose at the edge. Her friend was wearing a white skirt that came about half-way down to her knees. 'Who's winning?'

'Well, no one really knows the rules, or at least they don't agree on the same set of rules. Abigail's sort of in charge and is adjudicating on disagreements, of which there have been a lot already. Will *was* winning, but now Cian's hit his ball into the compost heap so Larry's in the lead.'

'Your turn, Rose,' Abigail said.

Rose moved into position and bent over to tap her ball towards the next hoop. This had the effect of exposing most of her backside. She was wearing a dental-floss-thin white thong, leaving nothing to the imagination. Shelley felt like clapping.

Poor old Larry, standing beside her, nearly fainted at the view.

'Christmas Day,' he said and sank to his knees.

Rose finished her shot and stood up, oblivious to the effect she'd caused.

'Right, that's it,' Larry said and sprinted off towards the woods.

'Where're you going, mate?' Cian called after him.

'I can't hold it any longer. Be back in five.'

Will and Cian fell about laughing.

'What was that about?' Rose asked Shelley.

Shelley smiled, and shrugged. 'I think Larry *really* likes you.'

Abigail wandered over muttering: 'I could teach that boy to control himself. It's just a matter of discipline.' She whacked the handle of her putter into her hand with a slap that made Cian and Will wince.

I like Rose too, Shelley thought to herself. In fact, she liked everyone.

Maybe another week here wouldn't be so bad.

That night, Rose was in the shower as Shelley got into bed. She closed her eyes and tried to forget the crowd of images in her head. Verity enthusiastically slurping on Dr Galloway's slick penis, Aidan striding brashly across the *Vixen* offices, Cian slapping his engorged member from hand to hand as he glared at her hungrily.

Rose came in wearing her see-through nightdress. Shelley was used to it by now and felt comfortable with the older woman's semi-nakedness. 'All okay, honey?' Rose asked.

'Yes, I'm fine.'

'Would you like to chat?'

'Yes, but not about my confessional, and not about sex at all. Let's talk about something else.'

'Okay,' Rose said, smiling as she sat on the bed. 'What would you like to talk about?'

'Oh, I don't know, house prices, politics, anything but sex. What about babies?'

'Babies?'

'Yes, you know, little noisy things, crapping everywhere and chewing on your nipples. Do you want babies? Slap me if it's too personal a question.'

'I think I do,' Rose replied, after a pause for consideration. 'But I need to sort myself out first, I know that.'

'You'd make a great mother,' Shelley said.

'Why, because I have child-bearing hips?'

'No, because you're a kind, thoughtful and intelligent woman. Plus you have pots of money.'

Rose laughed.

'I've never really understood the term child-bearing hips,' Shelley said after a pause. 'Does it mean you've got a wide pelvis to make it easier for them to come out? Or does it mean you have a sticky-out hip suitable for carrying a child around on?'

'I don't know,' Rose replied. 'Maybe both?'

'All I know is I don't have them,' Shelley said. 'Straight up and down, that's me. Even if I could force an eight-pound poo machine out without cracking my pelvis, it'd just keep slipping off my hip in Tesco's.'

Rose laughed again, leant over and kissed Shelley on the lips.

It wasn't a proper, passionate kiss. Just a sweet smack, but it was the most intimate contact Shelley had had with another human for some time and she was left speechless.

'You're cute, Shelley,' Rose said, climbing into bed. 'I'd like to keep in touch with you, after . . . all this.'

'I'd like that too,' Shelley replied and got up to turn off the light. As she lay in bed, she puzzled over whether Rose meant she wanted to keep in touch just as a friend, or maybe something else. Had that kiss just been a friendly peck? If so, why on the lips? And more to the point, was she, Shelley, really interested in sleeping with another woman? Or was she just horny and looking for affection?

At least all these new questions have stopped me worrying about tomorrow, she thought, as she drifted off.

Larry was in the room with a lap-top.

'I want to show you something,' he told her, sitting on the end of the bed and opening the computer. There on the screen, she saw a naked woman on all fours. Her face wasn't visible as the camera viewed her from behind. As the movie played, she saw a large cock glide into view like the Imperial Flagship in *Star Wars*. The owner of the cock eased it slowly inside the woman and began thrusting.

'Great stuff, isn't it?' Larry said excitedly, his hand in his pants.

The camera pulled back and Shelley now saw another man at the other end, getting a blow job from the brunette. The camera pulled back still further and she gasped as she realised it was Aidan. The camera began travelling slowly around the room until the first man's face could be seen. Shelley was unsurprised to see it was Dr Galloway. She was, however, surprised to see the face of the woman. It was her own.

The next morning was bright and warm. Shelley opened the window and took a lungful of the country air. She didn't feel too bad, even knowing what was to come later. The door opened behind her and Sandra came in with the bromide tea. Rose was still slumbering, her hair splayed sexily on the pillow; even in her sleep she looked every inch the porn star.

'Big day for you,' Sandra said, her hair tied in a bun, her face still showing the scrapes and bruises she'd got during her scuffle with Abigail. 'Time to face the music.'

Shelley eyed her suspiciously. If Sandra did know something about her, why didn't she just come out and say it?

'Nice new look you've got,' Shelley replied. 'What happened, get in a fight outside the chip shop?'

Sandra sneered. 'Save your clever words for the confessional today, some people will be listening very closely indeed.' And with that she left.

Shelley talked non-stop at breakfast, her anxiety spilling out of her mouth. She'd helped herself to a large doughnut from the counter, claiming she needed the sugar. She munched it now, eyes down on the table in front of her. The others sensed her nervousness and spoke quietly, not wanting to make it worse. She could feel their support, their love, and it helped.

Abigail tapped her on the shoulder and whispered: 'You'll be fine, Shelley. It'll all be over soon.' It was the first kind words the dominatrix had uttered, and it meant a lot. Shelley nodded and grabbed another doughnut from Cian's plate. 'I eat these things just to keep me going,' she said. 'Every time I eat one I find I have another twenty minutes' energy. The coming-down part always lasts longer than the high, though. It sometimes seems I spend most of my life crashing from a doughnut rush.'

'Don't replace one addiction with another,' Verity said.

Chapter Twenty-Four

'Okay everyone. Cian, please stop swinging on your chair. Larry, hands on the arms please. We're here this morning to hear our final confessional – Shelley's. Once all the confessionals are over, we enter the next phase of the course, but for now, please sit quietly and offer Shelley the patience and respect she has showed you.' Verity turned to Shelley and smiled. 'Go ahead please Shelley.'

Shelley, without thinking, stood and thanked Verity. This was it, she thought. The moment of truth. Could she get outside herself and tell a convincing tale of sexual excess? She certainly had the material, thanks to Aidan, and she was a journalist dammit! She was a writer and a story-teller. But did she have that heat, that passion that the others had? Or was she forever to be a frigid sexual repressive, doomed to run a mile at the remotest possibility of sex? No matter that there was another phase of the course to go. This was Shelley's final examination.

She began.

My name is Shelley Carter and I *am* a sex addict. For a long time I thought I was *the* sex addict. I didn't realise there were others. I felt like a character from a disaster movie, thinking I'm the only survivor. I've always loved sex and, as far as I'm aware, I've never felt love, not properly anyway. I can't stay with one man, or woman, for more than a couple of weeks. I crave new experiences, new partners, constantly. Everyone I meet I size up, thinking, 'Do I find you attractive enough to sleep with?' and the answer is almost always yes. I sleep with sexy people, with ugly people. Old or young makes no difference to me.

Strangely enough I started quite late, at least for my school. I was nearly eighteen and was at college. I knew all about sex of course. This was only seven years ago and we had the internet then. I knew what it was and I knew that I wanted it. I might have given Larry a run for his money in the self-love department. What I didn't know was that sex was easy to get. Especially for a young woman with lips, hips and tits. I know I'm no supermodel, but I'm not a total munter either. A friend of mine, Stacey, who was no oil painting to be honest, told me what I needed to do. 'You go to a school disco,' she said. 'You find an okay-looking, but insecure, boy and you dance with him. Then you put your lips to his ear and tell that boy exactly what you'd be willing to let him do to you. Even if he doesn't really fancy you, you can be pretty damn certain it'll be the best offer he'll get that evening, or probably that year. He'll go home with you, or out to the car park at least.'

Now this girl somehow always managed to get good-looking guys. No one knew how she did it. I asked her what she told boys she was willing to do that made them come back with her. 'Simple,' she replied. 'I tell him that if he comes back to my place I'll stick my tongue up his arse.'

The frontal assault is always, always the best option with men. Or in my friend's case, the rear assault, but you get my meaning. Men are simple, they like simple options and simple choices. Stay here and maybe get a dance at best from the school beauty, or come back to mine and get your first, and possibly last, ever rim-job.

No contest.

I had my eye on a guy called Richard Forster. Nice-looking bloke, though incredibly shy. He was a member of the Chess Club, which gives you an indication of the lack of girls he had hanging around him. I didn't care about his politics of course, just what he had in his pants. I found out via his friends where he'd be one Friday and waited for him to arrive at the club, sipping a cider and black and wearing a crop-top, leather skirt and no knickers. It took me no time at all to get him back out to the car park. It was exactly three weeks before my eighteenth birthday and within ten minutes he had his trousers down and was fumbling feverishly with a condom as I lay spread-eagled on his car bonnet, still warm and ticking, both the car and me, I mean. Richard scrambled up onto the bonnet and kissed me. I took his hand and shoved it down between my legs, desperate for something to press against me, to penetrate and invade. He was inexperienced and prodded and poked in all the wrong places.

'Get on your back,' I said and he obliged. I hitched up the skirt, hooked a leg over his body and leaned down to kiss him, biting his bottom lip as hard as I dared. He shuddered in expectation as my pussy lips brushed against his shaft but I wasn't quite ready. I carried on kissing him, rubbing my mound against him. He kept thrusting up at me, anxious to get inside, but I teased him and lifted my hips up out of the way. Eventually I decided he was ready. I held his cock tight and eased it inside me as I squatted over him.

It felt amazing. The pain I'd been expecting never came. It wasn't the first time I'd had something inside me anyway. I'd discovered you could get vibrators on mail-order some months before. He felt different though. More *forgiving* then a rigid vibrator, but more *giving*, if you understand, like he was expanding inside me. I'll never forget how good that first time was, even though he didn't last very long. Poor old Richard was over-excited and fired his packet up into me in a matter of seconds. I made him finish me off with his mouth. That was another trick Stacey taught me. If you ask a boy to do something, he'll probably say yes. And he'll probably find the fact you asked at all to be a real turn-on.

I made a reputation for myself that year. I haunted the clubs and bars on the weekend and sometimes on a school night too. I fucked guys in the car park, in the toilets, down by the canal, in cars, at my house, or theirs. Occasionally I'd take a guy home, screw his brains out then go back out and find myself another one. I was a predator, like Will. I'd cut a guy off from his pack of mates, take him outside and devour him, then next week I'd see him again and I'd smile as I walked off leading his best friend by the hand. Guys came to know me as the girl who'd do anything, or anyone. Girls knew me as that boyfriend-stealing slut. I didn't care. I saw myself as liberated. I read Sylvia Plath and Virginia Woolf and wrote God-awful poetry about being a social outcast.

My parents didn't approve of all the boys I was bringing back to the house. They couldn't keep up, but neither could the boys. It was time to move on, but where? I talked to the guidance counsellor and she asked me what I liked doing. I told her I liked to make people feel good and she suggested I should be a nurse. So I did. After college I went to university in London. I did my placements at Charing Cross Hospital in West London. I liked the job, and found university was full of young, attractive people suddenly free from the restraints of home and with their own beds.

I tried sticking with boyfriends, but there were so many other eligible young men and I never met anyone I was seriously interested in. A month or so after I started at university I was at some social event and met a guy called Matt. He was gorgeous. Big, strong, good looking in a dishevelled sort of way. Straight away I knew he'd got my number.

'You like to party, huh?' he said over the booming music.

'Doesn't everyone?'

'Some more than others.'

I shrugged. 'You here alone?' I asked.

'No, I'm here with my friend Chris, he's gone to get cigarettes.'

'Are you gay?' I asked. Well, a girl doesn't have time to lose.

'Do you want me to be gay?' he asked, smiling.

'Maybe I do.'

We danced for a while and eventually Matt's friend returned. He was also attractive. I began to suspect they were both gay. Matt went to talk to Chris. They looked over at me as I danced alone, watching them with interest, wondering what was going to happen. Then Chris nodded. Matt came back. 'Do you want to come to our place?'

I nearly asked what for, but I knew.

I nodded.

The question of whether they were gay was answered twenty minutes later as Matt's thick cock slid into me and he began thrusting. I already had my hand in Chris's pants and was fondling his swelling penis.

The boys hadn't wasted any time. They'd installed me on the sofa in their laddishly-decorated flat, cluttered with ashtrays and bottles. Chris had poured us all a drink while Matt put some Supertramp on the stereo. Then they came and sat on either side of me.

'We like to share things,' Matt said.

'Okay,' I replied. I was slightly nervous. I didn't know these guys from Adam and I wouldn't have been too surprised if Adam himself had suddenly popped out of the cupboard to make it a round foursome.

I turned towards Matt first, feeling some loyalty to the guy who'd picked me up. We kissed, gently at first, then more urgently. Matt cupped my cheek with one hand. I felt Chris nuzzle my exposed neck. It felt weird, but exciting to be kissed by two men at once. Why hadn't I thought of this before? Chris began unbuttoning my top.

I slid a hand up Matt's thigh and stroked the hard lump in his trousers. I could almost feel it trembling in there. Chris eased my top over my shoulder and unhooked the bra catch with a deft flick. Matt's tongue tickled the roof of my mouth. His hands had found my naked breasts and he lightly pinched my nipples.

Chris took hold off my hips and pulled me up until I was kneeling on the couch, still kissing Matt. Chris pulled up my skirt, expecting to find panties, but as usual, I wore none. I felt his hand flicker across my labia. I loved the sensation of being naked and totally exposed to these big rough guys when they were still fully clothed. I imagined I was an innocent waif being violated. Though of course the idea of me being an innocent anything was long gone.

I stopped kissing Matt and unzipped his trousers, he sighed and lay back as I slipped my hand in and hauled out his good-sized cock, already stiff as an admiral. I lowered my head and took him into my mouth, as I felt Chris's tongue enter my pussy. Chris knew a thing or two about how to please a woman with his tongue. I found it hard to keep my mind on servicing Matt at the other end. He seemed to enjoy it though. I moved my whole head up and down, gently mouthing his shaft, my tight lips slipping over the contours of his beefy cock. Warmth, moisture, softness. That's what men want. Don't ruin it by chewing the damn thing half off.

He stroked my hair with one hand and laid the other gently on the back of my head. I could feel the strength in his arm and I enjoyed imagining that if I tried to stop, he'd jam my head back down again.

I whined in disappointment as Chris stopped licking, but then grunted with appreciation a few moments later when I felt three of his fingers glide into my vagina. He worked me well, tickling my inner walls with the tips of his fingers and rubbing my butt-hole with his thumb. I could feel Matt was nearly ready to come and he seized my hair and pulled my head up. He didn't want to finish too early.

He stood and led me into the bedroom, Chris following. There Matt threw me onto the bed roughly and ripped off his shirt. It was incredibly sexy, I lay there, naked apart from my hitched-up skirt as they undressed, staring at me as they did so. I squeezed my thighs together, my pussy slick with Chris's saliva and my own wetness.

Chris was naked first and pounced onto the bed. We kissed, bodies coming together, crackling with sexual energy. Matt joined us and this time he came at me from behind while Chris positioned our entwined bodies so that both men had access. Chris slipped into me, I was so wet I hardly felt him go in. But I certainly felt Matt when he entered me from the other side and began fucking my ass gently. I felt shocked. I hadn't expected it, though what else had he been playing at back there? But my surprise stopped me objecting, he'd lubed himself up and it didn't hurt too much. In fact, it felt kind of good, especially with another cock sliding in and out from the front.

The boys had obviously done this before – getting the

angles right is not easy. I've tried it since with less experienced guys and it takes forever to get it working. I wondered if I'd met my match.

The thing I found hottest was the thought of them being able to feel each other inside me, you know, through the wall? As practised as they were, it was still difficult to get into a proper rhythm and after a while Chris pulled out and Matt flipped me over on to my front. Then he proceeded to give me a hard, pounding butt-fuck. I was relaxed and loose now and it wasn't nearly so painful as it sounds, but I wasn't going to come like that. I began clenching my sphincter in time with Matt's thrusts. 'Oh yes!' he called and I felt his cock jerk and he came inside me. I loved the way his body stiffened as his juddering orgasm subsided. As he rolled off and lay flat out and exhausted on the bed.

I lifted my legs and invited Chris inside. He entered me kneeling up, lifting my bottom off the bed a little to get himself inside me. His cock bent sharply to the right, I now noticed, and I could feel the head pressing against the left wall of my vulva. He pumped hard and steadily, fixing me with his fierce gaze, beads of sweat on his forehead. He came soon after that, lifting his chin, closing his eyes and growling like a wolf as he pulled out his cock, whipped off the condom, and sprayed his hot juice over my stomach.

I was sopping as I wiped it off with a tissue.

'My turn now.' I told them what I wanted. They looked at each other and shrugged, smiling, certain now they'd found the dirty girl they'd been looking for.

I lay on my side and lifted one leg into the air. Matt

dived into my butt and began licking my abused ring gently. God, that felt good. Chris lay down in a sixty-nine position before me and began lapping at my pussy. I took Chris's limp penis in my mouth as he ground his slightly stubbly chin against my clitoris. I made him hard again and deep-throated him as I climaxed explosively against the dual tonguing I was receiving.

Afterwards we smoked in bed and thought ourselves the nastiest little ménage-a-trois there had been since Versailles.

I moved in with Matt and Chris for a bit. The sex was great, I wasn't rolling in money and they didn't mind if I brought others back to the flat. When I started my placement at the hospital, the opportunities to meet and sleep with new people increased dramatically. I brought a doctor back to the flat once. He was cheating on his wife and got more than he bargained for when Matt and Chris came back to the house and hopped into bed with us.

I met a nice girl called Kelly, who was on my shift, and who told me she was bi on a drunken night out. I hadn't really thought about sleeping with other women, though that seems strange now. It didn't take much to get her round to mine when I told her about my two pet studs. I developed a taste for pussy that night. She whimpered as I ate her out and the nectar between her thighs was divine. Having a woman's head between your own legs is an experience all women should experience at least once. That soft, smooth chin, those sweet lips, knowing where to nibble, where to lick. Sheer bliss.

But mostly I liked a good, stiff cock pounding until it made my hips ache. I had to tell the ancient registrar I had a problem with my pelvis, so many were the times he found me walking around the wards hobbling like a geriatric. I know I'll feel it when I *am* an old woman. I'm convinced I'll be the first person ever to be diagnosed with an arthritic vagina. The registrar insisted on giving me an examination, and, well, one thing led to another and the next thing I knew I was face down on the exam couch while my sixty-year old boss gave me a sound fucking from behind. I could see his face in the mirror across the room, he looked like a gurning elf. I realised then that it didn't matter to me greatly what the person looked like. They say love is blind? Well, so is sex as far as I'm concerned. If the other person has a cock, or a fist, or a big toe, then why not put it in somewhere and see what happens?

I found something else out on that night shift. I love doing it in hospitals. A few days later I persuaded a shy young receptionist to pop into the supply cupboard with me. I pushed her up against the shelves.

'What are you doing?' she said, though she knew damn well why I'd brought her in; I had a reputation, remember.

I kissed her roughly, biting her lip and pulling it out. I slid down onto my knees, hoisted up her stiff white skirt, pulled her knickers to one side and buried my head in the soft-scented sweetness of her blonde pussy. She nearly screamed with the tension, terrified we'd be found, thinking she should be resisting, but powerless to stop herself thrusting her clit onto my questing mouth. I slipped two fingers into her as she writhed.

She slumped against the shelves afterwards and I wiped my mouth on the back of my hand and walked back out onto the wards without a word.

And it wasn't just the staff either. One day I was doing the rounds, this wasn't even a night shift, and I had to give a man with two broken arms a sponge bath. He looked miserable and groaned when he saw me.

'What is it?' I asked, taking off his gown.

'You're the worst,' he said.

'Oh, thanks very much,' I replied, used to ungrateful patients.

'No, I mean, you're so . . . sexy, which makes it even worse.'

I looked back at him, puzzled, then realised what he meant when I pulled the gown away from him. He was sporting the most magnificent erection I'd ever seen. I looked at his arms, useless in their great white casts.

'It's not funny,' he said. 'My balls hurt.'

'Oh, that old chestnut,' I said. 'Heard that a few times at school.' What I didn't tell him was that I invariably relieved the symptoms of that particular ailment when I encountered it. He looked at me with pleading eyes. 'My girlfriend won't do it,' he said.

I skipped over to the door and looked out; the ward was quiet and I came back and pulled the curtain around us.

Then I brushed my hand up his leg. He shivered. He was a big bloke, a little lardy to tell the truth and not at all attractive, but something about his plight made me wet, as well as sympathetic. I think also the fact he was trapped was a turn-on. I ran my nails up his pole and he groaned, his eyes burning a hole in my uniform. But I had no intention of taking that off. I could pretend I was giving him his sponge bath as long as I kept my uniform on. I gently encircled the tip of his cock with my thumb and forefinger and began squeezing gently. He lifted his hips, hoping for a firmer grasp but I left him hanging for a while. He'd waited a long time for this, a few more minutes wouldn't hurt.

Slowly I massaged the head of his fat penis. I wanted his hand between my legs, and I wanted to straddle him, but I knew I couldn't. Eventually neither of us could stand it any longer and I decided to finish him off. I thought about it for a while, then shrugged and thought, why not? I bent over and swallowed his cock. He grunted in amazement and appreciation and almost immediately fired a great sticky wad into the back of my throat. I can take a lot, but that choked me. I kept at him though. Here was a man in distress and I, as a nurse, had a professional responsibility to do my best to ease his plight.

He came for what seemed like ages, pumping more and more fluid into my mouth. When he'd finished, I gargled with a glass of water and finished giving him his bath. He lay there, staring at me in pathetic gratitude and I left with a pussy wet enough to keep goldfish in.

The burly security guard also got lucky that night.

Chapter Twenty-Five

I did well in my practical exams. I got favourable reports from a great many of my patients and the doctors. I also did well in my written exams and before you ask, no, I didn't sleep with anyone on the examination board. I couldn't find out their names. I am a good nurse, not just a good shag.

After I passed and gained my registration, I left to do a bit of a gap year, something I'd missed after college. My parents had friends in Hong Kong, so I stayed there for a while, exploring the New Territories and the Islands. My father's friends, Mr and Mrs Soon, fixed me up with some work too: I was asked to care for an aged relative, a Mr Chan, in Kowloon.

'He's very wealthy,' Mr Soon told me. 'He is a shipping magnate. He'll give a good salary for the right girl.' I wondered at this. What did Mr Soon mean by 'right girl'?

I expected to find some wizened old Chinese man on his death bed, but when I arrived at the building and showed the address to the security guard, he showed me to a special express elevator that shot me up to the penthouse suite.

I found the gentleman I was to care for didn't look that old, was not in the least wizened and was certainly not on his death bed. He was Chinese though. As I gazed out over the magnificent view of the harbour, impressive enough even without the dazzling lights of a Hong Kong evening, I felt a pair of hands on my hips and something hard pressing against my backside.

I turned my head to see Mr Chan's questioning eyes. He'd already taken out his cock, and it was standing proud – thin, but with a fat glans. I nodded briefly and his hands slid down my haunches and slipped under my skirt, lifting it up.

I watched those lights while we made love. Mr Chan liked me to ride on top of him as he massaged my tits. I rocked up and down gently, gazing out at the hundreds of soaring shafts reaching to the heavens, wondering how many of the tiny individual dots of light were from windows behind which people were stroking and licking and sucking and fucking. In my head the whole of Hong Kong was a seething mass of sex.

I didn't seem to have many other duties other than taking Mr Chan's blood pressure occasionally and checking his pulse as he lay exhausted after giving me a good seeing-to and I wondered if my father's friends had sent me there in the knowledge Mr Chan had been looking for a courtesan rather than a nurse. I didn't enquire. If my reputation had preceded me, what of it? I'd never tried to hide who I was.

I liked Mr Chan. From the window of his bedroom you could see all the way to the airport, and the sprawling dock area where he'd made his fortune. He was a randy old sod too. He must have been in his sixties, but he had good skin and firm muscle tone. He sometimes managed it twice in a night. I felt a bit strange taking money from him. I enjoyed the sex and liked spending time with him. Was I a prostitute all of a sudden? But I told myself the money was for the minor health checks I gave him. The sex was just a bonus, for both of us.

As much as I liked Mr Chan though, and Hong Kong, I grew tired of them in the end. I told him I was moving on to Tokyo and he cried, before giving me three parting gifts. First was a red envelope containing an eye-dropping amount of money. The second was the phone number of another 'sick old man', a friend of his in Tokyo by the name of Mr Iwasaki. The third thing Mr Chan gave me was a sound fucking. The enduring vision I have of him is his 'come face' eyes bulging, teeth bared as he jammed his cock deep inside me again and again and again till every drop was spent.

I left him panting on the $20,000 Persian rug in his living room with only a little regret. I was looking forward to meeting Mr Iwasaki.

Two weeks later I lay naked on the floor of a helicopter flying over the Sea of Japan. Yoshi, as I had come to know him, stood over me wearing an enormous Stetson, a pair of cowboy boots with spurred heels and nothing else apart from a corked erection. Oh, he carried a whip, which I'd already told him he wasn't to use on me. Instead he made me squeal as he cracked it out into the open air, a thousand feet over the foam-flecked ocean. Yoshi looked down at me, grinned and dropped to his knees. He wasn't attractive, but he had a boyish charm, despite being nearly as old as Mr Chan. Some of this charm came from the fact he was a billionaire who owned a large hotel in Shinjuku-ku. But his love of cowboy films I found endearing, as well as his ability to go at it like a rabbit for hours at a stretch. He wasn't big but made up in frequency what he lacked in quantity.

'Ready again?' he said. That was his favourite phrase. His English wasn't great, but he'd got the bedroom chat down at least. 'Do it doggy style', '69 now, please', and 'Don't worry, it could happen to anyone.'

I rolled my eyes in mock wonder at his stamina and nodded. He slid me across the floor until my head was hanging out the door and I could feel the slipstream whip my hair about. The howling of the wind blanked out any other sound, including the involuntary scream I let out. I felt him enter me as my head hung out the sliding door. The exhilaration and the primal fear of hanging out of a moving helicopter, coupled with the sweet sensation of a smooth, hard cock slipping in and out of my snatch was extraordinary. Yoshi pulled out after a couple of minutes and I felt his mouth replace his penis, his hot, hard tongue stroking my clit. I came for the second time on that journey, lost in a maelstrom of sensation.

We landed on a tiny island and the pilot turned into a waiter, laying a collapsible table on the beach for us as the co-pilot fussed about in the helicopter. Neither of them seemed remotely bothered by the fact we were both naked, apart from Yoshi's hat and boots that is.

We ate lobster and salad and drank demi-sec champagne. The sun was warm and after lunch we swam and sun-bathed, then made love on the sand. Yoshi was a receptive lover. He would watch my face intently as he stroked and licked, looking to see what I liked. Good sex is one per cent experimentation and ninety-nine per cent rhythm, once he'd found something that worked he'd keep at it until I grew sore or until I came. He told me he was intrigued to discover how many times he could make me come in a day, and I was inclined to go along with the experiment.

Now, how many girls in my situation would have sunk their hooks into this man and hung on to him for as long as they could? He was fantastically rich, good fun, good in bed and more sensitive to a woman's needs than virtually any other man I've ever met.

And he had a helicopter. Most girls would fuck a horse for the opportunity I had just then. But I'm not most girls. I was jaded by the time we got back to Tokyo. What else have you got, Yoshi?

Soon after I met a girl in a bar who was a qualified nurse who told me she was going to Cairns to work in a hospital, apparently they had a major shortage and were paying good money. I didn't need the cash, but figured it was time I did some honest work.

The high-life wasn't doing it for me. So I flew to Cairns and enquired at the hospital, soon installing myself there on the night-shift, which I didn't mind. I told myself not to screw the patients, or the staff for that matter. There were plenty of good bars in the town packed with bronzed tourists looking for a good time. There was no need to queer my pitch at work.

This worked out fine for a while and I felt myself settling down. I even managed to have a couple of relationships that lasted longer than a week. If I went out with tourists, I knew they'd be leaving soon anyway, so nothing grew too stale. There was certainly a great variety of nationalities to choose from: Germans, Australians, Brits, Canadians, Americans. I think the Swedes made the best lovers, if they were sometimes a bit clinical; I think they're trained in it at school.

Australian men I liked, though not so much with the girls; they tended to be big bags of repressed feminism. Look babe, just because I jammed my tongue up your twat doesn't mean I want to discuss *The Female Eunuch* with you all night. Now reach into that drawer and get the strap-on.

If you'd told me then I had a destructive addiction I would have laughed. Why would anyone else have a problem with it? It would be like when chubby female columnists write articles criticising everyone else for being too thin. Look girl, eat as many cakes as you like you like but accept that that's why you find it hard to breathe when you walk up a flight of steps.

All was going well, until I was asked to attend to a new patient. As soon as I stepped into his private room I knew I might have to make an exception to the no-shagging-the-patients rule. His name was Brad and he was delicious. Blond hair, bleached by the sun. Tanned like he'd never been indoors before. He looked bored until I walked in.

I looked at his chart. 'A shark took a lump out of your side, I see. Could I take a look?'

'Sure,' he said and shifted over to his side. I unlaced his gown, inspecting his rock-hard backside as I did so. I took the gown off him altogether. His wound had been bandaged tightly. I had to change the dressing. I moved around to the other side and caught my first glimpse of his magnificent penis. Maybe he'd be interested in shooting the tube with me when I did the night-shift tomorrow night.

I gently peeled away the bandages. He didn't wince. They build these boys tough in Australia. There wasn't an ounce of fat on him. All solid muscle, but naturally built, not artificial from too many hours in the gym while your brain turns to mush. I don't think I've ever been more attracted to a man. I wanted to nurse him in my own special way.

The wound itself wasn't too bad. You could see where the shark's teeth had punctured the skin, but it hadn't actually bitten much flesh off.

'How did you get away?' I asked.

'Poked the bastard in the eye,' he said casually.

'Hold on,' I said, 'this might hurt.' I applied some antiseptic and replaced his dressings, stroking my finger across his naked flesh hoping he'd feel the sensitive touch through the pain. This time he did flinch, maybe from the pain, maybe not.

Then I was done, I helped him into his gown again and left. Sometimes the pleasure's in the anticipation.

The next night, I went back to see Brad. The hospital was quiet; the only sound that of cicadas through the open window. I took off my uniform and stood stark naked looking down at the sleeping surfer, enjoying the cool night air on my bare skin. His muscles looked even more pronounced in the dim light. I took off his gown again, gently so he wouldn't wake.

He was sleeping on his good side, and his long cock, semi-hard, rested on the bed. I stroked it ever so softly and he stirred slightly, smiling as the member stiffened. Then I took hold of it more firmly and his eyes opened. He was shocked at first, but when he saw it was me he smiled, to my great relief. It could have gone either way.

'I'm not sure how active I can be,' he said. 'My stitches might pull.'

'Don't worry,' I replied. 'I'm a trained nurse.'

I pushed him over onto his back and knelt up on the bed, swinging my leg over his body. He felt my tits, first caressing then squeezing. I raked my nails down his hairless chest and rippling six-pack down to his pubes, then took hold of his thick cock and directed it into my wet snatch. I felt my inner walls straining. He grunted and tried to thrust back up at me. I shook a finger. 'No moving,' I said. 'Nurse's orders.'

He lay perfectly still as I rode him. I looked down between my legs to watch his thick, glistening shaft disappear inside as I lowered myself. He slid the back of one hand down my taut belly to my shaven mound and found my clitoris. The twin sensations of his fat cock filling me up and his thumb sliding across my slippery clit were almost too much to bear. I was here to make him feel good, but he'd taken control.

But Brad was experienced. He monitored my build-up

and judged it against his own, to ensure we came simultaneously. As it happened I knocked his hand away feeling suddenly over-sensitive and I leaned forward over him to kiss his sweet mouth. He hissed with pain as he came, unable to stop himself thrusting his hips upwards to fuck me all the harder. I kissed him tenderly then slid off, trying not to stretch his stitches any more than I already had. I helped him back into his gown.

'Thanks,' he said. 'Are you on night-shift tomorrow?'

But I wasn't to see him the next night, or ever again in fact. Because outside the ward, the night-duty ward supervisor was waiting for me. She'd seen everything.

A month later and I found myself in Darwin. I'm still not sure how I got there, I remember a combi-van full of surfers and tourists, a lot of skinny cigarettes, some great sex with people I don't remember, and there I was, in the far north, surrounded by crocodiles and mosquitoes.

I was running low on cash, plus I was lonely and wanted to stick around and meet people, so I went down to the hospital and asked if they had any work. I knew my slip-up in Cairns wasn't on my permanent record. The administrator there hadn't fancied doing the paperwork and asked me to leave quietly, saying nothing more would be made of it if I didn't collect my holiday pay. So I was able to get another job in the Northern Territory.

There was nothing available at Darwin General but the registrar asked me if I'd be interested in working in a provincial community hospital way out in the middle of nowhere. I shrugged and said yes. It couldn't be any duller than Darwin, and I was keen to see as much of Australia as I could.

How wrong I was. It was far duller than Darwin. It was a tiny town, with two pubs and a couple of dozen houses. The hospital had its own airstrip and plane, which was kind of fun to go flying in sometimes, but the novelty soon wore off. There are only so many rashes on so many shearers you can dab ointment on before you go out of your mind. That part of Australia is just thousands of square miles of featureless brown scrub-land and desert.

The only things to do in Warrumbungleburra are drink, hunt and shag. I didn't care so much for the hunting, and the local guys weren't much to look at. The two doctors at the hospital were no oil paintings either. I'm not fussy about looks, as I made clear, but there are some guys not really worth getting undressed for, you know? One of the nurses, Helena, was quite cute, but as a colleague, she was off-limits, and straight as an outback highway. So I drank. Everyone did. You'd start at lunchtime and carry on at a steady, slow pace right through until the wee hours. Then a few hours' sleep and you'd start all over again. It was the drink, the intense heat and the sheer boredom of it that made me abandon my professional ethics again. Plus the fact that one of the regular doctors went off on sabbatical and a rather dishy locum arrived from Sydney.

It wasn't hard to arrange things the way I wanted them. Everyone, straight or gay, married or single, has the same buttons, you just need to know where they are and when to push them. First thing was to take Helena to the slightly less dilapidated pub and suggest to her that the locum, Dr Marks, fancied her rotten.

'Really?' she asked, her eyes shining. She had a boyfriend but he was in Darwin, where she flew back to every so often, she worked ten days on, four days off. I could see those ten days dragged sometimes.

Then, over a drink in the other pub, I accidentally let slip that Helena had told me she wouldn't mind 'a quick root with Dr Marks' before he went back to Darwin. His eyebrows lifted. 'I thought she had a boyfriend?'

'Boyfriends are temporary,' I replied, sipping my cold lager.

He looked thoughtful, and I knew I'd done enough.

The next time they were on night-shift together, one of my nights off, I popped in to the hospital. The nurse's station was empty, so I wandered the halls until I heard a moaning coming from the maternity room. I flung open the door to find Helena, strapped to the bed, feet up in stirrups and Dr Marks standing between her splayed legs, his cock hilt deep into her pussy. They stared at me in horror. The doctor pulled out his penis, glistening in the faint moonlight.

'Don't stop on my account,' I said. I slowly walked over to the bed and trailed a finger from Helena's toes down her foot, up her leg and down into her dark pubes.

'What the hell are you doing?' she said, still panting from the shafting I'd so rudely interrupted. I glanced at Dr Marks. He held his cock in his hand and was staring at my hand, lustfully. Helena struggled to break free, but Dr Marks had strapped her in tight. I slipped a finger into her open pussy and she flinched at the sensation,

I guessed it was the first time she'd been intimately touched by a woman.

'Stop it!' she hissed at me. 'You bitch.'

I was taking a gamble here. I knew what I was doing could be deemed sexual assault if she pressed charges. But I figured she probably would do no such thing. One, because she'd have to explain why she was in this position in the first place and, two, because I fully expected her to enjoy herself once she'd got over the shock. I fixed her eye and began working her clitoris with my thumb. At the same time I inserted two fingers inside her and tickled her G-spot, a little trick I'd learned in Japan. Her muscles contracted around my fingers and I knew I had her.

Dr Marks slid up behind me and lifted up my skirt. As usual, I had no panties on and I saw Helena's eyes flicker downwards to watch his hand cup my mons and begin massaging me gently. His other hand deftly unbuttoned my blouse and slipped inside, his fingers searching out my erect nipple. I felt his lips tickling me.

Helena was breathing even more heavily now, and had stopped glaring at me. She was staring at my crotch and lifting her hips in time with my rhythmic strokes. The good doctor pushed my head forward, letting me know what he wanted to see. Without removing my fingers from her snatch, I lowered my head and began teasing her labia with my tongue. 'Oh my God,' she said, in a mixture of horror and lust. My tongue was swimming with her juices. I was sure I could taste something else as well. Dr Marks' pre-cum perhaps. Helena began humping her pussy down on my fingers. I slipped a third in for good measure and she growled with appreciation.

Then I felt the doctor's cock drive into me from behind. It felt so good it put me off my rhythm and Helena whined in protest. I got back into it, Dr Marks going easy on me. 'Fuck yes,' he said.

Helena came first with a great, rib-cracking groan. I continued lapping at her clitoris and pumping my hand into her until the last throes had died and she begged for me to stop. I shifted up slightly and kissed her full on the mouth. She kissed back hungrily, licking her juices off my chin. This was too much for Dr Marks, who came inside me with a swelling of his penis. He stopped pumping and held himself deep inside me for half-a-minute as his cock twitched and spasmed.

'That was incredible,' he said, after withdrawing. I stood up, wondering how Helena was going to be now the orgasm was over. We released her and she stood and glared at me. Then she slapped me across the face. She turned and gave Dr Marks the same treatment. 'That's for forcing me into your sordid little sex-game,' she told us. Dr Marks looked aggrieved. I smiled and shrugged. If that was the worst I was getting I was okay.

Then Helena kissed me again. 'That's for giving me the best orgasm I've ever had.'

'Really? I asked, thinking she was being a tad melodramatic.

'Oh yes,' she said.

'Well, if it's that good, then strap me down and do the same to me.'

She hesitated for a minute then nodded. 'You up for it?' I asked Dr Marks. He looked down at his half-flaccid tool. 'Let me take a little something and I'll be ready in five minutes.' He went to his jacket pocket.

'We may as well get started,' Helena said. 'Take your clothes off.' I did so. She inspected my tits. 'I've never touched another woman's breasts,' she said.

'Go ahead,' I replied.

She took hold of them, weighing each one and stroking the nipples till they were hard. Dr Marks had taken his pill and was watching us. I could see he was already stiffening at the show.

'Get on the bed,' Helena ordered.

She took her time strapping me down. The wrist bands were tight and I winced as she yanked them. Then she lifted my legs into the stirrups, pulled them apart and strapped me in, eyeing my shaven pussy and imagining what it was going to be like, eating that. When I was firmly strapped in, she leaned over and took my chin in her hands. 'Okay bitch,' she said. 'Now you're going to see what it feels like.'

I couldn't wait.

She turned to see the doctor was nearly ready and stepped in between my thighs. She leaned over me and kissed me on the mouth, biting my lip hard until it hurt. 'You're a quick learner,' I said.

'I've done this with my boyfriend,' she said. Then she dropped her head to my snatch and jabbed her hot little tongue into my pussy.

She was good for a virgin. I wanted to grab her head and thrust it against my mound, but strapped down, I was totally at her mercy. She looked up at me as she lapped.

'Does she taste good?' The doctor said. He'd come over and was stroking his erection. Helena nodded. She kept licking until I was twisting in ecstasy against the straps, then she pulled away.

The doctor took his opportunity and moved into position. I stared fixedly at his cock. It twitched as his heart pumped more and more blood into it. He positioned himself, then slowly slipped it into me. 'Yes,' I remember saying, 'yes, yes, yes.'

Helena came around and stroked my clitoris as Marks slammed into me, the stirrups allowing him to slide right up to the hilt. I came in shuddering gasps, delirious at the attention I was getting. It had been a long time for me since I'd come, and I felt the tension release from my body like an uncoiling spring.

My plan had worked perfectly, except for one thing. I hadn't counted on Dr Marks being even more of a pervert than I'd taken him for. I hadn't realised he'd placed a camera on a filing cabinet even before he'd got Helena to take off her clothes. Neither of us knew anything about it until we were hauled into the administrator's office individually and informed of the fact it had come to his attention there was a video clip available on the internet which had clearly been filmed in the maternity room and which featured two nurses and a locum doctor. Marks had long since returned to Sydney, where he had evidently decided the clip was worth showing to a friend, who posted it on the net, and next thing we knew half the sex fiends in Australia were watching our tender little threesome.

I wasn't too bothered about that, though it upset me to see Helena utterly crushed. I blamed myself and she blamed me too, even though it had been Dr Marks' video. We were both fired of course. She left town that night, and I left the next day. I went back to Darwin and phoned my brother Aidan.

'I need help,' I said. Though until the moment I actually said it I hadn't really thought I did. Once I accepted the truth though, I just sat back and let Aidan take charge. I told him everything of course. He's always been the only one I fully trust in our family. I was obviously not capable of running my own life, so I decided to let him do it for me. He sent me the fare to get back to London. By the time I'd touched down, he'd booked me into this place.

And here I am.

Chapter Twenty-Six

Shelley sat back in her chair, utterly drained.

Had anyone believed a word of it? It didn't sound very convincing to her. Who has sex with their head hanging out of a helicopter for Christ's sake? But then again none of the previous confessionals had sounded exactly commonplace. Well, she didn't really care if they believed her now. Her ordeal was over.

'Thank you, Shelley,' Verity said. 'I knew you could do it. Now everyone, we've over-run a bit, so straight to lunch, then back here at two-thirty for "Filling the Hole with Friendship."'

Cian came over.

'You keep on surprising me, Ms Carter,' he said.

Cliff and Cheryl were next. She stood and hugged each of them in turn. 'I'm so glad we met you, Shelley,' Cheryl said.

Larry rushed up and wrapped his arms around Shelley, giving her an enormous bear hug. He said nothing but as he let go and walked off Shelley was sure she saw a little tear in his eye.

Abigail stood before Shelley and nodded stiffly.

'Well done, Shelley. You're a tough cookie.' Shelley smiled back at her.

Coming from Abigail, herself tougher than fossilised biltong, that was the ultimate accolade.

'I knew you could do it, Shelley,' said Will.

Rose approached her last and gave her a huge hug.

'To think I've been sleeping a couple of metres away from you for the last six nights. See you in the dining room?'

'Yes, I'll be along in a minute or two,' Shelley replied.

She sat until the room was empty, then rested her face in her hands; she could feel the tension drain out of her. As she lifted her head, she realised someone was standing in the doorway, watching her.

It was Dr Galloway.

'Oh hello, Doctor,' she said brightly. Had he been listening the whole time?

He smiled, baring his teeth. 'Hello, *Nurse* Carter,' he replied.

Uh-oh.

'It is *Nurse* Carter isn't it? We haven't got that wrong, have we?'

'I don't know what you mean, Dr Galloway,' she blustered.

'Oh, cut the act,' he said, smiling. 'Come with me.'

Shelley hesitated but figured she had little choice. He led her down the hall, out of the back doors and across the gardens to his office. Galloway showed her to a chair and sat behind his desk.

'I've been doing some research, Ms Carter,' he began, picking up a manila folder.

How should she play this? Come clean, or go defensive?

'And?'

'Over the last few days I've checked every possible nursing register in the country. None of them have you listed. Maybe it was a mistake, I thought, and checked with the Warrumbungleburra General Hospital Infirmary and do you know what?'

Shelley shrugged.

'No one had heard of it. Isn't that strange?'

Shelley looked mystified, but said nothing.

'Perhaps she's using a false name, I thought to myself, not uncommon in these situations, so when your brother arrived to see you, I made sure our helpful receptionist checked his ID. Aidan Carter his name was, so that seemed to indicate you *were* using your real name.'

Galloway paused and waited for Shelley to respond, but she just sat and smiled as evenly as she could. She wanted to know where this was heading. Apparently Galloway still didn't know she was a journalist. Quite frankly she didn't care much if she was thrown off the course now. She got what she came here for, more than that in fact. Shelley felt she was a stronger person than when she'd arrived, she was ready for whatever Galloway had to throw at her.

'When Sandra came to see me and told me you were carrying around a BlackBerry, I thought you must be a journalist, come to get some juicy gossip on our more famous patients. So I came to listen to your confessional.'

Dr Galloway stood and walked around to the front of his desk, where he perched, once again. He continued.

'I've been working with drug abusers and sex addicts for twenty years now. I can spot a lie from a mile off. God knows, most of them are habitual liars. But when I listened to you today I could tell you weren't making it up.'

Shelley nearly fell off her chair.

'Oh yes. You obviously made up many of the names and the settings, I don't think you've ever worked in a hospital for example. But I could tell you had experienced all of the sex acts you described. You may not be a nurse, but you genuinely have a problem.'

Shelley stared at him blankly. 'We . . . well,' she stammered. 'You're right there. I most certainly do.'

He smiled at her, eyes twinkling. 'A helicopter, for heaven's sake, you are quite some girl.'

'So you won't say anything about this? I can continue with the course?'

Shelley didn't really want to continue with the course, but she was on a tightrope. It wouldn't take much more digging for him to find out who she really was, and then he could make things decidedly unpleasant. Legal action to force her to can the story was the most likely.

Galloway tilted his head and looked thoughtful. 'Well, that depends,' he said.

'On what?' Shelley replied..

'With cases as severe as yours, Shelley, I often recommend a series of one-on-one intense sessions, where we work through the manifestations of the addiction together.'

'Erm, okay,' said Shelley. In the back of her mind, she was thinking of more material for the column.

'It would involve you . . . shall we say, reliving some of your experiences and fantasies with me. Just so I can get an intimate knowledge of the worst excesses of your sexual depravities.'

The penny dropped. Shelley stared back at him open-mouthed. 'Are you suggesting you and I . . .'

'We can start off with the doctor and nurse fantasy you seem so obsessed with. I think I can rustle up a spare uniform. Size ten are you?'

Shelley stood. 'How dare you?'

Galloway remained unperturbed. 'Of course, if you refuse the hands-on assistance I am offering you, we could look at more difficult treatments. These would be longer-term, and might include a stay at another establishment.'

'This is blackmail,' she said.

Galloway shook his head. 'No, this is negotiation. I'm just trying to help you out,' he replied. 'It might not be so bad.' He watched her face closely.

Shelley shook her head. Galloway was a very good-looking man, for sure, and if he'd asked her back to his place after a drink or two she would have said yes without hesitation. But not on these terms.

'So Sandra told you I had a BlackBerry, did she?'

'She did indeed,' he said.

'Did she tell you what sort of BlackBerry it was?'

He frowned. 'Are there different types?'

'Oh yes,' Shelley said. 'Some of them have all sorts of additional extras, like web browsers, or phones, or . . . cameras.'

Something in her tone obviously tipped him off, because he twitched uncomfortably. Shelley turned around slowly and looked up at the little side window through which she'd seen Galloway getting a blow job from Verity Parrish.

'I wonder what sort of image one might get if one pointed a camera through that window at around . . . ooh, say one-thirty yesterday afternoon?'

Now it was Galloway's turn to look gobsmacked. He glanced down towards Shelley's pockets, obviously considering trying to grab the device.

'Too late,' Shelley said, smiling sweetly. 'I e-mailed it to my Hotmail account this morning.'

Shelley was hoping desperately that Galloway wouldn't demand to see the BlackBerry. She wasn't even sure there was such a thing as a BlackBerry with a camera. But apparently neither was the Irish doctor.

'This is blackmail,' he spat.

'No,' Shelley replied. 'This is negotiation.'

'And what if I refuse?' he asked, visibly trying to stay calm.

'Do what you like,' Shelley said, casually inspecting her nails. 'But be aware of two things. One, that I will never, ever sleep with you. And two, that I have no concern whatsoever for my own reputation. I have nothing to lose in that regard.'

Finished, she sat and watched his face as he struggled to still a nervous tic in the corner of his right eye.

Eventually he responded. 'Fine, I will say nothing if you keep those images to yourself.'

Shelley turned to leave, but then stopped and turned back. 'Oh, I'll need that Section Four document back. I don't want you holding that over my head.'

'I don't have it,' he said. 'Dr Jones has that in her office.'

Shelley headed straight for Dr Jones' office. In the hall she ran into Rose, on her way back to the Mountain Room.

'Hi Shell, where did you disappear to? We missed you at lunch.'

'Sorry Rose, I'll explain it all later. I have some personal matters to deal with.'

'Is this to do with that man who came to see you?'

'In a way, yes,' Shelley said, giving Rose's arm a squeeze before running up the carpeted stairs two at a time.

Shelley knocked on Dr Jones' office door. 'Come in,' a fragile voice called from inside.

Shelley stepped in, wondering if she might find Dr Jones as 'tired and emotional' as she had last time. But the doctor looked in reasonable shape.

'Ah, Ms . . .'

'Carter,' Shelley said. She walked in and stood before Dr Jones' desk. 'I've come to ask you to discharge me.'

'Oh?' Jones said, peering at her quizzically. 'And you are on which programme?'

'I'm a sex addict,' Shelley said. 'But I'm not dangerous, I am in complete control of myself and don't feel happy about being trapped here, against my will. Dr Galloway agrees.'

'Does he now?'

'Yes, he does. I just went to see him. Call him if you like.'

'Well, I'm afraid it's not up to Dr Galloway, it's up to me. And I will not consider discharging you until I've received notification from Ms Parrish that your treatment has been successful.'

Shelley had been worried about this. She liked Verity and didn't want to drag her into this. There was nothing else for it; she'd have to go nuclear.

'This centre is run by a private trust, is it not?'

'Yes, what does that have to do with anything?' asked Dr Jones.

'I just wondered what the Trustees would say if they were given evidence that the Medical Director of their precious institution kept a bottle of gin in her top left drawer.'

Dr Jones went still as a statue, then she reached for a drawer. Shelley thought she was going for the gin, but instead she pulled out a file and flipped it open. She pulled out the form, scribbled something across it, signed and dated it and handed it to Shelley.

'Thank you,' Shelley said politely and turned to leave

'It's a shame you didn't complete the course,' Dr Jones said. 'Looking through your file, you certainly need help with your sex problems.'

Shelley said nothing and walked out. She went to her room, packed up her belongings and walked to the stairs.

I'm free, she thought. *I completed the assignment, I pulled it off. I had everyone believing I was a globe-trotting slut. I've almost certainly knocked the smile off Freya's face. I've done it.*

But as she reached the bottom of the stairs, she heard a man's laugh from the Mountain Room. Cian. Then she heard an angry woman's voice. Abigail. Then, after a pause, the entire group clapped and cheered. Shelley felt she was missing something. She opened her bag and took out the Section Four form. At the bottom, Dr Jones had scribbled 'Treatment successful. Discharged.'

Treatment successful. Shelley thought. Well, sort of. In the last week she'd dated a rock star, kissed one woman and shown her bare arse to another. She'd masturbated at the thought of a porn star's antics and invented a debauched persona for herself that she'd felt strangely comfortable with.

But was she cured? She didn't want to be a sex addict, but maybe she'd learned something from those who were. Maybe she'd learned that there was a middle ground to be discovered. That sex with ugly people could be fun. That no one was out of your league if you were prepared to give them what they wanted, that it was okay to love yourself, that sometimes cheaters weren't the worst people in the world, that aggression had its part in life and sex. That sometimes you had to look outside your comfort zone.

And she'd learned all this not from Verity or Galloway, but from the others on the course.

'Welcome back,' Verity said as Shelley walked into the room. 'We were just asking Cian how he goes about filling the holes in his life. I'm afraid his answers weren't entirely helpful at first. But we've worked it through.'

'Sorry about all that,' Shelley said. 'I had some personal business that I couldn't ignore.'

'We thought we'd lost you,' Rose said, beaming at her. In fact, they were all smiling at her as she came and took her place in the circle.

'No chance,' Shelley said. 'I'm here till the bitter end.'

* * *

'Shelley!' Briony cried and rushed across the office to give her a hug, crushing her cardboard coffee cup and spilling latte over the only pair of black trousers Shelley owned that didn't have a shiny bum. 'You didn't tell me you were coming in today; I expected to see you at home tonight.'

'I wanted to surprise you,' Shelley said, struggling to breathe against the bear hug. Over Briony's shoulder, she could see Freya, shooting daggers. Evidently the news that Shelley had stolen the cover story had somehow got back to the office.

'Ooh look, everyone,' Freya said. 'Jackie Collins is back.'

'How's your column, Brie? Sorry I didn't ask before, I've been so caught up.'

'Don't worry about it. Plus ça change with me. I'm loving my life, but I've missed you. Banging a bloke against a wall isn't nearly so much fun if you're not on the other side yelling at me to shut up.'

'How about you, Freya?' Shelley asked. 'How's . . .' but she stopped. Something was wrong with Freya's desk. Then it dawned. 'Where are all your pictures of Harry?'

Freya pursed her lips, trying to keep her cool. 'Let's just say, Shelley, that Harry may have seemed perfect to you . . .'

'Um . . .'

'. . . but there were certain . . . problems, which made themselves apparent recently.'

'Say no more,' Shelley said. 'I suppose this means you're single again, like me?'

But Freya shook her head, the default smug look back on her face.

'Oh no, I was rather looking forward to playing the field a little, but fate had other ideas. I met a wonderful man just a few days ago. He was here looking for you actually, can't think why. But we just hit it off immediately.'

Shelley raised her eyebrows. 'What's this chap's name?'

'Gavin,' Freya said levelly.

'Gavin the Manga fan?' Shelley asked.

'Yes, I never realised just how literary comics could be. Most intriguing.'

Shelley fought the twitching in the corner of her mouth.

'He did say he knew you,' Freya continued. 'Oh my goodness, I've just thought, I hope I'm not treading on your toes, Shelley? Were you interested in Gavin?'

Briony was having a coughing fit.

'No, that's fine,' Shelley said in her best mock-serious tone. 'I'll get over it.' And she turned and marched past Briony, who was bent over with her hand on the water cooler.

Shelley sat at her desk and admired the new laptop someone had put there. Briony, having recovered, came over to join her.

'Things are going so well here, Shell,' Briony said eventually. 'And it's all thanks to you.'

'What do you mean?'

'Aidan put out a teaser mag, 100,000 circulation prior to next week's launch. He included one of your racy stories and advertising was swamped with calls. Half the media hacks in the country are attending the launch party on Friday; *Vixen* is going to be huge. They're all talking about your story.'

Shelley didn't have time to respond before she heard a voice calling her name.

'Shelley, in here, please!'

She turned to see Aidan was standing at the door to his office, looking serious. Had Fresh Paths' lawyers been on the phone?

She went into Aidan's office. 'Close the door,' he said. She was surprised to find he hadn't had any decoration done. The office was in exactly the same cluttered state as the day Kate had been fired. Even the mouse droppings were still there. Aidan noticed her looking.

'I didn't see any point in changing anything before the new editor starts. She can deal with it.'

'New editor?' Shelley asked in surprise. 'Are you leaving?'

'Oh no,' Aidan said. 'I'm not going anywhere. I'm staying on as publisher. I'm no fool, this magazine's going places and I want to stay associated with it. I'm just not cut out to be an editor. Plus I'm a man.'

'I did notice,' Shelley said, twisting a strand of hair around a finger. Aidan moved around to rest against the front of the desk.

'Look Shelley, what I'm getting at is that I want you to be the new Chief Editor of *Vixen*.'

The words took several seconds to register.

'Are you alright?' Aidan asked. 'Your lips are moving but no words are coming out and you've gone pale.'

'W-why me?' she asked. 'Freya's more senior, or Briony. I . . .'

'You're the one, Shelley,' he said. 'I knew that from the moment you interrupted my welcome speech to correct my grammar. Those balls and your attention to detail are just what I need. And what you accomplished at Fresh Paths was nothing short of miraculous. So, will you do it?'

Shelley paused for a moment before replying. The old Shelley would have said no, and thought of a hundred reasons why it was a bad idea.

But she'd left that person behind.

'I'll take the job on one condition,' she said.

'Great,' he said, smiling. 'What's that?'

'That you take me to dinner tonight.'

Shelley had never seen Aidan Carter gobsmacked before, and he looked even cuter than normal. 'I'll book a table.'

Chapter Twenty-Seven

'Shelley!'

She spun in the crowded tent and immediately picked Rose out amongst the heaving crowd of festival-goers. They bustled their respective ways through the throng and embraced.

'It's so good to see you,' Rose said. 'I wasn't sure you'd come.'

'What, and turn down a VIP ticket for Glastonbury?'

'Have you seen any of the others?' Rose asked.

'Will's at the bar and I think saw Cheryl on someone's shoulders in the crowd in front of Stage Two. I presume the shoulders belonged to Cliff, but who knows? Anyway Cian said if we can't find each other, we should all just meet him at his trailer; we can have a bite to eat and a proper catch up before his set . . .'

Shelley was interrupted as an arm snaked around her waist and she was lifted off the ground.

'Larry!' Rose exclaimed. Shelley found herself dropped unceremoniously and Larry turned his attentions to Rose. The two hugged each other tightly, then broke apart and stood awkwardly, grinning at each other.

Will wriggled between a group of writhing bodies, carrying a tray of beers expertly above his head.

'Sorry, they'd run out of Pimms,' he said. 'Got a few in when I saw the others had arrived.'

Just as they'd finished sorting out the drinks, and everyone had said their greetings, Abigail arrived and they had to start all over again. Then Cliff and Cheryl turned up.

'All here!' said Shelley.

'Except Verity, of course,' Abigail said.

They lifted their plastic cups sloshing beer everywhere as they were jostled. 'To Verity!' Will cried and they chorused in response.

'We'd better go,' Shelley said, checking her watch. 'Cian said to meet him at seven.'

They gradually made their way through the crowd towards the backstage area.

A group of bouncers blocked their way until Shelley showed them the special pass Cian had sent her, and they ran laughing towards the trailer with The Cossacks' insignia across the side.

A young man opened the door to them. 'Yes?' he said, looking harried.

'We're here to see Cian, he told us to meet him here,' Shelley said.

The young man looked sceptical. 'He's just about to go on; who the hell are you guys?'

'We're his support group,' Larry called from the back.

The man looked at his clipboard. 'Support group? There's no support group, this is Glastonbury.'

But then Cian appeared. He was wearing trousers so

tight they looked like they'd been first spray-painted on then shrunk in the bath.

'Wotcher!' he cried. 'Come in!'

They filed into the trailer. The air-con was blissful after the sweaty tent.

Inside was tastefully furnished with leather sofas and a double-sized fridge. A couple of guitars rested against a wall.

'Have a look around,' Cian said grinning broadly. 'Help yourself to booze or food.'

'This is bigger than my bloody flat,' Shelley said.

'It's got three bedrooms,' Abigail said, emerging from a corridor.

'Two of them are en-suite,' Cian confirmed.

'There's a telly in the loo!' Cheryl called.

'In case I need a crap during *CSI*,' Cian explained.

Shelley plumped herself down on a plush sofa and raised an eyebrow at Cian. 'Well?' she said.

'Well, what?' he replied, affecting innocence.

'Well, have you gone back to your bad old ways?'

'Have you?' he countered.

'I asked first.'

The others came in to hear the exchange, Will carrying a bottle of Moët and some glasses.

'Do me last,' Cian said. 'You got to go last at the centre, now it's my turn.'

Shelley shrugged. 'Okay, what about you, Rose?'

Rose glanced quickly at Larry.

'Well, I haven't slept with anyone since the course ended, but there might be someone on the horizon. I don't want to jinx it by talking about it. Other than that everything's going well, I'm working part-time in an office, and I've just started a book-keeping course. Who knows? Maybe one day I'll start up another business, and spend more time looking at the books and less time fucking about.'

Will handed her a glass of bubbly and sat down between her and Shelley.

'That's wonderful, Rose,' Abigail said. 'I'm afraid things have been a little less demure for me. I've managed to stay away from the dungeons, but I met this guy in my building, and, well, we went for a drink and one thing led to another and I ended up having to take him to A&E at four in the morning to have a boot heel removed from his backside. Damn thing snapped off. I knew I shouldn't have bought those cheap Chinese knock-offs.'

'Oh dear,' Cliff said. 'Was the guy okay?'

'I think so, he's coming around again next Friday anyway, so he can't be too shaken up.'

After the laughter died down, Cliff spoke up.

'Cheryl and I have been busy exploring each other again,' he said, gazing at his wife.

'We realised there are plenty of things we haven't tried yet,' Cheryl said, then sipped her champagne. 'We were always looking for more, and never realised that we didn't need to find other people to provide it, we just needed to look deeper into each other, and ourselves.'

'Oh shut up before I vomit on you,' Cian said. 'Larry, what about you? Still looking for porn stars?'

'Not any more,' Larry grinned, then went silent.

'Will?' said Abigail. 'How's Amanda?'

'She's brilliant,' Will said, smiling. 'Just brilliant. So is Jamie. We're doing just fine, thanks.'

'And no more lap-dances?'

'No, but Mand's bought herself a pole, says she wants to keep in shape. And that she wants to learn a new trade in case she ever decides to leave me again.'

'And you, Shelley?' Cliff asked, 'how are things with you?' They all stared at her intently. Too intently, Shelley thought. Suddenly she felt worried. A heavy bass line could be heard from a far-off stage; just outside a roadie shouted something incomprehensible.

'Cian first,' she said. 'My confession's a little different.'

'Okay,' he said. 'I can't pretend I've been celibate, if that's what you're asking.'

Shelley was surprised to find she felt a little pang of jealousy. Cian must have seen her look, but misinterpreted it as concern about him falling off the wagon.

'No, it's not like that,' he said. 'I've met someone. Just *one* someone.'

'That's brilliant,' she said. 'What's her name, what's she like, when can we meet her?'

'Her name's Gloria,' Cian said. 'And in a way you've already met her. You wrote a very imaginative story about her which I read on the internet.'

Shelley sat, stunned. Everyone's gaze was on her.

They all know.

'I'm rumbled then,' she said, feeling a little sick. Had they planned this confrontation?

'Yes, you could say that,' Rose said, with perhaps a trace of sadness in her voice.

'Let me explain . . .' Shelley began, then, realising that sounded like the worst cliché, started again. 'Look, I was going to tell you all, that's what I meant when I said my confession was unusual.'

Someone banged on the door and shouted 'Ten minutes, Mr O'Connor!'

Cian sat down and popped a crisp into his mouth, never taking his eyes off her. 'Go on,' he said.

Shelley laid her hands on her knees.

'I am a journalist, you all must have realised that if you've seen the articles on the *Vixen* website. I went into the centre a cynical, bitter hack. I had no respect for the course and every intention of exploiting your stories for my own career. I admit that.'

Cheryl glanced at Cliff who raised his eyebrows. Abigail stared back at Shelley like she was ready to pounce. Shelley swallowed.

'But as the course went on, I got to know you all better and I realised what wonderful, warm people you all are. I felt terribly guilty at the thought of lying to you and betraying your trust.'

'But you still wrote the stories!' Larry exclaimed.

'I did, I'm not trying to get out of that,' Shelley said. 'Things have changed.' She told them all about the success of the column, her promotion to Chief Editor, and working up the courage to ask Aidan out.

'That's great for you,' said Cian, when she'd finished. 'But what are we? Just rungs on your career ladder?'

'It's not like that,' said Shelley. 'Look, let me tell you what happened when Aidan and I were having dinner.'

* * *

'You want to do what?' Aidan sputtered, looking up from his steak.

He looked good enough to eat in his charcoal Bond Street suit. This was the second time she'd seen him lose his cool that day, and she was beginning to enjoy surprising him.

'You sure are purty when you're angry,' she said.

'For God's sake, Shelley, you can't pull the cover story. Your own bloody story. The story that the advertisers are creaming themselves over.'

The diners at the nearby tables had gone quiet. This was the sort of restaurant where everyone knew everyone and where everyone was desperate to find out what everyone else was up to.

Shelley ran her finger around the lip of her wine glass. 'Aidan, I know exactly what I'm doing.'

'It's all too racy for you?' he asked. 'You're uncomfortable with the explicit sex?'

'That's not it,' she said.

Realisation dawned over Aidan's face. 'You've gone native! You don't want to betray your friends.'

'That's part of it,' said Shelley. 'But there's a bigger story here.'

'And that is?'

'The course itself,' Shelley explained. 'I want to do a series of features on each of the people on the course. Each of them has a fascinating story which deserves its own article. I want to do a follow-up as well. I intend to wait a few weeks, contact each of them again and find out what's become of them, whether they've managed to beat their addiction. I want an objective picture of how well the course works, is it just some high-profile celebrity milking operation? Or a genuine programme helping the desperate and vulnerable?' She took a sip of wine. 'I'm not shelving the story, Aidan. I'm developing it. Nor am I going to reduce the sex content, I'm going to put it in context, that's all. Nothing wrong with a bit of smut, as long as it's part of a broader search for understanding. The advertisers will understand, and they'll end up benefiting too.'

Aidan stared back at her for a while, thinking this over.

'And what would you put on the front cover next week?' he asked.

'Freya's story,' Shelley replied.

'I thought you didn't like Freya,' he said.

'I don't, but it's a good story. Besides, I want her on my team, not fighting me.'

Finally he smiled. 'You *are* an editor.'

'I know,' Shelley said, watching him pour her another glass.

Two hours later, Aidan paid the bill, and watched the waiter leave the table.

'Any other plans?' he asked eventually.

'For the magazine?' she replied. 'Or for tonight?'

Aidan smiled and looked into her eyes.

'Either,' he said.

'I do have some other plans for the magazine,' Shelley told him. 'Perhaps you'd like to discuss them over coffee?'

'But we've just paid.'

'There are other places you can get coffee.'

'Oh,' he said, looking a little overawed. 'I have one of

those stupid coffee machines that never work properly.'

'Sounds perfect.'

Aidan helped her into her coat and gently slipped her hair out down the back.

He lived close and fifteen minutes later they were on his sofa. Aidan's machine had worked tolerably well but Shelley wasn't interested in the espresso.

'So,' he said. 'These plans . . .'

Shelley leaned across and kissed him on the lips. She pulled back, waiting for his reaction. The silence was broken only by the ticking of a clock on the mantelpiece.

'There was one thing I wasn't sure of about you,' Aidan said.

'What's that?'

'I didn't know if you'd be prepared to take risks,' he said. 'Sometimes an editor needs to take a chance, I was worried you might be too safe. That you might be too . . .'

He paused.

'Too stiff?' she suggested.

'Maybe,' he said with a smile.

'And what do you think now?' she asked.

He placed his hand behind her head and leant forwards. His lips met hers, his mouth hardly open. Gradually, gingerly, the kiss became harder, more urgent.

Shelley pushed back with her mouth, forcing his lips apart and darting her tongue around his. She forced him back against the arm of the sofa, then lifted her leg off the floor so she was straddling him.

She broke the kiss and looked down into his eyes. His hair was ruffled, and she felt his cock pressing against her.

'I've always been willing to take a risk,' she said, slowly unfastening the top button of his shirt. 'But only when the reward is something worthwhile.'

'One minute, Mr O'Connor!'

Other than the general hubbub of twenty thousand people swarming across the Somerset countryside, silence filled the air in the trailer.

Rose hugged her. 'Thank you,' she said. 'I'm so relieved. I thought I'd lost a friend.'

'Yes, thanks, Shelley,' Will echoed. The others nodded and murmured in agreement.

'Okay, Shelley,' Abigail said. 'Fair enough. I'm sorry you had to go through that.'

Shelley suddenly felt lighter than air. She hadn't realised up till now just what a terrible weight the guilt had been. She'd hated having this secret from her friends.

'You're very welcome to use our story in your magazine, as long as you change the names,' Cliff said. Cheryl nodded.

'Yes, mine too,' Abigail said.

'Thanks,' Shelley said. 'You will be paid of course.'

'Great, count me in,' Larry said enthusiastically.

'And me,' Rose and Will added together.

Shelley looked at Cian. 'And you Cian? Are you in?'

Cian looked back at her impassively. Shelley knew his sense of betrayal must have been great indeed. They had made a connection during the course. That evening at the pub had been a breakthrough for him. To find it had been built on a lie must have been hard to accept.

'Gotta go,' he said and rushed out of the door. The

others followed, wanting to get a good position. Shelley didn't move. She sat miserably, wondering if she'd lost something special. Rose paused at the door.

'Come on, Shell, you don't want to miss this.'

Shelley forced a smile and said. 'No. I wouldn't miss this for anything.'

'Oh, and I'm really pleased about Aidan,' Rose added, and they hurried across towards the stage. 'I'm so glad he's not your brother.'

'Me too,' Shelley said.

A huge cheer went up, presumably as Cian made his entrance across the stage. Shelley and Rose elbowed their way into the VIP enclosure, just as he was looping his guitar strap over his head and the drummer laid down the thumping beat to the first song. As the bass player and keyboard player came on and joined in, the crowd surged and Shelley found the others. Larry put his arm around Rose and landed a kiss on her lips.

So that was why they were both so coy.

Cian grabbed the microphone, and turned back to his band, waving his other hand.

'Quiet, you lot!'

In a diminishing cacophony, the drummer and bassist ground to a halt. The crowd went silent.

'Good evening Glastonbury!' The spectators roared back. 'I've been away for a little while. But The Cossacks have returned. Thanks for your patience.' A surge went through the crowd again. 'This song is called "Adverse Camber" and tonight it's dedicated to a very special lady. I have one thing to say to her.'

Cian reached into his back pocket and pulled out a

plectrum, then lifted it over his head. Everyone watched, transfixed, and Shelley's breath was frozen in her throat.

'I'm in, Shelley Carter,' Cian said quietly into the mic. 'I'm in.'

Shelley's gut clenched as he brought down his arm, thrashing the first chord.

THE EXCHANGE - CARRIE WILLIAMS

Love and lust in Paris and London…

London-based photographer Rachel and Parisian exotic dancer Rochelle, agree to swap apartments for six months, with unexpected consequences that bring new meaning to the phrase 'life swap'.

On arrival in Paris, Rachel succumbs to more than a passing interest in Konrad, Rochelle's fashion model boyfriend.

Rochelle, meanwhile, falls in with a rich London crowd. For a while a string of random sexual adventures fills the void left by dancing. But enlightenment ultimately comes to Rochelle too, she discovers that performing for an audience of one can be just as daring and titillating as showing oneself off.

Available at www.mischiefbooks.com

ISBN: 978-0-00-747928-3

UNDERCOVER – LUKE BRADBURY

He's sexy, charming and gorgeous. And he's yours – for the right price...

When young Aussie Luke Bradbury finds himself alone, broke and out of ideas in London, things look desperate. Until he spots a temping ad. Lured by the promise of easy money – and the chance to bed as many women as he can handle – Luke becomes a gigolo. It's a job millions of men would kill for.

Luke quickly learns all there is to know about women in his quest to give them the ultimate pleasure, climbing inside their heads as well as their beds.

But all too soon, Luke discovers the darker side of his lucrative new profession. Is he selling his soul as well as his body?

Available at www.mischiefbooks.com

ISBN: 978-0-00-747975-7